More Praise f

"It's good. It's really very good indeed. I loved it."
  Peter F. Hamilton

"Fast, lucid, and engaging throughout, vivid with inventive detail and sharp with unexpected twists snagging the unwary reader. . . . I can't wait to see how they'll tackle what comes next."
  SFRevu

"You get pulled in by the novel's sheer energy. The cross-genre pollination of various ideas makes for a quirky read."
  Deathray

Praise for *Keeping It Real*

"Entertaining fusion of SF and fantasy spiced with sex, rockin' elves, and drunk faeries."
  Publishers Weekly

"This is by far the most entertaining book Robson has written, a novel packed with memorable characters and ideas but that doubles as holiday-reading escapism."
  SFX

"Think an enthusiastic melange of Laurell K. Hamilton's *Meredith Gentry*, Tad Williams's *War of the Flowers*, Anne Rice's *The Vampire Lestat*, a touch of Marianne de Pierre's Parrish Plessis, even *The Bionic Woman* or *The Transformers*, and you get an idea of how much fun this book is."
  SFFWorld

SELLING OUT

QUANTUM GRAVITY BOOK TWO

SELLING OUT

JUSTINA ROBSON

an imprint of **Prometheus Books**
Amherst, NY

Published 2007 by Pyr®, an imprint of Prometheus Books

Inquiries should be addressed to
Pyr
59 John Glenn Drive
Amherst, New York 14228–2119
VOICE: 716–691–0133, ext. 210
FAX: 716–691–0137
WWW.PYRSF.COM

11 10   5 4 3

Library of Congress Cataloging-in-Publication Data

Robson, Justina.
    Selling out / by Justina Robson.
        p. cm. — (Quantum gravity ; 2)
    Originally published: London : Gollancz, an imprint of the Orion Publishing Group, 2007.
    ISBN 978–1–59102–597–9
    I. Title.

PR6118.O28S46 2007
823'.92—dc22

                                                                    2007027080

Printed in the United States on acid-free paper

CHAPTER ONE

Lila Black sat in the office of her psychologist, Dr. Williams. Her memory of her last mission was downloading through one of her WiFi outlet channels; key features streamlined for Williams's analysis by her AI-self, statistics ready-packaged for the medical teams that monitored her health, cybertronic readouts tabulated for the engineering experts, weapons and armour performance playing back for her master-at-arms.

Dr. Williams was reading as the information spread out before her on her flat screen. Lila was playing with the doctor's antique Rubik's Cube. It had been two days since she'd returned from the near total disaster of her first assignment, acting as bodyguard to the most famous rock star in Otopia. Well, it had been three actually, but she wasn't prepared to admit the first twelve hours they'd been holed up alone in a luxury hotel. That was personal, and as such she had deleted it from her AI memory.

There were many other things she would have liked to delete. The cold-blooded murder of a friend was top of the list, alongside the haunting memories of her family's appalled faces—the way she imagined they'd look if they ever found out what she'd done, and what she'd become; the first cyborg agent of the Otopian Security Agency. They thought she was missing in action in Alfheim, the elven universe.

In those old, long-lost days of innocence Lila had gone there as a diplomat's secretary. It was a great assignment, because Alfheim was one of the least-visited realms, and open only to the diplomatic corps from Otopia. She had been among the first humans to ever be permitted inside its borders. But the high-level meetings, attempting to forge a treaty permitting cross-border activities, had faltered. Lila didn't know the details, only that she had agreed to spy for the Otopian Secret Service and that it had seemed the most exciting adventure. The only thing she had to do was report on what she had seen in the course of her normal duties.

But then she met another spy, Vincent, and had gone into the deep country to check out the rumours of odd magical trading—weapons' grade magical artifacts being smuggled into Alfheim's heart. They had been caught by the elven secret service agents, the Jayon Daga. Vincent was dead. Lila had survived by the slenderest of margins, her body almost completely ruined by a magical attack. And then she had been sent back, a slab of meat, a warning to Otopia, and Otopian SS had made her into a multibillion-dollar hero. And that was only the beginning.

For the first time since those days Lila found herself glad that her family would never know the truth. She was glad that her psych profiles would show the redlines all over her shame and revulsion, because she didn't think she could speak about them aloud.

The luxury of self-recrimination is not for you, said a familiar voice from somewhere close to her heart. *We are already slaved to duty, and we must endure, and go on.*

You'd better keep quiet, Lila replied in the silent speech of thought. *I don't know how much of you the AI can pick up.* She sighed aloud without thinking and Williams glanced at her.

Lila gave the white-haired old woman a nod and a shrug, knowing that the substance of her report was enough to excuse a few heartfelt sighs. Having a "dead" elf living inside her chest wouldn't be one of the causes that Williams might automatically jump to.

In response to her words Tath coiled up obediently, a slow-whirling green energy. His *andalune* body was all that remained of him after Lila's sometime colleague, the elf agent Dar, had murdered him. Tath was a necromancer, and thus unique among the elves in being able to switch hosts for his aetheric self. His *andalune*—the magical body all elves possessed—had jumped from his dead body to hers when she had kissed his face in pity.

Regret it?

Shut up when you're winning, Lila suggested. She knew perfectly well that her survival and what success she'd had were in part due to Tath—the two days it had taken her to re-edit her memories of the mission, removing him, proved that. Waiting for a reaction to her download was agonising as a result. She kept thinking of all the inconsistencies, the mistakes she might have made that would give her and him away. Of course, as a good agent and a loyal girl, thankful for her life, she should have told everything. But she was no longer sure how much she trusted Otopian SS, even if she trusted these friends and colleagues who worked on her team. She had heard too much in Alfheim, and she had to look out for herself. She hated that. She wanted to go back to the first days, when it had seemed straightforward and honest in every degree, everyone trustworthy and Lila Black doing heroic information-gathering for the security and safety of the human race.

It was all she could do to bite her tongue and suppress a laugh at the idea now. But how she longed for it! Tears threatened. Tath growled internally, a vibration against the wall of her heart, and his impatience and the tickling sensation made her laugh burst out.

Dr. Williams looked up. "What's so funny?" Her face was serious.

"Sorry," Lila said. "Hysteria."

Williams gave her an I-don't-believe-a-word look and went back to her analysis. At that moment the door opened and two more of Lila's Technical Team came into the room.

Lila got up to greet her Aetherial Supervisor, the elf Sarasilien.

Since humans were incapable of sensing or using magic he was on loan from Alfheim to the service as part of yet another diplomatic wrangle. He had served the OSA since the early days of the realms' discovery, some ten years ago, and he had been the one who had helped Lila to survive her transformation from human to cybernetic organism. She hugged him in spite of his natural elven reserve and the situation. Although his physical self remained formally polite she felt the cool-water contact of his *andalune* body touch her with kindness.

/ Tath signalled, afraid that Sarasilien would go more than skin deep and see him. It was a great effort for him to stay so self-contained that nothing of his presence was detectable outside Lila's rib cage and every time they met another aetherically tuned being it was always going to be touch and go.

It's okay, she said to him and stepped back reluctantly from Sarasilien's fatherly embrace.

It's dangerous, Tath corrected her. *He feels affection for you, and his andalune is strong. He will be very hard to fool for long.*

When she stood back she could see the faintest hint of a smile at the corner of the older elf's long mouth, a sign most humans would easily have missed unless they were very familiar with his race. His long ears, the tips level with the top of his head, moved forward slightly. She could smell wintergreen in the long silky fall of hair that parted over his shoulders in fox tones, white and auburn. The aetheric symbols woven into his jacket sparkled.

His slanted eyes blinked slowly, "It is good to see you so well, Lila." Was that a special meaning Lila could detect in his words? Did he know about her and Zal, or her and Tath? Could he—smell it on her or something? She was appalled at the idea.

Behind him the team head, Cara Delaware, gave Lila a brisk smile and a nod. Cara was never anything but functionally social. Lila smiled in response and they took their seats, waiting for Williams to conclude her study.

Lila finished the cube puzzle for the third time and closed down her memory automatic archive so she could scramble it up again. Things which had seemed incredibly awkward, boring, and annoying to her about her cyborg self when she was originally made were now second nature. She glanced at the three faces quietly observing her and sighed, putting the cube down. It was worse than facing her parents after staying out all night.

Dr. Williams was, to look at, a kindly little-old-lady figure, like Red Riding Hood's grandmother, but in a white coat. Sarasilien was an alien presence in the high-tech environment of the Incon headquarters, an ageless elf sitting with the stillness of a statue at the point in the room which was least disturbed by strong electromagnetic fields from all the machinery, including Lila. Cara Delaware was a sharp suit from Langley, who looked as though she'd been born in a button-down white shirt and tailored slacks. None of them fooled Lila for a second.

She knew that Williams was a merciless and devious interrogator, Sarasilien a master aetheritician (why can't humans just say mage?), and Cara, well, Cara was the agency personified—a young and ambitious woman venturing out into an all-new world of five new universes, keen to make friends and influence people, desperate to know something about the sudden appearance of five new sets of dimensional neighbours: the elves, the demons, the faeries, the elementals, and the undead.

Lila was their instrument. No, all right, she meant a bit more than that, but she'd come to realise very recently (about the time she'd knifed her friend, the elven agent Dar, in the chest), that fifty billion dollars of research and engineering and the knife edge of interdimensional relations had bought parts of her she didn't even know were for sale. So she was sitting here, part employee, part volunteer, part slave, part friend, a little bit of daughter and a whole shitload of resentment, explaining to their quiet, experienced faces the grim details of how she had fulfilled her last mission.

Lila did her best to tell it in her own way, even though they all had
the benefit of the download.

It had been a success in its central cause—Zal had been saved from
a fate worse than death and was now playing stadium concerts in the
midlantic states. But the peripheral discoveries and events were less
than great.

Zal turned out to not just be a freak elf who liked playing mode-
X rock. If he had been that would have been enough, because Alfheim
saw that alone as sufficiently treacherous and defiant of their core
beliefs to exile him forever. But Zal was much more than that. During
his work for the Jayon Daga as an agent in Demonia he had somehow
changed his aetheric allegiance and was now—well, even Lila didn't
know what he was. An elf with demonic tendencies? Not quite half
and half, but definitely changed in radical ways so that the oppositional magics of Alfheim and Demonia were both available to him. As
a result of that, and his subsequent defection to the Otopian music
scene, he had become one of those magical items most prized by people
with really big ambitions.

One such person was Arië, a ruler in Alfheim's arcane monarchic
government, who had taken it upon herself to use him in a spell to
sever the realms altogether. In saving Zal, Lila had caused the destruction of a large part of the Alfheim ruling classes, indirectly caused the
death of Arië herself, and now Alfheim was in open civil war.

Still, it was even worse than that.

She had killed one friend to save another. She hadn't mentioned
that.

She didn't plan to.

She had a dead elf necromancer living inside her chest.

She didn't plan to mention that either.

She felt no loyalty, sitting there. She didn't know what she felt, but
it wasn't good. She had hoped, thought—well, she had had some
stupid idea that coming here and debriefing would be like a confession

which would absolve her. It wasn't. Didn't. She longed to go back forty-eight hours and to be in bed with the curtains closed, Zal's naked, sleeping body in her arms—when she hadn't had a care in the world and every fuse in the place was blown dead so that nothing and nobody could find her.

"Lila?" Dr. Williams asked her.

"Oh. Well. Arië was eaten by the water dragon and then . . ."

"What did it do next?" Sarasilien asked.

"I didn't see," Lila said, honestly. "It could still be in the lake for all I know. So, chomp. Which was lucky, otherwise I probably wouldn't be here. Chomp. Then we fell into the lake—everything fell. The whole palace collapsed when she died. Lots of people drowned and I caught hold of Zal and got him back to the surface okay and we made our way back out of Sathanor and then, here. Arië—there was a moment when I thought her whole spell to sever the realms was working but I don't know if that was true."

Cara flipped through the notes on her lap. "Extensive earth tremors were reported at that hour here in Otopia. It has been put down to crucial tectonic pressure shifts as several conjoined plates moved at once. Nothing too bad. Small tidal waves. Only a few hundred dead. Nothing since you came back."

Lila stared at her, wondering what kind of statistics Cara was used to dealing with that these seemed such small beer to her. "Arië was helped by necromancers from all the other realms, including this one."

Cara nodded. "A specialist team has been dispatched to attempt to reclaim or otherwise prove the deaths of those Otopians involved."

"Right," Lila said. "We were about two hundred metres down. It was very messy. They almost certainly drowned. I don't believe they could have survived."

"There was an aetheric shockwave," Sarasilien said. "Congruent with your descriptions. It was—difficult—to avoid." He winced. "All the other realms have sent us intelligence about the effects they have perceived. We are convinced Arië's efforts would have been reasonably successful if Zal had continued to function as the spell's axis. You are to be congratulated on a most successful outcome."

"Thanks," Lila said, wondering if she'd have sounded any more enthusiastic if he'd been inviting her to a funeral. Yes, she'd have been much more enthusiastic about funerals.

Dr. Williams made yet another note on her clipboard. Lila zoomed in on what she was writing but it was all in wretchedly tiny shorthand and on intelligent paper too, which concealed messages until it was cued to display them, so she could read nothing. Dr. Williams noticed her attempt, and made a note about that too. Lila frowned.

"As it stands," Cara said, "what interests us the most now is the connection between Zal's kidnap and the evidence concerning the Quantum Bomb fault underlying Bay City, which you and Malachi have uncovered."

"There's a link?" Lila said. She felt a tremor in her chest as Tath stirred with interest at the news. The quiescent, green shimmer of his presence opened out: alien spring.

"We believe that Arië was not alone in wanting to achieve fundamental separation of the realms. The recordings you found near the studios in Bay City were being taken by faery agents for their intelligence-gathering moot. Though our relations with them are somewhat hampered by the fact that we are all new to one another and have much to learn, they were willing enough to admit that they have been pursuing similar research in all the realms. They would not say what they were looking for but we believe it is closely related to the faultlines in Otopia which were created by the Quantum Bomb. As you know, faeries deny the Bomb as a fact, as do the other realms."

"Weird that they're so interested in evidence about it then?" Lila asked, recalling that it was faeries who had been key to Zal's kidnap in the first place.

"Yes. It is also known to us that Zal's own efforts are hardly limited to making money or music in Otopia. As you said in your report, your Jayon Daga informant . . ."

"Dar. He was called Dar."

"Yes. Said that it was not an accident where or what Zal sang. That he was one of Alfheim's principal defenders until he 'went native' in Demonia."

"Elf and demon aetheric usage is very different," Sarasilien said quietly. "Their cultures are built around those differences. Elves use language to mobilise and shape aetheric energy. Demons use music. We suspect that Zal is adept in a new, hybrid form of aetheric control. It is possible that he was made so by demon agencies and acts for them, or that he was deliberately involved in this spell of Arië's . . ."

"No way," Lila said.

"We are assigning you to discover exactly what happened to Zal in Demonia," Cara told her. "We need to know how, when, and why he was changed, and what it means to the demons, the elves, and everyone else on the aetheric block."

Sarasilien winced—Lila knew it was because of Cara's words. Clumsiness or imprecision of speaking were almost physically painful to elves. She was surprised that Delaware didn't notice. "Zal is no innocent bystander," Sarasilien said and Lila wanted to kill him, even though, of course, he was right and she knew that.

Dr. Williams made a note.

"You will go into Demonia under a scholarship ticket," Delaware was saying. "You have diplomatic immunity but you are there to study demon culture and lore, to covertly discover Zal's heritage and to bring back as much information as you can on whether or not the demons are also interested in Bomb faults or whatever they call them. Sarasilien has organised your entry with a friend of yours who is native. He will brief you before you leave." Delaware got up, looking at her watchface where it was scrolling with bright charts and schedules. "If you'll excuse me, I have other meetings . . ." She shook Lila's hand with formal vigour. "Feels just like the real thing," she said, with an encouraging smile.

"Yeah." Lila blinked, releasing the woman from her synthetic skin's grip. Since she had been in Alfheim she'd forgotten to keep remembering that her arms and legs were mostly prosthetics. They had started to seem her own, until now. "From the other side too."

Delaware glanced at her, revealing more sharp intelligence in that moment than she had all day. Lila shook her head, letting the matter go. "Good luck," Delaware said.

Sarasilien stood when she had gone. "I too must depart and prepare to meet with you this afternoon when our demon guest will be with us." He held his hand out to Lila and she shook it, feeling really stupid now until she realised he was only doing it as an excuse to touch her. His *andalune* body ran across her hand and arm. He held her hand in both of his and lifted one eyebrow in a very uncharacteristic invitation to complicity. "I look forward," he looked down at her chest, "to hearing more details of your visit to my beautiful homeland later."

Tath cursed.

Lila nodded. "Sure. Later." She wanted to hug him, to warn him, to tell him not to say a damn word about whatever he could see, but as she met the strong gaze in his slanted blue eyes she knew that he wasn't about to give her away. Not yet at least. The pointed tip of his right ear twitched—something like a silent smile. "Sure."

He left her alone with Dr. Williams, the one person that Lila really, really, didn't want to be talking to right now, though since all the formal information-gathering had been done there was no way she could put it off a minute more.

"Hello Lila," said the doctor with a gentle smile. "How are you?"

"I'm fine."

Dr. Williams sighed and turned her clipboard around. She tapped the paper with the end of her pen, activating it. It showed Lila that what she had taken for shorthand were a lot of drawings of little stick figures. They were standing in groups, shouting, and in the middle was one with robot arms and legs which had its hands pressed against its head. It was surrounded by a large scribbled circle of darkness. "Anything you want to tell me about in particular?"

Lila thought about it. "Dar, the elf agent who almost killed me, the one who was hunting Zal. Well, I nearly killed him, but then I saved him—in Alfheim. He saved me. I was having a bad time with all my metal. Like last time you saw me, it was all too powerful for my bones. I kept getting hurt. But after we did this healing in Alfheim I was fine. Better than fine. Zal said I have elementals fused into me now and Dar must have done that. I don't know. We . . . Dar and I . . . we worked together . . ."

"Not as enemies?"

"No! No, not at all. We worked together to get Zal free. But our cover got blown and I had to kill him just to stay in with a chance of finishing the . . . of getting Zal out and stopping Arië. He's dead. I think he was a true friend although there were lots of times when he . . ." She paused. She wanted to explain how the loyalties to state and friend, to family and self were so mixed up. But that wouldn't be the right thing to say now, perhaps ever, in her position, since it could only be seen as a weakness in her. "Funny how we always end up talking about Dar."

"Not really. If it weren't for Dar you wouldn't be here at all."

"No," Lila said. "I'd still be a desk cowboy in Foreign Affairs with all my arms and legs and family and I'd never have met him, or Zal, or you. Can I go?"

"Yes, if you answer me just one question."

Lila looked at Dr. Williams's gentle, sympathetic face. "What?"

"Was what you did in Alfheim right, or wrong?"

CHAPTER TWO

Lila looked at the doctor. "Everything I did was right."

Williams nodded, encouraging her to go on.

"At the moment I did it," Lila said, and loathed the qualification.

"I advised Delaware not to send you out immediately," the doctor said wearily. "But she doesn't like to listen to me. No doubt the rest of today is already scheduled up to its eyeballs with briefings and any number of other necessary checks and balances before you leave. So, you'd better spill the rest of it in the next five minutes."

"There is no rest of it," Lila said.

"You overused your Voluntary Emotional Override shunt so much that the logistics here advises me that you should have it removed for your own mental health."

Lila shrugged. "So remove it."

"I see that the Automatic Warrior setting or whatever ridiculous name it goes by these days functioned as it ought to."

"Yeah. The off switch actually worked this time."

"I'm glad to hear it. Tell me about Zal."

Lila was almost caught out by the sudden shift of topic, which was not accompanied by any change in tone or delivery. She hesitated. "He's very annoying."

"Are you involved with him? As they like to say when they mean, Do you love him?"

"None of your goddamned business."

"Congratulations. You may go."

"You know," Lila said, standing up. "You may think you know all about me, but you don't." The childishness of it surprised her.

Shut up when you're losing, Tath said, with a twinge of smugness.

"Call me," Williams said kindly.

Lila walked out. She was so angry she didn't know what else to do. Outside, in the warmly lit corridors of power, her colleagues and fellow agents greeted her with varying mixtures of friendliness, respect, and condescension that marked out very clearly to what extent each of them thought they knew something about her recent mission. She cued up the Voluntary Emotional Override and met them with interested politeness. Once she'd reached the women's toilets she uncued the VEO, vomited up her rage in one of the cubicles, and washed her mouth out at the sink.

She looked in the mirror as she dried her face on a paper towel. Scarlet hair, silver eyes. She watched her hands screw the towel up and throw it away. Their synthetic skin looked normal. She considered stripping it off.

Why bother? You look freakish enough as it is. Anyway, it will not get you what you want.

Oh. And what's that?

Another woman came in to put some water in a can for plants and to touch up her makeup. She glanced at Lila nervously. Lila said, "Hey," adjusted her shirt, and left.

To fit in with everyone else and be normal, Tath said.

I can get you extracted in a minute, you know. I don't even have an idea of what to say to Sarasilien.

How interesting that you know his long name, Tath said. *It must be worthless. I wonder why. Do your human magic experts not suspect?*

Perhaps it's a sign of mutual trust? Lila snarled. A secretary carrying papers and coffee shrank to the wall as she passed. "Sorry," Lila muttered aloud, trying to slow down.

If it is then it is the first of its kind. We should find out the truth.

No. I trust him. Don't even say things against him if you know what's good for you.

Do not reveal me to him, Tath insisted. *He may have noticed something, but it was not the fact of my inhabitation.*

We went through this already. Lila found the exit doors to the staff garden, an enclosed square at the heart of the main building. She walked out into the sunlight and fresh air and took several deep breaths. She doubted that it was even possible for her to have a private thought or feeling secret from Tath but she daren't think about that for more than a second at a time, because when she did the sensation of being invaded and violated got too much to bear. To his credit—his minor credit—if this was the case he was smart enough to keep quiet about it when it really mattered. She thought that she could detect when he was being truly withdrawn, because his energy signature changed and the electromagnetic patterns around him altered.

Now the opposite effect occurred as she walked across to the garden's two orange trees and leant against one of them. Tath expanded and flowed outward through her body and beyond it into the tree. She gave him a few minutes. It was nothing like a tree in Alfheim, nothing like the huge nature which made that place unique, and this Otopian tree had no magical aura she knew about, but the contact had a calming and regenerative effect on him in spite of those things. She knew he had to fight his corner against her now because he was so vulnerable to her. The opposite had been true in Alfheim, and might be again.

Lila connected to her AI-self and ran through the internal pharmacy she carried as part of her field medical supplies. There was nothing useful in there. It had all been used up treating elves and herself in Alfheim. The day's list of meetings—a collection of briefs, debriefs, and resupplies—scrolled obediently up over her view of the garden's mild morning colours. For an instant she imagined missing all of them.

A blue flash blinked on like a werelight dancing on the top of the yucca plants opposite and she took the private phone call, hearing the line link directly to her auditory centres with a soft click.

"I hope I'm interrupting something important."

Zal! Lila almost jumped with relief at the sound of his unique voice, soft because it was a flute pure as any elf's but at the same time as deeply harmonised as a demon's. She replied on internal voice only so that nobody could see she was online. *Where are you?*

"Bohemia. Not interesting without you. I have no idea what it looks like. How are you?"

Perfect. Was Otopia SA very hard on you?

"Your people are the model of tedious interrogative pursuit. Next time ask them to beat me up. I'm old-fashioned like that. It's hard to give away secrets without severe pain. Feels like cheating and I like to play fair."

Lila felt the snap and zing of wild magic crackle in the air around her for an instant and knew she was being played all right. The Game between her and Zal, a magical bond with severe forfeits and excruciating rules, was perfectly intact.

That'll be the day. What did you tell them?

"I stuck to the story we agreed on, though it could have used a few more years to get the paste straight over the worst of those holes. Your replacement thorn-in-my-side is a former model from Aragon. I think they hope she'll pillow-talk the truth out of me."

Lila's face prickled and the sharp scent of citrus peel shot up her nose. Far from hating the Game that tied them together with its barbs of mutual lust she found she was getting fond of it. *How are Poppy and 'Dia? Still talking to you?*

"I'm easy to forgive," Zal said. "I bet you're going into Demonia."

You keep guessing, o elf I am not supposed to speak to. Any other predictions?

"They'll crack this encryption in about another thirty seconds. When you get there watch out for the mafia. The highest families are the Cassieli and the Solasin. Oh, and the Ahrimani."

That would be your lot.

"Remember that the demon mafia value loyalty, just like the Otopian set. But in other respects it isn't like Otopia. The mafia are accepted as part of demonian government. Law is a mutable concept, depending on who applies it and for what."

Who can I trust?

"Nobody, obviously. One more thing. The Mephistopheli are involved in a vendetta with the Ahrimani going back about three hundred years, and they particularly want me dead. Long story. If they find out that you know me, they'll put you on the list, and if any of the demons catch a whiff of Tath, they'll be after you for all sorts of interesting reasons you don't want to know about."

Demons don't like elves?

"They like them like you like chocolate. Tath'll fill you in. Time's up. Give them hell."

Zal?

He had gone. There were three messages waiting for her attention, blinking red. She was running late but the conversation, laced as it was with dire warnings, had put her back in a sunny mood. *Come on, Tath.*

The elf reluctantly returned to his hiding place. *Your trees hardly count as alive. They have the aetheric energy of deadfall. You do realise that roots are for more than simply connecting them to the ground, don't you? What kind of idiot plants trees in concrete bunkers and expects to gain pleasure from their contemplation?*

No more compliments, darling, Lila said as she walked back inside. *A girl can only take so much in one day.*

She apologised to the microrobotics technicians for her tardiness. They exclaimed at how well everything had held up under the various loads. They couldn't find much to fix so they tested everything and gave her a clean bill of mechanical health.

The medical team couldn't understand what had happened at the junctions where her machine prosthetics were bonded to her flesh body. They wanted to keep her in overnight for testing but didn't have the authority.

"Is this the kind of thing that aetheric intervention can do?" asked one. "We need to start trading for that right away. Look at this. The tissue and the metal merge right into one another. The metal changes from crystalline to cellular and these metallic cells have their own kind of biology. And then the metal. Look at it. I thought we made her out of titanium-based alloys, but this has an even more efficient structure and it looks . . . I don't know, like it changes structure where it needs to, as if it had grown like bones in natural reaction to stress. How freaky is that?" The doctor looked up at Lila's face for the first time and into her eyes. "Are you suffering any pains or discomfort these days?"

"Not a thing," Lila said.

They resupplied her medical kit and she went on to the nuclear technicians, who said the reactor would go on its current fuel cell for another thirty years. She stopped at the armoury and reclaimed her weapons.

"Concealed guns only," the sergeant-at-arms told her. "And you're limited to what ammunition we can hide. That isn't much. And as far as we know demons are very resilient. There's not much research, but you have to get very lucky to nail 'em with firearms."

Lila checked the two guns that were stored in the empty spaces within her thighs and then closed the vents in her jeans over the top of them. The weapons in her forearms were all functional. She reloaded them and left, rolling her shirtsleeves down as she walked away. At the end of the corridor, behind special electromagnetic shielding, Sarasilien's office waited for her.

With every step she covered towards it she felt heavier and knew it was because she was going to lie to him, and nothing in her wanted to. She wanted his approval, but she didn't deserve it. It was easier when she was a bedridden wreck and he was the only one who could reach her, his the only touch that was light enough to bear. She knocked on the door. There was no answer. She opened it.

The only warning that anything might be amiss came from Tath. He uncoiled as the crack in the door widened, a shimmering, agitated bursting sensation under her ribs. He didn't need to call out to her. She could feel his "no" like a freezing jolt, but it was too late.

Her momentum carried her forward into the room, AI-self synchronising with her in that split second of unstoppable action. As her foot fell it placed her inside the aetheric energy field that had been set up to match the room's perimeter, a magic circle enveloping the entire office. To pass a spellcast wall like this was literally to leave the world behind, whichever world you had happened to be in at the time. The other side might be anywhere, if the spell was a portal, but this one was the so-called circle: in reality a sphere of space and time that had been temporarily disjointed or replaced by the conditions that the spellcaster determined.

On the other side of this barrier Lila found that she was still inside Sarasilien's office, and the office was much the same as usual, except for the strange general increase in colour saturation and the faint tendrils of visible wild aether moving curiously around the magical equipment racks. That and the fact that Sarasilien was seated on an altogether new sofa divan of oddly baroque design, draped with sumptuous carpets and thick white sheep's fleeces. He was his usual tall and upright self, stern-faced and attentive to the tiny and elegant pair of feet he held in his hands. The feet were attached to the long, shapely legs and infamously curvaceous bottom of Sorcha, Zal's sister. Sorcha was reclining at full length, leaning against the other arm of the divan. Her dress was filmy and perfectly designed to reveal nothing whilst appearing to reveal everything. She was eating a chocolate bar, her black-crimson skin sparkling with a raspberry glitter from within as she pretended to lash the elf's solemn shoulders with her arrow-tipped tail. "Harder," she snarled, in a voice that could have melted paving slabs.

Sarasilien frowned and dug his fingers into her feet with more concentration. Lila could see a sheen of sweat on his forehead and, in this aetheric world, could see his *andalune* body clearly; a blue-green shimmer in the air around him, its edges clearly defined. Sorcha's tail tip was catching hold of the substance of it behind his back and kneading it like it was saltwater taffy, stretching it out and letting it snap back into place like elastic only to dive forward and snag it again.

He glanced up as he noticed Lila and briefly closed his eyes and almost shook, ears flattening against his head in a clear elven gesture that was the equivalent of a human shrug of helplessness and embarrassment.

Sorcha quivered with pleasure and turned her head lazily to meet Lila's astonished gaze. "Hey honey," she said. "Welcome to Demonia."

CHAPTER THREE

"**H**ey," Lila said weakly. "I . . . um . . ." She didn't know what to say.

Sorcha had no such trouble. "Come and take a load off." She sat up and offered Lila the space directly behind her, patting it with her hand. To Sarasilien she simply murmured, "That's it, baby. Keep it going."

Lila simply couldn't believe her eyes and ears. She stared at her supervisor as he massaged the demon's feet, his aetheric body drawing the occasional pink spark from Sorcha's impeccably smooth skin where they touched. The sparks made the frown lines between his eyebrows deepen but Lila got the clear impression that he wasn't unhappy about the situation, only about being seen in it. She sat down where Sorcha indicated and the small, lithe demon leant back on her.

"Gods, I forgot you're metal!" she exclaimed. "And what happened to you? Who gave you the aetheric respray in Alfheim? I hope you weren't all unfaithful to my brother. Well, not more than once a day." Sorcha wriggled herself comfortable against Lila's shoulder and offered Lila a bite of her chocolate bar. "You can finish it. I need to save myself for the banquet."

"Banquet?" Lila asked, completely afloat in this strange unreality. She took the chocolate and sniffed it. It was not an Otopian brand. She took a bite. It was heavenly.

"Your entry to demon society is to be somewhat more of an affair than we had originally intended," Sarasilien said, keeping his gaze firmly on Sorcha's toes.

"Oh no," Sorcha said airily, licking melted chocolate off her fingers. "Nothing we wouldn't do for any visitor. Not like you queens of the prim frontier serving her nothing but leaves and all that shit. Even foreign assassins coming to murder us would get a decent meal before we tore their skins off and fed them to the dogs. She's coming in as my Otopian groupie."

"Your groupie," Lila repeated. Sorcha was as much of a pop phenomenon as her brother was a rock one, but their relation wasn't known about in Otopia and, even though she was sublimely beautiful and a great talent, Lila didn't feel in an homage-ous mood.

Sorcha snorted. "Okay. Friend. My geeky scholar friend come to assimilate our information for the Otopian homelands, ready to report back to all the glamorous magazines and medianets on the glorious realities of life in the perfect world."

"Report?"

"You are going to write journal articles, reports, and press releases for various outlets," Sarasilien said drily. "And some for the Demonian Tourist Board."

"You have a tourist board?" Lila's sense of unreality peaked. The soft warmth of Sorcha's crimson hair flames licked playfully over her chin.

"Of course, darling," Sorcha purred. "We are getting ready to welcome Otopians for city breaks, countryside retreats, and extended adventure holidays. Demonia enjoys the most cordial and free of trade relations and . . . Well, it will, in a few months' time. And you are going to prime the pumps. In return, I and all my esteemed contacts, relations, lovers, exlovers, adoring fans, and various multinational organisations, will release selected but important information to your lovely security services to promote interdimensional harmony and the spirit of cooperation and trust so that we can make beautiful money together." She wriggled her foot in the elf's grasp. "More."

"And you're another secret service agent, are you?" Lila asked. "What, is it a family business?"

"Me? No, honey. I'm simply myself. But I am acting as Demonia's representative here, and in my own interests, and mostly, mostly in Zal's interests, because you his baby, baby. And you'll need somebody like me fighting in your corner because of that. Somebody who's smart and popular, and who's got stuff on you. So I was just recruited."

"By?"

Sarasilien looked up. "I thought it would be best."

Lila gave him a wide-eyed meaningful stare, looking from his face down to his hardworking hands and back again. What gives?

His ear tips went pink.

"I thought elves and demons had oppositional magics and didn't like each other."

"We do. We don't," Sorcha sighed. "Have you ever had an elf, Li? What am I saying? Of course you have. Look at this." She snapped Sarasilien's *andalune* again. "That kind of hurts us both. But it's also kind of nice. Like picking scabs that are just about ready to come off. You know? It's fizzy. The magic is all attracted to each other, but then it meets and pow! It doesn't match and where it touches there's this reaction and zap! Ouch. Lovely. Really, really good. And then you do this." She penetrated Sarasilien's blue-green shimmer with her tail point and shuddered deliciously, "and it's like scratching the most intense itch—sooo gooood! But then." She pulled out. "You have to stop, or else you'll start to bleed and it burns—ahhhh! And you just know that in ten seconds it'll be itching like you can't believe."

Lila didn't think she should be listening, looking, or knowing about this.

"Miss Sorcha is trying to explain that there is more to our difference than simple alchemical responses or aetheric reaction. Culturally we are . . ."

"Well, you know them," Sorcha cut him off. "Captain Uptight and the Uptightathons. All serious and holy and pure and dull as the dullest thing."

"And I know you," Sarasilien said without twitching an eyebrow, "oh exemplar of the most exquisite indulgence. And you know that demons always say this about elves," he did something to her foot and she squeaked, "because you like to make fun. But you don't really mean it."

Sorcha lay back and rested her head in Lila's lap. "We do so mean it. They have some minor amusement value back home. That's all. Now, we have to get you some better clothes, and then we can be on our way. Oh, and your man here has to finish my massage, of course. Part of the deal."

Get her away! Tath pleaded. Lila could feel his anxiety and not a small amount of revulsion. He was cringing, and it wasn't simply with fear of discovery.

Sorcha, who wasn't privy to that moment, gave Lila a conspiratorial look and added in a whisper, "Silly Illy here took almost ten minutes to agree. Can you believe the nerve? Most men would be paying me their inheritance to do what he's doing and yet I have to *trade* with the idiot!"

Lila burst out laughing.

Sarasilien glanced at her and smiled. "You see? I knew she would be the right one for you."

"Ah!" Sorcha shrieked, her face breaking into an adoring expression. "Don't you just love him to death? All that elven arrogance and patrician garbage he puts out, but it's all about *you* the whole time. How cool is that? You gone up in my 'stimation, girl. Not that you weren't up there the whole time. Did you screw my brother's brains out yet? I didn't get a note telling me you were gonna collect on my bet."

It was Lila's turn to blush. "Um. No win yet. Still all ongoing with the Game."

"Oh. Tell me you didn't do him already. Don't you know anything about anything? And he was ripe for the picking, honey. He would have bailed, no question. Now it's gonna be much harder. But I still think you're gonna win, even if you do have to break his heart before you do. Now, what say we share this one here? He's not much of an aperitif, I know, but it's as good as it's gonna get this side of the border. Man, this place is a pleasure *desert*. I am so out of love with all the serious talk and diplomatic yar yar yar."

"Share?" Lila was sure she understood Sorcha this time. "That's obscene."

"Don't you use that language with me, lady!" Sorcha snapped and sat up. She grabbed the end of the chocolate bar out of Lila's hand and bit a piece off, showing her pointed white teeth.

Oh, thank you, Tath said fervently.

Sarasilien's adroit hands never stopped. "Sorcha's favours aren't lightly offered," he said calmly, as though they were talking about dividing a piece of bread. "Although it is common practice in Demonia to make little of great offerings. You must excuse Lila, princess of delight. She knows next to nothing about demons."

"Ah am appraised of that fact," Sorcha drawled and pushed at his abdomen with one foot, teasingly. "Listen to him call me a princess, like he thinks I don't know he's making butter." But the compliment had pleased her.

Lila used the excuse to get up. "If there's things I should get before we go . . ."

"Not you, moron." Sorcha plucked her feet out of Sarasilien's hold and stood up. "You and this frigid creature have to have some kind of long and boring talk, apparently. I'll go and see to all your stuff. No worries." She twirled around and sat down in Sarasilien's lap to put on her shoes—a pair of beautiful, almost strapless high heels. She smiled softly and changed in a second, from her pretended strop into a seductress, placing her mouth against the elf's and her hands on his shoulders, giving him a long and lingering kiss before bouncing up, light as a feather, and flouncing out without a backward glance. The door slammed behind her.

Lila stared at Sarasilien. In these few moments everything about their relationship had changed. She hadn't noticed him as a sexual being, and now she did. She had never had to think about him as anything but what he meant to her: security, reliability, parental strength, a protector, a fellow worker. Now she saw that he was a proper person, and that she had never seen him like that before. Her own arrogance amazed her.

The elf drew in a deep breath through his nose and blew it out very slowly through his lips before meeting her eye. "Cara Delaware is convinced by her demon advisers that you will be able to pull off this journalistic feat of investigation and reportage in Demonia. This is because no human has ever been into Demonia proper; they are all groomed to perceive what Demonia thinks fit for them to perceive at any given moment. Of course this is the way with all of us. However, her briefing materials, which she has given me to give you," he paused and reached down to his side, picking up a sheaf of paper, "are all exquisitely researched, but they will not serve you." He dropped them. "It is not remotely possible for you to enter Demonia and live there undercover. You must go as Sorcha's guest or not at all. And, speaking of undercover matters, perhaps you would like to enlighten me as to the nature of your suddenly acquired aetheric signature?"

Lila had to struggle not to squirm.

He means the metal elements, Tath murmured, distilled to a drop.

"I do not mean the metal elementals fused into the kind of alloys that the dark elves make in the foundries of night, though the gift of it is a startling revelation. But we need not speak of it now, nor fathom your story that it was given by Dar, which cannot be true, can it—else

Arië would have treated differently with you," Sarasilien added calmly.
He gestured around him with both hands. "You may speak freely to
me, as a friend, Lila."

Watch it, Tath whispered, afraid.

Lila looked around at the room, realising that Sarasilien was
emphasising the fact that his office was not part of Otopia any longer.
They were in Demonia. What he would never say in Otopia he would
say here, including criticism of Cara. And he would do . . .

"Sarasilien isn't your real name," she blurted, barely thinking it
through before she spoke.

"No," he admitted and Lila felt what was left of any conviction she
had possessed concerning the loyalties of those she knew dissolve into
nothing under her. "But here I am at least free to tell you so."

"What else do you want to tell me?" she asked, tears coming to her
eyes even though she did her damnedest to stop them.

"That I am still your friend, though I realise it must seem that this
day heaps one betrayal on another. Such is the way of our business. This
is how I can believe in your friendship with Dar, and at the same time
comprehend perfectly how it was between you at the end."

Who is he? Tath wondered, an itch in her thoughts.

Lila ignored him. "Do you mean that you'll kill me if you have to?"

"No," the elf said. "It is in all of our interests that you travel safely
and exit Demonia alive."

"Is this a secret cabal of *our interests?*" Lila asked, her heart hammering, feeling like it had been struck with a pickaxe. "How about you
tell me about that and then I'll tell you what's eating you about me.
And never mind that for a minute. How the hell could you do this?"

"Do what? Tell you the truth?"

"Is that what this is?"

"Lila." The tall elf moved closer to her and placed his hands pas-
sively into his lap, resting the backs of them on his legs. "Nationality,
statehood, these formations of mass identity are all false idolatry. It is a

heresy in Alfheim to say so, yet I am in agreement with Zal and those of Dar's party when they speak of the only true self being the spirit within (a contentious definition I will gladly speak with you of another time) and the only true relation of interest or value the friendship of equals. If I could give you my name and it not be a burden to you, because the knowing of it bestows a power that others will try to steal, then I would give it to you now. But I am not about to spend so unwisely for you or myself. I cannot give you anything concrete to anchor my faith to your trust excepting the token of some information. I am concerned that you have already given over much too much of this to another. Will you tell me about the *andalune* around your heart?"

"If you tell me how I can stop anyone else seeing it."

The elf whose name she did not know said, "Talismanic protection is the best I can offer."

"I'll take it, and if you stiff me . . ."

"If I stiff you, as you so eloquently put it, you will only find out too late." His voice was calm but he smiled delicately. "Unfortunately you will have to keep trusting me to discover whether or not I am worthy of your investment." He stood up and crossed the room to a fume cupboard. Beneath the glass hood of its extractor deck an old, much worn chest of drawers supported a marble slab. He unclipped the bindings which held the slab in place and hinged it aside, reaching into a narrow compartment beneath it. He returned to Lila with a delicate silver chain, upon which hung a garland of pink roses made from clusters of tiny gemstones.

Amethysts, Tath said. *Good enough against demons, and ninety percent of the elven population, which makes him in the top ten. That means noble families and I must know him, so besides the fact you do not know his name I think you might assume you do not know his face either.*

"Not your colour," Lila said aloud to her mentor, trying to lighten the mood, indeed, to do anything that could bring her back to the place where she could feel good about letting him into the sphere of her awareness again, with the solidity she used to have in him, like he was part of her furniture.

"Nor do I need it. I am beyond the ability of such items to affect me for good or ill," he said. "But I have charmed it to . . ."

"When?" said Lila and Tath at the same moment.

"As I took it out of its place."

Bad news. I didn't spot anything. No words. No nothing. He must be a synae-thete.

A what?

They do not require a medium to access aetheric power. Such people are extremely rare, one in a billion. If that's the case he may not even be an elf.

Stop now. I can't deal with this until later.

As you wish. Be on your guard. But it may be the demon was right about one matter. He is showing you clearly the truth of his nature, and that should either honour or appal you, for no being of such power needs reveal themselves to another.

Sarasilien—she could not think of him another way—placed the necklace around her throat and did up the catch.

I wonder what else is on this thing? Tath worried.

"Thank you."

He could be lying of course . . .

"The dead elf in my chest thinks you're lying about the necklace."

"Then they are a worthwhile ally. I assume that if you had wanted to be rid of them you would have achieved this or asked. Your secret is safe with me. But I wonder what motivates you. You struggle so hard to accept your change into a machine, why go further and become a boarding house to ghosts?"

"I like variety?"

The elf broke into a smile and then a quiet laugh.

CHAPTER FOUR

Lila sat in the Great Library of Bathshebat, chewing the end of her pencil. She was in a private turret, seated at a semicircular desk of exquisite workmanship, scrolls and books open around her. From their pages and runes a faint mist of colour and scent wove up into a pretty veil. Through this lacework she could easily see the pointed arches of the turret's fine windows and through them across the city's towers, parapets, pinnacles, domes, minarets, spires, and roofs. Jewel-like enamel and coloured tiles flourished in dazzling beauty everywhere beneath the sapphire blue of the sky. It was a riot of beauty.

The pencil tasted of lemonade. Her notes—all handwritten, because there was no electricity in Demonia, and because she must have something that made her look scholarly—fluttered gently on the warm breeze and would have blown away except for the pretty dark-blue paperweight that held them down. It was made of a smooth stone that Lila liked to touch, sculpted into the shape of a sleeping cat. She felt very content as she stroked it absently with her finger and let the tension drop out of her shoulders. Far from being the appalling assignment she had feared, Demonia was like a holiday.

The soft green of the library walls made a perfect frame for the soft yellow and apricot sky, she thought as she contemplated yet another spectacular demonian sundown. The batlike, birdlike, and aetheric forms of airborne demons skimmed and darted, and the pretty paper fans of the strange one- and two-person cars that floated like boats sailed soundlessly through lanes of air, their propellers whirring. The orange sunset brought out the beautiful tones of the city colours even more vividly so that the city seemed to hum or sing with hues, and between the buildings everywhere the canals wound in the perfect complement of aqua tones.

This was the problem with Demonia, Lila thought, drunk on its beauty one more time. It was devastatingly gorgeous. Every view was a postcard, every street a picture book, every store an Aladdin's cave, every coffee house a cornucopia of sweets and scents and divine potions. There was far too much art in Demonia, and most of it was good, unlike in Otopia, where there was quite a lot of art, but much of it mediocre. And for those who didn't think that beauty was the epitome of art, or evolution, or what have you, there were whole streets, movements, theatres, districts, societies, lunch clubs, guilds, and gangs devoted to exploring alternative philosophies. In fact, Lila had begun to suspect that if she toured the entire world she would find that there was no niche of political, intellectual, artistic, scientific, or aesthetic tradition that could not boast at least a tea house, a couple of galleries, a regular forum, and a devoted sect of followers. And this was before she could begin to take account of the social whirl of parties, dinners, breakfasts, wakes, impromptu theatrical productions, musical gatherings, orations, show trials, exhibitions, duels, fêtes, screenings, demonstrations, public experiments, engineering bees, concerts, recitals, spontaneous improvisations, races, fights, and shindigs of every conceivable kind which went on day and night, night and day.

In fact it was a relief to be sitting here engrossed by the day's offerings from the librarian who had been retained for her by Sorcha's family, and not to be still at the eight-day round of celebrations that had been her "preliminaries" and introduction to demon society. No debutante of any kind could have been more thoroughly exhausted than Lila by the talking, dancing, eating, drinking, and enjoying of fine things than she was—and she was fusion powered. Though recently it had begun to seem that she was canapé and champagne, or beer and pretzel, or coffee, tea, and cake powered.

Of course, demons themselves knew absolutely that overdoing a pleasure made it a chore, and so prior to her commencing study she and Sorcha had been shipped off to a spa and subjected to a week's worth of detoxification and relaxation. Again, this was a pleasure in itself that was prolonged to the point of torment; but this moment of having had a complete glut of a particular experience was the point. It had a name, eualusia, beautiful boredom, and the pursuit of the perfect moment of eualusia was one of the more important games, one of millions, that demons played routinely.

Lila had no doubt that eventually she would find the library's eualusic point, but it wasn't going to be for a long time yet. She glanced back down to her page where she was trying to write a basic tourist primer on Demonian culture.

"Demon children are serious, studious, and highly focused. Demonia is governed and administered in civil, military, and economic affairs by sub-nineteen-year-olds. They are born with inherited memories, full of the information collected by all of their genetic and aetheric ancestors. This equips them for mastery of intellectual affairs by the age of ten. They are expected to apply themselves monastically to academic, civil, or military duties until the age of majority (nineteen), when they inevitably drift off into more selfish pursuits, at least some of every day devoted to an art.

"A list of what demons consider art is so long as to be unpublishable. Any endeavour or project is elevated to artistic status by the energy, devotion, and skill with which it is pursued. The demon who exerts him or her self most completely and who achieves greatness in any sphere is considered worthy of the label artist. Those who also live the rest of their lives to the fullest expression are considered Maha Anima (great spirits) and are the most powerful of their kind.

"Demon adults are tricky. They reach complete adulthood at twenty-five, after which their interest in self-sacrificing affairs, such as government, declines. Demons view governance, jurisprudence, and the administrative affairs of their world as a tedious yet essential function. It is their duty to serve nine years of complete devotion to the correct practice of these affairs, after which they never again bother with it. They become much more independent, voracious, and sexually active (in Demonia sex is an art, of course; a social as well as a personal and physical one—and although demons can reproduce sexually this isn't their only means and reproduction is not considered an important function of sex per se).

"In old age demons become increasingly capricious, selfish, and devious. The highest mortality rates occur in the over-200s, who succumb to death matches and murders over petty arguments. The more petty, the more vicious. These squabblematches have consumed entire families, and it is unusual for any adult demon not to be involved in some sort of scheme, vendetta, or equivalent. Children are excluded from such obligations—they have the country to run."

She was aware, as she added the final line, of Tath's interest. Taking advantage of a quiet minute or two and her distraction he had leaked himself quietly down through her limbs and was making cautious contact with the air.

"Watch it," Lila murmured. "No glamourising me."

I am watching, Tath said, hovering at the level of her skin. *And it would be difficult to add anything to your costume. Zal's sister has execrable taste. Almost on a par with the faeries.*

Lila glanced down at herself. She was wearing what, in Otopia, would be considered a dress suitable for dancing the tango. It was cut up to here and down to there and clung to her skin by charm. Where it touched it was frosted with glitter and the glitter extended out on her bare arms and legs. Her arms looked strong and tanned. Her legs were the silver metal of their natural composition from above the knee down. Sorcha had insisted that this was better than any boots to be bought anywhere in the city. Through various bits of turquoise filminess Lila's tankini underwear showed dark blue. There was, she thought, enough eye makeup on her to make any Goth proud. She could feel its unfamiliar stickiness and again resisted an urge to rub her eyelids.

"Ah, don't tell me," she said, witnessing the merest flare of grass green *andalune* flip a piece of dress fabric contemptuously, "you wouldn't be seen dead in it."

And matching wit. Did nobody explain the complete lack of style in having coordinated accessories?

Lila got the feeling—not her own, but Tath's overspill—that he was enjoying himself. "You can wear it later," she promised.

"Oh . . . thank you," replied a voice as dry as dead leaves behind her.

Before she had a chance to move something flashed past her face and whipped around her neck. It was, she thought, oddly sleek and violet for a garrotte.

Time, as it does in those moments when only actions are of importance, slowed down, aided in obedience by Lila's processors accelerating her speed of thought and motion beyond human. Before the long thin line had a chance to bite into her she got the fingers of her right hand under it and then felt that it was no mundane line at all, but a wiry, curious flesh. It was deployed with great force however, and her own knuckles were soon pressed into her throat. If they had been flesh fingers she thought they would almost certainly have been cut in two. But they were not flesh and they did not yield to the terrible decapitating pressure of her would-be murderer. Her delicate skin became hard as metal, fusing tough around the site of contact and gripping the garrotte tightly. Then, with a kind of joyful fierceness amid the surge of all her battle responses, Lila pulled back against the line.

A bitter cold pierced her left shoulder.

At the same moment she felt Tath retreat to no more than a green-tinged haunt in her chest. He whispered, faint as a final breath, *Poison in the left strike seeks death. This is no game or casual play. You must show no mercy.* She thought he sounded afraid.

The line gave suddenly without any warning and her hand slammed down, through the desk before her, splintering it into smithereens and scattering her notes and books to the floor. In the second it took her to stand and turn she was stabbed three more times in the left upper back. From the wounds a great dullness began to spread, not cold itself, but grey and thick, like fog.

Her right thigh opened with smooth clockwork precision and she took out the gun, always loaded, that was kept there in the hollow where a bone would be. The first shots were out of it before the image of her assailant had resolved to more than a blur of lilac and blue in her vision. The ammunition was simple metal bullets—a choice she had made after Zal's warning, because they were not often fatal to demons. She had thought that if duelling was so commonplace and stealthy traps so often employed, she didn't want to accidentally slaughter someone attempting a lighthearted bit of maiming. There were few things more second eleven than counterattacking with excessive force. Hence, the shots were only to buy time.

She was already dropping the weapon as the demon surged to its feet. It was tall, and like a dog standing on hind legs more than like a human. In its right paw the long poniard it had used to stab her dripped with red. The fogging of her body slowed as emergency counteragents were released by her phylactery. She achieved balance and a good look at her enemy.

His long snout was snarling, showing long teeth shrouded in walrusy whiskers. Yellow eyes gleamed from narrow slits on either side of the long head where a ruff of spines rattled at her in orange profusion. The demon's broken tail whipped back and forth, scattering drops of blue blood which steamed and fizzed.

"What was THAT for?" Lila demanded. As she spoke she was weaving back and forth, balanced on the balls of her feet, letting her AI help her intuit the opportunity for a strike. She was ready to go in bare-handed but, as her assailant wove back and forth, arms and hands— there were four of them, disconcertingly—snaking in a hypnotic rhythm, she took the time to slip a blade out of her left leg's armoury and into her hand. Warm liquid ran down her back and she had to pass the knife across to her right side as her left arm slowly numbed.

The demon simply snarled in a guttural way for a reply. She feinted and it stood back, waiting for its poisons to take effect. Its eyes never blinked. Lila, desperate that her introduction to demon society should not begin with a miscalculated slaying, took a moment to digest the analysis of what was rushing through her bloodstream. From its filtration station in her liver her AI-self tasted the complex molecules of snake venom. Information rushed her mind, like an assault squad—it was deadly in a minute to anyone of normal human metabolism and very hard to synthesise a suitable anti-agent for in . . . Lila ignored the rest. She knew all she wanted to know. She reeled where she stood.

Convinced its attack was succeeding in paralysing her, the demon crouched and struck with a spring and a snarl. Lila used some heavy hydraulic assist in her hips and slid her torso aside in a move that anyone whose legs weren't more than two-thirds of their bodyweight would never have managed. The demon's blade, hand, and arm stabbed past her with a whoosh of cool air that lifted the delicate veils of her clothing with a soft movement like a caress. She brought her arm down and pinned the limb against her side with vicious determi-nation. The surprised demon landed against her, its shoulder against her chest, and suddenly they were eye to eye. Lila stared hard and brought her head forward with a sharp jerk, slamming her forehead into contact with its skull. Its skin smelled of sulfur and pine, and it was damp, like a frog. Her free hand brought her blade around and pressed the tip of it into the soft flesh just below the orbit of its large, shiny eye. For an instant she looked into that window.

That's not such a good idea, Tath whispered but he was cowering inside so small that his voice was more like a ghostly afterthought.

The dazzling gaze of the demon was captivating. Deep inside the black pits of its pupils she could see a strange kind of swirling. It was slow and dark and beautiful.

Magic, you fool. For all that's holy, stop! Didn't that traitor teach you anything at this spy school? Strike or be damned!

In her veins the poison and her body fought one another. Murky pain made her sluggish but her machine parts, unaffected, stayed strong. The demon made a tentative pull but it was stuck fast. She pushed the knife into its skin. Blue streaked down the blade and gave off a pale smoke. She was so close to it that she couldn't help breathing some of it into her nose. For a moment she lost the sense of where she was.

A dart of shadow shot out of the demon's eye and into her left eye. It was cold and it went straight to her heart.

Fuck! Tath said, discovered.

The demon sucked in a huge, fast, astonished breath and its free arm punched Lila in the head with the force of a sledgehammer. Only because she was machine did she hold her grip as her head rocked and bright pain shot through her toughened skull. The shadow in her heart began to expand and it was soft, like twilight. It made her feel sleepy and sad. The demon started to hammer her with blows. It jerked its head back and thrashed, kicking ineffectually at her armoured legs. The combination of poison and shadow made Lila feel as though she was swimming in mud but her grip on the creature was so powerful it could not wriggle free. She plunged her knife into its neck, angling up under the jaw and giving a good jerk to the blade as she did so. A gout of blue, like an ink explosion, burst out over her. Hot clouds billowed off it and blinded her. She felt needle teeth sink into her shoulder. Something pumped into her flesh, painful and tight. The shadow started to slow her heart.

She heard Tath chant some strange sound. The shadow disappeared into his green energy and then came the almost familiar prickle and tang of magic working as an emerald line of force extended instantaneously out of Tath's spirit form, through her, out of her eyes and into the blood slick of the demon. It shrieked, bubbled, and spat in agony. Lila felt a horrible voyeurism as Tath, using her as his proxy, sucked the life from the wound in the demon and from its blood. She felt Tath's energy grow in power and density. She felt him changing . . .

What are you doing?

It saw me. Demons have souls. Spirits. If this one reaches the realm of the dead with the knowledge of me there are necromancers aplenty here who will pull its story back to the living world. Death is no silencer.

Blood poured over her. Smoke billowed. The demon screamed and she felt its body go floppy, as if it was genuinely deflating. All its furious energy was passing through her. She could see and feel it but it was not of her. It was going into Tath. She was horrified and revolted. He was eating its soul.

For the first time this was not some drily recorded activity in a textbook. It was a frenzy; the destruction of something unique, beautiful, and fragile. Even though the demon had intended to kill her and she was killing it, or trying to, this seemed an atrocity far beyond anything either of them had meant. And moreover she could feel Tath's reaction to his own arcane power: he experienced it as an abomination almost beyond endurance but, at the same time, he gloried in it. He bathed in the demon's self as he transformed it into raw aether and he felt an intense, orgasmic pleasure as he drank that energy in. Tath swelled. Lila felt his presence intensify. His astonishment, fury, and self-hatred filled her up.

She dropped the demon's lifeless body and it fell at her feet with a meaty thud. Poisons—real, emotional, and psychic—flooded through her. Tath felt her responses and flared with anger and hate. For the first time ever she truly felt that he was capable of easily killing her, and always had been.

There was a flash.

She blinked blood out of her eyes. Standing on the window ledge was a small purple demon with a camera.

"Hold it, love!" it shrieked.

There was another flash.

"Perfect!" It grinned and then said, "Oof . . ." as it was kicked aside. Lila heard its angry protest as it fell and then saw another demon alight on the balcony. It was big and blue with a dragonish look and a long, horsy face. There were horns, whiskers, fierce gold eyes. Its eyebrows, arms, and legs had white feathers where a human would have had hair, some marked with violet and some plain. A mane of thick white plumes spread from its head down its back and along the spine of its tail to the tip where they ended in a heavy, soft burst of iridescent plumage. It was slender, powerfully muscled, and naked. The blue hide shone like polished vinyl and its powdery white angelic wings made a creaky sound as it furled them close to its back. It jumped down from the rail with the ease of flowing water and came towards her on its hind legs, grinning, suddenly almost human in aspect now that it was upright. A warm, sensual charisma radiated from it. Like an animal it crouched low, balanced on its toes, and sniffed around the wreckage of papers and the lake of blood. Its face was mobile and expressive—it raised its eyebrows and pulled its mouth into a surprised series of moves. It cocked its head and glanced down at the dead demon.

"Azarktus, my brother," it said softly and tutted. "You impetuous fool." A tear rolled from its eye and fell onto the body. When it landed there was a sound like a sigh and something faint, almost invisible, streaked up from the corpse and fled, wraithlike, out of the window. "I'd kill you myself if you weren't already dead." Then the creature stood up tall and held out its slender hand, smiling and showing all its sharp tigerish teeth.

"I'm Teazle," it said in a heavy demonic accent. "Pleased to meet you."

CHAPTER FIVE

"Of course," the demon continued, conversationally, whilst glancing between her and its outstretched hand in an inviting manner, "now that you have slain my blood kin my family is at war with you and I am bound by near infinite regress of ties and duties to seal your mortal fate at my earliest possible convenience, however . . ." It paused, glanced at the hand Lila had not taken, and then quietly closed it before abruptly coming to a change of heart and smiling and offering it again. "However, I consider it extremely inconvenient to do so and I expect that I will continue to consider it that way almost indefinitely which is technically not a crime though it violates the spirit of the law (though who cares for that?) and I wish you would take my hand because I am beginning to feel stupid."

Lila, woozy from poison, irritated by pain, and generally feeling in a bad mood, stared at the hand and then at the demon's yellow eyes. Straw to gold, she thought with annoyance.

Watch out . . . Tath whispered faintly . . . *beware of* . . .

Magic? Lila asked. She was heartily sick of his warnings and her own frequent memories of how easily it took her in. She did not feel the citrus airburst of wild streams which could bind her into some unwilling pact.

She dropped the blade she was holding and with her own bloodied hand took hold and shook firmly. The returning grip was strong and confident. The demon smiled cheerfully and its eyes narrowed in wrinkles of pleasure.

"Charmed," it murmured and tilted its head, looking mostly at her from one side. "And it feels so real."

Lila pulled her hand back. "It is real. Really."

"But of course." The demon flexed its fingers, remembering her grip. "Pardon my imprecision, it's not long since I left government and the affairs of state and, more accurately, the documentation and language of state, are slow to depart. I meant to say how fleshlike it feels, considering it is nothing of the sort."

Lila looked down. "You don't seem very . . . sad . . ."

The demon glanced at the body briefly and shrugged. "He is gone. There is nothing I can do about it. What I have missed of him through neglect whilst he was alive is my own failing but that is also gone. This," it rolled the corpse over with its foot, "is for the garbage collectors. Look, his face is very angry. At least he did not go to the endless shores in a self-pitying state. Really, our mother will be glad of that. Which reminds me. I was sent here to invite you to a party." With a quick jerk it tore a feather from its wing. "Burn this tonight at seven and follow the smoke. I'd stay and help you out here with whatever you were doing but I have to go deliver the rest of the invitations and my mother turns into a living horror if her parties go wrong. The librarian will send someone for the body if you holler. Pity about your dress, all that blood really has spoiled it. Nice breasts." It flashed her a grin of long, tigerish teeth and then hopped once, twice, onto the balcony and over the rail.

Lila stood and slowly straightened up to her full height. The body steamed. A light breeze ruffled the scattered, trodden on, and generally ruined pages of her scholarship. From behind her the soft padding of feet came into the room. There was a short, impatient sigh and a faint growl of anger.

"How many times must I go over it?" she heard the librarian mutter. "No duelling in the Reading Rooms!"

"I . . ." Lila began, seeing the old demon stoop and shuffle forwards, leaning on his staff with which he tapped a large brass sign attached to the wall beside the door. Lila had not really noticed it before. It said, "No duelling. No summoning of imps or other manifestations of elements potentially damaging to the records, including but not limited to: elementals, wisps, sprites, ifrits, goblins, vile maidens, bottleboys, basprats, toofigs, magshalums, witches, elokin and major, minor, and inferior spawn. No praying. No cursing, except by staff. The library is closed on public holidays. Donations welcome."

"I . . ." Lila tried again weakly.

"Not you!" he rasped crossly. "This idiot." He kicked the heavy body with one cloven foot and then growled with pain. "Arthritis in my knee. Janitor already fuming about unscheduled funeral arrangements—oh his job is not worth the grief, he is not paid to cart corpses about the place, he is thinking of forming a union . . . Curse you, whippersnapper!" His stave glowed and fizzed. He gave Lila a rueful look. "Can't curse the dead of course . . . and I suppose I should congratulate you but it seems a little like harsh sarcasm, my dear, considering you have voluntarily entered a vendetta with the Sikarzi family. They're big in this town, you know. One of their sons is the most successful assassin from Bathshebat to Zadrulkor, perhaps even the most successful assassin in the history of Demonia, although one has to say that just in case the bastard is lurking behind the shelving units." He rubbed his knee with one seven-fingered hand and stared balefully at the dead demon. "Not this one of course."

"No," Lila said, looking down, feeling sick and feverish as the discharge of contamination from her poisoned blood briefly overloaded her liver. "Of course not."

"No," said the librarian with vicious satisfaction. "This one was the runt of the litter and no mistake. If there was any justice in the world they'd send another son to marry you, you doing them a favour like that," he made a chopping motion and then a slicing motion, a common gesture in Demonia that indicated the importance of culling the weak, "but instead it'll be the endless war no doubt, depending on how long it takes them to kill every living relative you have." He glanced up at Lila and nodded with appreciation. "Weak and foolish but his mother's favourite. Doted on him. On all the sons of course, as they do, but this one more than any because he was weak and she couldn't stand the shame of having brought him from the egg so she made out it was all part of his character development and him some new experimental brave new breed to try out being more like humans—all snot and bother but no balls—no offence, Miss. Made it her mission in life to try to develop him. Her whole world, he was. How he must have hated her! And here you are, the human ambassador and a perfect freak to boot—everything he never was nor could be, like some kind of nemesis or foul doppelgänger sent to torment him, eh Miss? Ah well. He'll have been glad you came along, you see? Your public death would be the only thing that could have gained him any respect. Now he goes to the murk unmourned as the ass he was.

"Well, you can't walk around my catalogues covered in that muck. I will send you to your circumstances . . ." He whirled his hands in the air. A blue glow appeared around them.

"But . . ." Lila began.

And then she was back in her room at Sorcha's house.

The old male demon who kept the rooms free of wandering magics during the hours of daylight was there, collecting stray essences from the air that came in through the windows and sipping them from his hooly-bowl. He raised one, thorny eyebrow. "You look like you've had a successful day, Miss."

Lila felt herself cold, sick, sticky. She might throw up but that all seemed trivial in comparison to her new situation as murderer of a favoured son, subject of a vendetta and intended victim of the greatest assassin in a world of dutiful killers. And she had to go to a party, and her dress was completely ruined. "I guess," she said.

Look pleased, Tath said. *In their terms you just entered the big league. You should be throwing your own party and spending your inheritance on it, while you still can.*

I don't have an inheritance, Lila told him, walking directly into the shower.

Stop!

Stop? She began to turn on the water.

You have to go as you are. Wear the blood.

No.

Yes. It would be a sign of enormous cowardice to wash it off.

It smells.

You'll live.

That seemed like a promise. Tath assured her it was something like one. Wearily, she stayed her hand on the tap.

Zal stood staring moodily out of the window of the suite at the Beautiful Palms Hotel, watching the surf roll up and down the beach. It was a beautiful day. It was beautiful weather. It was all very very picture perfect. He was in a foul temper. It was because of what the faery behind him had just said a moment ago—words still ringing around his head in that acutely irritating way that happened when someone said something that hit a nerve . . .

"Tell her about your addiction, before it gets out of hand and she finds out another way."

Since the day, perfect though it was, provided absolutely no avenue of escape, he turned around and sat down in one of the armchairs and glared at Malachi for a few moments, but that didn't work either. Vague fantasies of a spectacular fight with the creature flitted through his mind but were squashed by the knowledge that this was one of Lila's friends and also by the fact that the faery's instruction was quite right.

In the other armchair Malachi matched Zal's steady gaze. There was a bouquet of flowers almost but not quite between them, placed on a circular glass table. Zal angled his feet away from Malachi and put his gaze on the flowers. He considered allowing his *andalune* body to spread out in the hope that it might put Malachi to sleep—elven aetheric bodies interacted with faery aetheric senses and caused an overload of some kind which put the faery straight into a deep sleep in a protective reaction.

"Don't even think about it," the faery said.

Zal ground his teeth.

Malachi smiled and it was not entirely pleasant. He enjoyed Zal's discomfort and Zal felt duly punished.

"Move back to your questions," Zal said. "I liked them better."

"As you wish," Malachi shifted to a position of greater comfort and crossed his legs. He was, like all faeries, a great and showy dresser, but whereas many of their ideas about costume were extremely peculiar to alien eyes Malachi had chosen, in his human form, to adopt a human style of plain yet extremely expensive looking elegance. His immaculate camel-coloured silk suit draped his tall, powerful form with insouciant grace. Against the warm colour the ink blackness of his skin and hair stood out, shining faintly with what Zal's nose told him was Unction: a rare and highly prized magical product, worn on the skin. It bestowed magical gifts, among them clairvoyance, protected the wearer from mortal harm, and it moisturised with a buttery sheen. He also radiated two contrasting attitudes in typical faery fashion—a good-humoured frivolity and a deadly serious self-confidence in his position. He was interviewing Zal in a more-or-less-but-not-exactly unofficial way on behalf of Lila's organisation, Earth Security, and he was enjoying it.

Zal also felt himself examined as Lila's new prospect, as if Malachi were her brother or father. He got this impression despite the fact that he did not know exactly what the relation between Malachi and Lila was about, but the fact that the faery was taking him so seriously made him resentful of the assumption and the intrusion and of the presumed closeness he must have with Lila in her working hours. And that led him to think about Lila on her own in Demonia and that made him crazy. So he stared at the flowers and willed himself calm.

"What we really want to know is why someone like you is in a place like this singing songs, Zal. And what does it mean to be both an elf and a demon? Surely you must understand your position here is almost intolerable to the authorities. Elven voices carry beyond the range of hearing and into matters no human even knows about. You and I—for all that either one of us claims to befriend them in their need to know our worlds—we haven't explained the half of what we know about each other."

"You keep quiet and I keep quiet," Zal said.

"Exactly," Malachi nodded. "All is honour among traders in secrets. No point ruining the delicate balances established over millennia for the sake of easing human anxieties. Trust must be gained with time and care. And there is so much to care about . . ."

Zal frowned. Malachi was starting to "wiffle" in the habit of faeries of his kind. Not that Zal had exactly determined his kind but he suspected from the clothes and the chat that Malachi was powerful. There were ways of discovering more . . .

"Want to play cards as we talk?"

"I thought you'd never ask." The faery reached into his inside pocket and drew out a sealed deck of playing cards, breaking the plastic wrapper with his thumbnail as he did so and shedding the cards into his outstretched hand in a single, flowing movement. The box ended up on the glass table, the plastic in his pocket, the cards in his resting hands. Zal had not seen exactly what happened, he realised. Malachi looked at him expectantly. A soft furl of wild magic, summoned by Malachi's invisible wings, crept between them—its presence was a guarantee the faery made that both of them would be able to detect magical forms of cheating in the other.

"No limits Texas Hold 'Em," Zal said, sitting fowards, starting to like matters much better now they had dispensed with the ridiculous human manners of simple talk and were playing. He flexed his hands and found them stiff. It was too long since he'd played for anything worth winning.

"Questions for answers. One question per game. Stakes on the Hoodoo Measure Rule . . ."

"You got the Hoodoo?" Zal would have to fetch one.

"Always, my man," Malachi assured him with a smile and from his jacket pocket produced a small handful of recently picked grass. With skilful fingers he fashioned a crude doll with the strands. He pulled a hair from his head and Zal did the same, handing it over so both were wrapped together before being wound around and around the grass to create a separation making head and torso; the hair was the noose that made its neck. "Good enough," Malachi said and set the doll on the table under the shadow of a daisy. He blew on one finger and tapped the doll on the head with it.

There was a faint burst of the scent of old battlegrounds, steeped in bloody mud. A tiny voice said, "Don't cheat and don't lie, or if you do I'll have your eye."

"Cool," Zal said approvingly. Whatever else he was, the faery was a good Maker, and Making was one of the most difficult of any magical art. He watched the black faery's hands shuffle the cards and the tiny Hoodoo doll sat down to wait.

Malachi shuffled the deck, his fingers moving in a blur, the cards shifting like water, in and out, round about. He dealt two and put the rest aside. Zal studied his cards with a nonchalant air. Queen of Spades, King of Diamonds. The faery glanced at his and waited.

"Impersonal noninteresting," Zal said, beginning with the obligatory stake of the lowest and least worthwhile kind of question.

"Impersonal interesting," Malachi said, raising him two instantly. The faery watched him closely.

Zal shrugged and yawned. "Impersonal interesting," he said, matching the stake.

Malachi dealt two cards on the table face up. Three of clubs. Nine of spades.

Zal felt a certain kind of sinking but strove to distance himself from it. He knew that everyone betrayed themselves but experienced liars only betrayed themselves to a practised eye that knew them and Malachi did not know him well enough. "Impersonal sensitive," he said.

"Impersonal sensitive," Malachi matched. He silently dealt out a third card.

"Impersonal acute," Zal said automatically, always geared to risk. He looked at the card afterwards: ten of hearts.

"Impersonal acute." The sixth card appeared.

Zal suspected the worst. They showed their hands.

"You had nothing," Malachi said with satisfaction showing a ten and a nine; two pairs. "So, should we tell the humans about the Others, do you think?"

"Nah," Zal said, gathering the cards up with a sigh and shuffling them himself. As he did so he watched the faery with considerably more curiosity than he had previously felt. How curious that Malachi would bring up such a taboo on the very first play . . . and something so apparently unconnected to his immediate concern. Zal added with some conviction, "They'd only worry unnecessarily and they have a lot of worries to get on with just through learning to know us in our least troublesome forms. Let's not go that far just yet."

"Mmn," Malachi said critically. "I thought so too. Deal."

Zal dealt with exact care and wondered if Malachi would take his word. In the faery world any of its ambassadors abroad might assume the diplomatic powers of the queen. Malachi did not only speak for himself, but for the entire universe he represented, even in minor dealings with a mere ex-agent like Zal, and his pronouncements had the force of law. It seemed a marvellously stupid arrangement of whimsical tyranny to Zal, but there it was. The faeries would not divulge a whisper about the Others to any human from now on. Zal was not sure that the humans really understood this feature about faeries or they would not treat them as powerless citizens so often. Still, buyer beware.

They played another round cautiously. Zal asked Malachi if there were remote activation codes for Lila's AI-managed abilities, codes which might override her own will. He had worried about this a lot, particularly as he grew to understand how little Lila herself knew about the way she was made. To his great irritation she did not seem to care, whereas he burned with suspicion.

Malachi lounged in his seat, idly spraying a waterfall of cards from one hand to the other. "I don't know," he said. "But it does seem like something that would exist."

"Lila wasn't made anew to save her life," Zal stated and the faery nodded slowly. "And if I made her I'd be sure to have some kind of insurance on my investment. Know why she was made, really?"

The Hoodoo doll sighed and said, "Rule violation. Do you really think it's worth it, elf? Left or right eye? Hurry up, I'm not going to last all day."

Malachi gave a broad smile and an expansive shrug. "Bet me for it."

"Bah!" said the doll, disappointed.

Zal sighed. They played again. Zal got a five and a nine on the original deal and things never improved. He lost. Malachi had made impersonal extreme importance.

"What are you attempting to do to the people of this realm, through your music?" Malachi asked.

"No circumlocutions," the doll snapped, still annoyed. "I can detect prevarication and dissembling at forty paces."

"That's not impersonal," Zal said.

Malachi looked at the grass doll.

"Sadly, he is correct," the Hoodoo confirmed, rustling. "And you've lost your go."

"So, not a state matter. Not a Daga matter . . ." Malachi said, watching Zal scoop up the cards as he privately cancelled his long list of possible activities that the Jayon Daga, the elven security agency, might have been attempting through Zal. Since the outbreak of the civil war in Alfheim it was a mystery as to whose allegiance lay where. He had doubted the claim that Zal was Charming with his voice but now he wondered what it could be for. Money, fame, what?

The questions that followed took three more hours to play for.

Zal won an impersonal acute. "Who are you really investigating me for?"

"Human security and faery interests. And Lila's interests are something I feel I have to look out for, inside the agency, her family, her partners . . ." Malachi gave Zal a long direct stare. "I don't know if I think you're such a great choice. You probably push every button she has and a few more. If there was a more unreliable character in the seven realms I find I can't recall the name. Hardly what I'd call supportive material."

Zal felt his hackles rise. He was not sure if Malachi was taunting him or interested in Lila for himself but he knew that Malachi could use influence with the agency to do pretty much anything he liked in terms of getting Zal incarcerated or exiled or whatever. He didn't like the threat. "Stay out of it."

"Unlikely," the faery said and dealt the next hand.

Malachi won personal minor. "Do you love her?"

"It's not minor," Zal said.

Malachi looked to the Hoodoo doll.

"Have another try," it said.

"That's cheating," Zal replied angrily. "That was a critical answer for a minor stake, and he gets another go?"

"Sue me, or offer me a limb," the doll snapped testily.

"Are you truly demonic in nature?"

"Yes," Zal said coldly.

The Hoodoo doll got up and began to shimmy with power.

"And no," Zal said, feeling a stabbing pain in his right eye.

It sat down again.

Malachi raised an eyebrow.

He won again. "What's your next single to be?"

"Disco Inferno," Zal said without a flicker of irony.

"Do you not feel that's selling out?"

"What am I, chopped liver?" the Hoodoo doll piped. "No extras. Faery eyes are as good as elf eyes any day of the week . . . better for some purposes. They last longer too, before they rot to mush."

Zal smiled with half his mouth. It wasn't a look Malachi really liked.

"I'm doing it with my sister," Zal added in an ambiguous tone of voice.

"I heard that from the brownies," Malachi said smoothly, "but I didn't believe it."

Zal dealt. Zal won.

"How many deep ambient faultlines have you found in Faery since the human bomb?" Zal asked.

The faery's jet black face darkened in expression and for a moment its fine lines, smooth angles, and handsome features shifted into something at once more animal and strange. Zal had just assumed Malachi would be some kind of cat-spirit with his style and manners, but that was not what he saw in the form that revealed itself for an instant as the faery's surprise beat his wit. He couldn't have said what Malachi was, not that every faery wasn't always faking something up for the sake of it and, as usual, that pissed him off. He listened to Malachi's answer with a bad humour.

"There are six," the faery said.

"An unstable number," Zal remarked.

Malachi gave the slightest nod.

Zal shrugged, "There are nine in Alfheim, far as I know. Even less stable."

The Hoodoo doll attempted to shake its head with disgust and fell over onto its side with a tiny, silent bounce.

Malachi conjured a vesper sprite with a wave of his fingers and sent it around the room, looking for bugs or telltales. When it returned and vanished he added, "Demonia has eight. And lucky old Earth has a hundred and nine. Mostly minor. So far. We haven't really finished counting."

Zal was privately astonished but he didn't show it.

"They grow like weeds here. Spread like lines on a crone's face come winter, and all the while in our old countries they creep on slow as ice marching, but still, creeping and listening to the whisper from the new land that talks of shredding and decay and the sundering of things to chaos. Sssssss, the web of the worlds undoing like silk slip-sliding and nothing to stop it yet," the faery said matter-of-factly as he collected the cards, shuffled, and dealt.

"Fucking indignity," the Hoodoo doll squeaked, "you don't understand or respect my powers, you imbeciles!" If it had had a fist it would have shook it.

Malachi set it upright again and it quivered with unexpressed feelings.

"It's nothing personal," Zal said to it.

"Save it for someone who cares," the doll hissed. "I'm drying out."

Zal walked across to the suite bar, opened the refrigerator, located ice, cracked it into a tumbler, poured scotch on it, and then set it down on the table. He lifted the doll by its head and put it into the glass.

The doll snickered and leaned back as though in a jacuzzi. "Take your time, boys."

This time Malachi took the cards and shuffled and did not deal. "I'm worried about Lila," he said. "I think she's cracking up."

"She was fine," Zal said defensively, thinking the same thing now that Malachi had said it. "Fine."

The faery stared at him.

"Maybe I'll pay a visit to Demonia."

Malachi nodded slowly at him and Zal felt manipulated and grateful.

"Thish time itsh for your HEADZ!" the doll squeaked in glee.

Zal reached over without looking anywhere but at Malachi, picked the doll up, and jammed it head down in the liquor between the ice cubes. "If you and your gang of fools does anything to harm or cause to be harmed by accident, omission, or stupidity, one tiny little bit of Lila inside or out I will make you all wish you had never been born."

"Likewise," the faery agreed with a smile.

They stared at each other and the grass in the glass slowly came apart until it was floating weeds.

Malachi glanced at it with a moment's regret. "I can't take responsibility here. You may pay for that."

"I pay for everything," Zal said sourly. "And I sell out to no one."

CHAPTER SIX

S orcha was thrilled to hear of Lila's situation when she returned from rehearsals that evening at a quarter past six. Her apartments were next door to Lila's guest rooms and in typical fashion she wandered between both of them as she went through the lengthy process of undressing, drinking a hot tea, taking a bath, dressing, and changing her makeup for the evening. None of these activities rooted her for more than an instant except the bath, during which she insisted that Lila circulate around the tub, handing her sponges, loofahs, soaps, towels, and alternate glasses of the tea and some cordial she was taking to improve her voice. After the bath, as she patted herself dry and showed no inclination to notice the clock moving inexorably towards half past seven, she stopped interrogating Lila on every detail of the day, flicked her long, black mane over her shoulders, and smiled with warm approval. "I knew you wouldn't let us down."

Lila felt her spirits sink another notch. She kept finding herself daydreaming about good reasons to return to her own world as she stood there, stinking faintly and feeling demon blood go dry and crackly on her skin. "I'm in this on my own," Lila said. "Your family aren't related."

"Mmmn," Sorcha hummed as she rubbed scented oil into her skin.

"You're our guest, honey. And we don't let guests die. Not on the premises at least. You're safe here. Safe as you can be."

Lila tried to look comforted. Through the open window of the bathroom she could see the glowing orange sun setting over the lagoon. Party boats and flotillas of pleasure craft dotted the open waters with beautiful colour and twinkling lights. In the skies flying jalopies, small personal air balloons, and winged individuals flitted and drifted. Close to the town the canals were alight with lamps and lanterns and the buildings were all outlined in electric fairylights of rainbow hues. Statues stood in arrested motion all along the skylines. The humid air was filled with the hum and swagger of coming night against a background of wild insect thrumming and the chorus of bull-frogs and other creatures inhabiting the darker regions of the vast delta that stood at the city's back. Occasionally the pulse of so much life was interrupted by the piercing shrieks of unexpected death.

Lila turned from the view. "You don't have any words up in lights. Just lights." She thought a change of subject was in order.

Sorcha threw everything she had used or that displeased her into the draining bathtub and put on an almost demure outfit of white miniskirt and blouse. She placed a diamond on the arrow point end of her tail and glued it down firmly. "We don't need words. The colour says it all. Just like on us." She inspected herself in the mirror and smiled with satisfaction. Her living flame hair moved with a slow motion flow all its own and her eyes gleamed like scarlet coals. Where her skin caught the light it glowed a soft crimson and where it did not it was a soft, pearly black. Superficially she reminded Lila of Malachi and reminded her that she ought to call him back and check in.

Lila shot a glance into one of Sorcha's many mirrors and saw herself standing like an automaton. The chrome metal of her legs was streaked with gore and the synthetic skin looked as waxy and ashen as the real thing. The stain on her hair and face where she had been magically scarred stood out in livid contrast to the blue-green demon blood that had splattered her from head to foot. Her arms were draped with towels and Sorcha's discarded clothes, each one sticking out to the side like a rail. She looked like a demented robot maid. She let her arms fall and everything slid off them. "What do my colours say?" she asked, having a dim memory of going into a department store with her mother and some woman there talking about colours. Something to do with what you should wear. The demon world was saturated with colour and everything meant something. It was not what you wore. It was what you were.

Sorcha gave her a critical look from top to toe. "Your colours say, Here comes some bad-ass bitch!" She laughed and slipped her elegant little clawed feet into high-heeled ruby mules. "That doesn't make you smile?"

Lila thought it over. "What do your colours say?"

"My colours say I am a raw creative force of nature—that's the impasto statement, the primary colours, always. Black is the colour of the Void, the final and the eternal, the ever-rising and the ever-falling rhythms of life and death. But I'm not just black; it's a rare thing to be one colour. I have this red sheen which is all good luck and friendliness. It's a dark red so I have lots of passion, but it's still red so I'm a civilised queen of what she surveys, not some green-hide barbarian. Then my hair is the fire of the day, showing my mood—that's where my flare is, where you read today's menu of Sorcha; what am I going to be like . . . changes all the time. Some demons have these on their backs, on their wings, wherever, but you have to show it so others can know it, right? And I wear white to show that demon mother whose party we're going to that I am sorry her son is dead, even if he was a lily-livered piece of scum from the bottom of a bog not fit to wipe my shoe on." She ended with emphatic contempt, then added demurely, "That's just politeness."

"Your eyes are red."

"I have an intellectual bent," Sorcha said with pride. "I am a scholar."

Lila decided not to mention that red eyes on demons in human terms usually signified insatiable evil though she wondered at it. "What about feathers?"

"They count as impasto—the portrait of the aetheric self. But you can wear or paint your bad self with secondary colours to say more about you; lime, indigo, that kind of thing. And those colours show up in the flare always . . ." Sorcha put on a purple necklace. "For my strong spirit," she said. "Don't worry. Nobody expects you to read the palette. They'll tell you what you have to know."

"If red isn't the danger colour . . ."

"White," Sorcha said without hesitation. "Always be wary of demons with white. It's also the colour of grief, hence my outfit. But you go as you are. Ready?"

Fantastic, Lila thought. She pulled out the feather that Teazle had given her. "Light this."

Sorcha held out an imperious hand and twitched the small thing out of Lila's grasp. She inspected it closely, smelled it, and licked it.

"It's white," Lila said helpfully.

"I see that," Sorcha replied, quietly. Her hair had turned to a brooding maroon storm of flame, lit with lightning flashes of alarming blue. "You didn't mention it was this brother that came in the window. What did he say?"

Lila told her.

"You know why white is so difficult? Because white is all colours in one. You don't know what the hell is going on with somebody who is white, all you know for sure is that they could be anything they wanted, no power they wouldn't draw on, nothing they wouldn't do. White is blindness. White is the display of power that hides every motive, every move." Sorcha spoke with a cold dislike that Lila could never have imagined was in her repertoire. "That assassin you were so worried about . . . this is his." Her tone became thoughtful. "But it has no evil charm. I can't feel a thing but a summons on it. It's like he said.

A party invitation. Even so, strange to pull something like this off your own butt."

"From his arm . . . under his wing . . ."

"Whatever." Sorcha smiled and with her free hand struck an imaginary lighter. A yellow flame shot up from the tip of her thumb. She stepped next to Lila so that they were touching gently at shoulder and hip and put the feather to the flame. It went up with a *pfft* of white and blue, the world blinked, and the two of them were standing at the head of a grand staircase.

The ballroom was huge, a natural cavern lit by crystals and torches, by dancing werelights and slowly drifting globes of feylight. Frosted crystals in the rock roof and on the branches of the petrified forest glade that acted as columns in this natural cathedral glittered and reflected everywhere. A grand table below them stretched out for almost half a mile, festooned with garlands, laden with sculptures in ice, in fruit, in other foods. Champagne and other drinks played in fountains and fell in cascades as though born of nature. Sublime, itchy-footed dance music played and instantly Lila felt Sorcha start to gently bounce to the infectious rhythm. The place was full of elaborate, saturated, incredibly coloured and decorated demons of every imaginable shape and size. Faeries were there too, their spectral wings visible in the thickened demon aether. Lila and Sorcha were atop a high dais—where arrivals all must come in. There was a queue forming at their backs between two white plaster statues of heraldic, naked dragonmen . . . when a beautiful baritone voice boomed out . . .

"Welcome the Magnificent Sorcha Azlaria Ahriman, Diva of the Nine Deities of the Fundamental Groove of Mousa. Welcome the Otopian Ambassador, Lila Amanda Black, Friendslayer, Lover of Azrazal Ahriman of the Cursed Race, Killer of Azarktus the Beloved Son of Our Glorious Hostess, the Principessa Sikarzi!"

The room went utterly silent. Every face and body turned to face Lila. Every movement stilled, except for the gentle dancing of Sorcha who went on quietly bopping as though nothing had altered, the model of relaxed enjoyment and pride at Lila's side.

Sorcha murmured with sultry assurance, "We rule, darling."

Lila's AI took a picture of the frozen throng.

You are famous, Tath whispered, hidden deep in her heart, pulled as tight on himself as any magic would allow. It didn't lessen his sarcasm.

The demon who had taken her photograph at the library was there, just starting to run away through other figures Lila began to recognise as guards and servers. Before he could get very far he was caught and, to her utter disbelief, ripped limb from limb on the spot by two lithe, red guards. They snarled and spat at each other over the little body, then let go of the dripping bits and started to fight over the camera like dogs.

She had just turned to confirm what she thought had happened when, as though released by that instant of savage punishment, the pent-up feelings of the crowd ripped forth in the form of a hail of missiles, all aimed at her. In the time it took for her to turn back from her sideways glance her AI-self had come into full capacity. Time seemed to slow down to give her enough time to relax into a defensive stance. As part of her turn to face the threat her left arm knocked Sorcha down and behind her. Her right arm and hand opened out and activated an emergency deflector that was usually housed in the back of her forearm. It opened out, as big as a tent into a shield of diamond-fine filaments which, like the airbag of a vehicle, would provide adequate defence for a split second before collapsing. Her legs shifted into combat mode. She got taller. She got stronger. In a blur of white and black metal her defensive and assault systems armed, targeted their most likely opponents, and offered a bewildering array of weapons to her hands. Hormones rushed her so that she felt almost like she was flying, was superhuman, could take on anything. Her left hand, coming back, caught the gun from its holster at the side of her leg and brought it around to bear.

There was a sound like a big, indrawn breath, and then the spatter of many items falling onto the stone dais around them. Lila's diamond net shield became soft as gossamer and began to float like dandelion fluff over her. A small motor hummed and reeled it back in, ready for a second cast.

A thousand flashbulbs went off from all over the room and there was a sudden great thunder of clapping and hooting. Lila, rooted, ready to defend her life, realised she was being applauded.

What a charming image, you the great heroic defender, the beautiful girl at your feet, Tath said witheringly, not without a trace of envy.

I'm the girl, Lila objected.

"Ow," Sorcha said, sprawling even more prettily beneath Lila's titanic stance. She smiled and posed for the shots with relish, scattering some of the poisoned darts, arrows, bullets, jewellery, bones, charms, and pieces of underwear that lay everywhere as she writhed obligingly. "Ow, ow, ow . . ."

Disgusting.

Lila thought she detected a trace of some other feeling in Tath but he withdrew completely before she got the scent of it. The music picked up again. Grey shadows came to pick over and clean up the dead press imp. Conversation resumed, all the words not meant for her ears—and that was almost all of them—sounding like yet more voices joining in the accompaniment of the songs as if the speakers were singers in a massed yet unconducted choir. Gradually attention was slowly withdrawn in a graceful way, though many glances were thrown back in their direction. Slowly Sorcha wriggled her way up to all fours and moved around, picking up items here and there. When she finally stood she presented two handfuls to Lila.

One was of little scrolls. "Duel challenges." The other was a collection of bones tied around with what looked like hair. "Marriage proposals."

Lila put her gun away.

"Keep it up," Sorcha murmured. "Looking good."

Lila left the gun where it was but remained in defensive mode. If it kept this incredible mass of interesting, fixated, obsessive creatures away from her then it could stay. Sorcha gave her the handfuls of tokens. "What do I do with them?"

"Who cares?" Sorcha tossed her head of flame and smiled dazzlingly at a tall green demon in half a tuxedo who had come up the stairs and offered her his hand. "Let's dance."

"Sorcha . . ." Lila began in protest but her guide was already descending the stairs.

"Mind the way!" said a voice behind her as a demon of beautiful yellow cheetah shape and with butterfly wings came forwards, the announcer calling names . . .

Lila wanted to step aside and give way but she knew that if she did all her grand entrance and show would count for nothing, worse than nothing. She shook her head and gave the cheetah a shove backwards, employing the AI systems to do her calm walking for her. Inside she was terrified, not knowing what she was going to do when she reached the bottom of the staircase. What had that announcer called her? Friendslayer? Her breath was short. She hoped her fear didn't show on her face, or come out in her smell or whatever they could pick up.

They like titles, Tath said. *Especially true ones. They love names.*

She looked around for the one or two faces she might know—Sorcha, who was disconcertingly far away in the crowd now, showing every sign of being courted by at least half a dozen individuals . . . and Teazle. Surely if he had invited her then he should be here to say something to her? But the last stair came and there was no sign of his blue, feathery being. She saw someone who looked like him but they had no horns . . .

The mass of demons parted gently as she arrived to let her pass. She kept walking because she had no concept of where to go or what to do. As she moved she heard distinct whispers rise from the musical throng . . . friends of the family wished her a lingering and painful death . . . curses of weakness . . . pleas for favour . . . anonymous bursts of admiration . . . explicit invitations for sex, for hunts, for adventure, for art, for dinner . . . It reminded her suddenly of the moment she had stood before the elf lady's court in Alfheim and the unspoken yet clear outpouring of their scorn, contempt, and hatred. The difference was that here, even the ones whose heartfelt desire was to see her head in a trophy cabinet had no trace of loathing in them. They gave her their ill will with absolute respect. And the ones who liked her . . . their adoration was boundless. It was clear that none of them had an ounce of pity for her.

She found a strange smile shaping her mouth and felt herself growing taller, though there was no more cyborg power to lift her higher.

Junkie, Tath whispered.

Jealous, she retorted.

Magic foamed softly around the table like the flow of bubbles in a hot bath. She watched people dip their hands into it and then it seemed to lead them, like a hand holding theirs. Many of them did it, with no more thought than they gave to picking up a drink or a canapé.

Moving closer to the table Lila pretended to cast a glance over it though she had long since learned never to look the food in the eye. As if she knew what it was for she dipped her hand and felt the foam tug.

That's right. Rush in, Tath snarled. *Magic you don't know, just touch it* . . .

If you haven't got constructive criticism . . . But then Lila saw where they were going and wished she hadn't.

The magical froth drew her gently but inexorably towards a gentle alcove lit by torchbowls of burning liquid with a throne at their centre. Carved with many creatures and the sigils of the Sikarzi house—a snake and a unicorn—it was filled by the tall and slender female form of a turquoise and golden Medusoid. Those heading to this seat were each in turn giving gifts to this person and generally doing things that looked to Lila very much like saying thank you to the party hostess.

I need a gift, she said to Tath in desperation, then realising her position . . . *I need an army* . . .

Show no fear, he said with sudden conviction. *And no shame. This is their world now.*

Lila began to switch on the emotional shunt.

No. They will sense that. They read feelings. It is one of their arts. You have to do it for real. The world runs on that here. Whatever stupidity they are about it must be sincere or it counts for nothing.

I can't do this! The queue to pay respects was rapidly dwindling and now the Medusa had seen her and Lila could feel her attention as if it were a searchlight in a world of darkness. *Even if they think it's trivial . . .*

They do not. I assure you.

Not helping!

Be true. Be strong.

Lila searched for Sorcha, but she was far away. Her turn arrived. The demon before her swept graciously aside in a swirl of fur and beads. Lila stood before her victim's mother clad in blood. She was as lost as she had ever been. Her life hinged on not screwing up. She thought of Zal. She imagined what Zal would do.

The Principessa Sikarzi stared at her with her yellow snake eyes, her beautiful woman's face as cold and expressionless as though it was carved by a perfectionist's hand. Her hair was made of golden vipers and all of them coiled, staring at her, their orange tongues flickering. All the warmth and enjoyment had left the demon. She was focused on Lila as though there were nothing else in the universe. The long reaches of her tail that had flicked and quivered in conversation froze. Lila felt the time given to her ticking away, leaking away . . .

Lila stared back. She channelled Zal in her imagination for all she was worth, trying to feel her way into his effortless self-confidence, his swagger . . . keenly aware that as Lila Black she wasn't able to contemplate murdering someone's son, but that as Zal she could do anything it took . . .

She swept a deep bow, eyes closed, arms wide, showing respect, but she was fast out of it and up to her full height. Did the eyes narrow against her? She wasn't sure. There was a kind of quiet around her as the others all watched. Without hesitation, arm animated by the sure responses of Zal instead of the hesitating doubts of Lila, she reached up to the shoulder of her flimsy dress and tore. She intended to rip off only a bit but the whole thing came away in her hand leaving her naked except for gore and her knickers. She dropped the dress in the Principessa's lap.

"Close," she said to the waiting yellow eyes. "But no cigar," and turned without a word, letting all her defence systems deactivate as she walked.

Her bare skin burned as she waited for the assault that was certain to happen. She reached the main room in a blur of terror which must have looked like haughty pride, and cast about desperately for anything familiar.

"That was nice," said a voice from behind her.

She turned but nobody was there. Then the dragonman statue close to the wall opened its eyes and cocked its head, looking at her with a gentle smile on its long, crocodilian mouth.

"Respect for the family, a very respectful present seeing as it's the only bit of him she'll ever get back, and then a show of strength at the end. Why, you might have lived here all your life."

"Teazle?" Lila said, watching as the large statue—white as snow, winged, muscled, and disconcertingly naked—shrank in size, peeled itself away from the wall pedestal it had been sitting on, and slowly moved forwards onto all fours. His long neck let him look up easily at her even when he was down, his shoulders no higher than her hip.

"I said it before and I say it again," Teazle said. "Nice breasts." He flicked his wings against his back.

"It's you, isn't it?" Lila said, feeling heat radiate from Teazle's lithe body as he stood beside her like a big dog. "You're the assassin they talk about."

"Now that I'm with you nobody else here will take a pot shot at you," he said. "Burn those daft duelling notices as well. Anyone who touches you answers to me. Including that elf of yours if he gets here unwisely. Fancy a drink? I'm parched." He padded off towards the main table and then waited for her to catch up with him. The feathered tip of his tail swung like a leopard's, soft and heavy.

"What?" Lila followed, feeling strangely comforted by . . .

Oh, please, Tath said. *Not the glow of attraction. Even you can't be so stupid as to . . .*

Lila ignored Tath. "We are not friends," she said as she caught up with Teazle who had gone bipedal at the table in order to fill two cups at a fountain of some kind of wine.

He handed her a dripping glass and threw all of his drink back into his long mouth with an easy gesture before flinging the cup away into the crowd. "Really? That's a pity. I was under the impression you wanted to find out what road your elf lover took in order to become one of us. But if you're sure you don't want my help . . ."

Lila gave the demon a long, hard look and for the first time since she had entered Demonia felt the solidity of a big conviction growing inside her. "Okay," she said, putting the drink down and setting her hands on her hips. "I know you like playing Games just like the elves . . ."

Teazle made a face at this but listened, his soft, cowlike ears tipping her way.

". . . but I'm done with all this operatic charade stuff . . ."

She was aware of the missile at the same moment as Teazle. The arrow in flight was so fast it tripped her sensors and cued her to duck even though she couldn't see anything. In contrast to her defensive move the white demon leapt up into the air with a single spring of his narrow, powerful legs. He opened out one wing and rolled as he jumped higher than the height her head had been at. The arrow hit where feathers gave way to skin and punctured straight through the tough web and flesh. Stripped of velocity it fell on Lila's shoulder harmlessly as Teazle's long arms and legs reached out towards the downshaft of a stalactite and took hold of the thick rocky substance of it. He pushed off from it in a huge leap across the table, wings opening, and skimmed across the heads of the crowd and the table itself, knocking over an ice sculpture of a fey princess. The ice form crashed down onto the splendour, splattering food over those nearest as Lila came up from her deep crouch, the arrow in her hand. It was slimy with faintly bluish blood. She was just in time to see Teazle kick vigorously off the heads of two partygoers, to shrieks of pain and protest, and loop his suddenly narrow and sinuous body up over the rail of a balcony close to the roof. He vanished with the speed of a rat into a tunnel. The half of the room that had watched his antics mostly shrugged and went back to their amusements. Lila looked after him and then down at the arrow in her hand.

To her surprise it was carved with little sigils she recognised as elven. Her AI scanned them and informed her it was simply a phonetic version of her own name. She looked back up to the balcony—why would he make a saving move like that? She had no doubt where he'd gone: after the shooter. Well, she'd had more than enough parties to last a lifetime. She kept a hold on the arrow and took a couple of steps backwards then in one big stride hurdled the table before her and kicked straight up off the floor in a jump taking almost all her power. It launched her up to the balcony in an arc that let her catch the rail in both hands and use her arms to lift her up and over, hands right and feet left. Then there was a narrow dark corridor full of people but they were mostly standing aside from Teazle's forced passage, some of them lying flat where he'd left them. She followed the trail of bodies, complaints, and turned surprised faces all the way up and up a long set of halls until they ended at a large opening with free night beyond.

This was the landing platform. As she left the structure of the mountain in which they had been entertained she saw the whole of Bathshebat spread out before her, far below. Its glittering lights and splendour shone off the water, and silhouetted against it were the huge, slow-moving shapes of various dirigibles and their balloons which had been parked here. The snort and scrape of living creatures betrayed a stables far off to her right. She heard some kind of babble and turned to see a humanoid demon in a uniform standing quite close to her in the relative darkness. She didn't need any certificates in demon culture to know a parking jockey when she saw one. "Which way did they go?"

The demon pointed out, towards the city. He vaguely mimed flapping, meaning they had flown, and shrugged because clearly she wouldn't be able to follow. Lila made the edge of the deck at a dead run and launched herself, arms wide, into the cold embrace of the night wind coming off the sea. Vanes opened from the lower section of her arms and at her hip. Her sensor arrays picked her target out easily against the dark background. The rocket systems in her feet ignited.

It was just incredibly cold.

CHAPTER SEVEN

Malachi left Zal in his suite and went out the easy way, through the open French windows and over the railings. He floated down to the ground slowly, thinking all the way and looking out over the city grid to check the traffic. Zal made him very uneasy. He had strange energy—not surprisingly perhaps—and the added factor of what was not a simple addiction complicated an already complicated person. Top him off with his personal problems, whatever was lingering in Alfheim to torment him, and the constant nagging from the record label and he figured Zal was about as reliable as a monkey-pookah. Whatever he said for the Hoodoo would stand, but Malachi wasn't convinced that Zal wasn't some kind of adept . . . who knew what he was able to do? He had the cojones to drown the doll so he was either hiding a talent for sorcery or he was already taking the kind of risks Malachi so hoped he would avoid until Lila's return from Demonia.

Malachi landed and walked onto the pavement. Even that small use of magic in this fundamentally magic-impoverished world had tired his wings out. Much to his disgust nobody commented on it. There were enough faeries around now that they were barely worth a second look. Malachi smoothed his jacket and adjusted the way it sat on his shoulders. Mention of the Others made him nervous. He had even begun to perspire.

He recovered his car and reviewed the list of suspects that had been trawled up after a forensics sweep of the old clunker Lila had found near Zal's recording studios several days before. They didn't match up with the unidentified fey driving the tankers that had successfully primed Zal's kidnapping and Malachi didn't recognise those drivers either. Given the talents for glamour in his world he didn't hold out any hopes from a photograph and the vehicles themselves had been burned out comprehensively, leaving nothing behind to use as a tip. The suspect list on the listening devices did include names he knew however. But his mind stubbornly refused to focus to the degree necessary to divine their whereabouts so he could go spy on them. He kept thinking about the way Lila had rushed off to Demonia like it was some kind of escape chute, barely enough time to grab her updates and the pretence of a cover story about being an ambassador and off she went. He would have bet his entire wages on her not having read most of the Demonia material. In her references from her diplomatic job they mentioned how diligent she was, what attention to detail she always paid . . . Malachi didn't recognise her from the descriptions. She sent his fey senses twitching with alarm signals that told him here was a person who did not deal with matters they found painful but had learned to sweep them under the carpet and the carpet would soon be big enough no more.

Such information was always of use to a faery of his situation, for whom sifting through the trash for truth was an essential preoccupation, an obsession, an unscratchable itch of curiosity that knew no fear or boundary. Many humans were like Lila in this way, but none of them happened to go around equipped with high-technology weapons on matters of interdimensional sensitivity. Upon this point he was in complete agreement with Lila's psychologist, Dr. Williams. But the doctor, himself, and Lila's mentor were no match for the determination of the agency and its addiction to speedy actions. For that to change there would have to be a spectacular disaster and thanks to luck and poor judgement on many parts the last opportunity for spectacular disaster had been averted. The elf insurgents seeking to divorce themselves from a dangerous continuum had been thwarted, Zal had been rescued, and all unpleasant matters that might have resulted had been forgotten as the elves commenced their largest ever civil war; a conflict that was waged across lines of class, species, heredity, magic, and almost any other parameter of power one could name so that even meticulous spies such as the Faery Fee could barely keep track of who was doing what to whom and why. Malachi was much less interested in the elven war than he was with Lila's carpet however.

The combination of her and Zal was, at the very least, ill advised considering the sensitivity of their positions, the instability of their personalities. And then of course Zal had to mention the one outstanding issue that bothered Malachi the most: Lila had been one of Incon's own, saved because of loyalty they said, but he was more than sure the truth was more like she got sucked into a job she didn't understand the depth of, was hideously damaged because of it, and could have been pensioned off with disability packages. That had happened before. But instead of that she was made into a one-person army and there were other things that did not involve experimental, pioneering technologies. The word "victim" kept playing through his mind like a bacchante's distant screech.

He decided to pay a visit to Calliope Jones.

Calliope was a brinkman, or, as they were known in Faery, a strandloper, one who was able to wander the edges of worlds. Even among strandlopers she was unusual, because Calliope was made, not born, with her talent. She had started life like Lila, unsuspecting and human. Unlike Lila, Calliope was made by accident and so far as he knew she was the only human ever to have seen one of the Others. Thus today she was good for two reasons and that set his intuition on a happy road, so he went to her.

The white body of Teazle was easy to track until he vanished in midair over a broad canal that lay between the mainland and the many
islets and sandbars of Bathshebat proper. Lila saw him fade from view
against the dark background of clear water reflecting the night sky. At
the same moment all trace of him slipped from her heat sensors and
radar. Whatever he was pursuing continued to flee, a blinking
enhanced dot in her AI vision, but then, in midflight of its own, it
crumpled for apparently no reason at all and then plummeted directly
into the water below. There was a splash of white water to mark the
spot and, a few seconds later, a bobbing body in the wavelets.

Lila slowed her swift descent and stood on her jets. Thanks to the
speed of the flight and her nakedness she was now freezing cold and
although many demons wore little or nothing she felt uncomfortable
and vulnerable too. Without thinking about it she moved into defensive mode. Looking down she saw that the person Teazle had pursued
was entangled in a silvery net which sparkled with magic. She was not
used to magic, even now. Her human senses were not the rare kind able
to sense whether such an enchanted thing was hostile or friendly to her
and she didn't want to touch it. The trapped person thrashed about
ineffectively and then became more still as they managed to get their
head above water. So, they had to breathe at least, she thought and
looked around for any sign of the demon.

A hot, damp breath passed over the back of her neck. She scanned
—nothing there apparently, but on the instant that Tath whispered,
Chameleon . . . she had already come to the same conclusion and did not
move. Undetectable even to machine targeting and scientific methods,
gifted with nonspecific, nebulous white power—she could easily
understand now why Teazle was among the deadliest of his kind. If he
had wanted to kill her she would be dead already, so instead of both-

ering with fear she said, "Who is that?" and pointed into the water. Her jets roared softly, making the patch beside the floating captive into a blur of frothy white and steam.

"Your prisoner," came the soft reply. "Your rules. I leave you to choose their fate." There was a hesitation, then, "If you decide to slay them for their insult I only ask you do it at the party, for my mother's sake. It would make her so happy."

Lila took a breath automatically to give her opinion on such an idea but there was a crack like a lightning strike, only without light, and in that instant she knew Teazle had dematerialised. Simple air rushed in to take his place.

Pathetic, abominable barbarianism, Tath said with real venom. *Disgusting excrescence of intolerant stupidity!* His sudden burst of hate for all demonkind and everything they stood for was hot and fearful in her chest. Lila reeled for a second with the impact. It was short lived. Tath got hold of himself in another moment and shrank down again to near indetectability; a residual shimmer of loathing.

"He teleports," she said aloud to herself, with considerable dismay.

There was some more thrashing in the water below and a few audible gasps for air. Lila extended a narrow fibre line from a reel in her right forearm and bent down to her lower leg where there were some small containers holding a few lengths of metal rod. Taking one out she bent it into a grappling hook and affixed the line to it with several carefully made bow lines. Then, careful of her jet wash, she manoeuvred herself into a position where she could catch a good hold of the net. In a few moments she was confident that everything could take the weight and locked her hands together to stabilise her grab. Moving slowly but surely she raised her captive from the water and began a stately progress up and up, over the water, rising until she was able to safely clear the approaching rooftops.

She did not head back towards the mountain retreat but instead took a route towards the flat landing deck of the Ahriman family mansion. At the end of her rope the prisoner, a relatively lightweight hundred and fifty pounds, twirled and dripped in silence. Then Lila felt a small vibration through the line and realised they were attempting to cut free. At this point they were several hundred feet in the air. Beneath them lay a labyrinth of tiny streets and narrower canals, covered alleys and tented squares. No doubt the fall was a risk worth taking. Lila would have taken it. Now she ground her teeth in annoyance, stood up on the jets, and gave the cord a furious jerk.

The net and its contents sailed up towards her and she dropped towards it efficiently, reaching out and taking a firm hold on the wet, cold body and the netting together. She exerted a great deal of pressure and heard the satisfying whuff of someone's lungs losing a lot of air very quickly. They struggled and she increased her grip to vicelike, then they stopped. With a subdued roar and careful manoeuvres Lila deposited both of them on the smooth landing surface of the roof.

The glowing lamps that ringed the area gave enough light for her to see well by without adjusting her vision, but no matter how she adjusted it she found she could not properly see the person she was holding. The net was clear as day, wet and fine and spiderlike, glistening with tiny silver sparkles of charm. The body did not glisten. It was greyish and matte, like a shadow.

It is a dark elf, Tath said with surprise and contempt. *Aether suckers . . .* his tone became disgusted. *Like Dar, but this one is magical and he was . . . less so. It is in shadow. If you release the net it will disappear into the wind.*

It feels solid enough, Lila objected.

The person was like a thin, two-dimensional silhouette to look at, but three-dimensional to hold. It was extremely disorientating. Breezes from the lagoon drifted around her, making her suddenly cold. She wished she had worn her usual clothing and not the stupid demon dress. She wished she had not made such a grand gesture as to throw the stupid dress away.

Anyway, why are you so hostile? I thought all the elves were of one brotherhood.

We are a divided species. Zal and I are of the diurnal type. This is nocturnal. We collect aether. They hunt it. They are the vampires of our kind. I thought you would know all this, you being the favoured human of such a mighty elf as Sarasilien, and he said the name with sarcasm.

Suddenly the complexity of your civil war makes perfect sense, Lila said to him, losing patience with his casual bigotries. *So, Dar was loathed because of his caste and his kind?*

That is correct. Loathed only in the light court of course. But no great deal to the dark court either, because he was not truly theirs. People like Zal and Dar are of no value to anyone, because their loyalties lie only with themselves. This is why Zal can never return to Alfheim.

I knew there was a reason it wasn't so bad to kill you, Lila sighed.

It is not a good idea to be powerful yet valueless, Tath said sharply. *I am surprised the school of politics, economics, and international relations lets you out alone.*

The simmering tension between them disappeared. Lila reckoned they were about equal. *What do I do now, then?*

It is entirely up to you, Tath said. *But if you plan not to slay your would-be murderer you will need to neutralise them some other way.*

You could talk to them.

I could, but then they have power over you, by being able to betray me to anyone here. Knowledge is power and whatever you have over someone else you should use only when it may be lethally employed. Value. You would be a fool to hand over knowledge without a great cause and this is not one. You will have to deal with it yourself.

Lila groaned inwardly, resenting Tath's schoolteacher primness and hating the fact that he was right. "Hey you," she said to the shadow elf. "What's your name?" She didn't expect an answer and didn't get one. "Great," she said to them. "And while you're at it don't thank me for saving you from drowning when you were ready to finish me off. Speaking of which, why were you trying to shoot me? Oh, don't tell me. I don't want to know. It hardly matters. But if you have any tips for getting you into safe custody before everyone else here decides to barbeque you for dinner, that'd be handy."

The elf took a small, shuddering breath and spoke a word. The world went pitch black and utterly silent. Lila did not lessen her grip. The net held. The prisoner cursed.

Light and sound banishing, Tath said. *That takes a lot of aether. Just hang on. It will get tired before you do. At least there is one advantage to your mundanity.*

She was almost dry by now but she felt even colder in the absolute darkness. She closed her eyes and when the elf moved she tightened her grip until it could barely breathe enough to live. After a long time the glowing lights of the landing began to glimmer faintly, or she imagined them, but then the Bathshebat night returned, soft and full of the sound of insects and many kinds of music.

If you want to get your answers, wait for dawn.

But Lila was bored of waiting. She used the net to tightly truss up the elf, paying no attention to what it looked like, and then with one hand caught in the tough webbing she dragged it behind her towards the door. The landing area was flat, smooth stone, so it would not be too painful. However, before she reached the door she realised that she had nowhere to save this person, nowhere to put them. The house did not have cellars due to being built on pilings, and although it retained a traditional Catchment where trespassers against the family could wait for justice, she didn't think that leaving an elf to the passing whims of a nest of demons was wise. She was lost in thought, staring out across the lagoon, when she noticed the coloured smokes rising from the Yboret Souk where aetheric trading went on. Somewhere down there would be a demon good at casting who would sell spells.

As Tath saw the idea forming in Lila's mind he bubbled with misgiving but she ignored him. "It's a good idea," she said, annoyed at how defensive she sounded.

It is a lousy idea, he said. *Even going there is a lousy idea that stands out in the brief yet terrifying history of lousy ideas you have had since I have known you. Naturally, since you have no magical awareness and almost no cultural sense here you will go immediately to the highly sensitive area of aetheric business dealings and attempt to duel wits with some of this world's most powerful and no doubt unscrupulous mages. You have a lot to hide, mostly me, so of course we must go straight to the place where we are most likely to be discovered and all because you cannot be bothered to wait two hours until the light of the sun uncloaks this shadow-monger so it can be made to talk, when, I have no doubt, it will inform you that it is loyal to some unheard-of faction back in Alfheim determined to exact revenge on the person they consider to be the catalyst for the war. We do not even need to bother asking. Just tip them into the canal and be done with it. In terms of honour alone you would be doing them a favour.*

Lousy, Lila said to him, going inside and then hoisting the netted elf over her shoulder for the walk down to her rooms. *Listen to you. You're getting more like me every day.*

!

She thought he was right. He was always right, sod him, and she could not admit it, at least not enough to make her change her actions. Maybe she was even doing this so as to not feel like Tath was the one taking all the major decisions. Yes, that hit a nerve, she thought, feeling her jaw muscles go tight. But now she couldn't go back because that would be a double weakness, it seemed, and so there was only onward.

The elf became suddenly doubled in weight and Lila almost fell over. It let out a piteous whimper that managed to be both very angry and very sorry for itself. Lila longed for the march to her room never to end. As long as she was moving she was okay and need not face the bothersome doubts about bullheaded stupidity and embarrassment which crowded her. But by the time this wish had formed she was already there and there was not even a moment's hesitation before she dumped the elf on the floor and left it to struggle feebly with the tightened net while she went to wash and get into some serious clothing. That was the problem with having to maintain control, you could not stop moving. She thought this, moving continuously, aware that if she stopped something waited to overwhelm her which, if she continued, could not rise up and show itself.

Zal screwed up the ninth attempt at a letter and threw it at the bin. It missed but he didn't care. His aim had been out on the other eight too. He looked at the hotel notepaper with dislike and then threw the entire pad into the bin where it lay curled up in the bottom, accusing him of profligate waste, selfishness, and cowardice. He walked across, recovered it and put it back on the desk, opened the desk drawer, took out the religious book there, and threw that into the bin. He suppressed an impulse to retrieve it and instead looked across to where Poppy, Viridia, and Sand were playing cards. They were using jumbled tarot decks and, after several attempts to decipher the game one time, he had realised that his failure to learn the rules was because faeries played with constantly changing rules, and the rules changed according to who was winning at the time or what the stake was or both. Because they mostly played in silence or communicating across some aether he didn't have contact with Zal didn't even find it particularly compelling to watch although the play absorbed the three of them, or any visiting fey friends, for hours. It was how Poppy lost most of her money and won all her pixie dust. She had a bad habit, and he grimaced with Malachi's accusation about his own.

Yes, he had told Lila truthfully that his conjuration of Zoomenon was necessary for his health now that he was exiled from Alfheim. But exactly how it related he had fudged somewhat and now his head was filled with explanations that sounded like excuses. He had started the practice when he was in Demonia. It seemed a long time ago. He had no idea what would happen if he really stopped. Thinking about it made the idea of Zoomenon seem suddenly important, vital even. He disliked that most of all. Addicts never wanted to think their preferences had a grip on them, but that was how control always worked at its most successful. Zal ground his teeth and derailed that thought with what he had been attempting to write in the letter besides the admission of weakness. He had wanted to tell Lila about his time in Demonia and that seemed the most inexplicable experience of all.

Incon had sent her there to discover the mechanisms of his transformation, he was sure. They'd asked him and he'd refused to answer. She hadn't asked. It irked him slightly. He had the impression that for some reason she preferred being separated from him by at least one dimensional shift and also that she wouldn't have trusted his story. Couldn't fault her instincts on that one, he thought. Even if he had been a great writer it would have been difficult to put into words and it would also have led, inescapably, to mention of the Others. Zal, like Malachi, was confident of human ignorance on this score and since none of them who liked to think they knew something about the subject really knew anything at all, well, a conspiracy of silence was the natural thing. He was so used to subterfuge he could almost convince himself it was in the humans' best interests.

He set his pen down and gave up. Ahead of him the day was filled with annoying small events: magazine interview, radio phone-in, rehearsal, some songwriting time he always penned in but had lost the habit of using. Thank fate Sorcha had offered him a duet role on her cover song or he'd have nothing to be doing. In fact the lack of stimulation here and the obsessive attentions of the fan club with its million human teenage elf wannabes and the rest of it was all too distracting. He needed a break. He should go to the place where music lived and find himself in that. Then he wouldn't even care about Zoomenon. No. He definitely would not.

He called Jolene, the band manager. "I'm going to take a break for a few days."

"You can't. You're booked into the studio the day after tomorrow for Sorcha's track and there's a concert a day after that."

"You can put it off until next week. This can't wait."

"No, Zal. You're always messing up the schedule. Just hold it together for . . ."

He ignored the powerless pleading in her voice, "I'll be back on Sunday. It'll be fine."

"Jelly will go ballistic."

Jelly was the owner of Zal's record label. No doubt that was true and he wouldn't have to face any of the flak. Jolene would get most of it and whoever was standing next to her would get the rest. He had a big mouth but he was mostly wind and noise. "I'll make it up to him. I'll write songs."

There was a moment of tense silence. "Where are you going?"

"Demonia."

"But you can't . . ."

Zal apologised for spoiling her plans, honestly, and hung up. He watched himself from a short distance of detachment as feelings of annoyance, worry, and uselessness at his feeble position flooded him with the desire to run, jump, sing, or throw all the furniture out of the window. He felt himself grow hot with inner fire, but did none of those things, just waited. After a time the horrible feelings slunk away and the fire dimmed to a glow. He went quietly into his room and looked through his things, spoke with the faeries about his plans just enough to keep them informed, and then left by the fire escape.

CHAPTER EIGHT

The flare and storm of demons fighting with the elements lit the dawn cloud over Bathshebat with many pretty colours and boomed through the air from the distant Playing Fields with soft vibrations that shook the crystal light catchers around the lamps in Lila's room. The elf, securely tied by the net but with head and legs freed, sat on her bed propped against the headboard with her eyes shut. Lila sat on the floor opposite, her wrists resting on her updrawn knees and her hands loose. They had been like that for some time.

The elf was not like others Lila had known. Her skin was grey-blue, her hair quite black. She had Dar's features, typical of the shadowkin, their faces seeming to be stretched from the tips of nose and chin, their ears also sweeping back like those of bad-tempered horses. She was dressed in poor, ragged clothing and was stained with soot and coloured earths in various ochre shades though much of this had run in the lagoon and become a muddy film. Her long, wiry body lay utterly still, as if she was dead, betrayed only by the slightest movement of breath in her belly. A soft shadow like the spill of ink onto wet paper covered her and, except where it was held fast to her by the net, spread from her into the air and over the bedclothes. It shifted and flickered slowly, larger than she was by several inches at all dimensions.

This *andalune*, aetheric body, the only one Tath had left, was utterly
unlike any Lila had seen before, and she had seen a few. They were not
generally visible in Otopia, nor in Alfheim, but in Demonia, apparently, they were. Lila had watched this for some time and saw it
changing frequently, forming appendages almost like fingers or tenta-
cles, or spongy, diffuse portions that spread wide, or other shapes; a
Rorschach mystery. She could not see it without remembering Zal's
touch, and shivered.

"Zhid'nah," said the elf suddenly. "Tubbuuk nan shivvuthek.
Zhayadbhalja mik seppukha."

Lila had never heard the language before but Tath translated
uneasily, *She asks for mercy at the cost of her honour. She wishes you to bring her
something to write with so she can put down her death poem and something sharp so
she may end her life with honour.*

I'm not going to kill her. Give me the words . . .

Tath supplied Lila's mind with the right phrases and his memory
guided her lips and tongue to the strange syllables. She only had to
think of what she wanted to say and, almost as normal, she spoke, "You
are my prisoner for now. You won't be harmed."

The elf sighed through her long nostrils and said with contempt,
"It will not be your choosing. You cannot protect me in this land."

"Of course I can . . ."

The elf opened her eyes for the first time. They were dead white with
fine slits in the centre and she had to squint horribly in the light. Her
voice was contemptuous. "You are lucky to be alive. The aura of the white
demon ruined my shot. It was a fine shot. Your death was in my hand."

"Seeing as we're on the subject," Lila said. "Why do you want me
dead?"

"Not I," the elf said, closing her eyes again and turning her head
away from the window. "I am the hand of another. If you do not kill
me the demons will, if they do not then he will and if he does not then
I will. Bring me paper and a pen. I demand a final request."

Do not give her any opportunity to make symbols. She may be sincere in her will to die but I doubt she wishes to go alone.

"Enough," Lila said. "I was going to haul you to the market and buy a spell to keep you at my side where I could see you. Then I thought I would get one that made you into a guard of mine, something along the lines of Do Me No Harm. Then I thought I'd add one that made you tell me the truth. But actually I'm sick of the whole business." She sat down on the end of the bed and looked at the prettily damasked walls, the beautiful curtains, the soft sweep of majestic loveliness that ran in a perfectly judged theme of reds and ochres through furniture, decoration, and placement of things. She did not look at the elf but addressed her with conviction.

"You don't want to talk but I do. You want to kill me for reasons I have no clue about and I think you don't know me at all, so as far as I see it you can damn well listen to me. I've been here a few weeks now. Most of what goes on here I miss because I have no ability with magic. Everything means something. That chair being there, for instance, it has a special meaning I can't remember. Something to do with the flow of aether in the room but also the significance of waiting and resting in relation to the outside air. See, I don't get most of what demons do, I just know that it's important to them to set the table right and important to them to kill for passion and those two things are about the same. Now to me they're nothing like the same but what can I do about that? Sorcha was supposed to help me out too, but all she wants to do is go to parties and shows. I get the feeling she's trying to put me off of something. So that sucks because I like her but I think she's in my way.

"And you elves—well, I know next to nothing about you either. I know there are day and night species or races or cultures or some kind of distinction and that there are castes and hierarchies that make you uptight as hell all the time because your social standing is so bloody complicated and important to you. And you hate the demons and the demons hate you because, as I understand it, basically you are savers and they are spenders. But the two of you aren't in opposition really. This is how Zal can be both elf and demon. You aren't different in the important ways. It's all in the expression. You are somehow the same. That's what I think.

"And I don't get how you relate to the rest of us, to the elements or to the faeries, but everyone is so preoccupied with how they're different I think that what bothers them just as much is how they're connected. And this story about the Bomb, that's just crazy. How could all the worlds' histories be different and still join? No doubt you wonder about that too. You say at no time in your past was Otopia not there. Demons say the same. Faeries say the same. Elements say nothing, obviously and the dead, well, we never met any of them after the crossing. And there's the hardest thing of all for me, you know. The realm of the dead. They say it's parted from us in temporal dimensions only, that it is panspatial and pantemporal, a dimensional 'verse transecting all points in which beings like us cannot move, though there are beings that can. Perhaps dragons do, and ghosts, maybe they do. But I wonder, how can it be? I can't even imagine it. Yet you say it's a place necromancers go.

"And all that's very interesting, kind of. But the thing is, elf, I don't care. The truth is I wish I wasn't here. I don't want you to tell anybody this, because it's important everyone thinks I'm a good worker and full of confidence and okay as a person, fearless and full of pep, but I'll be honest with you, since it doesn't matter a damn; I'm tired and I want to go home."

"Mizadak zhuneved?"

She says why don't you, then?

"Because there is no way but on," Lila said and then went silent. She moved the fingers of her right hand and heard the not quite inaudible sound of the machineries that moved her. She felt the slide and strength of metal and the responsiveness of electron flows. Her shoulders felt tense and heavy but her arms and legs and all her robot self was unchanging, numb to emotion of any kind. Her stomach was gripped by the cold understanding that her self-pitying, bleak statement was the truth. It tried to close around the fact like an oyster around a sharp piece of sand, to protect her from it. Her flesh felt it but there was so much of her that felt nothing at all.

"I have dreams," she said, without knowing that she was going to, "in which I run around looking for my arms and legs in the forest, until I realise what I'm doing. Then I fall flat on the ground and suffocate because I can't move my face out of the earth. Then I wake up. And it's a disappointment. I should be telling this to important people, you know, like Dr. Williams and Zal. But I could never tell them that. Just think of how disappointed they would be, how hurt, and how they would struggle to fix it and make it better. And I can't be fixed, so they can never know."

"Urshanta, hibranta mikitak nozherosti. Felyzi maszharan zhuneved."

She says that as long as she was able to live nothing could stop her return home if she wished to go there.

"I can't go home for the same reason neither you nor anyone else will succeed in killing me. For the same reason I can do what I have to do in this job," Lila told her wearily, staring unseeing at the beautiful things and thinking about Zal, suddenly realising that this was the reason she had been bold enough to try and love him when he was clearly far beyond her in so many ways and she so far beyond that kind of contact with any ordinary human. "Because I'm already dead."

Malachi returned to his office, a place that was often the first port of call on any visits to realms beyond Otopia. It was an outdoor room in the gardens, shielded on three sides by walls of old stones and on the other two sides by glass which could be clouded to prevent onlookers gazing at him from the other offices of the security forum. There was no roof, instead the open sky looked down on a floor of close-cropped grass, groomed to perfection by three miniature sheep. The sheep were sheltered by boulders and a tidy shrubbery. Malachi's shelter was a small yurt made from the hides of fey beasts and tented over poles of rowan, birch, and elm. Within its small circular gloom he lit candles and sat down in his ergonomically perfected seat—the one piece of hi-tech he preferred. His smart modern suit of human design pleased him as much as the chair did and both, thankfully, didn't impede business. He signalled to his secretary that he was going out for a while—a brief wave was sufficient for her well-trained gaze to pick up. She closed the windows to view with their blind of soft electrostatic fog and Malachi leaned back and let the chair tip and tilt him into a meditative recline.

Finding a strandloper was no easy task. He had first to discover one of their small number by searching anywhere in the insterstitial and he could only do that by a process of half-shifting—moving into a state somewhere between his natural fey form and his human shape and waiting there, neither one thing nor another, in the hope that one of the 'lopers would notice the disturbance this caused in I-space and come to investigate it. A faery was able to assume their own shape in Otopia, if they wished to. Because of their natures, most of them who stayed for any length of time did not wish to. In addition to the fact that their appearance could be off-putting, once in their true form they became more vulnerable to the charm of the elements, of places and opportunities that their natures directed them to want. Hence the faery singers of Zal's band never showed their horse forms lest they be overcome by the need to drown young men in deep water, a temptation that would even exceed the distraction of armed police officers bearing down with lethal weapons let alone mode-X rock music. Malachi waited until he heard the door lock before he even thought about moving. It was locked from the outside and finally, in the

moments that followed where he knew he could not get out nor anyone
get in, he felt safe and relaxed. He let himself take a five-minute nap.

On waking up he stretched and gently eased his joints. The wings
of faery were present but not visible in Otopia but he felt them, like
echoes of another life, and let them beat now slowly, shifting their soft
pattern between Faery and Otopia, fanning the aether of I-space back
and forth. The slow wash of disturbance in the magical element felt
like cool water. He let its energy break beneath the surface of his skin
and bubble upward. From the bone he shifted, the prickling and tin-
gling of metamorphosis just a tease at first, but then suddenly a gripping flood of compressive and expansive forces. To halt halfway was a
rare talent, one thing that anyone could learn but only a few could
master. His long years of effort had led him to fortune. He stopped and
balanced with seeming effortlessness, half fey man, half panther, his
wings blue shadows vibrating with the finesse of hummingbirds. He
saw with the triple vision of the half shifted, with human eyes, with
his fey sight, and with the vision of his element: carbon.

It was horrible. Malachi had never enjoyed the process of halting a
change, nobody did. There was too much information and too little
certainty. His senses were weakened yet expanded, mind barely able to
comprehend what it was being told. He saw I-space yet did not see it,
heard both Otopia and Faery, smelled the cold wind of Hibernia where
his spirit ancestors dreamed the long dreams and breathed the thick,
muggy atmosphere of an ordinary Bay City spring day. He was safe in
his tent in the ground of the five-sided sanctuary and he was whirling
particles connecting with aether in the fundamental realm and he was
gifted with the carbon sense that attuned him to all forms of the element in life and matter so he could feel structures and taste life. He
could not perceive I-space except as a feeling of suspension. It was a
grey fog that resonated with echoes of familiar things that never
resolved. It danced with potential that never brimmed into existence
and he danced with it and there was in the dance a terrifying uncer-

tainty that one day and maybe the brimming over the brink into one
world or another would never come and he would be here forever until
the winds of aether whirled him bit by bit away.

Still, he was still with his fear because he knew that this would not
come to pass. If you hung out long enough and withstood the feeling,
you realised you weren't being weathered away by the aether and that
although the limbo of metamorphosis was disorienting and unpleasant,
it wasn't going to be fatal. At least, it had never been fatal so far.

Malachi thought of eagles flying and wings soaring, of calls that
pierced the sky. The only language here was imagination because there
was no body. He had seen things here—the ghosts of course, and
maybe what might have been a dragon in the distance once. Among
the aetheric windstreams and fields he suspected there were many such
things, living lives he couldn't understand and barely glimpse. The
common forms of beings from the I were only forms that happened to
be able to move into other worlds. Their mysteries were still many.
Ghosts destroyed those they touched and dragons—they were legendary and elusive and when they did speak it was difficult to make
out a meaning. Their acts defied a story. He had been shocked to hear
Lila's tale of Arië being consumed by the lake dragon of Aparastil. Not
that he guessed it was the dragon of a lake, nor that it had exactly
eaten her for food. Dragons were frequently fatal encounters but he
had never heard of one ingesting another being. He detected no trace
of such a creature close by. Not far off he felt the chill of ghost movement. If one of those strayed too close he would have to abandon his
visit for days. They were drawn to positions of transit—where the
worlds had joined—and could loiter for a long time around the vortices in the aether that surrounded these phenomena. A storm of
ghosts he could live without.

His calls, animalistic so as to avoid distinguishing him as a creature of sentient power and aetheric potential, were well-known signals
between himself and Jones. Like hunters pretending to be owls as they

positioned themselves in darkness he and the lost girl of Illyria
sounded off when they wished to call one another; sounded and waited
for the answering retort. His vision of eagles drifted into the fuzz
blanch of the aether. He waited, his vision of Otopia and Faery beginning to dim as he became attuned to the incomparable pecularity of I-
space. Against his skin fragile vibrations in the aether spoke of distant
motions in space, time, and energy. Wavefronts like sound and light,
but neither, betrayed the conversations of those adept in magical arts,
and creatures natural to the region, and, amid all that, the occasional
strange whisper that Malachi had always thought must be the signature of one of the Others, because neither he nor anyone else he had
spoken to knew what those strange frequencies and shifts could be.

A shivering whistle came from far off direct to him, the ear it was
aimed at. Jones. He called again, hooting, promising information—
her only vice—and she piped a reply from a nearer point. He felt the
familiar soft trill of her navigation, a kind of sonar which she could
detect his unique aether trail along and follow to its source. Ghosts
trailed from the deeps in response to it too. He could feel them
forming like condensation in the spaces close by, coalescent, and
drifted off, shifting uneasily like a swimmer on the surface of an ocean
who fears sharks. He recalled Lila's documentary evidence of Zal's
encounter with a forest spirit, one of the ancient ghost forms that were
most common in Otopia. It had taken part of his substance, but he had
survived the loss relatively easily—only a handful of aetheric *andalune*
strength gone and him able to regenerate it without trouble, probably
because of the connection he had to Zoomenon. Now that was a phenomenon Malachi did not fully understand; even though he himself
had a similar connection to the elementals he was not able to draw any
energy from them, no. But elves could do it, if they knew the way or
else had the talent. Like so many features of the various divided races,
what was well known about each other was least powerful knowledge.
Now, in exchange for her appearance Malachi would have to find some

useful tidbits for Calliope to devour. For once he felt sure of a good audience. There was everything he knew about Zal for one.

The ghosts were blooming. He felt the cold of their density expansion as a numbing chill. Aether around him was pooling and changing state in chain reactions of exponential power. He danced away, lightly, pummelled and betrayed by Jones's sonar. Although nobody had detected any trace of sentience in ghosts, they were fearsome predators of organised aetheric energy—beings like Malachi, for instance, and beings like Jones. Malachi had learned to liken them to viruses for the purposes of explaining them to humans but although that was a good metaphor for explaining their similarity to parasitical life-forms it fell down when it came to giving good imagery for their particularities and their complexity. Viruses were RNA replicators. Ghosts were nothing like that. They agglutinated from raw aether—perhaps with some viral-like seed in the origin—and they took on shapes with meaning for the victims or locations they preferred to hunt. The mechanisms by which this occurred were the research remit of the Ghost Hunters, a crossworld organisation through which Malachi had first found Calliope. He had dealings with them through the secret service and she was one of their number.

Her sonar battery had become an almost constant song. She was close. An icy chill crept over his wings. Malachi felt his anxiety, constant but denied, become fear. He hoped Jones was close enough to mark his position when he shifted out. He had the impression of a great ship, black and broken, bearing down upon him across a silent sea. Its ragged sails howled with empty mouths. Deadly frost broke and shattered from its blunted spars and slithered off the decks. Ahead of its bow a wave of bitter hunger pressed forwards and he was lifted and felt the suck and draw of a ferocious pull in the nonexistent water of the undead ocean.

He flipped out without a second thought and opened his eyes wide, gripping the armrests of his chair and taking a huge breath of the warm, muggy atmosphere of the yurt. He still had all his fingers and toes. The presence of the ghost, transecting the space he had taken in the aether, was terrible in his mind, but only there. The narrowness of escape made his heart hammer and he grinned. It didn't get much closer than that. A few more moments and it would have had enough of a grip on him to drag itself through to Otopia with him.

"Still bottling out before the last second, pussycat?" said a soft, hoarse voice beside him, laughing with a dry rasp that became a giggle at the end.

Malachi spun the chair towards the sound. Jones was sitting on the rug that covered his chest of magical items. Planes of light sheared off her, gold and silver, orange and white, bending into dimensions not visible to the eye. Amid these distortions her human form looked oddly vulnerable—a gangly sixteen-year-old girl, with skin both dark and freckled, long brown hair that curled a little at the ends, sprawling with the relaxation of youth in a pale pink T-shirt, jeans, and sandals as if she had just walked off a beach somewhere. The ghost with whom she had been intercised was a faint shimmer around her; clouds and rain, occasional lightning as if she lived in a perpetual storm. Her thunder was beneath his hearing but it made the floor tremble. She gave him a wry grin with crooked teeth. *"The Fighting Temeraire* again . . ."

Malachi shrugged; the ship had appeared close by him before, most often of all the ghosts he had encountered in I-space. "Any closer to figuring out the attraction?"

"We're getting there," she said vaguely with a careless wave of her hand that indicated a lot of effort and hardship. "What do you want? Trade me and maybe I'll tell you."

"I had an interesting conversation with an elf today," Malachi began.

Calliope shrugged now, and smiled and spread her hands wide.

"We were deciding whether or not to tell the Otopians about the others."

Hard light sheared from the girl, burgeoning and then vanishing.

Her body was barely material. It was as hard for her to sustain form as
it was for him to disperse it. The concentration it cost her being disrupted, she exuded plane bursts of light and when she did so her storm
intensified and her hair lifted in the first breath of a hurricane he did
not feel. "But you didn't say a thing," she concluded.

"He knew about them," Malachi said. "You know the elf I mean."

"Worldwalker. Yes, I know the one," she said. "Ghostpuller. Demon-
heart. We know him." She considered for a moment, flipping her loose
sandal, playing with a curl of her hair in her fingers. Thunderheads built
around her temples. "But you are not here about the Others."

"No," Malachi admitted. Calliope had a gaze that he couldn't lie
to, strange because he could lie to almost anyone else. She didn't so
much look at as through him and he felt her eyes pin his intents more
closely than he knew them himself. It was probably an illusion of the
way she drifted between planes but it worked well enough. "I called
you because of Lila Black."

Jones frowned slightly. "And?"

"Can you see anything about her?"

The strandloper gazed through and at him, seeing things he was
unable to perceive with her once-human eyes. He felt the temperature in
the tent fall by a couple of degrees and the smell of rain suddenly filled
the air. "You should spend more time with us, Malachi," she said then.
"You would find out many things that are better shown than told."

"Ah, I was hoping for some advice."

"And you got it, sadly for you not what you wanted after all," Calliope sighed. "Come on, if we're quick we can catch the *Temeraire*
before she decays."

Malachi felt his jaw tense. The offer of a hunt was more than he
wanted by a long shot but it was the kind of offer that came once in a
lifetime. A trip to I-space was possibly more than he wanted too but
as he thought about it Jones was already beginning to fade. It was his
job to pursue all leads . . .

"How long will it take, Jones? I have things I have to do back here by nightfall."

"A year, a day, who knows?" She was more than half translucent. The bending light of her form shivered like curtains of heat on the desert floor. "Say yes or no, cat."

Malachi cursed freely in his imagination. "Yes."

Jones stretched out her hand in beckoning and opened her mouth to sing. Malachi felt the sting of serious magic prickle across his skin and through his bones, printing him to her, remaking him into a form she could better keep a hold of and tow into the interstitial world. Lines of intent bonded them together—a good thing or he would not last long. He let himself be dragged after her, losing integrity and finding his wings once again stronger. In I-space Jones was no more than a streak of light surrounded by the bleak forms of the huge storm ghost that she had intersected; living lightning.

The ship had sailed but the wake was there, a cutting in the grey strange of I-space that Jones followed without hesitation. Malachi was pulled after her, glad she was the one in front. He heard her calling to others in various spaces and their answering calls; as strange a mixture of voices as he had ever heard. From all directions and places, they came like arrows, like dreams, like rain.

CHAPTER NINE

Lila left the elf in her room, tied up in the bed with orders not to move if she valued her life. Things being as they were this was far from certain but Lila thought it really wasn't her business if the woman chose to die at the hands of demons. She went out of her window to avoid meeting anyone in the house and shinned down the building's wonderfully ornate and climbable exterior. An imp, which had been dozing atop a bird-limed bust of Xenaxas the Impolite (an Ahriman ancestor), muttered and woke up as she passed it and hopped down after her.

"Where ya going?" it asked in a high, curious voice, dropping from one stone sculpture to another with sparrowlike ease, vestigial wings flicking to keep its balance. It was hardly bigger than a kitten, looked like a scaly monkey, and was surrounded by a small aura of flickering red and orange fire.

"Nowhere," Lila said grimly, hoping it would go away.

"C'n I come?"

"No." She moved faster, hand over hand, feet able to see for themselves with sensors in the soles of her boots.

"You look like a woman in need of a familiar." It danced after her. "Girl like you all alone in the city. Can't come to any good. I'd do it for a nice rate. Make me an offer."

"Go away before I blow your head off," Lila said.

"All right. You've twisted me arm. I'll do it for free," the tiny thing said with a happy smile. "A quick exchange of names and the deal's done." It rubbed its hands together in proprietorial delight.

"I'm the Queen of Sheba."

"No you ain't. I met her and she was way prettier than you. Go on. You want me."

"I really don't."

"You do. If'n you doesn't why would you be climbing out a window the same moment I choose to wake from a beautiful dream about popping sheep's eyeballs and rubbin' me fingers through the hair of changeling children? That kind of a dream portends you know. Portends a moment of Significance in a demon's life. I open me eyes and there you are. I know you want a familiar because you haven't got one and here you are setting foot out alone in Bathshebat, Grandmother of Infidels and Broodmother of Extremities Beyond Imagination and you just a slip of a little anaetheric girl."

Lila had both her feet on the pavement now. She nodded calmly and activated the battle system in her right hand. Two guns, and an array of blades enabled themselves, transforming her human limb into a gauntlet of deadly promises. She held this up to the imp, at head level where it stood on the knee of a stone satyr. "Not today thank you."

The imp clapped its hands and hopped from foot to foot in delight. "Now that's what I call a penknife! I knew you was sent by Hell for me. Just goes to show you have to have faith." To Lila's surprise it hopped neatly over her hand onto her shoulder and took a thorny-fingered grip of her ear. She could hear but not feel the crackle of fire. "Walk slow, I get seasick."

"I said no." Lila reformed her hand and took hold of the imp. It dematerialised just as she felt its tough little form firm up in her grip. The hold on her ear vanished but the imp did not.

"Ah, come on, no need to be such a spoilsport about it," the imp whined. "I'll see you right. Need me you will, see if you don't. I charge nothing and I'll be worth every penny."

Even with all her sensors on Lila couldn't detect the imp by any electromagnetic means, but she could still see him on her shoulder and hear his irritating voice through the soft whuff and flap of fiery noises. She gazed at him stonily; rather difficult with her neck twisted around and her eyes at full turn. "What do I have to do to get you to leave me alone?"

"Leave you? Leave you!" shrieked the imp, clutching its chest with both hands. "All this talk of love is breaking me up inside, lady. Just go where you're going and I'll trail along behind you with my self-respect dragging after me in the streets like yesterday's chicken skins. Don't you worry about me though. I can take it. Don't even look back. But when you need me," he thumped the centre of his chest with one fist, blinking tears of red, his voice hoarse with emotion, "I'll be right there."

"Money?" Lila said. "Magic?"

"You can't buy love," the imp said, beseeching her with large, burning eyes. "Don't soil my soul with this talk. It's like you haven't got a heart."

"What I haven't got is patience for this kind of garbage," Lila told it. "Get this straight. I don't want you now. I don't want you ever. Get away from me. Scram."

"Here's what it is," the imp said in a more amenable tone. "I used to be a big all fire and brimstone kind of hellish lord but I fell foul of the damned Cassiels, providence rot them slowly painfully and eternally, and they put a curse on me so now I'm just an imp without any power at all. I can't even hex. Look . . ." It waved its hands in a manner that might have indicated some kind of throwing action or spell cast. Little orange fires grew between its fingers, then fizzed out like damp fuses.

"I don't believe you."

"See, that's part of the curse!" the imp exclaimed dramatically. "Proves my point. Nobody believes me. So I've been on the streets for decades, waiting to find a way out, selling myself to the lowest bidders for any old errands like some kind of bat-sprite. I live out of restaurant dumpsters. And now I have the eyeballs dream and here you are and you are it, baby, you are my ticket and come heaven or high water I'm gonna make you proud of me! Come on, can't you see? We're made for each other."

"Okay," Lila said, accepting the first defeat of the war. "You do what you like but at the first opportunity I am ditching you and if I have to end your miserable little life to do it, I will." She straightened up and put her shoulders back.

"That's my girl," the imp said with reassuring, paternal tones. There was a sharp pain in her earlobe and tiny claws stuck themselves into her combat vest.

"I hate you so much already I want to spit," Lila said and spat into the canal as she stood on the Ahriman jetty and watched the early morning light.

"Don't spoil me," the imp said happily. "Remember I'm a familiar and overfamiliarity with a familiar could be counterproductive to a beautiful working relationship."

The minotaur who tended the family boathouse came clomping onto the jetty and gazed at her with slumbrous black eyes. He snorted in the direction of his gondolas, "You want a ride out?"

"No thanks," Lila said. "I'll walk." She hesitated. "On second thought, do you know how I can get rid of this imp?"

"Oh my heart!" shrieked the imp, staggering on Lila's shoulder. "The things she says!"

The minotaur licked his muzzle with a long purple tongue and shook his heavy head, scratching at his sides with both cloven hands. "They are like the flies, mostly harmless, always irritating. You had better learn to ignore them."

"Fabulous," Lila said and scanned her internal map of Bathshebat. With a purposeful, determined tread she set out for the Souk. She was aware of Tath only as a kind of grinding discomfort in the centre of her chest. He knew what was going on and hated it but daren't uncurl even enough to speak to her with the imp in such close proximity. It was all just wonderful. She consoled herself with the idea that surely in the Souk there would be someone who was good at getting rid of imps. The thought cheered her up so much she found herself asking, "So, what are you the imp of?"

"Imp of?" the imp repeated incredulously. "I am a lord of the infernal and master of the aetheric sciences, not some wharf rat of minor torment. I am not the imp of anything. I told you but do you listen? No. Just like all the others."

"So, you're not the imp of anything. But you are an imp."

"For the time being, yes, it looks that way but looks are not everything. I may have been stripped of all the powers I have save that of my good looks and charm but I also possess all my knowledge and I was an old, old demon, almost starting ossification when this happened so I know a lot, baby, and that will come in very handy, you'll see. For instance, you are best to duel on the Harbinger Bridge unless you are facing a withering demon in which case you must make them go outside the city bounds to Wulsingore. Never forget that in a hurry. No ma'am. Why, I bested the Dread Rage Brutorian Malsotis on this very—"

"Not the imp of drivel?" Lila interrupted, striding across the bridge at ever greater pace, dodging the beautifully dressed demon traders who had prime site stalls ranged upon the broad span.

"So rude," the imp sighed sentimentally. "Almost like my own daughter. Now, on this street there used to be a whole frontage of the most beautiful late Rageblind architecture that was utterly breathtaking even though of course it was impossible to view directly without a slide into the most foul temper . . . I say, are you heading towards the Souk?"

"Looks like it."

The imp pinched her earlobe between two claws.

"Ow! By god you'll have a painful death if you do that again!" Lila hissed at it.

"We should discuss this," the imp said in a tone of command. "Turn left here and go up to the second floor. The café is rather foul underfoot with roach and asp-nit feasting upon the droppings from the tables but the tea is first rate. Have mint tea, keep your shoes on, and listen to me. It will take but a moment."

"I doubt that," Lila muttered but the pain in her ear was intense and she knew she would never hear the end of it or might possibly lose part of the ear if she didn't so she turned left as instructed, went through a greasy beaded curtain and up a flight of rickety steps to a room every bit as filthy as promised.

Three older demons were hunched in the corner, whispering and fussing over some cards and other items on a low table. They all smoked and were chewing some kind of herby stuff out of a jar, taking handfuls at regular intervals and spitting the result into an iron pot where it bubbled and gave off low vapours. They snorted this into their nostrils in a strict turn-taking round. As she took a seat at the least repulsive spot and feigned no interest in them they ruffled their feathers and spiked their quills but otherwise ignored her. Rough straw scattered on the floor seethed with insect activity. There was a strong smell of burnt frying fat, incense, and espresso.

"Well?" she muttered, watching the server appear from a hole in the ceiling. It was a spider form the size of a small dog, and clicked quietly across the roof upside down, extending a tattered menu to her on a long sticky strand of silk. Most of the hairs on its thick legs were singed and although it had no facial expressions she could detect among its eight eyes its body wore a strangely immaculate white band of apron that seemed to speak of a kind of hygienic pride. She took the menu and tugged it free. The line broke and clung to her fingers. She tried to wipe it off on the table but it just stuck more.

"It's enchanted. It'll evaporate in a minute," the imp said confidently. "Mint tea. And I'll have the double shot with just a dash of mare's milk."

But Lila was engrossed in the menu suddenly and not because it was stuck to her hand. "What is Essence of Humanity?"

"They make it by mage-pressing grave dirt with fresh spring water. You don't need to worry." The imp called up to the server, "She wants mint tea. I'm going for the double Arabica, if you don't have mare's milk then yak or bat will do."

"Milks of the world," Lila read, "see specials board . . ." She looked at the board. "Harp Seal milk?"

"Too fattening. Also it tastes of fish which does nothing for coffee."

"Milk of Mother's Tears . . . ?"

"Look, never mind all that. The thing is you want to go to the Souk and the other thing is that I want to prove I'm really who I say I am . . ."

"You didn't say who you were."

"If I could say my name I wouldn't be a damned imp, would I?" the imp snapped. "I have to get my name. And you have . . . some business that's probably important to someone somewhere so I was thinking I help you, you help me, match made in hell. You need someone who knows what they're doing around demons and you don't have that. I need someone . . . I need someone . . . so there we are. Perfection."

Lila sighed and shook her head, "I'm not telling my business to you so you can sell it all around town. Do I look crazy?"

"Yes, frankly. You *have* got an imp on your shoulder, and everyone knows that their entire purpose in life is to drive people crazy."

"With lots of lies. Which are pathetic, by the way."

"Just one shot. One. I'll get you something. Do something. Say something that will show you I'm telling you the truth."

"Nah, you'll just do it enough to convince me and then stab me in the back. Your entire MO is old news to me," Lila said with conviction as the server returned, via the door this time, and slid a tray off its pristine back onto the table. It bore a glass of mint tea, steaming, and a pot of coffee with a tiny cup and a small pitcher of milk.

"You see. I bet you're never usually that suspicious of anyone without some magical extra winding up your nerves. Of course you won't believe me, that's part of my curse."

"You're an imp. I don't believe you because of that."

"Sure, sure. Taste the tea. It's all good." The imp waited and Lila, because she had nothing to drink for hours, decided to try it. She put her finger into it first, in spite of the heat, for a quick analysis. It was tea. She raised the glass to her lips.

"Anyway if I was a real imp I'd have this hotline into your worst neuroses and be telling you that your boyfriend is too good for you, you'll never know the half of what goes on behind your back at work because it's in everyone else's interests to keep you ignorant and Tartarus will be under an ice sheet by the time you manage to conquer your fear of being alive. In the meantime you'll waste a lot of energy agonising about your old life and supporting your own denial with relentless activities that seem to be focused on work but really are just distraction tactics with vaguely work-related payoffs. Your heart is concealing something you'd really rather not face for reasons you don't want to look at so you'll spend what's left of your time keeping a lid on that whilst convincing yourself rationally that it's for everyone else's good that you do as you're told, don't ask too many questions, and play at being strong in situations that seem dangerous but don't matter to you so you can fool other people about how well you're doing. Of course, you know very well that you're turning into the biggest sell-out of them all.

"In your future alcoholism or other forms of addiction await you for when you get bored of playing at supergirl. You will become a cynical, bitter old woman who can only relate to small pets in order to avoid your intimacy issues, which by then will be of apocalyptic proportions and your loneliness will only be alleviated by certain great pieces of music which will also intensify its piquancy for reasons you never understand. There may be some dallying with literature or other arts as a way of faking contact with others of your kind but at a remove that allows your fantasies to remain untouched whilst never bringing you close to the ugly reality of genuine connections with the flawed and annoying monstrosities that are other people. You will die alone, like the rest of us, and making sense of your life in order to paint yourself the martyr will be the biggest fake ever hung in the big gallery of retrospective narrative lies and you'll know that in your final moments and in that second everything you have struggled so hard to hold onto will vanish like smoke on the wind but it will be too late.

"See, if I was a real imp, *that's* what I'd be saying."

Lila spluttered and swallowed a mouthful that was too hot and then put her glass down. The tea was really good. Her tongue was burned. She took a long breath over it, trying to cool it down. Tath spun in her chest; he was a little sparkly, like a gulp of champagne and Lila had learned to recognise that as laughter. There was a sharp pain under her breastbone that had nothing to do with him. For a moment she felt intense rage at the pair of them, little parasites, but then a cold calm took hold of her.

"Now let's get one thing clear," she said. "My minions don't gang up on me. My minions don't tell me the uncomfortable truth or the comfortable truth or any kind of stuff like that to make my life harder. My minions help me to the bitter end of their bitter little lives or they get sent through the nine circles to the Infinite Pit by any means I can find and, by golly gosh, if you don't think I have the balls to hold a grudge beyond all reasonable limits, demon, then you really don't have two powers to rub together."

The imp let go of her ear and pattered down her arm, balancing on her hand as it reached for the coffee pot and poured itself a cup. It disdained the milk it had ordered and knocked back the scalding brew with a single jerk of its head. Espresso dribbled down its chin, "Now that's what I'm talkin' bout, baby," it said with gusto. "You and me. Match made in hell. Had the eyeballs dream. Spoken like a real devil, my lovely. Let's hit the Souk. I'm itching for a battle of wits with those jessies."

Minions?

I didn't notice you protesting my valour. So can it.

Lila got up suddenly. The imp reached for another coffee, almost fell from her hand, and scuttled back up to its place. A sharp pain reported a fresh grip on her ear. She tried not to let the eye on that side tear up.

In the corner one of the large demons hawked and spat into the pot. Thick purple billows came from it and his companion sniffed deeply, reeled for a moment, and then fell senseless onto the floor. The other two cackled and scraped piles of small change from the table into their hands.

"Wait till he shrinks," one slurred.

"Yeah, so you can carry him out first . . ." the other said. "No way. I buy the percentage."

"Myeh, what you think he's good for?"

"Can't tell until . . . ah wait . . ."

The demon on the floor began to shrink. Nothing about it altered except that its breathing slowed and it got smaller, and smaller, and smaller.

Lila watched with unstoppable fascination. The demon, which had been just about her size, continued to diminish until it was no larger than a salt shaker at which point it took on a polished kind of sheen and a stony appearance.

"Crap," said the quilled demon. "Fucking chess set is what. You can have fifty-fifty on him. Think he'd at least have done for garden statuary, demon of his bearing."

"He must have been lying all these years about that witchery business. I said he was a bluffer. Gah, the money I've given him for enchantments. All up in smoke now, and I'll be lucky if we can get enough paint on him to call him a bishop." The feathered demon picked up the pot of bubbling mixture and flung it across the room where it splattered on the wall with a clang. The pot rolled away and the server came in and chittered in a high voice, spitting venom.

The demons attempted to get up and run for it but the server snared them in a sticky web until they paid up some sum. The quilled demon scooped up the frozen figure of the shrunken one, shook off a couple of roaches, and stuffed it into a pouch at its belt. "I'll do the fixings and sell him. Maybe there'll be some tips on eBay about the kind of things the humans like to buy. See you tomorrow for the cash up."

They shuffled out, weaving and bumping each other, unsteady on their feet and cursing frequently as they clutched at the walls for support.

Lila watched this without moving.

"True friends," the imp said on her shoulder with nostalgic longing. "Lovely that was. Just lovely." It had a quaver in its voice. "Oh, one more thing. We can't just roll around town with me riding here like some ordinary pestilence talking into your ear or nobody will trade doohickey with you. And I think rubies will go nicely with that big red streak in your hair. Nice touch that. Shows off your creative side."

The casual pinprick pain in Lila's earlobe became a swift, savage biting agony. "Oww! What the eff . . ." Her hand snapped up to her shoulder but the imp was gone, not even into its cold flame form. It was just gone. There was a cold, cut-sided stone set into her ear, like an earring stud. It pierced through and held at the back with a similar-size rock. Her fingers came away bloody. She could hear the imp almost as well as before.

"So, what are we bidding for?" it perked.

"Information," Lila said. "When the elf Zal Ahriman became a demon something happened here to him. I want to know what and how. And when I know, I'm going to do it too."

"Well that's easy," the imp whispered. "Every demon in the seven cities knows how you do that. It's the one legend of our world that never disappoints. You don't need the Souk at all, unless you need magic for something else. All you need to do is go through Hell."

Zal had gone about a hundred metres when he heard a familiar voice behind him and the sound of light fey feet running.

"Hey! Wait up."

He turned, grateful the back street behind the hotel was deserted except for an automated trash-collection bot doing the round of the bins. Poppy was bright, vivacious, sensationally dressed and together they could attract more attention in two minutes than a full-scale car crash at a city centre junction. His understated clothes and broad-brimmed hat, chosen to make him seem unremarkable in Otopia, were pointless beside her resplendent rainbow of clothing and her flaring green hair.

He waited for her, a soft spot under his heart always open to her in spite of the fact he found her over the top and she had tried to kill him on at least one occasion. She had a great voice.

She paused the regulation metre away from him. "You're going to see Lila, right?"

Zal made a face and sighed. She was sharp, despite having extreme blonde tendencies. He nodded.

Poppy bit her lip and drifted slightly across the ground, her invisible wings rendering her virtually weightless. She held something out to him in her hand. He took it. "What's this?"

The small packet was wrapped in a silk cloth and unwound to show a hammered silver pendant in the shape of a spiral attached to a grey silk ribbon which glimmered with the faint purple gleams of magical marks. It was a delicate object and looked as though the spiral should easily slip off the ribbon although Zal suspected that no earthly force and certainly not one as obvious as gravity would separate it from its band. It had a weight that was heavy to his *andalune*, light on his flesh hand.

"Just something I got her," Poppy said. "Kind of to say sorry from me and Vidia, you know, for the whole nearly drowning you both thing."

Zal folded the cloth again and put it in his pocket. "I'll give it to her."

"Don't be late back with Sorcha, me and V need some money." This statement came with the kind of offhand casualness Zal knew signalled great importance.

"I can give you a loan . . ."

"Nah nah, just be back on time, cut the track, that's good. Oh, and Boom asked me to give you this." She pulled a crumpled piece of hotel notepaper out of the back pocket of her trousers and held it towards him. She wouldn't meet his eye.

Zal flicked it from her grasp and read the scratchy pencilled handwriting. "What is this shit?"

"She wanted to keep true to her musical principles and . . ." Poppy began with rolling eyes and pulling her mouth into awkward shapes as she delivered the bad news.

Zal read aloud, ". . . will not record sub-vaudeville neo-romantic diva disco for the sake of a quick buck . . . spoiling the pure spirit of the hip-hop tradition . . . slave to corporate greed . . . less the spirit of punk than the seepage of neo-fascist marketing spunk . . . back to my roots in the souldance houses of Bay City . . . leaving your corrupting influence for the good of the genre . . ." He took a deep breath, "That superficial, ponced-up, jealous little two-bit hack programmer!"

Poppy bit both lips. "She was pretty good as a DJ."

"Well, screw her. What does she know about souldance Mode-X crossover anyway? The closest she gets to creative is sampling tracks out of the Otopia Tree Library Least Listened archive. I can get a better sound out of a demon technician than some bloody human. Good. Another damn reason to go back. Tell Jolene I'll find a replacement. Tell her I'll find two!"

"Zal . . ." Poppy began in a patient tone, clearly about to ask for some understanding in what was a major moment of band history. They both knew Boom was good and that she was pretentious and that she was gone and this would be hard to get over.

"No." He balled up the note and threw it on the ground. "We had this out. She was going to have as much leeway as she wanted to create a whole new sound and she bottled out of it. I don't want this bullshit about creative freedom and the history of fucking music. Let her go back to working clubs and selling her sad little story."

"The thing is, Zal . . ."

He looked into Poppy's smile-to-cover-the-story face and her awkward manner. A slow, weary sinking feeling spread across him. "You agree with her, don't you?"

"No, not exactly. But we were all, you know, feeling like it was bad to get attached to Sorcha's image too much and you know you were absent for the tour date and that was really hard for us . . ."

"Enough excuses. Are you going to bail out too? And who else? Do I or do I not remember you just telling me to get back fast to make some bucks for whatever stupid problems you and V have got yourselves into now? So it looks to me like whatever you think you're stuck with it."

"No no no. We're fine. We're all ready to do it. It's fine." Poppy backed away from him, her hands held up and waving in front of her in airy little gestures. "We just . . . we're worried, Zal. About you. That's all."

"Worry about yourself!" he snapped. "Worry about finding another DJ and worry about the money because I am not your damn problem." He spun on his heel and walked fast away from her, seething. For once he was glad there was no chance anyone could contact him via one of the ubiquitous Berries that the others used as electronic lifestyle aides. The worst part was that Poppy was right to call him on his absence. Even so, it was stupid elitist crap to say that any kind of music couldn't be good, no matter what style it was or what it was made with. Anyway, she was double wrong because disco was fantastic. He'd find some demon to help, someone who really understood the way all the grooves fit together, and had it branded in their soul like him.

His irritation made him more bad tempered, his awareness that he was bad tempered made him exasperated, his exasperation made him restless, and his restlessness pointed only one way. He walked the six blocks of back streets to where the warehouses of Ikea opened to the loading bays and climbed the wire fence onto the property. There was a shiver point so strong under the building that he could sense it even without trying. It lay along the same faultline that the recording studio in Bay City stood beside but here there was only the thinnest skin between Demonia and Otopia and a running torrent of free aether in I-space. Demonia's border, like the wall of a giant cell, softly billowed up from the aether depths at regular intervals with magmatic slowness. By the time Zal had walked in, unnoticed, to the self-serve area where the endless cabinets were racked, it had risen on its ten-minute turnaround and was practically right there beneath his feet. The boxes and pallets of furniture shimmered and a couple of bits were stolen by demonic fingers, right before his eyes. They vanished from the stock without a whisper. It was pure devilment as no demon would be seen dead with mass-produced items in their homes.

Zal opened his hands, released his *andalune* body to the floor where the borders were thinnest, and opened what he thought of as the inner fire in his soul. This was not a literal thing. Whoever you were, to get to Alfheim you needed some kind of portal. To get to Thanatopia you had to be dead. To get into Zoomenon you had to summon and find a spot where elementals liked to gather in sufficient numbers to help you out but to get into Demonia, especially if you were a demon, you only had to stand close to it and tune in to the ever-present beat of hedonistic joy in your heart—Demonia's music that was never out of key and never entirely out of reach.

He had the brief sensation of falling. It was always like that, like the dream where you step off the pavement into an unexpected drop and there's a heartstopping moment of being off-balance and out of control. It lasted a little longer than the dream, but not very much. He smelt brimstone and the sweet reek of rose-scented ifriti flowers, blooming with their love-drenched and fatal nectar saturating each

petal and suffusing the air around them. Otopian Ikea gave way to
Zhanzabar Walk's gardens. Next to Zal two sturdy horned demons
piled their looted flatpacks onto a wheelbarrow and hurried off.

"No scented candles?" said one with disappointment.

"They're not close enough to the shiver point," the other repeated
in the tones of someone who has repeated it a thousand times.

Zal stepped quickly out of range of the flowering bush and quickly
stripped off his jacket and shirt, allowing the flare on his back to be
visible. He folded the clothes and carried them with him in one hand
until a flitting sprite in the family colours came by, attuned to seek out
higher ranks and offer service. He gave it the clothing and told it to
send word that he was coming to stay at home for a few days.

The sprite took the parcel of cloth in its long fingers and rippled
its scales and whiskers with purplish delight. "Very good, sir. I will
have your things set out. Will you be dining at home?"

"Yes. As long as the guest Lila Black is attending."

"We expect her to be there. No events are on the schedule for this
evening. Drinks are served on the terrace at eight. Shall I alert your
wife that you wish her company? She is at the house in Tartarus
presently . . ."

"No, no," Zal said. "Don't disturb her. But if Zarzaret is in town,
I want to see him."

"As you wish." The sprite flew away on its dragonish wings,
bumping up and down with the weight of its burden.

The smell of the canals, thick and rotting, mingled with the far more
pleasant scents of the gardens and the wafting traces of various spicy foods
in the warm morning air. Zal took a deep breath and felt his ears prickle
with the amount of waste aether drifting about from all the sorcery that
burned on day and night in every house and corner. It was almost the
antithesis of Alfheim but just as abundant in its way. Not far off, among
a glade of deathflame trees, fire elementals spiralled like gnats in the thin
branches. The blue hiss and flare of methane burn danced in the heart of

the black flowers, carbon petalled. White and blue fire sprites darted between them, sipping, while their larger cousins whirled together into vortices of lazy fire, licking on the tar sap that oozed from the flat rubbery bark. Black smokes plumed lazily here and there.

At the centre of the gathering Zal, adept in fire, could feel the beginnings of a firestorm building. The outer elementals were whistling to their airy counterparts to beckon drafts into their midst, promising the lift of heat and a ride up through the muggy daytime into the cool, pristine heights of the upper atmosphere in return for a concentrated influx of oxygen. Between the roots of the oldest trees small pools of petroleum fractions shivered and hazed the air just beneath the fire blazers' gathering tribe.

Events like this were reasonably rare and fire blooms even more so, since he could never see one in Otopia short of wantonly loitering around fire stations waiting to be called. In Alfheim it meant volcano walking. But Demonia was rich with hydrocarbons and life-forms which processed the same. He thought it couldn't hurt just to take a look and moved closer. Other adept demons, attracted by the same sense of an impending surge, drifted in from the sky and across from various entry points into the park from the city. Two of them from the same Talent path as Zal, from the Mousa, had brought pyre flutes together with bellows-pump.

"Long-ears," said one of them to Zal, even though his own ears were at least as large beneath his curling horns. "Longtime we not see you in the Guildhalls, you been missing us, heh?"

Under the demon's attention and with proximity to the others, Zal felt the flare on his back grow warm and begin to blossom through his skin. Beside him the rest attuned themselves to one another and to the tone of the fires dancing in the trees, changing gently from reds and yellows to the hotter fires of blue and white. A surge of energy, the first ripple of a promise, went around them, passed from one to another like a torch. It lit their flares more brightly for the instant as it moved and with it the mages in the group began muttering some incantation to the elementals, attracting their attention.

The demon who had spoken to Zal produced a wind whistle and began to blow it. Compared to the tiny numbers of such beings in Otopia the gathering of elementals was shocking with its suddenness and ferocity. Within seconds the wind was strong enough to require an effort to withstand. Zal's hair whipped around, blinding him and lashing his face. He heard the soft fluttering of fire in the glade become a hiss and then, as the pools lit with a soft explosion a wave of heat physically pushed him back into the onrushing wind so he was caught between the flame and the air. The hiss became a ferocious roar. He and the other watching demons were suddenly all sucked forwards to the blaze by the backdraft, the mischievous hands and tendrils of air elementals tugging at them in passing as they hurtled into the heart of the flame.

They did not burn. The fire caused the natural fire of their flares to ignite and spread out into sheets of incandescent energy; aether channelled into flame, as individual as a fingerprint and as harmless to the one enveloped in it as his or her own skin. It was the fire that touched the living flames of the elementals as they gathered and united into a single storm entity, fuelled on the energy of the demons and the sap of the trees, lent power by the sharing of the air.

A spinning column of fire shot up into the sky. The demons with wings rode on it as high as they could and those without, including Zal, floated in the rotating pool at its base like swimmers, each barely visible to the others through curtains of blazing plasma. From their places the musicians flung their pyre flutes outward and down where their enchanted bases sent ceramic roots down into the fuel source. Air and fuel mixed and shot up through the pipes, sounding two burring notes of continuous burn at pitches calibrated by demon technicians to induce an even greater waveform for maximum combustion. The two tubes vibrated with the incredible sound, there as invitation for the god of Fire to use as a voice.

Since his rebirth Zal had not experienced anything like it. Once the burn had reached a tipover point the energy for which he had been only the conduit from his aether connection to the fire suddenly reversed flow. Now the power of the mighty elemental and his fellow demons began to charge him with enormous, astonishing force. The moment it began to happen he became simultaneously aware of two things. One was that this was exactly what he hoped would happen when he first noticed the elementals and pretended he was only curious about them. The other was that it was far more powerful than he had imagined and there was a third thing—he realised he was out of practice and couldn't handle it.

For a few brief moments the hit was joyous and a merciful release from the near-sterility of Otopian life. He couldn't imagine what had possessed him to leave an aetheric region for such a place. Nothing could compare to the incredible vitality of this! And then it was too much and what had been ecstasy became pain in his nerves and pain in his *andalune* as the vibrations—frequencies not natural to its ordinary elven system—began to disrupt its normal flow. He felt fire from the flare begin to eat its way through from the realm of the aetheric into his flesh body. If he did not discharge it in some way it could easily burst across the gap into a different form, its physical form which was more than able to burn him to a cinder.

Inside the vortex there was nothing to do with the energy but create more flame. He realised he had to get out and then his thoughts became a blur of roaring, singing noise and a voice said from the fire, "Sing for me."

He opened his eyes to the flat azure skies he knew well. Beneath him was hot sand and the dry air was hazed with shivering mirages and the colours of half-formed things.

"Fuck, fuck, fuckity fuck," he said and let his head fall back down to the ground.

He was in Zoomenon.

CHAPTER TEN

There was an instant when Malachi felt he would not be able to continue in this dreadful halfway world of chaos, that he must lose track of his forms: humanoid, feline, element, and dream. All his life he had shifted from one to another, mostly at his own whim and occasionally as a result of some charm cast upon him but he had only recently learnt to loiter in I-space and bear the discomfort of not resolving his state into one definite organisation. The desire, the survival instinct to do so was incredibly strong. It tore at him tooth and claw, a scrabbling, dry kind of fear rising all the time the more he delayed its gratification. This was made worse by the fact that he could make out almost nothing save indistinct masses of shifting aether with the occasional ghostly imprint deep in their midst. If Calliope let go of him in this place where most of his senses were useless and he was not even sure which way was up, or indeed any direction, he thought he would be lost forever. He knew, intellectually, that all he had to do was resolve himself into one of his forms and it would be done with and that he would be able to do that at any time, but the longer he did not do it the more doubt grew in him that he could do it.

"Step out," Jones said to him in a voice that came to his mind through the aether wave. He needed no other prompt.

Her pulling had altered the exit point. Although he had left from his Otopian offices he had made some transit across I-space and was now somewhere quite other. It was a place he didn't immediately recognise, but that was not surprising given that all he could see of it was a series of untidy rooms full of strange, humming equipment; both computers and other gear more reminiscent of the grand arcane engineering feats he was used to the demons building. Jones stood in front of him, grinning, and gestured at the hovel with pride.

Malachi stepped out of the one clear circle in the place and an empty card drinks cup crumpled under his foot. Behind him he heard the breath and movement of several others, arriving into four-dimensional reality with whuffs of cool air and the sharp smells of cold seaside days.

"Welcome," Jones said, "to the one and only Ghost Research Centre."

Figures of a demon, two other fey, and a shadow elf marched past him with the universal, preoccupied expressions of scientists focused on an important problem. With great energy they went to work at various places on different things. They barely spoke but moved with economy and ease, helping each other to do their tasks. Malachi shivered. There was about them the indefinable oddity of all brinkmen, a haunted quality, as if they were privy to some information about reality which was too awkward and horrible to impart. He had always guessed that's what they really were like, and now he was about to find out.

"Where is this?" he asked.

Jones's grin intensified. "Nowhere," she said. "It is an island floating in the aetheric deeps of the Interstitial. A created place, sustained by constant intent." She pointed at the pale grey walls. "Those are the limit."

What Malachi had taken for concrete and plaster was the border of their whole tiny world. He looked around and down at the floor. "Intent, as in enchantment?"

"Intent is the cornerstone of enchantment, the root," Jones said. "It comes before. Only intent is sufficient in I-space. No mere enchantment can hold the aetheric region back."

"But . . ." Malachi began. It had always been his understanding that yes, intent came before most things naturally, but how could it possibly be more powerful than enchantment? "Wishes aren't horses . . ."

"This kind of intent is highly focused. It requires constant, active attention." Jones beckoned and he followed her, stepping over bags and piles of broken equipment, boxes of unidentifiable instruments, clothes, litter. "No person would be able to create this kind of stability, so here we have our Watcher. The One Who Abides." She pointed to an undistinguished grey box. "The aetheric weather here is too forceful for enchantments to survive. The decay of organisation into entropy, which effects all spells, is so severe here that even the greatest sorcerers could not hold long against the erosion. As all energy in the material universe seeks to become stable through a transition into iron, so aether is the opposite, seeking always to become unstable through transitions into pure energy. Material energy and magical energy are dynamically opposed forces."

"Fighting for equilibrium?" Malachi asked.

"It is not known. To be sure, we are not convinced the two systems interact with one another at all in the sense that you mean. Still, our research focuses on the aetheric and in that world we are sure that chaos is the basic state of nature."

The box had wires running in and out of it, roped together with untidy cable ties. It had a single readout—a set of digital numbers flickered up and down within a couple of thousandths every other second or so. "What's that?" he asked.

"The AI concentrates on maintaining our space and privacy here," Jones said. "That's all it does. Its will forms the walls. It is a program of intent running on a single machine. Rather simple actually. Barely qualifies as AI. But as long as the generator holds out then it needs no rest and its concentration varies only slightly, as you see, according to the flows of electrons and the cosmic and various other minor disruptions that occur within its circuits." She gave the box a peremptory once-over and then led onward past a stack of still-packed bags and personal items that he realised were the piled-up goods of the individuals here, their sleeping bags and mats, their pillows, clothing, and so on.

"You live here?"

"Yes." She kicked through a heap of coats and went into a small room that was mercifully free of clutter. It had a functional food unit and was as clean as the rest of the place was not. There was a cleaning rota in red pen stuck to the refrigerator with sticky tape. "This is where we eat and drink, standing up because no room. No eating at the equipment . . ."

Malachi found that hard to believe.

". . . you can find the Otopian food in this cupboard and here . . . and drink whatever the unit makes that you like. The bathroom is here . . ." She moved out and through the only doorway with an actual door in it and put the light on in a poky wet room with a hole in the floor and a showerhead. "Pee and whatever it is you have to do down the hole, everything, in fact, down the hole . . ."

"Where does it go?" he asked.

"You don't want to know," she said and put the light off. "Now, you've got no gear but we sleep in shifts so just bunk down anywhere and . . ."

"Wait a minute," Malachi said. "How long a stay did you have in mind?"

Jones put her hands on her hips and tossed her long hair over her shoulder. "You have to see several important things. They're not exactly predictable, like weather systems, but they are reliable enough, like tornados. We know certain places and times are likely points for them to occur. Given reasonable odds you shouldn't have to be here more than a couple of weeks."

"Weeks!" he gasped, like a laugh. "I'm still at work." He glanced at his watch. "I don't leave the office for another five hours . . . I can't stay here that long."

Calliope stared at him, unmoving. Her cool grey eyes were like granite. They stared right through him. She spoke coolly. "If you want to know anything worth knowing, you stay." Clearly by her expression she was perfectly happy to share knowledge or for him to leave. She didn't give a toss but she would soon lose her patience. She was already looking like he was wasting her time and that haunted, driven look . . . that was ferocious. He was cat all through but he didn't like it on him.

"Something about the Others?" he hedged.

"And the rest," she said, and added, "We are self-funding, self-regulating. Nobody knows what we know. Nobody. Not any agency and not any government. You know why? Because they're too busy worrying about each other to worry about I-space. But they should worry about it. A lot."

Malachi began to see a reason. "You want me to bring it to attention."

She nodded. "That's the deal, pussycat. I help you with your issues and your case. You help us get something better than this two-bit operation without getting taken over."

He became aware of everyone else in the room suddenly shifting their focus to him. Of course aether responded to intent that strong . . . what could resist the demand of so many directed wills? He was aetheric and the response was strong, but he was trained and he detached from the need to comply. "What if I can't deliver? I'm hardly a major player and my evidence . . . depends how good it is."

Jones's eyes flickered around her colleagues, taking reaction. She glanced back at him. "We'll get your evidence."

He liked the feeling of her conviction. He always followed his instinct. "Deal."

"Now," said the imp beside Lila's ear as they reached the Souk entrance. "Where would you look for the best mages?"

Lila was transfixed. The Souk was in a particularly beautiful part of Bathshebat, an old town centre around which the great city had grown. Demon architecture, like everything else they undertook, was lavish and, as it constantly surprised her, exquisite. This old style was from an artistic period of great diversity and imagination but also an almost spartan attitude to materials and engineering. A thousand years ago the views on magic and materials science had been quite different to the prevailing vision of the modern era. Where now demons were joyfully inventing and researching with both disciplines as it suited them, at that time the two means of manipulating and discovering the world were kept separate and pursued by individuals who might never pay much attention to the alternative. Their domestic and civilian buildings were all products of material engineering. In the oldest parts of the Souk these were native substances that could be sourced in the area—petrified wood, ebony, magmastone, and locally made concretes in various lovely colours. Later, the imp told her with pride, stone, wood, and metals had been sourced from all over the world and these had given rise to the incredible buildings she now stood among, as rich in their own way as treasure houses.

"The Souk is the Hoard of Demonia," the imp said with quiet reverence. "The product of a backward age, but an age of enormous aesthetic power and spiritual integrity."

Lila stared at beautiful structures that reminded her of woods, of animals and natural things even though they were geometrically perfected and were absolutely mathematically manufactured. Demon buildings were symphonies for the eye. "This reminds me of something, an Otopian designer . . ."

"Antoni Gaudi," the imp said fondly, head on one side. "Of course, we were whispering in his ear and in the ears of many of your race down the long ages of your history. We have much to be thankful for."

"You were?" She turned to try and stare into the imp's ugly little face and he smiled with beatific pleasure.

"Oh yes, us and the others."

"What others?"

"Others of other races I meant," he said hastily. "Now, as you see before you, we are at the Palace of Seven Seasons and it is in here you will find the best mages because obviously it is the best place. Not like in some backwater like Alfheim where the best will always seek to hide themselves in spurious fake humility, sackcloth and monasteries and the like, which is ego run riot and hiding in mortified clothing. No, in Demonia if you see someone who looks powerful, ruthless, and ferocious then you may take it that they are, for we are true to our appearances. We play quite fair."

"What you see is what you get," Lila said as Tath muttered darkly and incomprehensibly something about waste and superficiality. He was far too nervous to unwind even enough to get a sentence out and she was oddly glad though she tried not to show it, thinking he would be hurt and that outcome would annoy her.

"Exactly," the imp said. "Except in my case of course."

"Of course," Lila agreed, not giving it credence for a second. "So, I have to do something with this shadow elf before I set off for Hell. What's your best shot?"

"Death is too good for such a creature, particularly since its assassination efforts were so puny."

"I'm not going to kill it." She gave a brief outline of how she had come by her prisoner.

"You could do worse than to torture it for answers before the lady at whose party you were fortunate enough to be attacked. Such a gesture would curry favour with her and her household and make the son who passed you the elf look rather good too. You would increase your standing with demon society for being so polite and your ruthlessness and willingness to get ahead would look well all over, I think. So of

course you won't do any such thing, being a human and stubbornly
lacking in sense and decorum. Therefore, the only recourse that might
pass in society, let your host family save face, and display graciousness
in the receiving of a gift like that is to buy some enchantment that will
bind the awful thing to you in obedient service for a reasonable term.
Say, not more than a hundred years."

"Slavery," Lila said, feeling a horrible weight slowly descending
upon her.

"It is the only civilised and acceptable option for such as yourself,"
the imp declared with a nod. "Since I guess you will not sell her for
profit."

"I couldn't just banish her from Demonia for eternity?"

"The coward's way out," the imp said with contempt. "It would
only serve to make you look weak and as soon as that happens you will
be regarded as everybody's meat. I doubt your host family could preserve you, even if they wanted to." Its tone indicated that it thought
they would be extremely unlikely to want to. "If you like, to soften the
blow, you could think of it as acquiring family of your own. Like me
for instance. She could be a sister to you and I could be . . ."

"You are an annoyance," Lila said firmly, rejecting the idea with
absolute horror. Sadly, its ideas about the elf did seem quite in
keeping with all her data on demon culture. She had thought as
much and now it was confirmed she was furious. The elf probably
thought the same thing, and would look for death at every opportunity. Lila would be honour bound to preserve her. The elf, wanting
Lila's death, would be bound to preserve *her* by the forces of aetheric
binding. It would all be just jimdandy. And since Lila didn't reckon
on living a hundred years it would last forever.

"You can avoid all the irritation and bother by simply handing her
to the hostess's family," the imp observed airily, examining its tiny
finger claws and giving them a polish on Lila's collar. "Easy peasy, pud-
ding and pie."

"Who will do what with her?" Lila asked, desperately hoping against hope that it would not be that bad.

"They may exert mercy in consideration of your humanity and simply eat her."

"Fuck," Lila said.

"After that no doubt," the imp sighed. "Well, come on, hero. How much money or trade goods do you have about you? What's on offer and what's not negotiable? What have we got to work with?"

"Let's just find what we need," Lila said grimly. She could see no good way out of her predicament. "You hide. I'll do the talking."

"If I might . . ." the imp began, clearly disagreeing with the plan.

Lila powered up her left gauntlet and exposed part of her finger struts to act as conductors. Sparks crackled across their tips as electricity began to discharge. She slowly moved her hand up to her shoulder.

"Of course," the imp said demurely. Again there was a piercing pain in her ear and then no imp but a blood-red stone, which whispered in a silent, niggling way directly to her cerebellum. *Same method as Tath*, she thought and then went silent, waiting to see if the imp had heard her thoughts like the necromancer could. But there was no response and she didn't believe the creature would keep quiet about it, so she took a gamble on it not being two-way telepathy. Yet one more thing to file in the AI and download for someone else to worry about later.

The Souk door was a hexagonal opening in the thick, old walls of soft red lavastone. The stone was weathered and pocked with holes and looked like sponge. The doorway was hung with a giant-size bead curtain.

"Every bead unique," the imp earring said, taking on the proud tones of a tour guide. "Shrunken heads, teeth, carved bones, dried berries, bits of old tins made into tiny racing cars . . . go and look you won't find two the same, I guarantee it."

Lila reached out to gently move aside some strands of the swaying, jangling curtain. "Don't tell me, if I want to return to Demonia I have to add a bead . . ."

"Dear Lord, no," the imp gasped. "These are the beads of the damned, fashioned from their treasured personal possessions by their own hands before the traitors were put to fire and the sword."

"Oh." Lila stepped through faster than she intended and wiped her hand unconsciously on her leg.

"It is an antitheft device of the highest enchantment," the imp added. "Try running through that with stolen goods and it rips the spirit from the body and shreds the spirit into pieces. The spirits of the damned are shriven and stuck in the beads you see, and if they can grab enough energy from thieves and brigands they can eventually break free and fly to Thanatopia's dark shores. Otherwise it's just curtains f'r ever and ever, amen. The sweet banality of it after lives of great drama and importance sacrificed . . . mmmnnn . . . you could never fault the demons for not understanding romance."

On the other side of the curtain the Souk itself was a labyrinth of broad streets with narrow ways leading to all directions off the wider avenues, and narrower channels yet splitting from those so that in layout it resembled three nets of increasing fineness, one laid over the other. Everything joined up eventually. If Lila had not had her AI to map and guide her she would have been lost within ten steps. As it was she tracked her route and let her inboard systems put an easy green line on her internal minimap so that she could find her way back, but otherwise she simply wandered, Tath a cold green clutch of dread around her heart.

There were many fey here, she soon noticed, clustered in twos or larger groups at almost every place, in every store. They moved in peculiar patterns, avoiding or moving towards magics that attracted them she supposed, though being human she could feel nothing and maintained a course in the centre of the alleys. Everything imaginable was on sale. She kept her face schooled to stony indifference to the living and dead animals, the pieces of things dried and preserved in jars, the fragments that she could identify not only as Otopian, but as human, among the collections. Her AI-self was perfect for the mission and she allowed its machine logic to overrule her feelings as she moved smoothly, taking footage of all she saw, recording every conversational whisper she overheard, analysing it, translating it, filing it. She was a moving library and she did not have to give in to care. Tath's repulsion was enough for both of them. A part of her clung to him and she strolled with relaxed ease through something she had anticipated would be a tourist's encounter with the arcane but which proved to be a catalogue of horrors. There were beautiful things, jewels and rich objects, weapons, treasures . . . her eyes flicked over them as they flicked over the severed hands, the shrunken flesh on ancient skulls, the pickled children of every race afloat in the amnion of formaldehyde and aetheric spirit.

Lila walked, fluid motion in body, frozen inside. If the imp had spoken she would have picked her ear off her head and destroyed it with any means but, perhaps sensing her hatred, it did nothing and she found herself longing for its voice and the excuse for a truly cruel vengeance. In those moments she felt her slightly embarrassed admiration of the demons alter into a much more complicated and difficult emotion and that extended to all the other magic users by a tenuous, horrible leakage. A prejudice she had not known she had, a fear she did not believe in unfolded from its dark seed and took root in her. The back of her throat dried and contracted. What a fool she had been to be sucked into the cheap superficial glamour of the demons' universe. All their art, their devotions to beauty and the pursuits of science, of greatness in intellect and spirit, their unrivalled exultation in every experience in the pursuit of the sublime . . . and beneath it all the time they said nothing about *this*.

And Zal was one of them.

Whatever interest she had felt in her mission here to find a spell to help her with her farcical elven prisoner situation vanished into insignificance. Let the stupid woman take her chances in the Ahriman house or starve to death waiting. She'd signed her own ticket the day she decided it was fine to shoot Lila.

And Sorcha . . . Lila could hardly believe she had felt such closeness, such friendship from her but that it was all this false front, this lie, hiding something as ugly as the true nature of demon magic. Arië's violence and plotting when she attempted to use Zal as her victim to destroy the link between Alfheim and the other realms, why, that was barely gracing the fringe of wicked compared with this casual, everyday traffic. Arië, twisted as she had become, was a positive saint. No wonder the elves despised this race and called them irredeemably corrupt.

She tried hard, with every machine and personal resource, to come up with an explanation that would lessen the nightmare but found none anywhere. It was as though in walking through the curtain she had stepped into a different reality. She wondered if Sorcha would have tried to conceal it, if she had asked . . . There was nothing about this place in her databases . . . Would the tourist trade include trips here? She wanted to laugh so that she didn't have to hold back the pain of not crying. She felt as though she was falling down a deep, dark hole and the circle of the known world, still in light above her, was shrinking. It was slow, but inevitably she could already see that there would be a moment when it receded to a dot in which nothing was discernible. For the first time since she had woken after Dar's magic had blown her to pieces she felt the possibility that even the dot may one day vanish.

"Now is not a good moment for an existential crisis," the imp whispered. "You are close to the clairvoyance of Madame Des Loupes. Her home is on this corner and her clarity of vision is said to be impeccable within the Souk if you catch her attention and there is no way that a beautiful freak such as yourself will escape that."

Lila felt a stabbing panic in her chest. She halted in the middle of the street. A faery bumped into the back of her and muttered something darkly as he floated around her, sniffing. When he glanced at her the irises of his human eyes were pinpricks in a blue field. He swiped at his nose and moved on, in a hurry. She found herself watching him go. He staggered slightly. His attention was on something else entirely. She realised that she had seen many others like that here, and in the city. They had been everywhere and she had considered it part of the fabric of demon life, that people took drugs or expanded their consciousness in many ways just as they might drink a coffee. She'd assumed that they were different from humans, much more able and in control of themselves, enlightened and educated, always so knowing about what they were doing and what it meant. But now she wasn't seeing exciting voyages in aetheric power and self-expansion. She saw an addict, wandering in the throes of his compulsion, lost to himself.

"What does Madame Des Loupes do?" she asked, barely recognising the sound of her own voice in her thoughts. "What's her thing?"

"You don't want her," the imp said with conviction. "We need a binder. Turn left here. Madame is a seer."

"What does she see?"

"Souls," the imp said with unease. "When she looks into your eyes there is nothing you can hide from her. She is able to speak of your past with perfect accuracy, and of your future with great insight, because she sees what you are and what you can be made into. She has allies who enjoy the challenge of making great things from poor materials too, and they will all attempt to engage you. She sees potentials everywhere, what you might be, and who. And that may sound so intriguing but I must warn you it is not something to do lightly. Madame knows so much about so much, and of course her knowledge is power. Those of us with secrets go no closer than the end of the road where she lives. Even then, who can say what she knows about us? We treat her as a goddess here, for fear she will betray us."

"Betray you?"

"Madame is old. In her youth she was the president of our world, the head of government. Nothing escaped her, and nobody. Under her guidance we soared in all our enterprises. But as time went on and she grew out of responsibility and duty and into the reckless abandon of adulthood she led her precepture to great power through trades and combats which she all foresaw to her advantage. She cannot be deceived. Without the limit of her conscience working any longer a group of great sorcerers devised a binding upon her to put her under house arrest. If they had not succeeded in restraining her she would have enslaved our world as she once ruled it in fairness."

"But she didn't foresee this happening to her?" Lila asked.

"She permitted it," the imp said. "She knew what she could become. She saw that most of all."

Lila found a grudging admiration for that. "Or maybe this way her ultimate goal was better served?"

"We may have to admit that as a possibility . . ." the imp conceded. "In any case, she is the oldest of all of us and she shows no sign of petrification. Other demons as they use their powers age and become as stone. This is the price of metabolising aether. But the limits have kept her almost free of such entropic damage. Year on year her strength increases but she does not waste. You should turn left."

But as he spoke Lila was looking directly forwards at the corner house. It had a first-floor verandah, with an ornate balcony railing about which grew luxurious trailing vines—a caged bird's cage, she had been thinking and then even as she thought it the bird appeared. A delicate womanly shape, with the head of a raven and the wings of a hummingbird stepped out and put her elegant hand upon the rail. She turned her head and with one black eye looked directly at Lila. Lila heard her own thoughts joined by another's like a voice speaking in harmony—the caged bird's cage. Then the new voice continued alone, "To enter Hell you must find one who opens, a gatemaker. When you do not find another, find me."

"Leeee-eeft!" whined the imp. "She's looking this way."

The demon turned her raven head, cocking it abruptly to look down into the square below her where a few ordinary crows were walking about, looking upwards with one side of their heads, then the other, clearly waiting. She threw something down to them that looked like scraps of meat and they hopped and scrabbled over them in a storm of wings. Lila saw a train of peacock feathers where most demons would have had a different kind of tail as Madame Des Loupes went inside and closed the shutter.

"Did she . . . ?"

"No," Lila said. "I think she was just feeding the birds."

"They're her eyes and ears," the imp said. "Most of them not here. Always be careful when you talk business not to do it within earshot of a crow."

"Binding, binding, binding . . ."

"Just pick someone," Lila said. She had been about to make an excuse and ask the imp to do it all for her. The sight of the birds stamping down on the bits of flesh and tearing it with their beaks, gulping shreds, had almost pushed her to a place where she could not contemplate carrying on and she didn't know why. She'd seen worse than anything here. Done things almost as bad without much more than a flinch.

A shadow crossed her shoulder, a cool patch running over her bare skin where the strong shoulder padding of the assault vest gave way to a short sleeve of net. It was her only warning but her instincts and her AI all told her to move and she was more than ready for that. She dropped her weight, slid her hips sideways, twisted and ducked, coming around and away in an arc that moved her towards the shelter of the closest building, its side in shade. The attack missed her by a millimetre. She felt a breath of air as a spinning blade clattered into the stone paving and shattered with the force. Its trajectory would have set it in her neck—a bold and accurate shot but one she felt could only have been half hearted, perhaps a distraction.

As she swung around she let her natural twisting motion carry her through a sweep of the area, her AI senses on full alert, looking for the patterns of reaction and movement in people over a wide area to detect not only her assailant but anyone responding to the incident. In the second it took her to slow and straighten, free the firing ports in her forearms, and arm up the weapons she had taken from her cache back at the Ahriman house she already knew the demon in the air who had distracted her wasn't alone.

It was a small, agile-winged creature which was already fleeing the scene at top speed. She didn't bother shooting at it. The others were in groups of two and three, walking as if they were not really together through each one of the arteries that led towards the square of Madame Des Loupes's house. On the rooftops another three figures, lying close to the tiles, moved with spider confidence across sharp angles and over buttresses. They were converging on her with a clear purpose—to corral her in any of a dozen useful dead ends close to the square. In the sky no less than five airborne creatures spiralled out of the afternoon traffic and floated lower. The small number of pedestrians in the Souk who were not involved moved about a fraction more slowly, more idly. There were not enough of them to shield her.

The shadow of the large central route dirigible moved slowly across her, plunging her into a sudden pale fog of mystical advertising: words and images floated towards her with scents and sounds like fleeting dreams . . .

When you need a clean that's fine, use Rapstallion's Burnishing Powders. Suitable for all colours of scale and chitin. Does not scratch. Usual disclaimers apply.

Cheap, cheerful, and always ready. Punty Maroon's Downhouse Tavern serves Surprise Meat of the Moment—at any moment!

Kiss of Death . . . this last was just a name and a feeling of closing cold, the image of a woman with black hair and purple lips leaning near, then darkness . . .

Lila moved with the last short-lived seconds of this shadow, crossing the narrow alley at its speed. She had no plan, there was no time to plan. She held out both hands, palm forward and in the last stride made her smart, artificial skin into speakers. She sent out sound waves in a specific pattern and read them as they returned. Without a pause she made both hands into fists, braced her feet, and punched through the wall. Demon stone was bonelike—friable and soft. She barged the edges of the hole with her shoulders and felt her skin tear but her strength and the speed of her blow was enough to create space for her whole body to fit through. In a flurry of dust and dry mortar she emerged into a dimly lit space full of incense. By the time the dirigible passed on and sunlight claimed the alley she was into the third room of the magehouse, going through any door that caught her eye.

Demons and other—things—shifted in the darkness and the flickering light of lamps and candles; mages and their clients started at her passage, though some of them were deep into whatever they were doing and did not notice her darting from one side of their room to the other. But, as she knew there must be, there was soon a room with no other door except the one she came in by. As soon as she stepped over the threshold she knew it was a mistake.

She had collected a trail of protesting demons who attempted to follow her to this point but once she crossed into this room they turned back without another word. Unlike the other rooms this one had only one lamp and it cast a faint violet gleam, barely enough to see by. It was a big room and it smelled musky and dry. There was no incense. Colours moved on the walls, all of them as near to black as could be. They shifted in patterns that made symbols and then undid them, created pictures as if by accident on their way past each other. At first she thought the room was empty but then, in the farthest corner, in the dark, she heard a movement and then looked that way and just made out the glimmer of lilac light sliding over a dark body; a spike, a scale, and then the surface of an ink-black eye.

Get out.

She hadn't heard Tath's voice in so long it startled her. She froze for a moment and in that moment she heard the hissing sound of a long intake of breath through narrow, refined nostrils. Something ephemeral, a spirit voile, brushed her shoulder where the skin was raw. On the wall in front of her the colours moved into an image of sudden clarity, dim and barely there but there nonetheless.

Get. OUT. NOW.

But she couldn't move. She was frozen, staring at the sight of her mother, standing at the kitchen sink. She was in her nightdress and her hands were shaking. She held a glass in one and an open bottle of pills in the other. Lila knew it was twenty fourteen, the year before the bomb, and she was a little girl and it was the night that grandma died. Classical music was playing on the radio, a song she could hear right now—*Clair de Lune*. She hated that song.

Her mother looked at her, across time, across the night. She picked up the bottle of pills and tipped them down the sink. They weren't needed any more. They made a tiny, tinny rattle in the metal bowl, exactly the sound they made that night. Water rushed from the faucet automatically and flushed them into the waste disposal. It made a sound like grinding teeth. The colours were so dark that Mum's eyes were dark pits, her mouth a slice of black, like a skull.

This is one of your marker points, Tath's voice snapped, cold and powerful with a command Lila was grateful to hear. Move away quickly before the anchor is created. Think of a different time.

Because the association was so obvious she began to think of that, which led to the night they met, the night he died . . . Her mother vanished and she saw a pale, dead body lying with a blade in its chest . . .

Not that one!

By now, through AI and intuition she knew she had stumbled into the path of a necromancer. All the Otopian data on such people amounted to little more than a list of names and a few speculations. Even Tath himself, whom she had begun to trust almost as a part of her with her usual foolish disregard she seemed to bring to the essential spy armoury of personal boundary setting, had never revealed anything of his profession, except in that single moment he had slaughtered Teazle's brother. The pale body had already dissolved and in its place she saw the twisted limbs of the demon, felt herself coated in sticky blood . . .

Not that one either!

She got it. Nothing involving death. But as soon as she tried to think of anything except death all the deaths she knew about shot through her mind at the speed of a bullet. She felt seasick. Around her the darkness thickened as the demon sensed so many potentials . . . Aether seethed like heavy vapour and smarted where wild tendrils snapped at her skin and investigated the elemental nature of her metal.

It searches for entry points to your life matrix. At least too many is almost as good as too few but if you are to save us think of the living!

Lila smelled citrus peel. The game potential rose at the same moment as she felt the demon—still invisible in its own darkness—prepare to pounce upon one of the fleeting images that raced across its charmed atmosphere; the traces of her past. She smelled fresh blood and only then felt the sting of a blade on her bare shoulder. As her blood ran, the images became suddenly three-dimensional and the room began to fade.

Without thinking she immediately sprang to the opportunity to start a game. "I bet you can't beat me in a straight fight."

What?!

The room returned. The citrus smell vanished. There was a clear, fresh burst of air and the static crackle of an aether discharge. In the ordinary gloom she looked across the stone floor to her adversary. The bleeding stopped as her enhanced platelets sealed the wound. The indigo demon slavered and stared up at her from its lizard sprawl, slowly getting up from its belly to its hind legs. The challenge was accepted. Her Game was on.

If there was a chance, you just lost it, Tath informed her with the frigidity of shock.

But you sucked the life out of the other one . . . Lila protested inwardly, battle systems activating in an almost silent explosion of perfectly operating components. She got bigger, stronger, faster. She armed her guns.

That was just an ordinary demon, Tath said. *This is a necromancer and where it has spent its entire life practising the art of the pursuit of death in this room, I have done my best to avoid every opportunity to exert my abilities. It is a master and I am barely qualified . . .*

Why NOW?! Lila screamed at him inside. *Why do you never tell me anything important BEFORE it matters?*

Who knew you would run directly into this lair? Necromancers are rare . . .

Tath, how do I kill it?

Decapitation. If that fails you have to find its phylactery.

Its what?

A special vessel, object, person, or document in which its life is stored.

Great, where's that?

I do not know. If you had the whole of space and time to hide such an object in, where would you put it?

Lila stood for a moment and then put her guns away and took a large blade out of her left thigh and another from the inner right where it lay just beneath her armour.

The demon snickered and lifted its long saurian head, exposing its narrow neck. With one clawed finger it made a slashing motion across its own throat and cocked its head at her, eye glinting with grey and purple light. It stabbed the finger towards the imaginary line and hissed, "Cut here . . ." Then it laughed and raised its heavy, scaled brow in a clear, amused taunt.

"Oh that is so not fair!" Lila exclaimed and stamped her foot, letting her blades drop to her sides. "How does having a phylac . . . philac . . . life hidden away count as FAIR?"

The demon paused and said in a normal, much milder voice, "I had it before you challenged me. I didn't conceal it and you didn't ask. So according to the rules, it's fair." It then resumed its taunt pose, complete with glaring eye. Then it paused and relaxed again. "How did you know about that?"

"I . . . it was a good guess . . ." Lila said, bringing the blades up automatically as the creature suddenly advanced with a much more serious expression on its long, lizard face.

"My ass," the necromancer said. It made a throwing gesture, languid and graceful, and a sheet of dark fell across her, and through her; a voile so soft it barely existed as a trace. Tath shuddered and twisted but he could not avoid its caress. Too late she recognised the aetheric equivalent of x-rays. It had scanned her for magic.

It pointed at her chest and fixed its gaze there. She set a defensive stance and prodded at its hand with the tip of her knife but it ignored her . . . it stared and gaped, yellow throat pulsing with basic reptilian surprise. "Acolyte!"

Now he has to die, Tath said, doing the internal emotional equivalent of throwing his hands up in the air and casting eyes to the sky in despair.

All suggestions gratefully accepted, Lila said and, without pausing, launched into a blur of normally fatal blows. Without hope of killing she thought she'd settle for a good mincing and see how that slowed it down.

At speeds beyond human perception, battle blades catching the grey light, her arms seemed to move in blurs the shape and density of faery wings, their lethal tips striking with machine precision. A haze of sickly purple flew from their dance as they sliced flesh and bone, and the spraying blood of the necromancer collided with itself drop upon drop smashing each other to ever smaller parts. Lila glided in a mist of gore and the clean form of the demon vanished into the lilac storm of slaughter with unnatural ease, as though passing through a flat plane that destroyed it; as if it had fallen into a shredder.

She stopped when she reached its tail.

Tath was a moment of frozen surprise. She felt him peering through her at the twitching, snakelike lump of meat left in the pool of chunky purple and lime goo. A faint patter of blood rain fell on her skin and hair, on her glistening armour and into the murky puddles. Lila felt the side of her mouth twitch with satisfaction at his response and some pleasure in her appalling ability . . . as bad as the Souk . . . yes . . .

"Now that's gotta hurt!" The imp's voice came from the doorway, full of delight and admiration.

Lila turned around, senses primed and the world seeming slow to them as they were in battle mode. Time was watery.

The imp scampered across the floor, up the wall partway and then leapt to her shoulder, sinking its claws into the padding. It beckoned to the ominous figures that followed it. To Lila it said, apologetically, "Boy, I thought you were way worse than that so I went to get us the only help I could think of . . ." It hesitated and the two shapes came out of the corridor and into the near darkness. Lila saw them easily. They were tall and narrow humanoids with hulking shoulders draped in black sacking that fell around them in tatty festoons to the floor. Their heads were the bare skulls of giant carrion birds, with ravenlike beaks. Instead of eyes, maggots moved in their sockets. They had limbs like insect arms poking through their robes. They stank of raw meat.

". . . well, they were more or less on the way anyway . . ." the imp added more quietly as the two approached with the slow measure of coming night. "I just helped a little bit. But I did help. I was very useful. They'll remember that part."

Lila shifted her weight into a ready stance and raised her daggers. The pair of raven demons halted just out of reach. They tipped their birdy heads and regarded the jellying mass of the ex-necromancer and his tail.

Before its ghost recovers the phylactery we ought to depart, Tath whispered urgently to her. *It will not be caught like that twice, and now it will be furious.*

The bird demons moved as one and lifted their heads upright. One extended a black, pincer-ended limb. It was holding out a white business card.

Lila extended the tip of a dagger and, after a moment, the demon impaled the card on it. Keeping her other blade ready she brought it close to read. The card simply said,

"Madame Des Loupes requests the pleasure of the company of Lila Amanda Black and her companions at her earliest convenience. Tea and small fancies will be served. Formal dress is not required."

Lila read it twice—companions—and said to Tath, silently, *Don't tell me I have to assassinate a perfect clairvoyant as well as a deathless necromantic fiend or I'm going home.*

CHAPTER ELEVEN

The radiation counts in Zoomenon were high, always. Partly this was because of the raw lodes of uranium and plutonium that it contained, scattered hither and yon in patterns that defied analysis. That accounted for the electromagnetic interference that was like having elfin nerves scraped with sandpaper, let alone their flesh mortified by damage. Partly it was because of the aetheric concentrations and fluctuations that created enormous turbulence in the panspermic raw aether atmosphere. These concentrations took the form of elementals, both primitive and agile. Zal watched them with the apparent disinterest of a sated tiger watching deer in the forest. He nursed his sore body and the nauseating headache that the twin radiation had given him and from which there was no obvious respite. Inside his *andalune* body the surge and rush of the fire elementals whom he had permitted to transect him burned on, purging the worst of the damage from him with swift cautery. He knew that if and when their power abated he would soon sicken and die in this hostile, monophilic world. So he watched the elementals flock and disperse, watched their play, their moving and breath and death among the eerie perfection of the rocky world around him. Overhead the Zoomenon sun, a solar of pure white energy more powerful than any natural star with its endless raw fusion, flooded him with merciless light. He lay and considered his position with an ironic sense of the ridiculous that was rapidly growing old.

He had not been to Zoomenon before. Well, that was slightly inaccurate. He had been in Zoomenon. He had simply not been to it. When he created his magic circles and excluded the world from his universe he had summoned the place to him. It had come forth and enveloped him, spawning through the fissure he was able to open up with his small aetheric abilities. To his knowledge very few mages were powerful enough in their control or adept in their understanding to create genuine transits across the realms. But under the influence of the elemental storm, possessed by the essence of his own elemental relation, he must have been carried here as the beings themselves used their massed energy to return to their home. This was their nature of course; they enjoyed flitting among the realms, even Otopia, but as with every other creature, they felt best in their natural environment and, more than most, took every chance to trip back to it. He supposed it was something of a scientific coup to have discovered their ability to transport nonelemental matter (himself) with them in this manner. But it seemed he would have no chance to share his knowledge. Zoomenon was a place of purity and nobody with any sense came here, even if they could. Of course there were expeditions . . . but these were few, even among those who dared to scavenge here. The problem of Zoomenon was that it was the least permeable realm. And what came here in complexity tended to leave as components . . .

He got to his feet but that was horrible. The merciless glare shivered off the salt flats and glanced off outcrops of crystal. It hurt his eyes and that hurt his head and his head already hurt with the thrumming horror of the aetheric weather which seemed worse further off the ground for reasons he didn't understand. On his hands and knees he crawled into a patch of shade. An earth elemental materialised beside him, as though it had been waiting for him to join it in its shelter. It condensed out of the aether with easy speed and sat with him upon a small stone, at his shoulder. It was a stocky humanoid with somewhat globular, muddy limbs and a potato-shaped head, black pebbles for eyes. It smelled of rich, wet, alluvial soil. Where it touched the ground it was one with it.

Zal didn't speak. Elementals may take certain forms but the outer appearance was not matched by inner capacity. The best he had seen were about as intelligent and individual as cats, and with as much inclination to conversation. The worst were simply forms without reason of any kind. They did not need reason. They simply borrowed it, he understood, from millennia of elven research. But not always. They enjoyed aether. They were considered expressions of aether, as the elves were expressions of the divine will to intelligence and self-awareness; nature's reach towards itself.

He didn't feel like a divine intelligence. He felt hungry, thirsty, sick, and stupid. The earth elemental grew more solid and fixed him with a curious stare from its oddly attentive eyes. Perhaps it was looking forward to the entertainment of seeing him disintegrate. Zal wondered what he would reduce to. Humans that had been found here were patches of iron-rich dust surrounded by the white crystals of a few salts—their water having evaporated by the time the expeditions arrived. Demons left behind shards of various crystalline components and many curious globules of condensed aetheric matter, and various stains like shadows upon the places they left behind. Of elven fatalities there were no records but he suspected that these had been scrupulously erased by the secret service since it was hard to believe elves had not attempted to come here and died in the grip of the conundrum that faced him. Magic could bring you to Zoomenon, but it could not take you away. Nobody knew why. They came and went with the death of their fiendishly expensive portals and if they missed their moment the curious died here and left only their own elements to mark their passing.

"They say," Zal decided to strike up a conversation with his new friend. "They say that the aetheric structure of this place is so tight to keep the electromagnetic problems under control that conditions don't permit creative acts like enchanting."

The small elemental stared at him with boulderlike calm and understanding.

"Yeah," Zal said. "I'm with you. I think it's horseshit. I mean, if that was true how would you guys just trip in and out so easily?"

The elemental kept its views to itself.

"I like you," Zal told it, trying not to notice how much its smell was making him want to squeeze it until a drink of water came out of it, no matter how muddy it was. "Strong and silent. Just my type. I like when the bartender just listens. I have a lot to say and other people's comments just get in the way of my thinking. That faery, for instance, the one who tried to beat me at cards. That cat. I got the feeling he liked my woman rather a lot if you know what I mean. Now, she's gone into Demonia on some mission all on her own and I was meant to help her but I had a little party with your fiery friends and I'm here instead. I was hoping the guilt would eat me alive before something worse happens but I have a nasty feeling it won't.

"Of course, the trouble with me not being there is that my woman doesn't know about my wife. Or my other mates. Being a human she's bound to assume it's all about sex and that's just going to make life a bitch when I have to explain it later and tell her why I didn't explain it at first. I was hoping to be there, you know?"

The potato-faced creature tipped its spud head to one side gently as if it couldn't be more concerned.

"Yeah, you see how it is. It looks bad. Probably it is bad. But there's a lot worse things out there for her than just some horrible shock about demon lifestyles, as I'm sure you'll be well aware. For a start there's the vendettas. But she can handle them. The real shit in the fan is the necromancer she's got stuck in her heart. Lots of demons will be able to see him. And he's an elf. They'll really like that in the worst kind of way. Ruins her status either as a journalist or a diplomat or even a party fiend. She could play it to her advantage but not if she doesn't get some help fast and I don't think she'll tell Sorcha about it so that won't be any good. Plus Sorcha's obsessed with music and the Precepture problems she's got so she might be busy. And that faery had the nerve to suggest that disco was unmanly. Can you believe it?"

The elemental oozed some mud from a side bulge and a couple of pebbles fell out of its body and clitter-clattered to the ground.

"Exactly. Total shit," Zal agreed forlornly, pausing to put his head down and breathe. Internally, nausea and the foam of primal fire energy swirled and danced with each other. He felt blissful and disgusting at the same time.

"And here I am, stuck in Zoo with you and no idea how to get out. Facing death. The end of what could have been a rather promising career in the music industry. Soon I'll be some kind of green ooze, like you." He wallowed for a moment in the luxury of total self-pity, but then took a breath and brightened slightly. "Still, could be worse. I could be in Hell."

Tea with Madame Des Loupes.

Lila sat in her black combat fatigues, dripping a little lilac blood onto the marble tile and the soft velvet upholstery of the exquisite chair upon which she rested. At her side the imp crouched on a tasselled cushion, eyes fixed upon the elegant form of their hostess as her slim, black human arms carefully handled a fine porcelain tea set. She poured milk into cups first, from a wide-mouthed jug, then the tea after, before placing two lumps of sugar and a silver teaspoon on the side of each saucer. Her huge raven head tilted almost entirely sideways so she could see what she was doing, the beak always facing away from her guests. As she moved with perfect grace Lila photographed her, capturing her from as many angles as possible. She was the most extraordinary being Lila had ever seen.

The sleek black feathers of her head fanned gently down to the base of her neck where their blackness, tinted with the oil sheen of many iridescent colours, became ever more blue and green until it blended seamlessly into the tiny vivid plumes of a hummingbird. These tapered along her spine, and branched out across the skin of her shoulders to become small wings that were tucked against her lower back and sides. At the base of her spine they fanned out suddenly into a broad bustle and train which Lila had at first mistaken for a dress but now saw was a train of real peacock feathers growing from Madame's body. Where the eyes of an ordinary peacock feather would have glowed blue and purple as dark marks of reflective glory instead these feathers showed living eyes. They were not real eyes, they were images on the feather, but living images which blinked and looked about, every one differently coloured: human, animal, demon, fey, insectile, and of other kinds.

The front of her body was no less unique. Her neck feathers lay flat over dark, smooth skin that was faintly mottled with a pardlike pattern of spots in an even deeper, duskier hue. Generous breasts were supported in a delicate filigree of the loveliest green and blue lacework, like the wings of dragonflies, their cleavage a rich, warm, and sensual promise that played out down the length of a flat, powerful belly adorned with a single emerald placed in her navel. Her skin there was dusted with a kind of golden pollen caught in fine hairs that gathered and once again became feather along the length of her naked groin. Here their tiny prettiness jewelled her upper thighs where an open-fronted skirt of silk let her body show through to display, at their centre, a handsome, relaxed phallus covered in shining emerald scales and marked with rattlesnake diamonds in sapphire blue. Its head had scales of red that denoted eyes, but they were only markings, like those found in nature intended to deceive. Beneath the silken skirts shapely legs ended in soft, cloven feet like those of a camel, meant for walking in the desert. The two large toenails on each were painted and decorated with sugar pink varnish.

Madame Des Loupes lifted and held out a cup and saucer towards Lila. She kept her head with its massive beak averted but nonetheless managed to convey the tea with a gentle bow. Her voice was soft and warm, "You come battle-clad in the gore of your enemies. It is a high honour I will not forget, Lila Goredad."

Lila stopped taking pictures and focused on the teacup. It rattled in the saucer as she took it and she had to cue some robotics to steady herself, trying and failing not to know she was alarmed by the presence of the demon itself. "Thank you."

She watched as Madame went through the same process of giving the imp his tea, but seeing as the cup was half his size and he had no chance of holding the saucer without tipping himself onto the floor she settled it in front of him in the fullness of the cushion. Although she had only the beak, Lila could have sworn she was smiling as the imp immediately seized hold of a sugar lump in both hands and began crunching on it.

Madame returned to her special seat—an embroidered stool—and picked up her own cup. "I know you don't take sugar," Madame continued, "and usually I don't either . . ." She added two lumps to her own cup and stirred gently. "But I find that after trying moments or in new situations a little sugar doesn't do any harm."

Lila glanced towards the door of the room, where the two stinking raven demons still stood, then across to the open balcony where she had first seen Madame from a distance. She kept tracking in order to try and control her thoughts, even though a lot of different concerns fought for her attention. But they were always suppressed by the idea of Madame's powers. Beside her the imp crunched frantically, spraying sugar everywhere. Lila put a cube in her tea, then the other one. She tasted—it was delicious and just what she needed. Then she half remembered something about not eating the food in the netherworld and glanced guiltily at Madame.

"You're not there yet," Madame said in her plummy, fruity voice— that warm mature woman's voice that had no business issuing from a bird's throat or a beak. "Merely in the waiting room. No need to go, if you don't want to." She sounded slightly teasing, because, Lila assumed, she really did know exactly everything that was going through Lila's head.

"Can you just skip to the part where you answer my questions before I have to ask them?"

"Of course," Madame said, "although I do rather prefer to have some small talk before we get down to business, you see, despite the fact all I wish to know is open to my sight it interests me much more to learn what you think about your situation, and mine, and the world. And that is something revealed only in your choices, about what to say and what to remain silent over. Do you see what I mean?"

"But can't you see that too?"

"Perception is an act of creation," Madame said, pouring some of her tea from the cup into a wide, shallow dish that Lila had thought was an empty biscuit plate. "And creation happens in the fall of the instant. It is unpredictable. Unknowable before it takes place. So no. I cannot. My talent only allows me to see what is, and some of what has been. But the truth of what is . . . appears differently to all who perceive it. I get close to its fundamental reality, but even my gaze is coloured and focused by what I am—an imperfect being in a perfected universe." The demon bent down and laid her beak sideways in the dish, imbibing tea and then tossing her head back to swallow it down. She wiped her beak clean with a lace-edged linen napkin and composed her hands upon her lap, head to one side, listening.

Lila was not sure but she felt an exultant stab from Tath, somewhere near her solar plexus, and trusted that he would be able to fill her in at an easier moment. She took a second drink of tea and did begin to feel a little better. She let her thoughts spill out since there seemed little point in concealing them. "Are you married, Madame?"

"No," Madame glanced, following Lila, at the raven demons. "Ah no. Such alliances do not interest me as I stand little to gain from them. I would marry for love, but I have not met the creature who stirs that passion in me. These demons in my house and who serve me in the world are minions, ones who came to me in the spirit of a marriage in spite of my refusal. Unrequited suitors if you will, they desired my compact at any price and so they willingly became my creatures. Once they were independent beings like yourself, but now their will is mine. They are enough of a responsibility that I do not require more."

"Lonely at the fuckin' top!" snickered the imp, coming to the end of the first cube and plunging his head down into the teacup with greed. Slurping and gulping sounds choked off his remark.

"No doubt you face the same problems," Madame added, looking closely at Lila. Her black eye, so large for a bird's, so dark, narrowed slightly from the bottom in an almost human expression of wry knowingness.

"Me?"

"One may marry or enslave anyone for business purposes, but true partnership can exist only among equals."

"That was a compliment, 'case you missed it," the imp said to Lila, scrubbing its face on the cushion to dry itself and starting in on the second sugar lump with gusto.

Lila found herself taken aback. What the demon said sounded so callous, as much of their culture seemed, and she had images again of the dead fetuses in their pots and jars, of the death she had dealt herself. She looked down and suddenly felt the sticky, congealing goo of blood on her hands, her shoulder, her face. She leaned forward abruptly and put her teacup down with a rattle and slam on the occasional table to her left. "I'm not your equal. I'm nothing like you. I'd never marry anyone like you. I couldn't. I . . . ." She stopped. Words jammed in her throat. For an unaccountable reason she was reminded of the shadow elf, tangled in silver netting, trapped in her mansion room. What time was it? How late was it? She looked outside at the sun and inside at her clock at the same moment.

"How interesting," Madame Des Loupes said with more than a trickle of condescension. Her head did one of those sudden, birdlike motions that made both Lila and the imp start involuntarily.

Inside Lila's chest Tath somersaulted with fear.

"What do you mean?" Lila stalled, grabbing inside for something chemical, something machine she could use to shore up her sudden and inexplicable sense of falling. Her AI came online and decanted stimulants into her bloodstream, and serotonin, to reassure her.

"You are a liar," Madame said. "You are already bound to the elf-source demon of the Ahrimani. Not to mention the alfidic spirit with which you share your body. Further you entertain the marital interests of Demonia's beloved son, the phase-shifter Teazle. Yet you speak with the passion of truth. You conceal much from your self. You use your alchemical power to enforce it. A strong will. It will be hard to break, more's the pity for you."

Lila was frozen with outrage, literally frozen, a thing until now she had considered something that only happened to people in books. "I'm not married to Zal! I certainly have nothing like that to do with . . . with . . . the elf spirit . . . and I never had any intention of accepting anything from that white monstrosity!" She stood up and involuntarily glanced at the imp who was cramming his mouth as full of sugar crystals as he could, hands clamped to his face. She gathered from his fear that one did not speak like this to the most powerful of demons but she wasn't bothered by it. She was furious, but the drugs were taking hold too, and she knew that if nothing else this was no way to further her greater aim; to discover the truth of Zal's demonic making. She mastered herself and sat down, the effort costing her any remaining ability to speak. Though she didn't want to notice it she couldn't help feeling that her responses were nothing short of racist, intolerant abuse but she pushed this notion down hard.

Madame casually poured herself another draught of tea and took it down. She was as lovely and studied as a geisha as she picked up a tiered tray of small iced cakes and offered them to Lila. "Petit fours? Dinner is served very late in Bathshebat."

Lila declined with a barely managed shake of her head. The imp leaned over and seized the nearest, a lemon square, and plunged it directly into his tea cup where he watched as the soft cake soaked up the dark liquid, his face a rapt picture of pure, avid lust.

"Do you know my favourite human story of the devil?" Madame went on in a skilled effort to preserve social calm. "It goes like this: god and the devil are observing Adam as he takes his first foray out of Eden and into the wider world. Adam has recently eaten of the fruit of the tree of knowledge, thanks to his wise wife, and is taking stock of all the things he is able to see. God says to the devil, 'So, what will you do now? Steal all this marvel away from him and create in its place a chaotic nightmare?' And the devil says, 'Oh god, no. I'm going to help him organise it!'" Madame put her tea dish aside and cleaned her beak. "I mention this because you want to know about Hell, Ms. Black. I can tell you plainly all you wish to know, though it will not help you one bit because you are a liar."

Lila stared with a terrible combination of loathing and attachment at the beautiful creature that was talking. The tension between her and Madame was a thing she could feel, like a long flat blade, resonating. She was not able to stop herself listening. She had to, but she didn't want to. Of course a demon would play this game . . .

"I do not play with the aether, Ms. Black," Madame said quietly. "I have no need to. I see what is, and that's all. You feel I have insulted you, but I am only telling you what you already know. You are a liar, a cheat, a thief, a traitor, and a murderer."

Lila had become still with fury. She wanted to move but the stillness sat upon her like a lead jacket.

Overcome by anxiety and desire the imp leaped up, grabbed two fistfuls of soggy cake from in front of him, and then sprang to the table in one froglike bound. He hopped into the wide, white maw of the milk jug and vanished from sight with a small splash. The jug wobbled briefly and then stabilised. In the ensuing silence piglike noises of gluttonous eating and drinking carried quietly across the room.

"You are untrue, reckless, and careless. You rage. You are love's bitch, in heat as it is in heaven . . ."

"Enough!" Lila was on her feet. Her voice carried much further and louder than she knew it could have.

Madame looked at her from a single, gleaming eye. That eye stared at her, unbending, unblinking, uncaring. "This is all you need to know about Hell," the demon said after a long moment. Neither of them looked away, though Lila's eyes were burning. She would not, would not give in to this stupid fight . . .

"What are you talking about?" Lila said scathingly. "Stop talking in ridiculous riddles and slander and trying to get me off balance. Open the gate and send me to Hell. I don't have time for this crap."

Madame Des Loupes sighed. "As you wish," she said, spreading out her hands upon her knees and sitting more upright. She gazed out of her balcony a moment in what might have been composure, though she looked as though she were listening to a distant drum. "Though you ought to know that there is no special entry point into Hell. And when you enter the world of the damned you enter it alone. Your companions may be with you, but they cannot help you in any way. Isn't that so, Thingamajig?" And she looked at the milk jug.

The imp's face appeared for a second over the rim. "You know my name," he said, accusingly.

"I cannot tell it to you," Madame shrugged.

Lila felt she was starting to lose her mind. "What? What has that to do with it?"

This time when the demon's head turned to her it gave her a direct gaze from both bulging black eyes, the beak aimed squarely at the centre of Lila's chest. "Because, Ms. Black, the fact is that it was never in my power to send you or anyone else to Hell. Thingamajig here is in his state because he entered that place and will not or cannot return. His only way out is to remember his name. If I tell it to him he will not be better off. And you, like him, like all the rest, need no portal to enter the realm of the lost souls, for you already have all the necessary prerequisites, to whit, you are a liar. My role here is not to show you the way into a great test or trial whose success I might judge and whose rewards I can bestow. My only power is to be the one who sees what is. I will be the one you come to when you are ready to leave. I am the one everyone comes to when they are ready to leave Hell. I am not the way in, I am the way out."

Lila stared at the exquisite demon, feeling a wild hatred. She stared at the imp, wet and dripping as it rested its sad face on its paws, clinging to the lip of the jug. Towards it she felt rage and pity. "Talk sense!"

Madame Des Loupes shrugged airily, "There is never any need to conjure Hell, Ms. Black. We all go there in our own time. It is a place created in the moment, an act of perception. I am the keeper of Hell, for I see what is, and those are the limits of Hell. There is no need to send you anywhere, for you are already there, and you have been there since long before you came to Demonia."

"What crap!" Lila snorted. She gave the imp another glance to see if it was coming, because clearly it was time to leave and she was leaving, no doubt about it. "Are you coming?"

"You cannot save him," Madame said sadly.

"I don't want to save him!" Lila snapped. "He owes me a mage spell."

The bird demon tilted her head to one side and considered Lila. "There may be hope for you yet," she said and then reached over and tipped the imp out of the jug onto the tray. She looked up at Lila. "Always beware of males who wish to return to the tit." Then to the imp she said sternly, "That porcelain is made from the bones of my enemies. You were fortunate not to number among them on the day I had it made. Begone and do not hinder this one on her way. If I find you more meddling than ornamental I will have your hide for a handbag."

The imp scampered across the furniture, leaving a trail of milk droplets, and raced up Lila's arm to her shoulder. A familiar pain pierced her ear as he clutched hold. He was quaking.

"Return when you are ready," Madame added to Lila. "I will await you."

"Go to Hell," Lila said.

"Been there, done that," Madame replied. "Be firm with your minion. They don't understand kindness." Her beady gaze was fixed on the imp.

Lila stared at the demon for a moment, beyond speech, then turned on her heel and stormed out, barely noticing the hulking shapes moving aside to let her pass.

CHAPTER TWELVE

Calliope Jones rode the crystal flow like an old rodeo hand easily taking the humpbacked punishment of a wild bull. She moved as Malachi watched her from the security of the Ghost Hunters' barge and put her feet on the blazing torrent of aetheric hard light, changing from rider to surfer in a fluid move that she must have done a thousand times.

At Malachi's back the demon heeled the barge hard over as the crystal set in its prow started to make a keening noise and struggled visibly against the delicately engineered bonds that held it in a trap. The flow of channelled aether streaming from its focus whipped and twisted like a snake. Within the light that made it up Malachi could see fragments of runes, words, and programming that made up the schematic that the Hunters had been creating over the last day and a half. They had encoded their instruction to the crystal matrix and now it was working to create—Malachi didn't exactly know what although the theory had been drilled into him at exasperating length. Faeries rejected technology mostly—not because they hated it, like the elves, but mostly because they didn't see the need for it. And they didn't have the attention span for science. He'd tried to follow all the jargonistic hoohaa, but he was comfortable enough to know that Calliope was riding an ocean of saddled aetheric light in order to set up a trap for the formation of ghosts.

The barge, *Matilda*, was a mongrel creation. Like the Hunters' base it was magical and material at the same time but its exclusion field was the most important part of it. It let them float around and look at I-space without actually being in it. Only Jones was in it, riding the stream, sliding along its length far into the blurry greyness of the in-between. Somewhere out there the immense nets and spongelike tangles of half-formed aetheric matter were visible as they congealed out of the uniform greyness of I-space. Jones would see them first and the crystal-shaped stream would run under her guiding feet to a point where she would harness them into a ring and then spin the ring to a sphere. Within the sphere aetheric potentials would collect, attracted by magical gravity created by the crystal force. At such a point it was only a matter of time before they witnessed Immanence, Jones had promised him. The end of several months of hard labour at much less glamorous and exciting tasks, programming and building. As ghosts attempted to form within the shell of the crystal sphere the aether stream would feed information back to the instruments on the barge and they would see with their strandloper sight things Malachi would never see—how ghosts were made.

That was the theory anyway. Malachi was more interested right now in watching the other hunters. He'd thought he knew them at first; knew their race. But after spending more time around them he realised they were like their instruments, peculiar hybrids. This wasn't a physical alteration. It was aetheric. Jones was human but she had an active aetheric aura, a spirit body that could take up all her material form into itself, and remake it anywhere, or not make it. A faery like him was in a similar state in half-shift but he could hardly sustain it. She had no trouble, and they were all like her.

The demon at the ship's wheel fought hard against currents of aether flowing at them from the unstoppable, unknowable vastness

beyond. He kept them stable between those forces and the warp of the
crystal stream, the strain visible on his face, a sheen of dark-yellow
flame-sweat flickering from his eyes and nostrils as he used his colossal
physical strength to its limits. Servo motors thrummed in tune with
him, obeying the commands the same as he did as they came from
Matilda's onboard systems. The demon's spirit form spilled out in a
direct contact with the ship itself, joining him to its processes and its
aether field. Malachi was impressed with the jerry engineering—all
down to the solemn, near-silent elf and another demon who sat in the
bow in positions of meditation. He wondered how they had done it, so
few and all alone; they could not be alone of course, and he added that
to his growing store of assumptions for future consideration. The ship
reminded him of Lila and that brought a fierce smile to his predator's
face. Then he remembered he was supposed to be helping.

Jones was out of sight, the only connection to her the weaving
hawser of charmed light. Lightning crackled as electromagnetic forces
were created by the computer system's power supplies hitting resonant
harmonies of important magnitude with the unstable aether field . . .
flashes of blue, red, and orange flared in zags and sheets across the
metal-plate deck of the ship and flared harmlessly against Malachi's
gleaming polished shoes. He noted that as well, trying to commit to
memory what Lila would have effortlessly recorded—he missed her
scrupulous fieldwork now more than ever. As it was, there was just
another rare and inadequately understood phenomenon happening
under his nose and he would probably misreport the important part
since he had no real idea of what it meant. The demon at the wheel
snarled and heaved to. There was a whining note from the crystal that
briefly threatened to deafen Malachi eternally and then it resolved into
a major chord of beauty.

The meditators in the prow leapt to their feet and began chanting,
their hands braced forwards in a spellcasting action Malachi was most
used to seeing fey warlocks adopt when mastering elementals and

other unreliable creatures. Behind the background of action the featureless drift of pale grey seemed at once distant and closer to him than his own breath. Where aether massed against the ship's field it condensed into a thick, oily liquid and briefly skirled across the surface before evaporating again. He thought it tried to form shapes but he was not sure it wasn't just his imagination. Where it was sucked into the crystal's supply fans it became a distinctly treacly kind of white gas before being flung into the facets of the machine. Before him simplified readouts leaped in bands of bright colour.

He watched a yellow stripe rapidly decrease, "Fundamental potentials dropping," he said, feeling important and proud of himself as the second demon worker reacted instantly to this and began working hard at various valves on the juddering engine that sat amidships. The contraption jiggled and groaned and the flow of aether increased as the fans whirred, their enriched gemstone blades humming a complementary note to the main crystal song.

An orange stripe dipped. A blue one peaked. "Energy inflow maximised. Stability above ninety percent." It was indeed very exciting!

"Drop the anchor!" screamed the second demon into the mists.

There was a silent interval of no more than a second and suddenly all was quiet. The streaming power calmed to a trickle of steady, almost flat-lined beam. Malachi's colours faded in intensity and dropped to steady states. The barge seemed to enter a sudden doldrum and the demon wheelmaster gave a great sigh. The casting pair released their control over whatever they had been holding. There was quiet.

Malachi turned his attention to the sweeping readouts of his secondary panel—the proximity detector. He had forgotten it until now and was relieved to see no dotted telltales of ghosts or the streaks of dragons marring its empty perfection. For a few moments there was a beautiful silence and the aether furled against their bubble with pearly luminescence like a particularly expensive brand of nail polish or the reforming blankness of a violently shaken Etch-a-Sketch.

Malachi was lost in admiring this instant of loveliness when his sonaron began to blip and then belch concern at him. A spirit was coalescing out of the aether, moving at high speed inwards to the barge like an arrow building itself sharper and more lethal in every instant of its flight. It paid no attention to the trap or the humming lure of the line.

"Incoming!" Malachi screamed with sudden alarm and then he heard the big demon laughing with a sound of boulders being rolled around a disco by a very amused Barry White and several of Barry White's bigger cousins.

A streak of silver parted the gas, punctured the barge shield with barely a ripple—and the ripple closed over the wet, shaking head of Calliope Jones, her brown hair in rats tails, her vagabond's clothing coated in a shimmer that evaporated even as she straightened up and flung her rope-riding harness to the deck. The casters got up and one handed her a beer which she cracked open with a strike of one hand and drained half of in one go. The elf woman laughed.

"Yeeee-haaaa!" Jones cheered and spun around to look at Malachi, still stunned, at his post.

"Defensive!" called the demon at the helm and they leapt as one to new positions, except Malachi, who was scheduled to remain on monitor duty no matter what happened, mostly for his own safety. He was still gathering his wits over the strange sight of Jones materialising from one universe into another with such ease, trying to figure out if he had to revise his ideas about strandlopers, trying to figure out if he trusted this band of lunatics . . . when a fuzzy blot appeared on his radar, or whatever it was. It looked like radar. He wasn't fussy about the details. Something had sensed the bait of what Jones called "morphic" energy, promised by the crystal line and secured upon the position they had cast.

In response the team cracked open some more beers and the atmosphere of party and celebration aboard the *Matilda* increased. Someone put on some music. The No Shows doing a soft soul number with aching Mode-X bass—it was more like a party than most parties Malachi had been to recently.

"Too late . . ." Zal's haunting voice soared across the ship, "for making nice . . . too late for good advice; your smile is on my mind but I'm not the dancing kind . . ."

The groove deepened and they were all dancing, to the irresistible bass beat and the individual rhythms of their own machines as each of them flowed to a pitch of attunement Malachi recognised and revelled in as he joined them: the high of someone doing what they loved the most, out of time, beyond tick and tock and the rules of ordinary days. With the music they drifted into the eternally brilliant groove of mind, body, and spirit united; like the greatest fuck or the most wonderful food or the moment of a smile unexpected . . . he was dancing himself as he watched the strange blur move towards their trap with the soft sways of a late-night drunk. Deep and away in the aether a bell sounded; clang clang . . . clang clang . . . the warning two-notes of an approaching vessel lost in fog or darkness.

"Oh man!"or some such phrase, he didn't quite catch, breathed the elf, "it's here . . . so close all the time, just like we hoped."

"Category Five," Jones hollered . . . "Whoo-hoo it IS the fucking *Temeraire!*"

"Yeah, baby," endorsed the demon behind Malachi as he used a length of a hawser no human could have lifted to secure the barge wheel into a locked position.

Then about fifty other points of light, faint as fireflies seen through an evening mist, began to show up on Malachi's radar. "Hey," he said. "What's this . . . Got a lot of," he searched for the right term and gave up before it was too late, "little ghostettes moving around . . ."

"*Tem* comes with a whole flotilla," the demon rumbled, for the first time sounding anxious. All the others hesitated for a moment, Malachi couldn't help noticing.

"Flotilla?"

"Category Five apparitions are highly developed, complex creations that have accumulated Category Four and Three spectrals into their mythos," the elf said. "They're semisentient but the Cats Four and Three probably aren't yet. Look for Twos and Ones and proto activity around them too. Log it all." She had the tone of someone trying hard not to be impatient with the new, stupid member of the team who hadn't done enough homework.

"Ghost ships," she added with a sudden turn to him, fixing him with her green stare. "The Lost Fleet." She sounded nervous too, now. Everyone tensed as she said the words. Malachi watched her swig down some potent-looking elven brew with faint misgiving. "We got a history with the Fleet," the elf said to him, staring into nothing for a second or two before shaking herself free.

"They won't actualise," Jones yelled with confidence over the No Shows' effortless segue into thumping dance-floor rock. "Focus on the ship herself! C'mon!"

There followed a bewildering array of screamed instructions, one to another, focused on the trap and the securing of the giant ship *Temeraire*, whose rigging Malachi had spied only a few hours before sailing away from him into a threatening dusk of aether. He knew more about it now than he had at the time, which was a mercy then and a bane now: the *Temeraire* was the name of a ghostly sailing vessel which was part ironclad battleship and part pirate clipper, part spaceship, and part steamboat, and possibly also some kind of submarine akin to the famous *Nautilus*. She had the features of the first great boat of her kind, the long lines of oars that heaved at *Argo*'s sides, and the pompous majesty of the Titanic and the awful, grim promise of the dreadnoughts of earlier times, loaded with cannons and suppurating, unstable dynamite. She had unspeakable engines of light. More than that she had a personality, made from all these legends, that was uniquely described by the image and name of the ancient painting by the long-dead artist Turner. She was the glory and the loss of all seagoing vessels since the dawn of time. She was a primal.

Nobody knew if she had a crew or a captain. They thought not. They wanted to know. It was part of discovering what made ghosts tick and the answer they wanted to find (in order to secure funding for further research, if not because it was the actual truth) was this: ghosts are constructs, a form of aether that happens to brush upon the consciousness of some being or other and picks itself a form. Thereafter it seeks the same from others it encounters, sucking it from them along with their energy and their life and their material structure in a great siphon of meaning-bearing energy—information and power. The *Tem* was a big, old ghost and to see it forming, as it went through the various stages before actualisation, was to read some of its history. So the Ghost Hunters told Malachi, and who was he to disbelieve them?

This information would provide the beginnings of a theory of how aether became actualised in all its forms. The implications for the aetheric races were pretty clear—evolutionary theory was headed their way and science was there to punch it home with solid data: data Malachi was instrumental in collecting! Then they would only need to complete the work on the Aetheric Relativity Theories and a science of aether would be well on the way to full integration with the physical sciences of old Earth—a theory of everything! He felt as high as a kite for a moment. Then the barge shuddered.

The line had been tugged. The morphic energy laid down, promising more information as well as energy to the aether form, had been picked up without hesitation.

"*Tem* always grabs like a fuckin' shark," muttered the second demon, locking her feet and tail into special grabs placed on the decking at regular intervals. "Hold tight."

The barge slewed sideways with a sickening lurch. Malachi felt his harness bite into his humanoid body and then three of the minor spectrals lit up and focused to points. "Three Actual!" he screamed, with the automatic reaction of his drilling at Jones's hands.

"Fuck!" hissed Jones and at the same instant the crystal started to whine, the engines roared up several notes, the barge started shaking like it was going to disintegrate, and the energy line flowing down to the trap snapped taut. Malachi didn't need to be told over the next few seconds that they were being towed . . .

"How can that happen?" the elf asked, cool as though she was observing some dull play.

"*Tem*'s passing energy . . ." Jones guessed. "Always thought it would. Joined to the Fleet. They're not really separate."

"Should we cut the line?" the helmsman asked, nervous, his Barry White turned all to fluttering in an instant.

"No, stay on it," Jones insisted with what Malachi well recognised as the zeal of the mad and the genius. Trouble was, he wasn't sure which one she fell under.

"*Nina, Pinta, Santa Maria* . . ." the elf logged calmly. "The Fates . . ."

Malachi's head swam—the Fates? Had he heard right?

"Threes are bad shit," the second demon declared. "I say we abort."

"Stay on it!" Jones ordered. "Focus on the *Tem*, forget the rest . . ."

"Cut it!" Malachi heard himself shrieking over the scream of the barge engines, rising to accompany the crystal's drain of power. He knew about the Fates. Too much. Plenty. If these ships somehow partook of *their* mystery then he wanted nothing to do with them. He was suddenly and coldly certain they would not survive the three ships and at the same moment in his mind he heard a little, sweet voice sing: *I saw three ships come sailing in* . . .

"They're connecting!" he screamed, realising that a link between the ghosts and his own mind was building, sudden and fierce. Arcs of lightning jagged towards him from the crystal.

"Fuck!" screamed Jones with anger and defeat. She brought her hand down on the control panel like a fighter slamming an opponent to unconscious defeat. A cage of iron sprang up around the crystal and a clockwork mechanism triggered a lead jacket to clamp shut around that. The beam vanished. The engines gave up with a sigh, taking the music with them as they went into emergency down mode. All the instruments went dead. The *Matilda* stilled.

There was quiet, except for the lonely tolling of the warning bells.

"You didn't say anything about the Fates," Malachi said plaintively into the furious, accusatory seconds that followed. "You didn't say anything about the Fleet."

Zal pushed his pile of pebbles across to the silent earth elemental. "You win again! I think you're hiding cards up your sleeves." He had run out of pebble currency. The elemental had a medium-sized pile of stones set in front of it, enough to buy the whole casino, Zal reflected, as he collected the tiny scraps of a ripped up till receipt he had found in his pocket and attempted to shuffle them. A capricious breeze that had been around a few times already got hold of a piece and blew it away, chasing it across the long shadows of the rocky outcrops. The sun was going down. Zal peered at the rest of the papers. They were mostly covered in dirty fingermarks so he couldn't read the little magical marks he had placed in the paper hours ago.

"There goes the three of hearts," he said. "And that means I don't want to hear any more straight flush calls from you," he wagged his finger at the elemental. "Now I'm willing to bet . . ." But he couldn't think of anything it might want. More stones lay a few feet away but he felt too sick to go get them. He wondered if it had been such a good idea to wait for sundown to get moving. He'd thought that without the light powering up the worst of the crystal interference with the aether weather he'd be more able to get around but there seemed to be no discernible difference in the forces around him. "I'm willing to bet that if I stay here with you, my dear friend, I will never get out of this place alive. Possibly even dead." He knew by the dull force of resignation he felt that this was surely the truth. He let go of the rest of his cards and the little zephyr came by and chased them all about in a tiny storm of paper flakes. A few of them stuck to Mr. Potato Head and slowly absorbed some of his moisture, turning brown and grey. The tiny sigils Zal had forced on them gleamed like the dials on an old clock, reminding him even more that though he couldn't feel it he was being zapped by fearsome frequencies.

He accessed the soft colouration of his flare and felt the fire energies renew themselves, burning through him with something not entirely unlike pain. They were considerably weaker than they had been. He had not seen any fire beings here at all, in spite of his closeness to several vents in the raw ground where steams and smokes issued at irregular intervals, promising some kind of underground sources. Weak air zephyrs continued to amuse themselves with his cards, and soon scattered them far and wide. None of them burst into flame. They simply blew away. He was going to have to get out on his own.

"I hope you'll forgive me," he said to Mr. Potato Head with solemn sorrow. "But I must take my leave. It's been fun."

The elemental slowly assimilated the five of diamonds with a thoughtful slide of gloop down one side of its body. It rejected the paper a moment later, having stripped it of its remaining magic.

"I knew you were cheating," Zal said wearily and set his teeth together as he pushed himself up to sitting. His *andalune* felt sickly and weak, pushed through by the fire energy of his demon flare in ways it was never attuned to. His dual nature was pulling itself apart. He groaned and threw up on the sand. Mostly it was just dry retching. He spat stomach acid and grimaced against the taste. It was highly mineralised. He was starting to evaporate.

He pushed the thought away and forced himself to his feet. The air zephyrs snatched at his hair. He held it aside and stared across the shimmering flats. No direction suggested itself but to one part he thought he could see a change in the shapes of the stones and the suggestion of rocky outcrops that might provide shelter, if they did not harbour lodes of deadly elemental deposits, and so without further contemplation he set one foot before the other.

He had gone about forty agonised paces, not allowing a pause even for dizziness or stumbling, when he heard a soft sound behind him. He turned cautiously, too weak to defend himself against any great threat, and saw a ball of mud roll to a stop beside his feet. It ejected some sand in a kind of shake and then resolved itself into the familiar head-to-side lumpiness of the earth elemental. There were two kind of holes that were eyes, but no other feature of note, just a head, a body, a stare.

"Wrong person, pal," Zal said. "I'm a fire guy. We had this out before when you stiffed me out of all those rocks." He returned to his path and began plodding. The sun was down now and the temperature was soft and dewy. Water was gathering in droplets in the air. It was the complementary energy to his natural fire and he felt it as a dampener, literally and aetherically, neutralising what remained of his excessive energies. He got weaker, but he started to feel better and for a time he was able to walk without too much difficulty, feeling nothing worse than a hundred self-inflicted hangovers.

As he did so he heard the occasional sound of sand shifting or small stones being rolled close behind him. As the land darkened and the sky grew pink at the edges, then lavender, then blue, he kept on without pausing. Then at some point he stubbed his toes hard on something extremely solid and stopped without thinking, grunting in pain.

It was dark. He realised, with a great surprise, that there was no moon in the sky, only the blaze of stars which cast a very weak light . . . mostly because there were not many of them. He looked for the splash that would mark the position of the galactic main body, but for the first time in his life, he could not find it. He heard the wet glop noise of serious mud ejecting a stone close by. "Where the bejesus is this?" he said aloud, forgetting all his aches and pains, his sickness, in the surprise. He thought that surely some spatial displacement was possible between the realms, though theories of transparency and mutable dimensions had floated around the elven realms all his life . . . but he had never seen proof that at least one of these places drifted beneath different skies.

Elf eyes were good in low light, but not this low. Zal bent to rub his foot and let his *andalune* body spill out slowly into the surrounding air and ground, replacing his primary physical senses with everything that it could tell him. He felt the first numbshock that always greeted the extension of his aetheric body into worlds that did not contain any viable akashic sentience for contact. It blurred and then it shifted. There were no conscious things there with him—not exactly . . . but there were things with him all right.

Zal straightened up, suddenly more awake than he had been. Elementals of the sort that crossed the borders and flitted to business in other realms were always reasonably well-formed individuals, and usually at least as conscious as most animals. These things were an order of magnitude dumber than that, but they were aware of something—others and themselves and, of course, him. In fact the more he stood there and expanded his sensitivity the more things and varieties of things he could detect. They moved in fields, as if fields were a kind of cattle, shifting in herds of greater magnitude, or shoals of fish . . . big shoals of very big widely distributed fish . . . no, his metaphors were packing up under the strain. Things drifted, skeins and nets and the bodies within them, playing with the beginnings of form. Some coalesced into microfragments of physical elements: carbon, vanadium, cobalt, sodium . . . Some became the aetheric elements of fire, air, metal, water, and earth . . . But some had stranger properties, things he could only call abstract. They were no more than energy in formation, a cluster of pulses . . . he realised with a gasp of unadulterated delight—they were *numbers*.

"Mr. Head!" he said into the starlit night. "I declare, there are more of you than I thought." He assumed the earth elemental was still following him. Maybe it thought he might yield some suitable components for it . . . For a minute or so the discovery and this possibility amused him, until he remembered why he was there and where he should have been instead. "But we must go on, Mr. Head," he said wearily, vaguely aware that not only was he witnessing numbers in existence, he was also getting the notion that yet more oddities were out there . . . things like . . . the elements of forms—triangle, circle, square—and the elements of propositions too, the building blocks of communication.

"Helluva time for a big discovery, Mr. Head," Zal said, feeling his way around the rocks and moving on in the direction he seemed to remember was right. "Take a note of it if you would and keep up. We must have a record of what the expedition discovers." The notion of being a great leader and expeditionary scientist and visionary was very pleasing. It kept him going for hours of moderately uncomfortable staggering and occasional dry heaves, all the way until the moment when he trod on the bone and snapped it under his boot.

The next stride crunched a lot more.

Zal stopped walking and sat down to wait for dawn. It wasn't going to be great, but he'd found something that hadn't decomposed entirely. So it wasn't that old. And it used to be something that was not an elemental and that meant it had come from outside and that meant . . . he daren't think about a way out, or about rescue parties setting out to look for their missing ones or about Jolene detecting his absence and hiring Lila to come save him . . .

He felt the presence of the earth elemental approach him. He felt a shower of loose particles shower his boot and felt peculiarly comforted. The ground seemed friendlier here, or he was much sicker than he liked to think. The aetheric distortion was minimal, like a distant toothache instead of a hammering migraine and the fields of swirling proto-elementals were less organised, as though this was a younger zone where nothing had really got going yet. The energy was almost as indistinct as wild aether, but—there was no wild aether here. None at all. It was all formed or in the process of being formed. He composed himself into the meditation posture of his youth and winced as his knees protested but this way he could sleep sitting up. He didn't want to lie down here, not knowing what he had been walking in when it felt so biological. "Take a note, Mr. Head," he said with a weary sigh. "The lack of free aether in this realm means that any transits from here including portals must all draw power from beyond its borders."

His spirits sank as he said it. He hadn't realised that he had been clinging to a fantasy of finding a trail of wild magic and using it to create a circle of either transit or protection. But his *andalune*, even damaged by radiation, was sure on that point. There was nothing wild here. He heard and felt the vibration of a small pebble being ejected from a lump of mud a few inches from the ground and coming to rest on something hard, but light and friable. With his fingers he felt out the shapes of what they were sitting on. It felt like light wood that had been carved into smooth shapes . . . he was holding a scapula. It was as big as his own. It was very much like his own. He put it down carefully and closed his eyes to wait for moonrise or dawn, whichever came first. To stop himself obsessing about scapulas and their previous owners and the possible fates of said previous owners he started to hum a little song and then, effortlessly, this became writing a song and that absorbed him entirely so that for a short time he forgot all about his troubles.

Lila reached the Ahriman mansion at dusk. She had taken a diversion via the communal bathhouses at Magisteria, a district of the Musicians, and used their escalating chain of increasingly hot and caustic waters to scrub every last bit of necromancer out of her hair and clothing. Her insystem had given her a corrosion warning and a lot of fine print about some kind of warranty violation and at that point she had given up. The imp was no more than a passing pain in her earlobe. Tath brooded, an emerald weight in her heart. Only her jet boots kept her floating high and safe above the evening masses of demon life, swelling the streets and the city air with their homeward-bound legions.

She could still smell the carrion stink of Madame's companions. Or the wind was blowing from the charnel houses of the south shore where the butcheries lay open to the seaward air; meat drying, meat fresh bloodied, meat part buried and festering until it was ripe enough to sell. There was also hanging meat, flyblown meat, maggotted meat cultivating special kinds of fly and wasp larvae which could be served in the meat or on their own, live or dry roasted. They had done everything with meat that could be done. Of course they had. Cookery was an art and within it all kinds of other work was an art—cake icing, for instance, or extracting the important glands from bor wasps. Lila stopped dead in her tracks, momentarily paralysed by the enormous, lavish detail of demon cuisine, provided by her AI memory as it cued up on the charnel district. Cooking Precepture. And then, her olfactory module objected and said that the world didn't just smell this way because Mama Azuga was cooking up blood sausage and vile ribs again. Some of the smell was coming from the house.

Lila slowed down, waking up with cautionary alertness. She zoomed the house on high res and saw the guards and servants were mostly stationed outside, or at doors and windows. Tath unwound as he sensed her dread and stretched out a little into her torso, connecting his spectral self with her enchanted alloys, tuning to her with a subtlety she belatedly realised he'd just about perfected. She hardly felt it.

Two demons in the brown sombre flares of officers of the government were descending to the mansion roof from the ladder of a small dirigible bearing the insignia of the Department of Official Justice. A figure emerged to meet them—Sorcha, her crimson and black body almost entirely hidden in the white robes of mourning, recognisable only by her emergent tail and its scorpion tip. They all went inside and the servants began securing the dirigible to the roof anchors.

Lila, still fuelled on righteous outrage at Madame, landed with care and began to march inward to discover what was going on. As she proceeded the servants all glanced at her and then busied themselves more fully with their tasks. They noticed her and then they turned away . . .

Are they—cringing? Lila asked Tath silently in her thoughts, letting them channel to him however they did.

I believe that is not entirely accurate, the elf said. *I think that what you are seeing is a shun. Whatever has occurred to the family within the House, they clearly blame you.*

Her AI confirmed it. Those who brought disaster on their families were routinely ignored by lower orders and . . .

I believe you should exercise extreme caution in meeting any members of the family, Tath said, cutting through the detail. *Whatever their personal feelings for you they may be honour-bound to exact vengeance.*

But I'm not one of the family . . . Lila said. She did slow down however, and allowed her systems to prime Battle Standard, the unique AI that would enhance and supersede her human limitations. She thought the best thing would be to find Sorcha, privately, and took some quiet passages and stairs towards her room in the hope that she could reach it without meeting anyone. She was in luck. The servants and household were distracted elsewhere and she navigated the maze of ways alone.

Sorcha's apartment was open and airy—it had been recently cleaned and the smell of blood came from far away, closer to the heart of the house. Lila's neighbouring room was open too—the door ajar. Foreboding closed on her like the touch of a cold hand. She didn't let herself pause but went forward, pushing the door fully open with her fingertips and letting her AI and full senses scan for danger. There was none. There was nothing. She stepped through and there her momentum stalled.

There was nothing but an enormous mess. Everything in the room appeared to have been systematically destroyed, and in the middle of it, on the floor, lay the tangled remains of Teazle's silver net. A closer glance at the door revealed the stain of shadows around the lock and handle. There was also a scattering of dust on the floor . . . Lila bent and touched it with a fingertip. She put the fingertip into an opened slot on her opposite forearm where a microanalyser waited. Steel dust. The lock had been fragmented.

Sub- or hypersonics, Tath said. *Nocturnals are good with sound. They use it as a weapon.*

Is that how she got out of the net? Lila went forward to examine it, careful not to disturb anything, though it was difficult. Shredded bedding and the dust of other ruined items lay everywhere.

She lifted a part of the net carefully. It weighed almost nothing.

Looks torn, Tath said uncertainly.

No, Lila corrected him, letting her eyes bring the ends of each fibre of the spider silk into absolute focus. Some strands were worn and frayed, warped with recoil shock, but most of them bore a clean edge. They were cut.

Maybe she had a concealed blade?

Lila straightened up, frowning. She was sure not. Someone else did this . . .

Several pairs of footsteps sounded on the tiled floor outside and with them came the murmur of voices. Lila turned and saw Sorcha and one of the officers standing in the doorway. They were both surprised to see her.

CHAPTER THIRTEEN

As if the drinking could get any heavier, just when Malachi thought they must have run out of beer, the demons produced a fourth keg. The Mode-X music had been replaced by Vivaldi's genius at maximum volume. Malachi felt them all soothed by alcohol and music. They were nearly ready to talk to him.

The bubble station drifted in the I, calm and collected. No ghosts were near. The machines hummed, a vibration he felt in his bones as he lay on the rough decking with the others, huddled in their sleeping bags around a mess of opened fast-food containers. He had no idea how much time had passed in his office but he was reasonably sure— contrary to his expectations—that he was not in any way in his office any longer. He was with these people, entirely in the I, floating in a bubble within the tides and flow of Akashic space. It was the fey term: Akasha. I-space. The Interstitial. The Void. The Aether.

The female demon—Rhagda—held the beer barrel (an entire hogshead! Malachi noted; they would not rise for a week) firmly and the male demon who had been the captain on the *Matilda*'s abortive voyage took up a mallet and bashed in the tap unit with a single, slow resigned blow, as if he were putting the final nail into a coffin. Malachi felt that the time for explanation might be upon him. "About the Fates," he said and they all lifted their heavy heads to look at him. "They're well known to us."

"Us too," the male demon grumbled, setting his cup to the tap and drawing off an expert stein of ale. He licked the froth with his thick, pointed tongue. "But they not demons."

"Nor elf kind," said the female elf scientist, sniffing and wiping her nose on a delicate handkerchief. "But we have met them in Alfheim from time to time."

"All ghosts cross over," Jones said firmly. Malachi thought he detected the zealot's conviction in her tones and hesitated.

"We know what they are. You know too. If they're connected to the *Tem* and the Fleet then, even if they are limited here by their ghostly forms . . ." Malachi trailed off. He didn't know what he was talking about, he realised suddenly. Could the Fates be limited by form? Insight rushed him like a mad bull and he looked at Jones with his faery sight. He could see a thin wall of grey and red around her head and shoulders, the shield of deception. "You wanted them. Not the *Temeraire*."

The gazes that had been on him switched to Jones. She glared at the floor.

"By the Namer," said the Demon softly. "Is it so?"

"Jonesy," said the elf man. "You would not risk us . . ."

"We have to get something incontrovertible," Jones said, glaring at them defiantly through her fringe. "You know that."

"Humans!" Rhagda snarled, flinging her beer away with a grand, angry gesture that sent the cup and most of its contents sailing straight out of the room, through the fields of the bubble wall and out into the great magical nowhere. "No sense of danger. No wisdom!" She spat at Jones, hitting the girl where her hands clasped her bony knees. "The *Matilda* sails no more until you are back home in Otopia where you belong!"

The silence that followed was acute, desperate, and final. They all felt it, none more keenly than Malachi. Jones stared at him with dismal loathing as she wiped her hands on her jeans. He shrugged helplessly. Fey had no tact. He wished it was not so at that moment and got up, swaying slightly on his feet.

"I should go," he said. He turned to Jones. "Don't go chasing them again." The sullen quiet was waiting for him to depart so it could erupt. He felt that he was throwing her to the lions. "Not until I get you some decent protection for that barge." Oh, where had that come from? As soon as he was saying it he was already regretting it but he was back at the centre of attention again. Seven hopeful gazes on him.

Well, he thought, he could use the family charm and probably blag something out of someone, even if it wasn't Incon. He probably could. He could convince the fey that they should support the Ghost Hunters' science. Just had to not actually mention the Moirae as such, only more generally in some bigger and more vague kind of mention of the Others. Curiosity would drive things forward where his convictions faltered. He knew enough of his own race to momentarily welcome their greatest weakness as his advantage. Nothing would stop them wanting to find out more on that one subject. And since he could pretend a degree of ignorance with reasonable cause he would not be in personal danger, most likely.

How was it, he wondered, that one always thought of these excellent schemes AFTER one had committed to them and not before?

Jones was giving him a mixed look of gratitude and annoyance. He made some awkward farewells to the others and then slunk away as unobtrusively as he could to the far corner. He hated to be seen shifting. Maybe it was a cat thing.

He slipped his humanoid skin with haste, barely felt the split instant of I-immersion, and was back in his offices in the flat atmosphere of Otopia before he had time to blink. There was a brief but unpleasant itchy feeling inside his skull, like a badly tuned frequency crossing his awareness. In Otopia with its endless deluge of radiowave shit polluting the entire electromag spectrum it was common but for a horrible moment he rather fancied it had followed on as something which had started in I-space. Then it was gone and he stretched out in his wonderful chair, made sure all his comms were turned off still, and took a well-earned forty winks.

It turned out when he awoke that it had been more like a hundred and forty winks, and, reading the clock, that his stay with Jones and her crew had consumed thirty hours. No wonder he had been sleepy. Time shifted too, if he had any say in it, because he'd spent at least two days with them. He made his notes for Incon dutifully and then, finally, switched on his messaging systems.

"You're late," his secretary said with her regulation slightly addled anxiety. He didn't blame her. With him as a boss she had a lot to keep up with and she was only human. "Delaware wants to see you," she added. "I'm afraid there's some bad news."

She paused and Malachi waited. When he didn't prompt her she said, "Lila Black's parents are dead."

Malachi winced. He'd kept an eye on the family for Lila, taken surreptitious photos, ensured she got as much news as possible. It had been his special thing. "She doesn't know," he said, filling it in for himself. Of course she didn't. She was on assignment and they would never pass that to her until she got back.

"How?" he asked, getting up and studying himself in the full-length mirror he unrolled down a length of wall. Man, he looked dreadful. He raked his hands through his hair and tried to dab at some of the marks on his suit but it was a pointless effort. With a snarl he turned away from his reflection, not wanting to notice how damned guilty it looked.

"I don't know," Sally said. "Delaware said she would brief you. It looks suspicious."

Demonia, death, family. It was goddamned predictable is what it was Malachi thought furiously. Humans! He was as sick of them in that minute as the elves ever were. They didn't even know where to

fear to tread, or why. But it never stopped them long enough to listen.
The idea of facing Delaware's cool expense account attitude, after
Jones's deathwish ambition, made his claws suddenly appear. He had
to wait ten minutes before they would retract far enough to head out.

Cara Delaware's office had panoramic views out over the Bay City area.
She was the top of the department, the head of the world. Malachi knew
that he and Sarasilien and all the other seconded diplomats here tolerated
her rule only because it suited them. He never was sure if she knew that
or not. Either way could account for the hard-faced manner she deployed;
disappointment or ego, they were two sides of the same coin. He spent a
miserable minute holding his predatory instincts in check as she made
him wait for her. She was reading something at her desk. He got to pace
restlessly by the windows and pick out potentially suitable victims from
the pedestrians he was able to see walking at varius points downtown. The
cooling air conditioning soothed his temper but dried out his nose. He
sneezed, three rapid cat sneezes. He felt superstitious about three. He
made himself do another, but it wasn't quite the real thing.

Delaware looked up, her heavy brown ponytail swinging heavily
behind her head. She was as immaculate as he wanted to be. "Malachi,
you were away a long time."

"Important business elsewhere," he said. "I'm still writing the
report." He hadn't even begun to consider what pack of lies he was
going to set down in it. He didn't try now. He needed his concentration not to give away through his body language that he and she were
no longer exactly allies all the way from top to bottom. He relaxed in
his usual manner and took a seat in one of the easy chairs Delaware
kept for guests. He crossed his legs and found a fried chicken wrapper
stuck to the sole of his shoe. He crossed them the other way.

"You know that Agent Black's parents are dead," Delaware began,
giving him the full width of her attention, her desk silent.

"I heard," Malachi said quietly. Then, unable to contain himself he
added, "They were killed, right?"

Delaware nodded.

"Demons," Malachi said.

"Maybe. We aren't sure." She cued up something on her private screen and turned it towards him so that he could see.

Malachi leaned forwards. He felt his jaw loosen slightly and his hackles rose. Tiny hairs stood up along the length of his spine and he felt his nostrils flare, taking in air in a futile search for telltale scents. "Necromancers."

"Yes. So, they could be of any race, technically. We don't know. And also . . ."

Where she paused he had no trouble filling in, "Also you don't know if they're all that dead. What have you done with the bodies?"

"Freeze suspension . . . attempted . . ." Delaware said stiffly, clearly fighting to control her feelings and keep herself calm. She managed of course. "Just in case."

"You need a magical suspension," Malachi said, turning away from the picture of the scene with a curled lip. "Not so nice to come back from the final dance and find you're a corpsicle. Die next to the frozen peas, screaming."

"Do people return?" Delaware asked, looking him straight in the eye. She was strong. He shrugged.

"No humans ever have. It's assumed your bodies decompose too fast, even if you could port back to them. Fey sometimes. Don't know about elves or demons but I'd bet if they were careful they could make it. Thanatopia's an aetheric place. But not exactly. You need to talk to someone who knows. I met a returner. They weren't quite . . . like they used to be."

Delaware nodded and made some note or other. She looked up. "I need you to find Lila and tell her."

Malachi nodded silently. "What about the sister?"

"We're watching over her. Round-the-clock surveillance."

"Hn, and what does she think happened to Mom and Dad?"

"Funeral's on Friday."

Malachi shook his head. "Two empty caskets I take it?"

"Malachi," Delaware ignored his resentment. "Do you think there is any possibility at all that those people could be returned?"

"Anything's possible," Malachi said, getting up and pacing to the door, trying not to know how bad every step suddenly felt. "But as your faery wiseguy, I'd have to say that no matter what you think about it, I would never try to do it. Burn the bodies and be sure. You don't want to mess with the kind of people who traffic in the dead. If there was one thing I could make you humans do it would be to never take up hope of those you lost coming back from Thanatopia. Because they don't come back. They come forward and they miss out the middle and I have the feeling the middle might be important."

"Malachi," she said again, stopping him with his hand on the doorknob.

He looked back over his shoulder.

"Find me a necromancer, or a returner. I want to know."

"What shall I tell Lila?" He gave the slightest nod to let her know he'd heard her. "Will you let them die for certain? Have you signed them off the registry, like you did for her?"

Delaware looked at him, flat, a long minute. He took it as a No Way I'm Telling You and a clear passing of the buck. He shook his head at the stupidity and left the door wide open as he walked out without another word. He toyed with the idea of walking straight back to Faery without any plan to return, but first he had another trip to make.

He went home to get washed and changed and in some kind of shape. Sure, he was putting it off. He'd put it off forever, given half a chance.

"Adai Tzaba, like all demons, had a talent," Sorcha began. "Now how strong and how useful it was depends on who you talked to. She had a gift of Presence, which means a ranged gift that's passive, you don't turn it on or off, it's part of you. Everyone within range of Adai could see the truth of their own lives. She was of the Voyant Prefecture, Inward Facing. She was included in the scope of her talent too, so she was never able to do any of that useful shit like deny what was going on around her, or to her, at any moment. And when you got next to her you were in no doubt about exactly how much bullshit you had believed about yourself in the past, and also the actual truth of what happened to you and what your friend meant when they said 'nice hair' that day you were nervous about your first stage appearance . . ." A curl of smoke came from Sorcha's mouth with the last words, but she mastered herself and continued.

"Now in Demonia telling the truth is one of the essential arts, but don't let that fool you. To be a liar in Demonia is to be the most successful alpha-class bitch. Yet holding to the hard truth is what is most valued because only truth can set you free. You understand me?" Sorcha tilted her head and looked Lila in the eye with a hawklike stare.

She is as clear as mud, Tath grumbled, excessively disapproving but understanding all too well.

Lila hazarded, "Um, if you tell the truth you're honoured but if you manage to lie and convince others you're telling the truth then you get one up on all of them, and that's better?"

"Is so," Sorcha agreed, nodding. "Exactly so. But danger always lies in lies. They addictive, like Juju. The thrill of success . . . thrills. But the thrill is hungry. It is the hunger that can't be satisfied. It makes more and more lies. And always you are in danger of being exposed by clairvoyant talents of some kind. Like Adai's." Sorcha took a deep breath and let it out slowly. She was looking down at the floor, her sight cast inward to her memories, and they seemed sad ones Lila judged, by the way the demon frowned and pressed her lips together.

"So," Lila said, to clarify for herself as much as to show Sorcha she was listening, "Adai was in great danger, because people saw the truth when they came close to her. She exposed how they'd been tricked. That made them shamed. Of course nobody wanted her around, making them feel weak."

Sorcha nodded as though her head was heavy, "But she was also one of the great medicine spirits, Maha Bhisaja, because the danger of bullshit is that you come to believe your own. The path into Hell begins there." Sorcha looked up at Lila and glanced at the red stone in Lila's ear.

Lila touched it without thinking.

"Imps sense weakness," Sorcha murmured. "Wish I had paid more attention to you. Zal will blame me . . ." She sighed and then suddenly straightened, and arched her back and roared in frustration, a musical but terrifying exclamation of feeling that made Lila's heart jump. Afterwards the demon relaxed again with a rueful expression. "I blame myself. I should have guessed you were more fucked up than fifty genies in the same bottle." She looked at Lila with interest, to see if Lila was going to dispute the statement.

Lila found her jaw clenched but she didn't say anything. She was aware of the fragile remains next door, and her part in their making. Let Sorcha say what she liked. She was probably right. Lila listened inwardly, hoping that Tath might deny this out of a need to deny everything the demons stood for, but instead of rebellion she sensed only a sad quietude and that, more than Sorcha's assertion and Madame's warnings, made her hesitate. Sorcha's red gaze was searching.

"Once that road is taken, few return. Demons take it to prove themselves. Most never do. And outsiders, if they want to become of demonkind, they must travel the path. But Adai was the cure for the Hell road. Every good intention was shown to be self-serving, riddled with contradictions, based on dreams. There was no escape. So though you might be found out through her, you could find your way free again, back to the Via Maha, the True Way."

How ironic, yet again that the one person who could most have aided you is dead, Tath said drily, and Lila felt herself twice attacked, and twice hurt.

Sorcha shrugged. "She was a damn painful experience to have around for anyone not pure in heart . . . and because of her liabilities nobody wanted her around. She was destitute when Zal married her. There were plots afoot to get rid of her all the time. She spent her money and time avoiding death, little girl mouse. She gave them no excuse for murder. Her family were powerful too. They wanted her least. Their secrets were in constant peril. Nobody wanted her at parties. People used to run from her in the street, shout names, and avoid her. The worst part was, they all knew she was better than them. She would never sink to Hell. She was the angel who fell from heaven we don't know when. Blessing and bane."

Sorcha shook her head. Her fires were slumberous now, embers and soft smoke around her head. She folded her hands and sighed. "Zal married her, his only wife. The thing about Zal is . . . actually he's the most powerful member of this family. He went to Hell and came back on his own. That's why he's here. He doesn't need marriages. Now me I try to steer clear of them too. I don't want to waste my time with all that family shit but I only escape it by never being around much. And I make my own money. Money buys a lot here. But Zal has real power. Nobody's sure what exactly it is. But some big bad-ass mojo, that's for sure. He's demon, real demon, in a way he was never really elf. Who knows what that means? Who cares? Point is, he saved her from a miserable life—nobody would cross him in a hurry—and gave her a place to live where she could be safe. And she loved him, not for that, just anyway. She wasn't supposed to come to town. But she must have found out he was coming, so she had to rush up here, see him. He hasn't been here in an age. Been with you lot, like me. Taking turns to fight, then run. Only difference is he ain't running from Demonia."

Sorcha finished and closed her lips in a final silence. She and Lila sat for a while and the evening washed gently past them.

"What did the elf do to her?" Lila asked. She could hear the subdued voices and movements from beyond the door that signified the police at work. Barges on the canals below them twinkled. Bats flitted, catching insects. The calm seemed unreal. Everything did.

"Shadow filth are aether suckers. Best of them tap a little from a lot. Worst of them are like spiders. They inject their *andalune* body into someone else's and pump in some kind of elemental poison. It liquidises every aetheric mote. Whatever a person was, they get blended into raw aether. The elf sucks it all in, converts the aether to its own form—getting hugely powerful as a result—and leaves what you saw. Just the imprint, and the shadow. The only damn good thing is that they can't pick up talents or knowledge. Just juice. But they get kinda strong. Wherever it went, wherever it's hiding out, it'll take more than an ordinary power to find it now." She looked down at Lila's shackle. "You plead ignorance. True enough. But you're all they've got. And nobody likes a killer on the loose outside the law."

"I don't suppose I get any consideration because of . . . the Hell thing?" Lila asked.

"Nah," Sorcha snorted. "All you humans mostly in Hell all the time. For your species, it's not a mark of devotion."

"I don't understand it," Lila said in a quiet voice. "It's not a place."

"Sure it is," Sorcha said. "You carry it with you wherever you go."

"In Otopia, Hell stories say it's somewhere you go after you're dead, to be tortured for eternity . . . by demons . . ."

Sorcha laughed and the night lit up with its sound, a glowing, sparkling few seconds. She thumped her own knee with the palm of one hand and coughed, "It never gets old, sweetie." She straightened up and composed her shoulders, letting them drop, and her face returned to a stern confidence. "You look around the worlds and see who the experts in tormenting themselves are . . . where is the torturer and their shadow? Then you be out of Hell."

Lila took an impulsive risk, "Madame Des Loupes said she was the gateway."

Sorcha's eyes narrowed and oranged. "She was Zal's opener. Adai was of her Precepture. With Adai gone you could use an ally there. I hope she doesn't take news of Adai's death too literally . . . but perhaps she knew it was coming . . . and called you . . ." Sorcha looked disturbed and Lila shivered, feeling the air had become suddenly very chill though the sun was not down. The tinkly notes of a distant piano came floating up to them.

"I like jazz at night," Sorcha said quietly, "just don't tell my fans."

"If you don't have to be born a demon to be one, what do you have to be?" Lila asked.

"Know thyself," Sorcha said, and her voice took on a power and authority that pierced Lila to the bone. Even Tath felt it. "And accept all. That is the heart of a demon. And ride life like riding the wind. Seize it, love it, never let it go except for the moment when you must let it go, or else see it change into the shadow of itself, the living death of the fearful and the weak. Then abandon it without a hesitation, before you spoil. This is the essence of the divine as it is shaped into the form of demons."

"No selling out," Lila murmured.

"No selling out," Sorcha affirmed. She rose and shook her hair back, inhaling as she drew herself up to the haughty, proud figure of the diva again. She inclined her head in a gentle movement that Lila was surprised to acknowledge as respect, walked to the door, released it, and went indoors, leaving Lila alone.

Lila sat and looked at the soft glow of the evening. She put her head in her hands and cried.

Dawn in Zoomenon. The sun rose swiftly, a blaze of merciless pain, refracted through the billion indices of pure crystals that grew in profusion from the sandy desert. Colour shimmered. The aether whined with torment and weather patterns began to emerge from the night's calm as pressure zones developed in its distribution. Zal withdrew his *andalune* body automatically, shrinking from the cacophony, but there was no real escape.

The light revealed that Mr. Potato Head at least had had a good night. He was the size of a pumpkin and stouter in form than before, but, as Zal groggily woke from the fevered rest he had endured to find that his meal of the dead had sustained him, the earth elemental shifted slowly and contemplatively into a little humanoid figure, with rudimentary arms and legs, a blob of a nose, and a slash of a mouth. It stood and looked around, managing to appear slightly surprised.

Zal reckoned he must look pretty sick considering the state of decay he was fighting, but he was more surprised, he was sure of it. In front of him, as far as the eye could see—skeletons.

This made no sense. Only pure forms could exist in Zoomenon for any length of time. Still, Zal didn't care too much for scientific anomalies at that moment. He got to his hands and knees, crawled over the fine dust that was what remained of his dinner, and fell face-first down onto a crumbling heap of rib cages with an almost transcendental gratitude.

He lost count of how many corpses he pillaged. The only things he was aware of were the influx of aether, the surge of elemental fire force that came after that, and the burn of resurrection that it brought. He guzzled himself stupid. And then he lay in the bottom of the hollow he had found and stared at the painless sky. He held his hands in front of his face and saw that his *andalune* had reemerged. Instead of the elven green he would have seen, it was yellow and orange fire. He looked as though he was burning up alive. He giggled. This was very funny. Surely he was insane and death not far away. Around him the field of bones lay stark white against the dull brown of the silicate sand. He found that he was able to see the aether residue they contained, like a kind of faint light that glowed out of them. He didn't remember being able to do that before. He felt suspicious, and after a few minutes that seemed more interesting than death, he sat up.

There was something tickling his back. He wormed an arm around to scratch fiercely between his shoulder blades, but before he touched skin he felt a thick, syrupy resistance and then the slightly sticky but unmistakable shape of a feather. His wings were out, unsummoned. That explained some of his optimism. His demonic self had become stronger, probably because the elementals he had absorbed were fire and it was his demon nature that bore the fire affinity. He felt better. At least, half of him did.

He took a quick inventory and reckoned there was enough aether in the bones to keep his material forms organised enough to survive for several days. But then he began to notice more things about them; which he had not noticed before because he was too busy being grateful for their energy. They were deeply familiar. They were elf bones.

His euphoric minute seeped away. He glanced guiltily at the earth elemental. It had settled to a slump of dull clay and regarded him steadily. "You don't tell anyone about this and I won't tell anyone . . . I won't . . ." His attempt failed him. He stared back out across the battleground. No, not a battleground, he thought. There was no damage, only decay, and this strange persistence in a region that ought to have dessicated all aether to raw state long since.

His curiosity rapidly outweighed his revulsion at his cannibalism. He studied the slopes and the shape of the bowl in the ground where most of the bones lay. It was formed from a series of circular depressions—many of them, hundreds, that had been created randomly, one on top of the other . . .

Zal got to his feet slowly and began to walk along the edge of the field. It did not take him long to realise that the circles each contained the same number of people—always six. Where they fell across one another the bones were jumbled and piled higher, some destroyed. He began to see a history of something that made no sense to him at all. These circular dips were the imprints of powerfully cast magical circles, rings of binding and porting. All the occupants were, without exception, elven. The rings were of a diameter Zal knew from his childhood; the scale of a double-eight cast, a charm that required sixteen equal sorcerers to make. That kind of power was rare—elf sorcerers of skill were hermits who tended to live in the deep woods, far from contact with others. Their *andalune* bodies were so powerful that they disrupted the natural flow of the spirit in others. They usually took voluntary exile and devoted themselves to the shepherding of plants and the practice of alchemy. The only person with authority to summon such a cast was a Lord or Lady of the First House . . . so if he knew the age of these then he would know who sent them. They puzzled him greatly, for he had never heard of anyone making so many sendings, nor calling so many circles. Casting into Zoomenon was common only among shadowkin.

That made him think of the war. Long coming, now on, and him nowhere near it, though he had been instrumental in its making. And Dar. And other things he had not thought about since Hell.

He heard a stamping sound and turned to find Mr. Potato Head close by, mimicking his stance almost exactly, clay hands set to clay hips, his eyeholes set to regard the worn white sticks with an intense frown shaping up above them.

"I didn't intend to leave the war to others," he said to the little figure.

The clay man simply stared.

"This can't be part of it."

Mr. Potato Head seemed uncertain about the claim. His stare beetled unwaveringly.

"It's too old." But he wasn't sure about that. The more he looked, the more it occurred to him that the ageing processes of Zoomenon could be incredibly deceptive. These could be recent. Or else they were the product of something very old, very strong, and very strange. A feeling of deep unease made him sit down where he was. He picked up the femur of a skeleton at his feet and felt its lightness. The flames on his fingers danced out over the bone. His elven abilities let him sense the energy latent in its fragile structure. Woody, almost papery, the structure held just enough power to keep it intact. It was not decaying, even though he was. Why not?

He picked up another, then another, and found the same thing. After a time he began to remember some kind of charm he'd come across before, during his years in the Alfheim secret service. As an agent of the Jayon Daga you were expected not to let yourself give information to an enemy. In the event of capture and interrogation that could not be resisted, with no hope of escape, you committed suicide. But first you incanted your body and sealed part of it against deterioration, reforming its aether to hold the information of your imprisonment and some small part of your memory for eventual recovery by another agent . . . one who knew the unwinding spell. These bones—he could have sworn they were here only because they had been acted upon by a charm like that. But all of them? There weren't even this many agents in the Daga entire.

"I wonder if you can cast on someone else," he said, consulting his assistant who continued to stare across the legions of dead. "Never thought about it. But if you knew they were going to die . . . if you knew that and you wanted to try to save their memory for a long, long time, as long as possible. You cast on bone, because it lasts longest." He looked at the field, and it changed before him. He'd seen survival. Now he saw another kind of harvest. "You cast on them all. You're there every time. It's the only way you can think of to tell someone what you did. Hope they get found. Hope someone knows what they're looking at. Has to be an agent. Not much chance. But you do them all. You want to tell someone. But you don't stop what you're doing. Why not?"

The earth elemental marched stiffly to his side and sat down, absorbing its legs and becoming a lump with arms. It picked up a bone and held it like Zal did.

"More to the point, Mr. Head," Zal said, "why bother with such an elaborate death? If you want them dead, why not kill them an ordinary way? What's so special about this place?" He looked at the elemental and the answer came to him as clearly as if it had spoken. "That's right," he said approvingly. "Because nobody comes here and if they do they never stay. Your chances of having the bodies found are about zero." He leaned over and held his hand out to the small creature, "Welcome to the Near Zero Club, pal. Good work."

And then he was even more perplexed because he didn't recall any history about large numbers of missing people. Unless . . .

Dar was Zal's only direct contact with shadowkin. He'd referred, once or twice in bitter moments, to some long-lost bit of shadow history called Winnowing. Zal hadn't paid too much attention at the time. He'd been too keen on surviving training and then gathering enough strength to try and follow his own convictions. He didn't feel any particular interest in shadow history. They were a divergent species and that was enough for him. It was difficult to manage even one friendship and keep it alive in the atmosphere of loathing that the hugely dominant diurnal Light elves maintained against Dar and his kind. History had just been one more stick that the older ones use to justify their bigoted hate, he'd thought. He couldn't have stood adding the injustices of the past to those of the present, not and keep his focus, he daren't, so he never studied the history of the shadow. Now he racked his brains for some clue about that elusive word—winnowing. Beating grain from chaff, it meant. Keeping the goodness and throwing the useless things to the wind. It was also a part of the harvest.

"Ah, very wise," he said as the earth elemental put down its bone on his knee with a look at him that seemed quizzical. "I should try to unlock it. You're quite right." He didn't say that it was clear that at least one reason for casting on the bones of your victims was confession: the first step towards an absolution for a crime you couldn't face being responsible for in reality, only in another reality, where you were already long gone—the future.

He looked out across his field. "Time to reap, Mr. Head," he said quietly, his voice almost lost in the soft burring sound of his fire body. He took the bone in his burning hands and closed his fingers around it. The unlocking charm was easily made, the power of the binding of structure cost the person who bound it, not the undoer. So this binder was someone of great power, that they could fix all these people into their mortal shape against the entropy of Zoomenon . . . and with that he wondered what it was hiding in his hands. More than information?

He had no urge to continue. He sat there for some time, contemplating the kinds of things you could stick into a whole skeleton, and he didn't like the idea too much. He couldn't have done it himself, but he was reasonably sure you could reposition a spirit body into their frame. If you were really good. If you were incredibly strong. He'd come across it when Ilyatath had Crossed Over. It was part of the necromancer's bind, the way they anchored their spirit selves to their physical body when they chose to voyage in time.

There had not been a necromancer First Lord in Alfheim since times before humans had walked across their world. If this was the case, then these bones were more than old. They were ancient; prehistoric.

"Mr. Head," Zal said uneasily, remembering standing guard over Ilya's body long ago when he, Zal, was still playing the loyal pack animal, knowing that he could sunder the elf forever from the material planes with a single spoken charm. It had been his job to do so, Arië had instructed him, in case Ilya came back wrong. Necromancy was a chancy art. The best-trained adepts often went astray at the first voyage.

He'd never have said it, but he felt it come quickly to his mouth now: a sound, a call, a word that must be obeyed.

He turned to the earth elemental and said, wishing it were a longer line, "I'm going for a little journey. I may be some time."

What did he have to lose? He could only die here with them. He had hours left at best. Nobody came to Zoomenon. Nobody left. So, what else to do but dance?

CHAPTER FOURTEEN

Lila?

She knew it was Tath, and Tath never used her name, so it was important.

She took her head out of her hands and savagely wiped her face on the backs of them. The synthetic skin felt a bit rubbery suddenly, and too cold. "Fuck," she said and cast about for anything to dry her eyes on, but aside from ripping a few leaves off the nearest ornamental bush there was nothing. She yanked up her military vest and used the hem. "What?"

Little feet with claws on pattered on the bench next to her. It was a green imp, larger and fatter than the one she was used to and it looked at her with a contemplative greed. "Piss off," she said, but it only sidled closer and reached out towards her with a clammy paw.

There was a pain in her ear and she felt Thingamajig suddenly explode, his voice shrill with atavistic, possessive passion, "Get off my . . ."

The green imp exploded. Bits of it splattered across the bench, the floor, and the pretty flowers. Lila looked at the gun that had assembled itself over her right hand and gently relaxed the fingers. The gun took itself apart and placed itself back into storage in her forearm. Her skin molded itself over the metal and carbon surfaces. It looked like putty. She curled her lip and flexed her fingers.

There was, she felt, a stunned silence from her shoulder, where a light weight swayed gently. "I want to be alone," she said.

"Yeah," the imp said. "I know. I was gonna go get you a pack of wetwipes. Be right back. Shops are all open late . . ." It hopped down and scampered over the balcony rail hastily, soon lost to sight in the growing dusk.

"Don't bother," Lila said to the empty space. She slid sideways, away from the worst of the mess, and then looked at her hands again. She made guns. She made grenade launchers. She made fists with spikes and fists with razors. She made hands that were almost but not quite right.

Lila.

"I know," she said. "Tell me something, Tath."

The elf waited. She could feel his attention all on her, for the first time, a cautious, careful attention. She thought that was a very bad sign. But she didn't need it.

"Do you really hate me?"

There was a pause. *No.*

"Oh," Lila said, lightly, she felt, considering. A fragment of imp slid down her face like a piece of wet cake. She brushed it away absently and flicked it to the ground. "Then it must be me."

Lila . . .

"Not now," she said. "There's a good boy."

But the elf was unwinding. She felt his spirit body unfold and spread with liquid slowness through her chest, her guts, and into her limbs. He left her head alone but he could still hear her. Thanks to the metal elementals fused into her once-mundane prosthetics he could even reach through them without being nullified by the anti-aetheric properties of electromagnetic fields. It had been a long time since he had done anything but crouch inside her and hide. The last time he had been out was the day he ate the soul of Teazle's brother.

She couldn't help but cringe inside when she remembered, but the shrinking wasn't from him alone. He was more than she ever realised. His presence was steady, and alive, as she shrank away from her own body, and tried to do what he did, and wall herself off somewhere deep within that had never been touched by magic or engineering. Tath unfurled. They might share physical space and one another's thoughts and senses, but they were nothing like the same. To Lila he felt old, full of secrets, and young and full of unused potentials. He reminded her painfully of Zal and the facts of his unknown agendas, history, and abilities wore at her. She could go nowhere and do nothing without his witness.

These people are savages, Tath said, lying calm like a smooth lime river in her veins and circuits. *You must understand their culture is nothing like yours. They hold life so high, but they throw it away in an instant. It is their pride.* His tone left no doubt in Lila's mind that he despised this attitude, but also held a grudging admiration for it. *The dead woman isn't someone cherished and lost to them, she's a bargaining piece in an endless game. They will not judge you like humans. You should not either.*

"What are you talking about?" Lila snapped.

Lila, do you know what this Hell is that they speak of? He sounded less chiding now.

"Self-doubt or something," she said. "I was never that great at analysis and the spirit stuff. I like to just," she drew a line in the air with one fingertip, between her head and a distant spot, "let the doctor suck it out and see what she says."

She felt Tath's disturbance grow but he remained calm. *I know what it is*, he said. *And I only know one useful thing about it. Once you start to go through Hell, keep going. Lila, you are beginning to stop. But you carry me with you. I am in Hell too and I will not stop.*

"Talk sense or shut up," she said. "I'm sick of it already." She felt wretched. She should go in, do something, report, write a paper . . . She sat on the stone bench.

You must stop pretending, Tath said.

"Pah!" Lila spat, standing before she knew what she was doing, head down, stance ready. "How dare you of all people say that to me. We agreed to stay out of one another's way. You'd keep your lying little secrets and I'd let you live. Or did you forget that deal?"

You cannot answer every challenge with death, Lila, the elf said, for the first time in a tone that she could have sworn was laced with concern that wasn't entirely for himself. *Will you shoot everything in the world that comes to tell you that you are running out of time? And I am not speaking of your job as spy or your personal need to discover Zal's story or anything like that.*

"I don't eat people's souls," she retorted, not even sure how that was supposed to make sense except that she hated being taken to task by someone worse than she was. "And you're not my conscience so shut up or . . ."

Or what? A tendril of green *andalune* wound slowly out from the side of her right arm and enveloped a piece of imp flesh that lay seeping beside her on the seat.

Flesh without the spirit is such a strange thing, Tath said. It has everything needed for life, but life. And the aether decays instantly . . . gone. The shadowkin would have consumed him by now. To her it would be a crime to waste what is no longer needed. They eat their dead, you know. The dead offer themselves to be consumed, and some of their memories pass with the substances of their being.

Necromancers use similar techniques, but we do not eat the aetheric body. We mine it for its unique organisation—for the soul. Souls are our mounts that we ride into death. Time stamps. Constellations. Compasses. We cannot get there without one. Only the dead may cross over. Or those shrouded in the mantle of a soul fleeing into death. But you have to pick the moment. Dar, for example. I could have gone with him. But I did not.

He had nobody to offer himself to when we took his life. All his line and their moments, wasted with him. Fifteen thousand years of brave and defiant continuity in the face of chaos and destruction, gone with the blow of our blade, as if they were nothing. But you were human. I was light born. And everyone else there was a bastard he wouldn't give breath to. Who had he?

I would not make him my horse and save him, like I saved the demon I yet contain, for when I need an energy ride into the hidden land. But I have that demon. One ace in my hand. His tone had become soft, but she could feel its spite as strongly as ever. *Once I was a boy who dreamed of other things.*

As he said this last Lila found her mind suddenly suffused with soft pictures of incredibly high trees, their leaves a billion shades of green beneath the sun. She was running in the dappled glade beneath, watching her hands catch the golden coins of the light as it fell through the slowly moving foliage. There was an animal beside her, running too. Their spirits were joined in friendship and they were lost in the moment. Not far away others were around, higher in the branches, and their animal companions were with them; all kinds of beasts were there, each of them vivid to her. With no more effort than thought she could see through their eyes, feel the beat of their hearts. They were part of a special tribe. They were free and it was good to be alive.

Then the little montage of Tath's lost dreams faded and she was left seated on the cold stone, the demon night around her, the forest replaced by the hoots and whistles and shrieks of endless struggle.

"Why are you telling me this?" Lila had felt herself slowly frozen during the revelation, all her resentful fire replaced by cold uncertainties and a sense of being so far from home. She was slow and calm.

The elf was still and silent, just spoke the words quietly to her, no rancour left. *I wanted to share one moment of my Hell with you. We are all alone in Hell. But we are not alone in being there.*

Lila looked out into the night. "I don't know why everyone else but me is so confident of that analysis. I don't feel like I'm in Hell. I'm in Demonia on some assignment that got out of hand. Probably it's no worse than what most demons face every day, I mean, look at them! I just screwed up a bit. I can fix it. I can do . . . things . . ." She realised she was scrubbing her hands against her leather leggings and stopped. She felt sympathy. It wasn't hers.

"Don't you dare fucking pity me!" she screamed out, leaping to her feet. It shocked her almost as much as it shocked Sorcha, who reappeared at the door, her hair blazing as she looked around for trouble.

"Who are you talking to?"

Tath diminished, swift and subtle. Lila stood staring out at nothing. "Nobody."

Sorcha looked baffled for a moment, then shrugged. "Someone here to see you."

Lila stared at her. She glanced down at the shackle.

"A friend," Sorcha said.

"But I don't . . ." Lila began and stopped. She took a deep breath and nodded. "Here?"

Sorcha stepped aside. Lila was astonished to see Malachi walk past her onto the terrace. He was the last person she had thought to see here . . . nearly the last anyway.

She felt a confusing surge of gladness and anxiety and then a moment of awe as he emerged fully from the dim interior into the torchlight. Malachi just looked like a jet black human being in Otopia. A jet black human with yellow eyes and a style not far short of the 1940s, suits and shoes always perfect, walking slightly off the ground sometimes, like walking on air. In Otopia she never saw the wings but here, like the elven *andalune* bodies, here they were.

Lila had never seen him in his natural fey form before. Malachi looked much more like a cat than she remembered. He had whiskers on his top lip that spanned out in ebon arches, shining, as wide as his shoulders. His hair was softer and more furry, it tufted at the sides as though he had ears like a cat. He had wings that transected his jacket and camel-coloured raincoat without damaging them; transparent, floating wings like the thinnest gossamer, veined with ink black lines so fine they seemed to draw the outline of wings on the air, two sets of them, butterfly shaped with ragged edges and glittering with rich grey anthracite dust, twinkling and soft.

His large eyes, orange, slit pupilled, took in detail and narrowed as he sensed the degree of disturbance in the scene. Above his eyebrows two long delicate lines she had taken for other whiskers revealed themselves mobile, questing through the air. They were mothlike antennae. After a moment they folded back and were lost in his hair. "Seems like you get in trouble everywhere you go," he said, though he wasn't entirely lighthearted about it. His face was taut.

Lila restrained herself from moving forward to greet him, because his hesitancy made her self-conscious. She brushed at something wet on her arm and then let her shoulders slump, "Ain't that the truth," she said.

Behind Malachi, Sorcha signalled a servant to go get something, or do something, but she didn't leave. Malachi looked at Lila's shackle and made an awkward hunching motion with his own shoulders, "I . . . Can we go somewhere?"

Lila gritted her teeth, "I don't want to go out. People everywhere." She prayed that Malachi would understand how it was when you were new and strange in town here. He seemed to, because after a second he moved towards her, his expression resigned but determined to offer her a sign of friendly affection. He put his hand on her shoulder and set to give her his customary kiss on the cheek but as he leaned in he was suddenly yawning instead. Lila felt awkward and did nothing. As usual fey proximity had a slight fogging effect in her circuits. He leaned back and covered his mouth with one hand, nails long and clawed upon it.

"Must have taken more out of me than I thought," he muttered, mostly to himself and smiled at Lila with a smile that soon faded until his mouth was as thinly drawn as a wire.

"What are you doing here?" she said. "Problems?"

"I came to . . ." His hesitancy and seriousness were uncharacteristic, and it was a relief when he gave up the effort of making a show and said simply, "I have to tell you some bad news." He looked over his shoulder at Sorcha, who smiled at him with a cold elegance that said she wasn't going anywhere. Malachi shrugged it off and turned back to Lila, walking forward to take her arm—pointedly avoiding a smear—and leading her to the very end of the terrace where date palms in giant pots provided a nominal kind of shelter. Behind them the summoned servants appeared and began cleaning with great haste and efficiency. Sorcha brooded and skulked around them, trying to listen in.

Lila was strangely grateful for the distraction, no matter how bad it was, but Malachi hesitated again and washed his face with the back of one hand—something Lila had never seen him do before. "You're going feral?" she asked, trying to make him smile. He liked silly jokes.

"Are you going to sit down?" he asked impatiently.

"No," she said. "Are you going to stop stalling and start talking?"

"Lila, your parents are dead."

She saw Sorcha jerk slightly in the background. A moment later, in the long quiet, Thingamajig bounced back up onto the terrace railing and looked around for her; it opened its mouth and received Sorcha's tail in it at something slightly less than a hundred miles an hour. It vanished over the edge again with a muffled cry.

"How?" she asked. She felt so calm it was really quite odd. She felt like a big space opened up inside her, around her, and what had just been important was receding on the perimeter.

"Car accident."

"Really?" She wanted it to be that. She looked at him desperately, hoping it was not the overspill from what she had done. Praying . . . and distantly aware that it was odd to pray for death for people you loved.

His burning orange eyes fixed their gaze on hers steadily. "I didn't see that."

Oh. Something the agency were covering . . . that was . . . "Demons?"

He shrugged—he really didn't know. His wings shed a little dust and it sparkled in the air, a cloud of almost weightless magical matter, soon borne off on the breeze. "Later," he said in a low voice. "Not here."

"Are you sure . . . I mean . . . there couldn't have been some mistake . . ."

"I have a picture of the scene," he said in clipped, near silent syllables and gave a slight shake of his head.

Lila swallowed hard. "Can I see it?"

The faery backed off a step.

She held out her hand, "I mean it. I can handle it. I need to see it. I have about thirty vendettas out on me and I want to know . . ."

"It's probably not a good idea," he said. "Don't you think . . ."

"Show me," Lila demanded, losing all patience. "Give it to me! I have a right to know!"

"And I have a business to protect you right now," Malachi countered, polite but unshakeable, his chin lowering with determination. "You'll get to know when the time is right."

He has a . . . Tath began.

You shut up, Lila snarled inwardly. To Malachi she kept her hand out and balled the other one into a fist. "Give me what you got, partner."

Malachi didn't miss the load on the last word. She saw him flinch. He wrestled visibly with his conscience for a second, then slowly reached into his inside pocket and withdrew his Berry. He flipped it open and cued the screen before holding it out to her.

All her conviction left. She didn't want to take it because it was going to hurt, only, she didn't know how bad. Everything was suspended, until the second she saw and it was true. She was okay, until she looked. She was aware of Sorcha staring at her, of the world being still and silent, of Malachi waiting. She wanted to live in this moment forever.

She took the Berry and turned it towards herself. The AI in her skull offered to take away everything but the facts; it could detach her from emotion and even deal with all the deductions. At all costs she had to remain a functional, capable agent, responsible for her awesome power, her duty foremost in her mind. It was there to help when that was too hard for an ordinary person. It wouldn't be cheating. It was essential. It had protected her from the impact of so many things since she was Made. The only time she'd ever cut it off completely was the night and day she spent with Zal in his hotel room.

The prospect of using it again made her feel weak, grey, and flat. Empty; she was the robot girl who never had to deal, who downloaded her passions, who bypassed her pain, who had infinite energy and the strength of a thousand men and the heart of a zombie. And no change, not ever, always the smile of the medicated mind and the comfort of the hot guns. And nobody asked her. They saved her. Oh . . .

She shut it down.

Lila . . . Tath was afraid for her. She knew it was real concern and she was glad of it, no matter what fucked up shit else he was keeping back for another day.

No. You're right. I thought when you said lying you meant to you, and to other people. I didn't think about me. I have, ever since . . . since Vincent died, or even before. Yeah, maybe before that, before the bomb even came. (She thought of weddings and school and a feeling she had never named, a deep dissatisfaction with the prospect of a normal adult life, her parents' visions of what it held in store. Within her shock, was there not just a tinge of . . . relief? Yes. She felt herself fragmenting, almost grateful that her missing limbs and pieces were not here to see what she had come to because she did not feel like a horrified, upset, dutiful child. *At last*, said some old, old voice in her mind. *We can stop now.* An exhaustion came over her so profound that she had to lock her limb mechanics to hold her up. She thought she could lie down right there and sleep for a thousand years.) *I'm so tired*, she said and looked at the image in her hand.

"Oh," she said.

Her mother was seated on the sofa—a new sofa, all beautiful hand-tooled leather and Italian design like she'd wanted for so many years, but when Lila was at home it had been an old divan set—she was relaxed and slumped. Her mouth hung slackly. Her eyes were wide open and rolled up, just the bottom part of the iris showing. Her dad was the same, but he half lay on the sofa, like he'd been draped there. A string of saliva hung from the corner of his mouth.

They didn't look dead, just passed out. On the table in front of them was a box and a lot of silver and white wrapping paper, ribbon and tape, scissors, and a card tucked into the fold of its envelope. It bore a picture of two bears holding hands, one in a tux and one in a veil—"Congratulations!" Next to it was a half-finished bottle of vodka and her mother's chunky glass, leaded crystal. Ice cubes in it had melted almost down to nothing and the glass ran with water on the outside. A deck of her mother's trademark Lucifera casino playing cards had spilled off the corner and lay in a scatter on the carpet next to two unopened packs, their crumpled cellophane wrapper beside them. In the corner of the image she could see the curve of the white baby grand piano her sister played, covered with silver-framed photographs of the family that always used to ring faintly whenever someone hit a high F. They were dusty.

"How did you get there so fast?" Lila's voice didn't sound like her own. She was barely aware of speaking.

"I didn't. I got the picture from Delaware. A neighbour called the police. She heard screaming."

"That was lucky," Lila said without thinking.

Malachi frowned with incomprehension.

Lila became aware of a coldness in her chest. Tath?

I cannot tell which of two possibilities are there, he said, calm and gentle. *Either they were soul-sucked by a necromancer, or they were eaten by the shadowkin or some creature of that kind. I have seen this petit-mort often, but without a close inspection I cannot tell the cause.*

Petit mort?

The little death. Those taken out of time are spoken of this way. To die in the body by more natural means is the grand mort.

She handed the Berry back and turned away to find Sorcha staring at her. The servants were gone. The place was pristine. Lila felt a grim determination fill her.

"Sorcha," she said. "I need to go home."

"I . . ." began the demon.

Lila cut her off, "If you would keep all my duel notes and just say I'm delayed, and send a No to all the proposals and business plans while I'm gone, I'd be grateful. I'll leave you some money for the messengers and sacrifices and all the stuff you need for that. Now, I understand I have to take on the Mantle of Vengeance for Adai, and I'll deliver the notice on that as soon as I find who did it. I believe that frees you from debt to her family."

Sorcha nodded, her face serious as she matched Lila's change of mood. "I will also send out the wedding invitations."

Lila frowned.

Malachi groaned as he got a grip on the facts, finally. "Of course. Li, you inadvertently caused Zal's wife's murder. You have to replace her with a like value."

"With what?" Lila asked.

Sorcha rolled her eyes, her brief interlude of solicitous patience over. "Will y'all be wearing red or black?" she smouldered, giving off a slumberous purple vapour, her flare lit with scarlet and cerise.

"You can decide," Lila said, ignoring everything that wasn't of essential importance. She had no intention of going through with a wedding. She could deal with it later however.

"Red, then," Sorcha said. "No sense in being half-assed about it." She looked pleased, her tail became lofted and perky.

Malachi seemed to have come to the same conclusion. He put the Berry in his pocket. "I will summon a taxi to take us to the port."

"I need this thing off my wrist," Lila held up her shackled arm. "What can I do?"

"Nothing." Sorcha dismissed the notion with a wave of her hand.

"I will inform them of the situation and they'll give you Leave of Mis-
ericordia. Five days of free action."

Lila nodded at her and then said to Malachi, "Let's go."

He spread his wings and lifted clear of the ground. "I will fetch a car."

He disappeared into the night air. Where he had stood a small pile
of black coal dust blew into a ring and then glittered briefly before it
faded entirely to nowhere.

Sorcha curled her lip at it. "Cheeky creature. Still, what do you
expect from cats? Marking themselves on everything. At least he
didn't piss on the plants." She glanced up at Lila. "I don't know what
gives in your world, but if a demon did this, we pay. We always pay
for our mistakes and we always keep our end of a deal. Even if we ain't
the ones making them. We take a strong view on it. You understand?
Adai—I know you meant nothing there. I'm just sore is all. If you need
help, send your imp. They're a useless gaggle of crap, but they can send
messages fine."

Lila nodded. "Mine says he's a lord of Hell."

"The old ones are the best," Sorcha shrugged. "It'll be fine."

Lila guessed she didn't mean the imp with the last line. She tried
for a brave smile but didn't make it. Sorcha snarled for a servant and
instructed it to retrieve Thingamajig. Her face was deadly serious, an
expression Lila had never seen on her before and hoped never to again
for it was like seeing a sunny day turn to the point of a sword. She fixed
Lila with a steel gaze.

"You're one of us now. Do as we would do, or be damned."

Without thinking, acting only on her feelings, Lila snarled in
return, "I'm not one of you and I'll do as I will."

Sorcha glared at her then laughed, "No less!" She sobered as an
aircar appeared from the night, balloon swelling like a second moon in
the torchlights.

It approached rapidly, fanning all the flames to flat streaks of light
with the wind from its propellers. Beneath the gasbag Malachi leaned

out, one hand on the rail, the other held to Lila as they walloomed close to the terrace with a whirring and the jingle of a chain ladder being unrolled expertly into position. The ladder shone faintly and seemed feeble, but a large and capable-looking baboon swiftly swarmed down its links to the terrace rail and secured the end of it with a piece of rope cast into a knot faster than Lila's eye could follow.

"Hup, lady," it said to her with some difficulty around its large yellow canines. "Be so kind. Master y'ave paid and we is hurry. Otopia Portal close in the quarter mark o' the clock."

Lila, stone inside, heavy and numb, sprang up without the use of the ladder and set her foot to the deck, taking Malachi's hand. The aircar swung heavily down at her side and dropped a few metres, slackening the ladder until it was horizontal. The baboon raised its eyebrows, loosed the knot, and leaped the gap, barrelling past both of them wth a rattle as it stowed the lines. The pilot, a monkey-headed humanoid, turned the wheel, and they moved steeply away from the Ahriman mansion. Lila turned to look back. The house looked huge from the air at this angle, as many lights as an office block, but of strange shapes that were inhuman in their setting. Coloured banners draped it, now being replaced by the white streaming trailers of mourning even as she watched. The stonework on her side moved with shadows that did not seem entirely in keeping with inert architecture.

Malachi's hand gripped her shoulder.

"How long until we arrive?" she asked.

"Otopia Portal will open to Bay City. Did you live far away?"

"Half an hour," she said.

"I got my car. Twenty minutes then."

"I should call my sister." She activated a line link into the Otopia Tree before she even thought about it, then cancelled the call. She'd been gone for years. What would she say?

CHAPTER FIFTEEN

The bone did not open its secrets. Zal sat as the sun rose and his headache grew and blew out through his lips, a sigh of defeat. The earth elemental was drying out across its back where the light fell on it and from the warmth that Zal's fire body gave out. Periodically it would stop watching him and roll itself into a ball, then reform its little humanoid shape.

"I think," Zal said, "that the charm I know to open this is not the one that was used to seal it. Which, given the age, seems quite likely. Spells change. Fashions go in and out. Knowledge changes. Usually for the worse, for reasons I never got . . ." He had quite a friendly feeling towards the bone now. He'd been holding it so long. A cough interrupted his talk—a dry, itchy cough that tickled with flame. "We need a drink," he said and looked around.

The bone field was as dry a place as he'd seen. There were no water elementals around, in fact nothing he could detect except for himself and Mr. Head. He rubbed his head where it itched with the heat and saw several strands of hair come away on his hand. "Radiation sickness," he said and deliberately did not open up any more knowledge about it. It wasn't his problem. Over the pocked land, hazes of the primordial numbers appeared as clusters of light that flared for an instant and then were gone, with the fleeting speed of notion. Maybe Zoomenon had regions where certain kinds of elemental spawned and died, ecologies . . . just his luck to find something useless and abstract instead of a blazing vale of plasma. He decided he had to leave the field and move on. It was tempting to just lie down and die but that would have spoiled what interest he had left, and he had some. He got to his feet and promptly fell over.

He was too sick to go anywhere. But he had one resource, even though he was reasonably sure now that eating the long dead here was erasing their knowledge and whatever message was left in them. His shadow blood had never been strong enough to let him preserve the dead, as a true shadowkin did, taking their knowledge to his own memory. This was why the shadow had no written histories, and why the light ones trailed around libraries all their lives long, forgetting and losing important stuff. The reminder of his early years and the irritation that his unusually good memory had given to his guardians brought a smile to his face. He put his bone aside—it seemed important—and moved along the sand on his belly to another spot before closing his eyes and letting his aetheric body find what it must and sunder it to nothing. To prevent himself thinking or feeling too much about what he was doing or what Lila might be doing, and where, he worked on his song in his mind. Zoomenon didn't really lend itself to disco. Even the beats and the melody wanted to revert to a purity of form that he'd never been drawn to before: one drum, one voice.

He became aware of a tapping addition and looked around to the source. Mr. Head was counting time with two ribs by tapping them on a small stone, following his line. The situation struck him with its full absurdity then and he laughed soundlessly, his body shaking against the ground as the fire aether sucked on the last juice of the long murdered and started to burn hotter. Emotion filled the flames and they danced out happily across the dry field. He felt so much better suddenly, and recognised the groovy feeling of getting dosed with surprise. Close to his face he felt the soft reports of bones cracking in the sudden heat. He put his head up and opened his eyes.

Almost half the field was on fire. Sprites of flame—the first stage of elemental formation—were coming into being above the burning bones. They were barely more than candlelights but swiftly darted down to join the conflagration to add their heat and hunger. As the blaze intensified they rose again, big as torches, and gathered in groups before plunging in again.

"Holy shit," he whispered. Burning all the evidence hadn't factored in his plans. Then he saw the fire that limned his own body, his *andalune* demon fire. Its normal orange glow, the flare of the creative, happy-go-lucky individual, had fuelled up to an intense yellow-white burn which glowed with a steady, furnace-like blast rather than its more common tealight flicker. That explained the feeling of exaltation and furious power then. Also the niggling sensation that if it got much more potent it felt like his *andalune* was going to ignite and fry his brains and most of the rest of him into something crispy. Technically demon fire was an expression of energy, not a hot flame of the sort that signified combustion. It was aetheric plasma, not matter burning. But the fire elementals had complicated the whole thing out of the window and out of Zal's, and possibly anyone's experience. They seemed happy with aetheric plasma and electron plasma on more or less equal terms, feeding on one to the other without a flicker of shame. He could see both types out there, and both in elemental form.

They liked his fire. A lot.

As he stared at the destruction for an instant he felt rage and annoyance that some idiot hadn't come here a long time ago and sorted out the technicalities of how Zoomenon actually functioned. Then he figured that they had probably tried, they just hadn't lived long enough to get very far. On the plus side, nobody would be around to care that he had just ruined a piece of elvish prehistory that could possibly rewrite some of the currently popular histories fuelling the war. Only him, and he wouldn't be around very long.

The flame surge suddenly hit him with some force—in the mind. Wasn't this how he got to Zoomenon? Ingesting elementals? Shadowkin talents plus demon affinity for fire plus an innate curiosity equalled . . . well, mostly it equalled social ostracisation and daily danger of death but in a more positive light it equalled the ability to do more than just crank up on elemental jazz like an ordinary elf. And then he remembered Lila. She had been suffering until Dar was with her. Dar was shadowkin, full blood and aether line. He had done the other shadow trick with her—the opposite of eating—feeding. A light elf could have healed her but only temporarily. A light elf could heal the flesh and living material. It would have been energised by the elementals fooling around with her metal, but it would never have been able to ingest the elemental power and spit it back out into her metal body, doing the same to flesh, fusing the two incompatible parts of her into a seamless being. Dar had transmuted her metal to a kind of living metal, one infused with the essence of metal spirits, which were aetheric in nature, alive. Just like now, when they were using that same technology no doubt to forge living weapons and cut the light elves to pieces, like the old days . . .

While he was thinking his hair was singeing. The awful carbonising smell and the growing heat made him refocus fast.

He did a quick calculation along the lines of eating aether from bones plus attracting fire elementals, plus eating fire elementals eating said bones, plus changing flare colour to increasingly whitened tones and yellows . . . white the colour of pure creation and yellow was transfiguration.

Some of the new creatures were entering third generation as he watched. These shapes had humanoid elements—they were gaining conscious abilities . . . paraconscious ones anyway, it had never been too clear since they didn't speak even in their highest forms as pure spirit avatars. Meanwhile, the flames were spreading and pulling him with them. And the bones were shattering, their aetheric information being converted to aether plasma without passing through anything like a mind first. He tried to pick some up but even before he touched them the blaze of his *andalune* overspill set them alight.

Zal jerked his face around and shouted at the earth elemental that stood beside him still holding its two drumsticks, "Save the bones, Mr. Head! Save them!"

The clay man turned its noseless and mouthless face to the pyre. It looked down at the rib sticks in its hands with expressionless consideration. Then through a wall of golden light Zal saw it roll backwards into a football-sized lump of thick clay and then go rolling off.

"The bones!" he screamed after it, upright on his feet before he was even aware of moving. His eyes and nostrils began to hurt with the temperature of the air around him. Somehow the material and aetheric fires were getting out of hand. He had to close his eyes and focus then, drive the material burn down and away so he didn't go up in smoke with everything else. It was a feeling, that was all, just want to do it and the *andalune* reacts . . . he wanted to live, he wanted the knowledge, he wanted the power. On his back he felt the flare erupt into a new kind of power as the elementals entered fourth generation. Now they wanted him. They wanted awareness. Wanted life. They dove into his *andalune* and out again, ripping themselves free with glee and seizing what they could of his spirit body for their own only to know, by their growing instincts for survival, that if they were going to make it they had to get enough organisation going to escape the terrible dismembering gravity of Zoomenon's aether fields.

In an instant of superclarity it became obvious to him that he had never been the one doing the exploiting in the elf-elemental relation. What they had always taken for a mutual attraction was interest and greed on the elf's part and a parasitic necessity on the elemental's. Elves had the upper hand in terms of knowledge and complexity. Elementals had the mojo. The weakened ones who survived in places like Otopia and the other realms were easy enough to subdue for a being like him, but here, where they bred and rose and where he broke up and died . . . here they were king. In another few minutes his fleeting shadow abilities would be history because they were eating him alive, mindlessly destroying in their need for a mind of their own. At the same time their power added to his own, for the length of their immersion in his aetheric body. It was glorious. He felt his wings open, bigger, broader, more powerful than they had ever been in any other region. Fire rained on him from the barren sky and from beneath the bodies added spectral heat on heat.

He engulfed the pyre and the firestorm engulfed him and they became as one.

Things happened in a chaos then. Zal was aware of much more going on than he was able to perceive in any way—the truth was beyond his senses. But the following things became clear, more or less in a sequence.

He stopped burning.

The bones began to incandesce.

All the fire elementals of every stage rose up suddenly like a flock of birds startled. They swarmed together rapidly, motes of light and fiery blazes with rudimentary features, whirling into a vast cloud. They raced about in seething ribbons of sheeting flames that flashed through every colour of the rainbow, making a roaring sound and creating a wind that slapped up the sand and used it to scour Zal's skin and the exposed ground, whisking through his fragile *andalune* and turning to glass beads in flight.

A boulder roughly the size of a builder's skip rolled up and came to a halt where Mr. Head used to stand. Its terracotta clay with admixed grit formed up into the shape of an android figure, somewhat larger than Zal by half a metre. Two dark eyes formed as it shed unwanted gravel from its skin. It turned and mechanically began to pick up bones from the last untouched edges of the pits. It placed the bones against its body and took them in, arm bones to arms, leg bones to legs, and so forth. It created a vast maw beneath its eyeholes and consumed half a skull. What did not burn, Mr. Head placed within himself, picking indiscriminately and without count.

As Zal watched this in amazement that briefly won out over his other amazements, the whirligigs of fire elementals abruptly came to some decision, bunched together, and flew directly at him with the force and accuracy of a guided missile. With more will than idea he tried to move away. His wings beat and he lifted just off the ground in time to be hit midchest by the swarm. His body remained untouched, in a different dimension, but his aether body, burning, white, furious, deranged with survival instincts, instead of resisting, took them all in and ate them up.

Zal opened his mouth to scream and with his voice a huge jet of fire spat out into the swiftly circulating air, where wind sprites were massing, attracted by their fire cousins storming and raising of the weather. The fire jet and the sonic scream, an elven expression of savagery containing all Zal's great need to live, caught Mr. Head full force. Things went white, and then red, and then they went black. It was, Zal felt as he collapsed, a whole big elemental thing right there and happily fitting as a colourful end. He would have objected to a lack of balance and maybe the need for a few secondary powers if everything was to be considered artistically perfect, but he was already out cold before that notion had time to become a thought.

He woke up with the mother of all headaches and a pain in his spine so severe he thought he must have broken it. He tried hard to be unconscious again, but it wasn't working. He also felt sick and there seemed to be a lot of minor pains like burning sand and rocks around so he figured he was still in Zoomenon. A big grin spread across his face. Not dead. Result! Then he threw up.

"Mr. Head," he whimpered into the ground when he was done, "this is all very instructive stuff, but I have to confess a certain boredom in the dying scenario. It's getting to operatic proportions." He looked up. The dimpled ground was free of bones. It was free of everything. The air was stagnant and flat. He racked his brains but no new memories of anything prehistoric were in his head. The pain made him lie flat a while until the sensation of being burned by the sun got too much. The ground was a desert.

Zal thumped a fist weakly on the ground, "Drinks! Shady palms! Overpriced hotels and malls full of air conditioners. That's what this place needs!"

A cool stripe fell across him. He felt a slight shudder. Then, from nowhere, a trickle of water splattered down onto the back of his neck.

With great difficulty he rolled over. A twelve-foot-tall terracotta elf with the physical dimensions of a brick outhouse was standing over him with its arm extended, hand in a fist. The water was running out of the fist. Zal watched drops land on his chest. He was naked. He had no *andalune* at all and panicked for a moment until he tried reaching out to the aether and saw a yellow-green flame lick from the tips of his fingers. The pain was receding in his back. He was glad. He worshipped whatever caused that to happen, put his hands under the silty trickle, cupped them, and then drank.

After a short while he felt much better. Then he could look up at the enormous figure and move more comfortably into its sizeable shadow. Shading his eyes against the glare of the light he got a better look at it.

"Mr. Head," he said. "Why, I do believe you've . . . evolved."

The golem creature released its hand and the water stream dried up. It looked like shadowkin, if they had been into bodybuilding in a major way and made out of malleable wet clays. It even had hair, but that moved in hefty blocks as it flowed around its massive shoulders. It was naked, as he was, but had no sex organs or genital openings at all, just a smooth shape, like a plastic action doll. Otherwise the detailing was superb. Its eyes were long and slanted. They even blinked though they were not wet. But their centres were dark hearts of emptiness. Very deep. As Zal looked at them he thought they reached into a blackness that was more than just a shadow and, in spite of his heat and discomfort, he shivered.

Mr. Head put his arm down and shifted with colossal slowness on his thick feet. His ears, backswept and much longer than usual, were not the narrow tipped ones like Dar's, but flatter and thinner with ragged edges. They were wedge shaped and got wider the further they reached from his head, like the vanes of a demon pleasure boat. Close to the head they were pierced many times and hung with rings. Not a fashion Zal had seen on any elf other than ones in museum paintings.

"Can you speak?"

Mr. Head opened his mouth as if for a dental examination and out of it came voices. There were many of them, female and male, all elven but not speaking any language Zal was overfamiliar with and so many at once it was both deafening and crowded out. They were all frightened and desperate sounding. They made Zal's flesh crawl.

"Very good. Enough for now," he said supportively and gave Mr. Head what he hoped was a grin. "Welcome to the world of the semiconscious. Give me a hand."

The golem closed its mouth and there was a blissful silence. Zal held up a hand. The creature reached down and took hold. Its skin was dry and leathery and much more flexible than Zal had thought. It felt like—it felt exactly like an old fired earthenware pot. It lifted him up without effort and then stared down at their hands. It let go. Zal was relieved but attempted not to show it.

"I don't suppose you have any special powers of the ancestors about you?" he asked hopefully. "We're still going to die here in a few hours, miraculous rebirths from elemental fusion notwithstanding."

Mr. Head lifted one gargantuan arm and pointed with a finger. His resolute, immobile face followed that direction. Then he returned to his akimbo stance—waiting, apparently with the patience of a rock, for Zal to decide what to do.

"That way?" Zal looked. It looked like every other way. "Good. You must know your way around. Better than me anyway. You go first. Then I can walk in your shadow."

Mr. Head took a step forward with a purpose and impetus that reminded Zal of something . . .

"My girlfriend—fabulous woman—walks like that," he said, stepping into line behind it and trying not to notice the muscular action apparently going on in the granite-style buttocks in front of him. "Well, I say like that . . . no, actually, just like that. She has buns of steel. Really. And the same kind of . . . unstoppable mechanoid ever-ready action. I thought was all down to well-lubed pistons but now I'm not so sure maybe it's a strength-to-weight thing. Yes. That'd explain it. I used to worry she'd crush me but as it turns out she's so strong she can move as if she's as light as a feather as long as some bit of her is in contact with the furniture. Bit expensive on the furniture, mind you. Next time I should call ahead and get some reinforced pieces in, though the bed was all right once all the legs had broken and it was flat on the floor. Hotel were very understanding but then, Jelly paid for it so it was fine.

"You will stop me if I get boring, won't you? Only, I like to talk when I'm feeling anxious and the whole being-lost-and-near-death business has got me a bit rattled. Usually I keep it all under control—you can't cry in a war and all that—but seeing as it's only you and me left alive out here I don't think the old agency will mind me showing my elvish side and I'm kind of hoping that if I just go on long enough maybe just maybe you will learn to speak something I can understand, Friday. Because you have elf ears, sort of."

Mr. Head plodded onwards without reacting.

"Or not," Zal added, saving his breath for the walk, which was

looking like it might be a long one. The horizon they were headed to
seemed as flat as an absolute straight line. "Friday Head. If anyone
asks. That's your name," he said then. "Mr. F Head. Or . . . Mr. Head
anyway. I wonder what you are." And he did wonder, all the way to the
crack in the desert from which nothing radiated, or shone. Mr. Head
stopped before it.

"Faultline," Zal said looking at the matte un-ness of the Void.
"Akashic region opening. Very . . . dangerous. Very . . . in betweeny.
Very universal instability."

The giant clay elf stood like a statue. Occasionally it blinked.

"If I were a faery," Zal said, patting the massive arm next to him
consolingly, "that could be really helpful."

Mr. Head leaned over and stared into the Void. There was nothing
to see. It wasn't a thing you could see. It was a wasn't. Zal knew you
crossed it when you opened portals, but that was less of a crossing than
a pulling of two worlds together until you could punch a hole for an
instant. You didn't go over the Void, or through it as such. Necromancers did, to reach Thanatopia. Fey did, during their own moments
of unstitching when they shifted form or universe, but he had no idea
how it worked. And Brinkmen wandered in the depthless, beginning-
less, endless nothing without losing themselves—an arcane twist of
fate that, one that was a mystery to all, even those who had the trick.
From the Void came the ghosts. From the Void came raw aether, so the
demon scientists claimed, and from the Void came wild aether, mani-
festing into Alfheim in ever greater abundance, to the dismay of all his
kind. *What is not mastered lies in wait* . . . isn't that what those ancient
elves used to say?

Mr. Head pointed at the crack with a firm decision.

"We can't," Zal said, leaning back larily. "For you and me there's no
trifling with That Which Cannot Be Spoken. Speakers, elves. Singers.
We talk the world, and what you can't say you no can do. Portals. We
persuade stuff to come together. We don't do immersions and crossings

and trips in the Unmentionable. Even demons don't do that . . ." He trailed off, not convinced by his own presentation. He had been brought here, and not through a portal. "Maybe you can. But I can't."

Mr. Head remade his gesture. He reached out and took hold of Zal's forearm in a grip that had all the negotiability of time itself.

"Listen," Zal said quickly, "I know you're new to the world of ideas in general and this may be your first and a very good effort it is too but I have to tell you as an elf of the world that you are mistaken if you think that just because we're friends and you like me so much that you can pull me with you somewhere I can't actually go without . . ."

Mr. Head opened his mouth and the thousand Shadow voices spoke at once in their ancient tongue. Zal understood one phrase though . . . out of the million words . . . because they all said it together and he knew it, a name really . . .

"Abida Ereba."

In modern Alfheim it was blasphemous to utter the names of primordial powers. Especially that one. To call something of which you were not the master was always a very, very dangerous business and in the long list of things that most elves never mastered Abida Ereba was pretty close to number one. If there had been a fight between Abida Ereba and the Void itself, Zal would have given even odds but he'd put his money on the name.

He didn't want to be the biggest wimp in the universe, so when Mr. Head put out his foot to jump in Zal copied him and made it look like he wanted to go even though he'd have cut his own arm off not to go.

If you pretended you did, maybe it would seem better, and if you had to go, then you should set out like you meant it.

He was still the one screaming at the top of his lungs though, as they dropped out of the world and into the uncontrollable, unknowable, and ineffable. He tried to make it sound like the roar of the warrior and in the second or two in which there was still air, and therefore sound, he felt reasonably pleased with the attempt.

CHAPTER SIXTEEN

Lila's hair blew in the wind and battered at the sides of her unnecessary sunglasses. She'd always wondered why your hair blew forwards if you were in a convertible and Malachi's vintage '65 Eldorado was no exception. Now she could know why, complete with a detailed moving graphic of airflow dynamics, almost as soon as she could wonder. She was glad she'd turned off the AI. It spoiled things indefinably—too much information when the interesting part was the experience, and not the explanation . . . She sipped from their shared Diet Coke and rattled the ice as Malachi took the huge boat of a vehicle up to a stately sixty on the autoroute. There was nothing technological about the car. It was like a kid's toy, all huge steering wheel and big numbers with plastic indicator needles. She liked it more than she could say, and it had a ride like a sofa lost at sea, made worse by her uneven loading of its suspension. Above the wind noise the sound of Malachi's favourite girly-funk tracks on the stereo were almost lost.

"We're going to my place first," she'd said. He hadn't baulked, just turned the car out of the office lot and taken the bay road instead of the bridge. He knew her address. Driving there was a lot like it used to be, she thought. They could have been cruising back for pizza and movies after another long day training. She pretended it was so and ignored the throbbing pain in her ear and the green density in her chest as if they were the results of a minor accident.

The Eldorado, pearly green and shiny, dwarfed pretty much every other neat and zippy little personal car on the highway. Lila felt herself whale riding, moving in a world set to a different kind of scale and speed. The car turned into her driveway with a head-rocking shimmy as it met and danced over the curb, then silently stopped before the main door. The sprinklers were out on the apartments' grass, fanning the green with diamonds. Lila got out of the creaking leather seat and turned to face Mal.

"I'm just gonna get a few things. I won't be long."

"Want me to wait here?" Meaning, did she want him along as wing support.

"Nah. I'm good," she said, lying with a clear conscience. "Be a few minutes."

He nodded like he was supposed to and drummed his fingers on the steering wheel as Pink sang shocked about the state of people's hearts. ". . . they knew better, still you said forever . . ."

Lila's building let her in with a near silent click of the lock. Inside the atrium it was cool and perfumed. A faery mistlamp gave off the comforting smells of home. She ignored the waiting lift—at this time of day most of the people here were at work except Mary the escort, who was at work too, only usually at home. Up one floor and turn to the back garden view, past the public patio terrace with its maintained barbecue and serviced jardinette, its fragrant flowers, its executive vistas across the Lower Bay and Steamboat Pool. Government stipends paid for a lot, at least they did if you were a hotshot experimental cyborg who had to be compensated for the loss of a lifetime.

Her door was the second on the right. She didn't feel a thing as she opened it up. The only hint that something was wrong was the way that the air felt as the door moved in, like it pushed a little against her because it was already moving into the rooms from another place. She felt the guns in her hands open up and arm. They were a little noisier, or was it her imagination? They were a little slower.

Over the scent of baking biscuits, cinnamon, and ocean came the slightest tang of lemons. Wild magic, and its bearer, looking for trouble.

Allow me.

Tath spilled from her skin with the ease of a lover falling out of warm sheets. Lila was uneasily comforted by his familiarity and strength as he clothed her in his aetheric body and his glamour and she shrank within, the hidden iron hand inside the velvet glove. For some reason she wanted to cry.

Tath's senses were better suited by far. In an instant he was relaxed with the aura of a fighter who knows it's only a second away. He withdrew once he had discovered the facts and animated her from the centre, her trusted puppeteer for those moments where she was out of her aetheric depth. She wanted to hug him.

Aloud he had her mouth speak his voice, "Come out. Nobody's playing and I see you already." With her legs he strode into the living room.

A dark shape, like a curled giant cat, undid itself from the Persian rug and stretched out. Its colour shifted as it moved in a bewildering change of purples and lilacs, blue and white. Besides the colour the shape altered too. As it rose it showed long tail and wings unfurling, long neck and horsy head with fans, big eyes, long arms, hugely powerful body naked and shining with natural sheen. And then, as it straightened on two legs, it became much more like a man, absorbing all its natural demonic form and smoothly morphing into a handsome, slim-hipped white guy in his early twenties, silver haired and blue eyed and wearing pale blue clothes that came out of nowhere, wrapping themselves around him in strips of cloth like lovers' arms which became the fabric of a beautifully cut shirt and trousers.

Tath handed back, the perfect tag-team buddy. Lila lowered her guns. "Teazle?"

The young man bowed his head a fraction, amusement giving him an endearing monkeyish grin. "Clearly you expected someone else." He glanced at her guns.

She put them away and flexed her hands, feeling a moment's pain in her shoulder, but it was gone almost before she knew it. "I expected to find my house like I left it. Cut to the chase. I have to leave." She would have been pleased to see him, even as an intruder, at some other moment, she was surprised to realise, but now she didn't have the inclination. She walked past him to her bedroom and opened up the wardrobe, looking for something she could wear that wasn't military issue and that would cover her up from neck to ankles. Everything in it looked strangely foreign, like they were someone else's. With annoyance she began to fling things onto the bed.

Teazle followed her, his presence like a vibration on the end of her nerves, but what sort of vibration she wasn't sure. Right now it felt like irritation.

"I'm here to give you service," he said without a trace of humour.

Lila snorted, throwing a bizarre ginger-toned two-piece suit out with astonishment she had ever thought it was suitable for anything. She used to wear it to business meetings. The idea made her shudder now, the idea of all those serious faces, telling her how it had to be and what she was to do, how she was going to live—all worked out. And she would be there nodding seriously too, taking it all in and inside she'd feel like she was dying out and hoped it didn't show in case they thought she was too weak. "I don't need it."

"Yes, you do," he said. "And even if you didn't I have to give it to you because I gave you the shadowkin."

"I could have given it back," she said.

"But y'didn't. And it was no fair gift. It was a test."

"Nice," she said. "And I failed. Not your problem."

"I failed," he said. "So, I'll take all this down to the garbage and then . . ."

Lila spun around and spat, "Get this through your thick head. I don't want you, in any way. Not now and not ever. You're free. I absolve you. Get lost and play your sick jokes on someone who gives a shit."

His eyes widened and his mild expression altered to one of interest. "No. I know the demon that hunts you and I know the shadow that stalks you. You need me. And you are Hellbound. The journey is sacred to us. Pilgrims will be looked after on the way. And I am champion of Demonia and what I say I do, I do. Here." He held out his hand and slithering from his fingers, as if from the sleeve of a conjuror, a fall of dark blue cloth.

"Plain clothes will be fine," she said, turning back to her almost empty wardrobe and staring in disgust at the shapeless, sexless corporate uniforms hanging there in white and black and grey and brown.

"Treat me as your servant," Teazle said, moving up behind her. He gently touched her arm with his hand. "Made by enchantment but absolutely mundane."

Slimy little trickster.

Lila suppressed a smile, but it twitched at her mouth. She looked down at the clothes.

"You lived here?" Teazle asked incredulously as she took them from him without a word and went to the bathroom. She heard the demon sniffing the air behind her and felt subtly violated.

He can smell me, Tath said and curled up smaller. Lila thought his green increased.

She took off her military blacks and automatically put the underwear into the washing machine, checking and packing the vest and combat pants with precision into her overnight bag. She was still fully gunned and most of the loads she was carrying were chambered and hot to go. She took a minimum of spare kit with her, fitting what she could into her dusty makeup case and throwing out dried mascaras and eyeshadows she'd bought but never used—who wants to draw attention to eyes hidden behind impenetrable shades? Their pastel colours spoke of contented secretaries, boyfriends, homes . . . she shoved them into the bin. Some moisturiser, a lipstick, a blush compact, she took those and tried to arrange them on top of the flat black-metal packs of explosive bullets and heavy jacketed grenade rounds, the cargo net and the colourful vials of the pharmaceutical spares. They didn't exactly cover it. She pulled a pink and orange sarong out of a drawer and tucked that across the top instead. Knickers and bras down the sides. Shoes she could wear since her boots were really mostly her feet anyway . . . they were three sizes bigger than she used to wear but you could still get a decent court style to fit.

She pulled Teazle's tailoring over herself, put the shoes on, and then took a gold necklace off the dresser and added that. The few charms it bore were all birthday and graduation gifts from her family. The old item had a familiarity that caught her by surprise. For an instant she felt almost authentic.

She looked at herself in the mirror. The long skirt and jacket were at once extremely conservative and, with their high collar and fine seams, deceptively sexy. The plunge front didn't help much. Her bra showed in the middle and it was too plain and the necklace was girlish and too small and tentative for that kind of jacket. Her freckles stood out, and the magical stains on her face and neck and hair blazed brilliant scarlet in the dim light. Her silvered eyes . . . she quickly slapped on some foundation, cover stick, and sunglasses. Better.

She was about to whistle out of habit, then remembered Okie wasn't there. An unopened box of dog treats had gone out of date on the dressing table but a few of his hairs were still there, beige and white. She picked them up and stuck them on her sleeve then took the overnight bag back out into the bedroom and saw Teazle standing with all her clothes in his arms. He was fooling about with the mirror, looking into it and altering himself. "You need a hairdresser," he said, not taking his eyes off himself as he stuck out his tongue—thick, pointed, and blue—examined his teeth, and then sighed.

"I don't want a posse going everywhere with me," she said angrily. "Put them down and just go."

"Posse?" the demon asked and glanced at her ear. "An imp is negative posse. Is there more?" He kept hold of the clothes. In front of him the doors opened themselves to the kitchen. She heard her entire couture set go down the rubbish chute. She wished she cared but she knew it wasn't worth the fight. Nothing in the apartment felt like her. Without waiting for him she went out and back down to the car.

Malachi turned as he felt the bag land in the backseat and looked over his own shades at her. "Lookin' good."

"Spare me," Lila said. "Drive."

A big white object landed on the hood with a thump. Both Malachi and Lila jumped back at the sudden appearance of Teazle, in his demon shape.

"Groupies?" Malachi asked, though his smile was grim and he bristled visibly, hands clenching on the wheel and gearshift, locked in place. A bead of sweat appeared at his temple.

"Get off!" Lila stood up, reached over the windshield, and swatted at the big, skinny creature with her hand. She didn't manage to connect.

Teazle leapt with froggy speed and morphed in midair, landing in time for his ghostly dresser service to kit him out once again. He smiled and gave Malachi the honour of a male-to-male solid *fuck you* glare.

Lila sat slowly down and stared straight ahead though nobody was in any doubt that she was addressing Teazle when she said, "I don't have time for this shit. If you want to help me, protect the rest of my family from whatever the hell is going on. Otherwise get out of my way or I'll put you out of it for good. Mal—drive."

Malachi pushed his shades back up his face and returned Teazle's look with interest as he lazily spun the wheel and took the car in a sweep backwards around the demon. He rested his free arm on the seat back and took them back to the road in a cloud of dust, sparkling with black motes.

In Lila's ear, in a voice only she could hear, Teazle whispered, "Your servant."

What the hell was wrong with all these people?

She closed her eyes and let the wind mess up her hair.

". . . I'll be so much better, I'll do everything right, I'll be your little girl forever . . ." Pink sang.

"Stop at the store," Lila ordered. "I want cigarettes."

"You don't smoke."

"I'm starting."

"You know . . ." Malachi said, with nervous fey wisdom.

"Finish that line and you will eat this car," Lila promised him honestly.

He didn't even pause, bless him. "Menthol or lite?"

"Whatever," she said.

At the store parking lot Malachi promised to do the walky-talky necessities, and she let her head fall back against the rest and closed her eyes, bathing in the warm sunshine. Hearing the ordinary Otopian birds, traffic, and voices was a relief after Demonia's raging beats. A stream of metadata from her AI about all her missed calls and urgent messages and so forth blurted from the one bit of her insystem she couldn't turn off where work placed its most important information. It was annoying that the damn thing always reset every time she set foot back on home turf or came close to a port where Otopia Tree was active, but once she'd let it pass unanswered it went onto a sleep cycle for another hour.

She relaxed and thoughts of Zal drifted into her mind. Her reluctance to log into the Tree fought briefly with her longing to hear his voice and lost. She linked in and placed a call. When there was no answer all the sad weight of the day became crushing. Flat, she listlessly dialled for Poppy, hoping he had just disconnected and was maybe with the band or somewhere easy to get hold of.

Poppy's automatic answer system came online, the recording of her

bright tones quite saccharine and nauseously perky, "Hi! Poppy can't
answer your call right now because she has gone back to Faery for a short
stay and for the May Queen Festival. Don't panic! Poppy will be in
Otopia from Thursday morning onwards to do whatever you like and to
return to the stage for another sellout show of all perfect No Showy goodness! Next stop Transylvania. For other dates in Bohemia call Jolene . . ."

Lila hung up. She wasn't sure she could face Jolene's Angel of Death
act if something else had gone wrong with the band's schedule. Viridia
and Sand—she didn't feel she knew them well enough to call. She
phoned Luke, the bass player. He answered, muffled and half asleep.

"Shanny, listen baby, I was . . ."

"This is Lila Black. I was looking for Zal."

There was a moment of silence and then, "Oh," surprised but, she
thought, relatively pleased. "Hi. Um . . . he and the DJ had a fight and
he's gone for a few days . . . it's kinda sad because she came back
looking for him yesterday but he's not in the Tree. I think Jo said he'd
gone home for some personal thing." In the background a girl's voice
murmured something mildly complaining.

Home? "Thanks, Luke." She hung up, and then added, "Have a
good day." Home? But why? She'd been a bit disappointed he hadn't
magically appeared in Demonia but assumed he was finally taking
something moderately seriously and keeping to the tour dates in
Otopia. Sorcha hadn't said anything about a visit . . . but then she
remembered. Adai had come because she knew Zal was going to be at
the house in Bathshebat by now. Luke made it sound like he left a
while ago. So where the hell was he?

What little comfort had remained in the afternoon vanished like
mist on the wind. She sat up and opened all her ports to the Tree, maximum bandwidths, security bypasses installing. Within seconds she
could view camera feed of his arrival in Illyria at the airport and his
transit to the hotel. She could see his room, his room service bill—
pretty hefty, nothing too unusual . . . a deck of cards . . . She speed-

viewed the day she left, looking at the hotel lobby, the activity records of the doors Zal used. She saw Malachi walk in, take off his coat, ask the receptionist something, and head to the elevators . . . There were no feeds in the rooms, obviously, and as far as she could tell he didn't leave by the door that day. Zal was not recorded as having left the hotel, at least not checked out, but his activity there stopped about three hours after Malachi's arrival. Then, nothing.

She phoned Jolene. "Hey, it's Lila."

"Oh, thank goodness. I suppose Zal is with you, is he?"

"Uh, no," Lila said, feeling a cold ball beginning to form in her stomach. "I was hoping you'd be able to tip me where he'd gone."

"I assumed he was with you." The sound of Jolene's tight-lipped anxiety snapped right across all technology and made Lila's nerves ring. "He swanned off the day before yesterday, insisting he had to go to Demonia. Clearly that was a lie, but then I thought so at the time."

"But he said that's where he was going?"

"For what it's worth." Jolene managed to sound both royally pissed off and pleased at the same time. Lila didn't bother to wonder about the reasons.

"When I find him I'll tell him you're worried," she said and cut the call.

Malachi sat back down, an open brown paper grocery bag on his lap. He shut the door. Lila turned to him and took off her glasses.

"You didn't mention you went to see Zal."

Behind her eyes huge flashing messages were instructing her to report to Delaware immediately, to return to the offices, to debrief, to download. She dropped out of the network and closed down the AI once more. There was too much to explain and too little time to try.

Malachi sighed and his shoulders slumped, "I woulda," he said. "But there was all this other more important stuff I had to tell you first."

"He's missing."

"Nah," Malachi said. "He was going to see you."

"Yeah, and?"

"So, he's probably doing something first if he didn't catch up with you. It's only been," he shot his right cuff and looked at his watch, "forty-eight hours."

"Since what?" Lila demanded. "Since you took a trip all the way to Illyria to see him in person. Why?"

Malachi drummed his fingertips on the wheel and stared ahead before turning to face her. "I was worried about you."

She stared at him, checking his inscrutable orange cat eyes for signs of deceit but she didn't see any. He looked grim, and vaguely pre-occupied. "And what happened?"

"We played cards. Talked. He seemed to think you could handle anything."

"But you didn't."

He took a deep breath and his chin dropped as he fixed her with a blinkless gaze. He was deadly serious. "Li, you're not long out of reha-bilitation. The last month has been full of major shit and for some reason you and Delaware are about the only people who don't seem to notice that you're generating one mother of a psychic wake. Probably 'cause you and she are fighting for the lead role in *Cleopatra, Queen of Denial*. The only reason the turbulence isn't killing you is that you run so damned fast. But you can't keep the speed up, baby. You just can't. All of us adepts can feel your pain." He glanced at the red jewel in her ear. "Even Zal can't do it. You're going to crash and I don't want you to burn."

"I . . ."

Malachi cut her off without hesitation. "Nah, you're just doing what most people would do. The interesting question here is why Delaware is doing it too. I never had much feel for her. She's got the aetheric sensibility of haddock. It's in her interests to make sure you succeed. But instead she overrules Williams and Silly the elf, and everyone else in sight. You have to wonder about that. Except, you're kept too busy with all this distraction and that suits her fine. Nothing was nicer for her than the moment you hooked up with Zally and gave her a primary link into one of the biggest and oddest mystery people in the seven worlds. Without that she'd have had to hire an entire division just to follow him around." He nodded and soberly held out the brown paper bag to her.

She grasped it as she stared at him. Her mind was turning over what he'd said, slowly, like looking at a fragile jewel and suddenly noticing it was much more complicated than you thought. So many faces. "Six," she said automatically. "Worlds."

"Yeah," he said. "I was thinking of Samurai."

She looked at him a moment longer and saw that his frank, flat gaze meant that he knew perfectly well what he'd said, and meant it, then noticed the bag was cold. She opened it and saw a pint of mint-choc-chip ice cream and a wooden gnome spoon (see it here, see it there, things taste better off faery-ware!).

"Worry about it later," he suggested, starting the engine and backing them out expertly. Without asking the directions he drove the way to her sister's apartment—the long way, through the country park drive. Lila ate the ice cream, careful not to drip any onto her new suit. When she was done she threw the spoon into the grass at the roadside, ready for the gnomes to collect, and crumpled the empty carton and bag in her hand. The car drew to a stop. They were there.

She fumbled her shades and put them back on her face, pushing them right up close to her eyes. Her hands didn't shake but she felt like they were. In a flash she remembered the first time she'd seen them. They were so convincing she hadn't known they weren't hers until she reached out to pick up a glass of water and shattered it. Her hand closed into a fist and it didn't open until a doctor with a portable keyboard came and plugged something in behind her back. She'd thought he plugged it into a wall socket. Later she discovered he'd plugged it into her spine. It took a few months to get the calibrations right.

"I can't do this," she said, mostly to herself. As far as her sister knew Lila had gone to Alfheim on a work trip over a year ago and never returned. Nobody who knew her had seen or heard from her since. The reasons for that had always seemed so good—make sure you're better, make sure you work, make sure of this and that . . . don't want to get their hopes up and then . . . Lila, you can be our best agent . . . you have no choice but you can be it. And then don't call because what to say? She felt like they belonged in a different universe to the one she moved in now. She wasn't allowed to talk about any of it. What could possibly explain it, then? And the guilt was overpowering, crushing, because of course she should have called them to say she was alive the moment she was able to speak. How could she have said that she didn't want them to see her like this? They'd treat her the way they always had, and she'd want to kill them, because she was nothing like the same and their presence would be an eternal reproach—you left us and now you refuse to turn back. She'd be there, but she wouldn't. The Lila they knew didn't exist any more. It was easier now to live without them. She'd often thought about them dying—that it would be better. No more worry about them and knowing they couldn't think about her any more. They were dead and that era was over, dead with them. And she was free.

Where was Zal?

"Want me to come up with you?"

She shook her head mutely and put the balled up paper back in the door side pocket before pulling the ancient handle and getting out. As she straightened a sleek black car drew up in a spatter of gravel and hissed to a halt beside them in the lot. The door opened and Cara Delaware got out: perfect black suit, black shirt, black glasses, sleeked hair drawn clear of her face, perfect lipstick, killer heels. She looked about five degrees cooler than the surrounding air. Her door closed with a soft whisper behind her. Cara walked forward with a professional smile, her hand held out to shake.

"Welcome back," she said, warm and friendly with that hint of viper overtone that Lila had always admired. You knew where you stood with Cara. Nowhere.

Lila pushed the Eldorado's door closed and enjoyed its heavy slam. "What're you doing here?" She didn't take the hand which was withdrawn calmly.

"At such a difficult time I felt it was only proper the agency offered you full support. It can't be easy." She glanced at Lila's clothing with what may have been a hint of envy and more than a hint of mild disapproval.

"Nothing's been easy," Lila said. "But I'm fine. I've got Malachi."

"Ah yes, Malachi," she stepped around Lila and leaned her hands on the Eldorado's hood. "Now that I'm here to take care of things you can return to your investigations at the office." Her polite textbook words did nothing to hide her order.

Lila bristled with loathing. "I want him around."

They were interrupted by the door opening. Two dark shapes rushed out of the gap, across the porch, and down the steps, barking. They barrelled straight for Lila for a moment and then both stopped and hesitated, sniffing and looking, their heads to one side, then the other, tails wagging uncertainly, lips twitching.

"Rusty! Buster!" Lila crouched down instantly and put her arms down, hands to the floor in let's-play position. She was so grateful and happy to see them for that minute she didn't care about Delaware or whatever reason she'd chosen to show up.

At the sound of her voice they dashed forward, confident they'd been right the first time.

"Hey dogs! Hey boys!" Lila stroked heads and ruffled ears as the two ancient retrievers bashfully licked her face and wagged themselves off balance in apology for their moment of nonrecognition. She felt the softest glimmer of a strange kind of feeling from Tath inside her chest, something so unusual from him she didn't know it at first, until she realised it was the same fleeting sensation she had right then, amid the hearty bustle of thrilled-to-bits dog buddies: happiness. From behind them inside the house a figure appeared, running a few steps and then pausing . . .

"Lila?" Maxine's amazement was held back a fraction, waiting to break out. Her voice was tight and creaky, the sound of someone who's been crying too much.

Lila looked up, a smile on her face from the enthusiasm of the dogs, and Buster buffeted her with his nose and knocked off her glasses.

Maxine gasped and her hands flew to her mouth as she took in the sheer silver surfaces of Lila's eyes. "Oh my god! What happened?"

Lila didn't really blame her. Dogs were creatures of the nose. People liked to look you in the eye and that wasn't really possible with her anymore. "Hey Max," she said, straightening up with a big sister swagger she thought she'd forgotten. She was aware of Malachi getting out of the car behind her, and Delaware, closing in a step and then thinking twice about it. Rusty and Buster made happy noises, snuffling around her feet and examining her skirt hem for news of where she'd been.

Staring for another minute, Maxine came down the steps and glanced left and right at the other two, and the cars. Then with a moment of courage she decided to ignore both strangers and enveloped Lila in a tight hug. "Where did you go? What happened to you? Why didn't you call us? Where have you been?"

Don't notice, don't notice, don't notice, Lila thought as she hugged back and felt the fragile form of her always-too-thin sister. If possible she was even taller and thinner than Lila remembered. Her body felt soft and friable. Her face was grey and there were dark-brown half-circles under her eyes—still their usual hazel brown. She smelled of cigarettes and her breath was full of last night's wine.

"I was in an accident," Lila said with the airiness of an almost utter lie and glanced sideways at Delaware. "I've been in hospital."

"Buh . . ." Maxine let go and looked at the others with more unease, referring back to Lila for information with a face full of uncertainty.

"Oh, this is my partner, my colleague, from work, a friend, Malachi," Lila said clumsily and quickly in an attempt to dismiss their presence, which she didn't want. "And this is my boss. She's come to pay her respects."

Max shook hands with them both as if it didn't matter too much to her. Her eyes slid off their faces and into a distant nowhere with a greasy flatness that scared Lila more than anything that had happened to herself. "Fey," Max said with a smile at Malachi that didn't quite make it beyond the corners of her mouth. "A lot of you were with the police. I never saw so many before. I didn't know . . . Liles worked with outworlders." She finished her sentence as though she'd already forgotten the start by the time she got to the end.

"Max, you look awful," Lila said rapidly, cutting off that line before it could go anywhere. "Can I come in? They'll stay outside. We need to talk."

"Oh, sure." Maxine shivered suddenly and clamped her arms around herself, hugging her ribs through her thin T-shirt, then, part way through going back to the house turned and said, "Can we go down to the beach instead? I hate being here. We can take the dogs. They need a walk." Rusty and Buster rushed up to her at the sound of the word "walk" and bounced around for a few moments until their elderly legs had enough. They turned towards the narrow path that ran between the houses here to the road that led to the shore.

Max walked after them, stiff-legged herself, and Lila followed, glancing once over her shoulder at Malachi, who gave her a nod and indicated he'd wait in the car for however long it took. Delaware stood uncertainly, unable to enter the house or to follow. Lila was pleased but it didn't linger as she set off after Max and the dogs. Even without her assisted senses she was aware of the pale blue clapboard house behind them with its white-edged windows watching them go. They were always running out of it, along this sandy, grassy pathway, past where the expensive houses sat on bigger lots with beachfront views and crisp green gardens like giant bowls of salad, constantly cleared of sand by the eternal rain of sprinklers waving celebration fountains. Oh, she'd wanted one of those.

Ahead of her Max's shoulder blades stuck out at awkward angles. The T-shirt looked like she slept in it. A familiar, but forgotten, grinding pain started up in Lila's belly. She wanted to run and catch up, but at the same time she didn't. She didn't know what had happened, and she was afraid to find out. She walked faster and put a hand on Max's shoulder, pretending not to notice the flinch that happened under her hand. She put it down.

"You first," they both said at the same moment and for a second their gazes met and they were grinning, like the old days, when that kind of thing happened a lot and they were hoping the other would come up with a better story, a better plan.

"You look like a Regency action figure," Max said. "So, get well a long time ago?"

Lila absorbed the accusation and the observation and set her teeth. She wanted to get on with Max, not aggravate her, though it was hard. "About six months ago."

"We didn't go anywhere. Still got the phone connected. Surprising really. How lucky that the government paid out so well on your insurance . . ." Max physically bit her lips together until they went white. Then she sighed. "That was the wrong thing to say. I was gonna save it until later but your sudden return from nowhere got me on the wrong foot."

"You never needed time."

"Hah, no," Max said, "but the thing is, this time it's gonna be harder. I took your room and most of your stuff. You know. Missing means dead. And Mum and Dad, they were always such airhead optimists . . ." She stopped and put her hand over her mouth tentatively though there didn't seem to be more words to stop. They had reached the shoreline. The dogs bowled steadily over the sand, determined to enjoy themselves.

"Max, how long have you been like this?" Lila asked, trying to cut past the indirection and not notice how much she sounded like Dad. He'd never had the patience for a roundabout way of anything. He was slow, but direct. She wasn't slow.

"This?" Max plucked at her shirt and ran a hand through her hair. She coughed theatrically and smiled at herself, cynically. "This is pretty new actually. Just since the day before yesterday."

Lila was prepared to take it at face value. Max had never had much time for eating and the necessities of life. "Did you find them?" She almost winced herself at that one.

"Yeah. And I saw a thing too." As if Max hadn't been a bad colour before she paled further and shivered under the hot sky. "It was right there in the room. Hm! D'you remember before the bomb? None of these things were real." She sounded spacey and reached out for Lila's hand, finding it, then rejecting it out of spite, the way she had to when she didn't want to look weak.

Lila's heart ached but she knew any show of kindness would be wasted, until later. She stuck to the brute facts. Toughness was Max's preferred mode. "What did you see?"

"A great . . . big . . ." Her hands came up in front of her, holding an image for her mind's eye. She worked her jaw, lost for words. "Blue and white, like a huge dog, but with a snaky neck and it, oh, d'you remember those violet lights in nightclubs that made everything white shine? It glowed like that. Like it had negative light, or something. It was surrounded in that. It kinda looked like it wasn't really there. But it was. And it looked at me, Liles. It looked right at me, like I caught it doing something. I guess I did. It had these great, big, yellow eyes and a sort of snakey face. And then it faded right away. And there they were. Dead." She gave a single burst of a laugh that wasn't remotely funny and then turned to Lila, cold sober. "But of course it couldn't have been there. I imagined it. That's what the police said. They said there had to be an autopsy because it was strange, but they kept asking questions about intruders, strangers, people. I said it wasn't people."

"It was there," Lila said, looking into her sister's eyes with conviction and what she fervently hoped was reassurance. She couldn't bear to imagine the strangeness of seeing what Max had seen, the horror, and then the days alone with only the questioners for company. She had to protect her, but part of that was the truth, no matter who wanted it buried or why. "It was there. I've seen things like that." And she prayed it wasn't her doing. How could she say that part?

Max nodded, silent, and resumed walking along the dunes, stumbling here and there where the sand fell away beneath her, Lila reaching out, never quite grabbing her elbow because that would have been an end between them. The uneven ground was very dry. Lila sank deeply and slid now and again. Her hip hurt and the muscles that still attached to it twinged as she slipped once further before they made the tideline's smoother way.

"Is that why you're here? That woman. I saw her before," Max said dully. "She came to oversee the . . . when they were taken away. She took stuff from the house. I wanted to go in the ambulance but she said no."

Lila mentally drew a black line around Delaware and coloured it into a big, black block. "She's part of the government."

"Thought you were a diplomat's secretary."

Ahead of them Buster and Rusty snuffled around in the banked seaweed and driftwood. Their pace was slow, steady. They didn't look at each other.

"I was. She's part of the same department. His boss." Which wasn't a lie. His boss in the secret service, not his boss in the foreign office. "I work for her now that he's retired."

"And she made sure you didn't have a phone."

Lila drew in a hissed breath between her teeth. "I was really hurt."

"Weren't we all?"

They walked another hundred metres.

"You know, after you were gone a man came to tell us that you went into Alfheim and just didn't come back. It was all very hush-hush. He gave Mom and Dad a big cheque. Compensation. I always wanted to be in a spy thriller. Didn't you? Sure you did. Something happening to us instead of the good old ordinary way." Max's voice had taken on a loathing tone. "Of course, they pissed it away. Mom's half was her big Making-It stake. Dad's was the vodka and the golf club and all that. We had garden parties. We had a big service for you. Horses, the works. Dad gave thousands to some guy who went looking for you. Never came back. I thought he was a con artist but they'd never let go of any hope."

"What did you do?" Lila said quietly.

"Me? I worked at the Organic Café, making veggie burgers the hard way, throwing things in the juicer, putting in the hours. My girl-friend, May Lee, she met another girl, so I moved back home for a while. I saved up for a motorbike." For an instant her posture and face lightened. "I walked the dogs. I went to tai chi and did all the good health shit. I wrote you letters at first. They all came back. Course, my friends helped me a lot. I'm going to move in with Addie and Ydel next week. They've got a duplex in the Heights."

Their walk had taken them beyond the houses and the regular streets that opened onto the shore. They kept along, around the curve that led to scrappy woodland and the cliffs where the riptides were so fierce nobody swam.

Max was quiet for a while, but Lila sensed she was the one who got to ask all the questions, so she said nothing in turn, only kept her pace and felt the soft, receptive presence of Tath, who had been very quiet since her entry into Otopia. It never occurred to her he hadn't been here before. He wasn't about to intrude but he couldn't withdraw any-more. He just rode along.

Max dug in her jeans pocket and got out some matches and a folded paper pack of cigarettes. She lit one and disposed of the match with an expert flick of her wrist that put out the flame and sent the stick into the piles of bladderwrack by her feet. The sea rippled softly. The dogs explored the grassy parts of the dunes that rose towards the woodland. Max jammed the cigarette in her mouth and her hands into her pockets, looking out beyond the cliffs. "Let's have it then. What could possibly make you want to abandon a cook, a gambler, and a drunk?"

Lila recognised the look she hadn't seen before in Max. Self-hatred. It rang a chord in her that was undeniably powerful. Her stomach churned. There was a sharp pain in her ear but the words were already on their way out under automatic. "Don't talk about Mom and Dad like that!"

"Why not?" Max was almost cheerful. The cigarette moved up and down between her lips like a judge's gavel. "It's the truth. Can see why you would. Hell, who wouldn't? We spent our fucking lives on this beach dreaming about getting rescued by pirates."

"They had their shit together!" Lila roared, full of anger. "They got us out of Bella Vista. We went through school! We had a good time . . ."

Max laughed, her head thrown back, skinny neck and Adam's apple sharp against the blue sky. "We ran like there was no tomorrow. You got to be the one who got away. Nice white-collar job. So smart. Then your accident or whatever. And now you look like you dress on Berkeley Square and your boss in the government is here to smooth it over for you. Congratulations."

"It wasn't like that." Lila bit back tears with the hot teeth of anger. "I never meant to leave you . . ."

"We both wanted to, Liles. It's no big. So, what happened? Total the big man's car?"

Lila turned, her mouth full of poisonous things to say.

Keep going.

But she wouldn't. Max was only being that way because she was so hurt. Mom and Dad—they'd only been like that because they'd had it bad, tough starts, wrong decisions, bad luck . . . She could fix it, if she got a good job. And she had. If she got enough money, if she did the right things, worked hard, was a good girl. And she did, she had . . .

Max turned to face her, eyes full of a frankly undiluted fuck-you stare that was full of love and hate and, worst of all, jealousy.

"We . . ." Lila started, and stopped, because she wanted to say, *We had a perfectly good childhood,* but it wasn't true. "You . . ." *You're just talking out of grief,* but Max wasn't. "I . . ." *I only did what anyone would have done and I never wanted to get away and leave you with them . . .* but she hadn't, and she had. "I'm . . ." *I'm a good person, not this self-serving bitch.* But then again . . .

And then she stopped. She just stopped. Lila could not move or talk any more. It only lasted a moment but she realised inside it that what hurt about Max's spite was that she shared it, always had. Holidays were coming next year. Dad would stop drinking as soon as he could find some work. Mom didn't need to play cards except with the ladies who held bridge lunches on the terraces of the country club. She'd made their money and she'd stopped. Things were going to be better in the future. Real soon. Hard work at school, and then hard work in jobs, and then maybe something like a relationship with a house and more work and then the kids and some more waiting and hoping and wanting with the mysterious pain in the middle of things always there because nothing was Now and everything was on the line, all the time, and they lied, nonstop. *I'm fine. It's great. I'm fine. I'm fine. I'm fine. They're only tired. My heart is not breaking. I'm fine.*

In that minute all her anger went out. She took a breath and felt it leave as she breathed out. The whole thing. Gone on the wind and blown round the headland, towards Solomon's Folly, the place where she'd met Zal, where this journey had started. She looked at her sister, her tall, skinny, tomboy, brave sister, whose head was always partly cut off in family photos, who met her silver eyes hesitantly, not knowing where to focus her attention exactly, then looked away.

They were alone on the beach, beyond the curve of homes.

"Max, I gotta show you something."

Max gave a short little nod of someone who can't do much lest they break, expecting another lie.

Lila took off her clothes. As they fell on the sand Max snickered and took her cigarette out of her mouth, "What's this? Going freaky on me . . . whoaaaaa!!" As Lila stepped out of her skirt in her knickers and bra she also let the simulated skin-colour of her metal prosthetics fade away. Where the simulated flesh covered her hands and forearms she allowed it to separate away and pulled it off, like gloves, to reveal the black and chrome metal of her true arms. She stepped back, making sure she had room, and then just cued up Battle Standard.

The familiar whine and snick of metal moving was quiet but distinct against the sound of the surf. Lila went from a five-foot-seven medium-build redhead to a six-foot-some mech warrior, limbs bristling with weapons, changing into weapons, her normal human motion altered into the soft, sinuous mechanoid movements calculated by her array of intelligent targeting and defensive systems. In constant, weaving motion, she was set for lightning reactions.

The cigarette fell out of Max's hand.

CHAPTER SEVENTEEN

In the car, Malachi reflected for a few minutes. He felt a strong pulling inside him, and recognised it as his soul starting to separate into pieces. Pecadore: the state of falling into parts inside the soul and so becoming divided from god. In faery lore it was a grave misfortune and one to be corrected immediately, before any other ill could befall one— as it was bound to do to anyone with so much shattered negative energy surrounding them. Unreflective as he often was, at these points he knew it was worth the discomfort and effort. He was sure the Pecadore wasn't due to the politics of the situation getting antsy—no faery could care for such Vannish (this was the word for un-fey behaviours) stupidities.

He did not mind the implication that he had revealed the existence of the Others to Lila, nor the fact it went against what he had agreed earlier with Zal, who was in no position to complain in any case since he didn't speak for Alfheim, nor that it disagreed with his instruction to the other fey not to do so. No doubt they would heed his law as long as they remembered it (which in the case of the flower fey may be up to an entire minute) or until a countermand appeared, which was all one could ask.

He did not feel disturbed by the fact that Delaware was probably attempting to cover up some demonic dirty work here, perhaps with plans of her own to use Lila's parents as further experiments in her ever-experimental explorations of what power humans might wield in the newly formed (to them) post-bomb universe.

He did not mind that Jones had double-crossed her friends for the sake of staying true to her self and her driven reasons. It was almost noble, given the stakes at hand.

He wasn't disturbed by Zal's disappearance. Perhaps it would be temporary and perhaps not, but if there was another single being he was confident could take care of himself, it was Zal.

He didn't care if the tourism treaties being wrought with Demonia all failed due to a breakdown of relations here nor if the GDP of Alfheim threatened Otopian economies nor if the casual disregard of any rule by the fey was a matter he was supposed to be resolving, pointlessly, with the stone-minded humans. He didn't even mind who had killed Lila's parents, only that they had.

He was not significantly concerned about his promises to the Ghost Hunters to provide faery gold to continue investigations into the Fleet. He was sure he could achieve it. He briefly considered the Nornir, the Moirae, but they were another matter entirely. No, they were far at the end of the list of concerns and in a separate category, marked Do Not Go Here Under Any Circumstances, No Really. So he wasn't bothered about them.

He *was* concerned about what Lila was going through, and this was the fracture point. He was concerned that Delaware's bosses had created Lila in the first place and whether or not it would come to harm her more. The separation taking place was between his job, which demanded loyalty to Otopia (Vannish foolery to expect he was capable of it), and to Lila herself. He could feel Delaware as a heavy, dark presence over his right shoulder, where she sat in her own car, seething or doing some business, or both. Waiting in cars was the order of the moment whilst in front of them the empty house sat, door ajar, drapes swinging in the breeze.

Malachi considered his position. It hardly served any fey interests to trudge along with human designs here. Besides which, what was eating him, like a slow worm in his gut, was Zal's suggestion that Delaware and others might have a leak into Lila's head. So, anything he said to her might trickle out of her and down some wireless link into a grunt's daily stack of data to churn over and somewhere, somehow maybe they'd have drunk enough coffee or pumped enough smart drugs to figure out he'd mentioned the Others. And it might be two-way. He zoomed all his senses on Delaware for a minute and considered whether she was capable of ordering a takeover of Lila using her fickle AI. Would the woman have a secret code—the equivalent of a True Name?

After about half a millisecond he concluded that of course she did. If he were a dumb human with no magical senses and had invested the value of a minor city into an experiment who was supposed to . . . a-ha! He realised. Supposed to be able to operate in any area . . . of course. They must have been waiting and hoping for a candidate . . . they must have planned it out. Now his curiosity really started to itch. Between the itch and the worm and the Pecadore he was in serious need of fey antidotes to his ills. And he realised with a smile that he hoped Cara couldn't see in the mirror, that he had the perfect idea.

What the humans really needed was a distraction, to give him enough time to snoop around and discover the scoop on Lila. Two scoops, but even so . . . he began to grin as his idea moved up a level and became a Very Very Good Idea. Faery wasn't only home to the fey who enjoyed trips to the other worlds. It was home to a great deal more including many things that humans would consider monsters. But he didn't want to kill anyone, not unless he had to upgrade to save his skin. Meanwhile he was starting to see how his Very Very Good Idea could fit rather nicely with his promise to Calliope Jones. It was in fact becoming an Excellent Plan. Fortunately time moved quite differently in Faery to the speed of progress it made in Otopia. He could get things done nicely and be back without anybody knowing better.

He stretched and got out of the Eldorado to take a leisurely stroll around to Cara's blacked-out window—as if she thought that made her invisible to anyone of importance! He knocked on it and it slid down. "I need to take a whizz," he said. "I'm going to the garden at the back." He was pleased to see a twitch of distaste at the side of Delaware's mouth. She gave a nod and the window went back up. He didn't like leaving her alone with the house—seemed cruel to the house—but it would hardly take a minute.

Hands in his pockets, moving slow, he observed as much as he could as he passed between the wall and a fence, and into the backyard. The room where the parents had died was visible in the akashic range—the aetheric spectrum was disrupted and distorted, weak of course because it was in Otopia where aether barely permeated, but still, noticeable. The chaos focused on a single spot, where Malachi assumed the responsible party had stood and worked its powers. Must have been disturbed to create such a messy scene, but then, maybe it figured the investigators for mundane and stupid, so it didn't care. An ugly, spectral shadow of grey-violet jags hung in the space, moving slowly, and he knew that for the aetheric time-signature of Thanatopia. It took a powerful necromancer to create ad hoc portals, drawing the dimensions together into a moment's seamless whole. True collision would have negated the universe. You had to be very deft to avoid that. Very confident. Overconfident. A bit of a nutter, in fact.

Malachi felt his face stretched by a narrow grin that bared his long feline eyeteeth. A nutter was good news. Nutters were unstable and you could get good leverage on them. Their instability might tip them into armageddon of course, but it was a whole lot better than the odds against someone who had attuned personal power under the harness of reason. Now, all he had to tangle with was Lila's stability—an issue he fervently hoped could gain some resolution by this unhappy forced conclusion to her unwillingness to face reality.

The presence of the imp bothered him, but not just because imps fed on the leaky energies of unstable people and accelerated their decline. It was just that he'd never known an imp to be able to shift form that way. Their MO was to ride the back of the victim, talking incessantly, until death. This one had a neat trick of knowing when to flip into mineralisation and when to shut up. In fact, the mineralisation was the most bothersome part. All demons who had attained purity of crystal shifted to another mode of being entirely. Those few Maha spirits who had become free left the purified residue of their existence behind as stone and became creatures of aether, the avatars of Akasha; and the rest were just dead or trapped for the ages inside their solidified carapaces like djinniya in bottles. It was quite an incentive to enlighten up fast. Not least because mineralisation was a one-way trip. But here was a demon who used it like a parking lot.

And then it struck home—the obvious thing so close that he'd missed it all along. Just as he came into the roughly mown yard and saw its semineglected borders with all the shrubs overgrown, he realised how ordinary it was. Very few people in any kind of life were extraordinary, but Lila had picked up one and everywhere he turned now there they were, uniques, all becoming involved in matters that included her. Even this necro, possibly just executing a vendetta contract in the normal manner, was one big leap over the odds.

He felt a momentary fall in spirits—*he* was not extraordinary, unless you counted extraordinarily well dressed. And then . . . with a shiver he recalled Teazle's appearance. Not only the ex-Chancellor of Demonia, but a white blue-point demon on the verge of adulthood who looked at Lila with what Malachi was confident was more than a friendly interest. No, Teazle was either in love or in lust and it was hard to say which was going to be worse to try and handle. He supposed it was only to be expected. Power called to power. Thankfully that was Lila's problem.

Malachi stared at the shrubbery contemplatively and pretended to spot a lost object in the shadow between a rhododendron and a laurel.

He bent down and, as he felt the shade close over him, shifted scale into the vibrational frequencies of the flower fey. He removed his human clothes and stored them on a clean stone under an overturned leaf for safekeeping. Then he shifted form, felt an instant of the cold, grey, shining clutch of the Void, and emerged into Faery in his natural shape, in his natural place. That was the honest way to cross, through Akasha, none of this pulling things together, tying and cutting knots in a cosmic cross-stitch.

He shuddered and stretched, yawning widely and then shaking himself before licking his whiskers to calm himself. Sewing made him think of the Moirae and the less they came into his awareness the better he'd like it. What was moved into one's attention awakened . . . no, let them sleep on. He'd have to talk about them and that was bad enough without adding extra huge alert stickers all over his psychic self with big red arrows on them and signs saying "Primal Powers This Way, Look At ME!" Hunger came over him then, like a saving angel. He decided to think of food, but not to get any, since that would be a great help in keeping him alert. The worst thing would be to go out hunting and eat a bellyful of fresh meat, fresh, red, juicy meat, and then fall asleep in a sunny patch and spend hours in the dreamworld, unable to alter course away from what bothered him. He might be stuck for several eternities of dream on some dreadful hunt for the very things he most feared, then be pursued by them until . . . So, no dinner was a smart move. The jungle was safe for another day.

He left his lair at a leisurely pace to begin with, following a favourite trail (one which only he could see) down towards the main pathway which connected this part of the jungle with all the other parts. It was a warm afternoon, but on the dry side. His black and khaki-grey tiger stripes fitted perfectly to the shadows, concealing him from any observer . . .

"Hey, Mal! Long time no see you! What's going in the human world?" The high voice belonged to a tree sprite, one of the hamadrayadi; his girl next door. She descended from the upper foliage of the Cycad in one long green dollop of transmuting aether and assumed her humanoid form leaning against the thick bole of alligator skin bark.

Malachi sat on his haunches and commenced to clean a forepaw as he spoke. Fey voices did not require actual speech except for odd moments of calling attention, as the hamadrayad had done. Minds were enough, and the will to be heard. Given that language of the vocal kind was off, they communicated with a far more effective complex of meanings that were utterly unambiguous, transmitted from intent to recipient without the awful fouling of a medium.

[Friend in trouble. Humans stupid in usual ways (he used a symbol here that was a nod fey used to signify a proposition of universally acknowledged eternal standing). They want power in all realms.]

The hamadryad showed him a complicated visual joke about the humans trying to negotiate and/or build an embassy in Faery. They kept asking for the capital city. However, fey did not live in houses nor gather at any particular spots for any reason. Being creatures at one with the nature of their universe they existed in what, to human eyes, appeared to be a pre-Adamite unspoilt paradise. The dryad chuckled and told him the humans had been sent on a goose chase culminating in an audience with the fey who were pretending to be the Seelie Court—a thing noted out of a book that a faery called Detritus had once filched from an Otopian library about faeries. The humans were impressed and terrified and duly returned home to make more plans.

In spite of the urgency of his situation Malachi took time to laugh about this with her. "Mapuko," he said, using her daily name as she had his, "what will we do next time they arrive with a construction site?"

[The fey built a giant ark on the Shiadasi River; a thing like a showboat with sails, outfitted in the manner of an Otopian cruiser. It sails the world. Travelling players. Humans think it is parliament. Local fey get aboard, do business, get off. But is entertainment only. Calls to all ports. Job of interpreter most wanted job in Faery. All take turns to be Bamboozler. Broadcast of most funny moments.] She showed him one from memory: ["But who is the Prime Minister, or King?" a human official was demanding, rather piteously. "I am!" said the nearest fey, and all around nodded yes. "And me," said the next one. "And me!" said the third . . . beaming with sincerity, so pleased to be of help.]

He laughed so hard he thought he was going to burst something. Tears ran from his tiger face and his tiger jaw ached. He stretched out and raked the grass vigorously with his claws and did a little spray marking just to say he was home.

The hamadryad sniffed and held her nose daintily, "I not missed that!"

"Mmn, sorry," Malachi said humbly. "Carried away."

Mapuko reached out her hand and scratched behind his ears and, thinking of the time sadly being so short, Malachi assumed sovereignty and issued his global statement to every faery in the world. He explained the Ghost Hunters, their project, the Fleet, and then, carefully, inserted a code into the thoughts that alerted the listeners to beware of the next statement since it contained the Name of A Great Being, and something they shouldn't think of until it was quiet and they were alone and quite in control of things and certainly not all listening and hearing it at once and then being startled and repeating it to themselves all at once and creating one of the biggest summonings in the history of summoning. Then he said the least powerful of the names of the Moirae: the Graceful Ones, and put it into a neat image, thus reducing its power further. And fey curiosity about cosmic things of power, gods, and monsters would do the rest.

He was immediately assaulted by a cacophony of demands and put his head under his paws, though it did no good. Eventually the shock wore off and people retrenched to places they felt secure enough to determine what the hidden name meant for them. Malachi's mind became quieter and he was able to establish a comfortable psychic barrier between himself and the rest of the fey.

Mapuko was still scratching his ears—she was a good friend—but now she was sitting beside him in a slight fug of expressed sap, staring straight ahead with alert interest, the quintessential pose of a faery on the trail of an idea. She was of the Mica nation and almost as black as Malachi with a gleaming lustre to her body that made it seem as if it was made from billions of tiny flat planes and not skin at all—a reasonable inference since that is exactly how it was. Her hair by contrast was thick strands of vegetable fibre, the same as her spirit tree bore in its thick leaf stalks. By necessity they were gathered into greenish grey dreadlocks. Her vivid green eyes moved with the soft dark shadows of the forest and her wings opened and closed gently by just a few millimetres, their vast butterfly architecture supported by networks of green and black vessels with clear crystal between. Their sheet facets made them look like huge crystal windows.

When she spoke she was only repeating the words of any fey. "We have always longed to know more about the three."

"Aye," Malachi said, purring gently and laying his head down upon his folded paws. "Almost as much as we want to know about the Others."

"And Agent Black."

[Humans are very curious also. Secretive. Busy doing something we need to know about. Need to distract them while I find out more. Major distract. Must involve security agency at major level.]

Mapuko considered and came to the obvious conclusion. Malachi agreed with her and felt the glut of contentment that came along with an agreement—one of the fey's most favourite sensations.

[Mothkin.]

CHAPTER EIGHTEEN

Zal's childhood was not a happy one.

He rarely considered it these days but it snapped to the front of his mind with the clarity of a fully digitised recording that you could get off an Otopian Berrycam. He was rather amused to find that his brain considered itself sufficiently near extinction to warrant a quick review, and slightly more sobered to notice that this was the edited highlights version and not the director's cut.

The only physical sensations he had were the grip of his hand in Mr. Head's much larger, grittier hand and the greyish void of the Void—which was the universal experience everyone produced when their senses continually searched for something and came up with nothing. In the absence of all stimulation and without any knowledge when the nothingness would end, it was good to have an internal entertainment system willing to do some overtime. He didn't miss the irony of himself clinging to Mr. Head as a child to a parent, hoping to be led out of trouble. He didn't mind it. Elves had no ability to engage with the Void, if that was a phrase that even made sense. Other beings did, and maybe Mr. Head was one of them. It was the only hope of survival, and so Zal was quite happy to go with it. In the meantime, the showreels were spinning and he was still full enough of breath that he wasn't suffering.

With the speed of light, his memories played out.

Due to his mother's constant need to avoid being poisoned by members of the High Light Hegemony she moved around a great deal between safe places when Zal was a baby. After his first five years he was handed to the care of an aunt who lived in the most distant, wild, and remote parts of the Tiger Isles off the coast of Verivetsay where even bold sailors rarely dared the ferocious reefs and deadly tidal flows. The voyage there took place in a floating ship that rode the air above the waves. Zal remembered his mother at the helm, her robes flying in the wind and hair whipping around like snakes of gold. Her pearly *andalune* body covered the entire vessel and sustained its flight as the winds blew it over the whitecaps. She was singing, and her words directed the wind as her voice lent it strength. There was no crew to tell of their voyage. It was the last time they were alone together. He sang with her and played his drum and she directed the little drum to move the oars that ranked the sides of the ship. Invisible galley slaves heaved the blades of shining oak through the spray-drenched air at the tap of Suha's fingers, and around their masts birds of the ocean and the land circled together. They had both been laughing, wild, without a care.

His first name gave away the cause for his exile: Suhanathir, Half Light. His mother had discarded the offers of noble elves of the line and taken off to the Nightside to find herself a shadowkin mate. At the time this was the equivalent of finding an animal mate to the Dayside elves but Tanquona Taliesetra did not have a moderate bone in her body. She acted directly on what she loathed, determined to correct stupidity where she found it, and nothing was more stupid than the vicious racism of the Dayside, in her view. She was one of the most powerful sorcerer priestesses of the line and had no intentions of doing anything reproductively that wasn't of benefit in demonstrating that the future of the elven peoples lay in uniting and not in their lengthy and bitter cold war. At the time her insistence on an evolutionary history for the elves (something she had picked up from Otopian study), rather than the notion they had sprung from an avatar of godhood speaking directly to the plants and creatures to unite their powers and bring forth a supreme form, was heresy. Also, she had a theory about power that needed testing—that crossbreeds would be better aetheric adepts and, Zal suspected, she had had distant visions of a united race brought together by her daring activities. Proof of spirit, proof of love. She was a romantic.

But although Zal was half dark, his half-light side was respected by the 'kin and they didn't try to do anything other than put him far from polite society.

Zal was well aware of it all and tired of it by the time his aunt, Mysindrina, took over his care. She was also an exile. Where her sister Tanquo had been born with immense magical talents that were too valuable to let out of sight, Sindri had no aetheric power whatsoever in a race for whom such a thing was unheard of. Well, it was unheard of because they hushed it up, as Zal discovered when he made his home with Sindri and eleven others, who were all the same or worse. The blood of the dynastic families had suffered from voluntary eugenics. It threw up individuals of enormous power who were consumed by their own energies before middle age, and also individuals with peculiar weaknesses. The powerful rose to the top, because the Light worshipped power; for a bunch of creationists they had no trouble placing Survival of the Fittest as their watchword. Suha hated them all.

Sindri was slow, weak, and her *andalune* body was as delicate as gossamer and easily disrupted. Ordinary elven life was too stressful for her with its constant melding of one *andalune* flow and another; it would have torn her spirit apart. She wasn't the only one there. Around her others that Tanquo sent gathered themselves: the Hegemony's shameful runts without power or skill, barely able to survive their own world. Only among them Zal stood out as vital and strong, but because of his shadow parent he was without question one of them and they were his family and the windswept islands became their home.

It was because of them that Zal learned early how to completely control his aetheric self, to do no harm, and to heal if needed without destroying the other.

There was enough incident in those times to fill an easy hour of whole-life-before-you moments, but one stood out.

Between two of the islands, not more than ten metres apart shore to shore, lay a vicious strait that was as deep as it was narrow and through which the tides raced at furious rates. The islands themselves faced one another cliff to cliff and at some time in the past a rope bridge had been put across but in recent years it had rotted and fallen away. They were working on a new one. After Tanquo had made a visit that year and raised two pillars of stone on either side to act as anchors they had spent months developing cables using what materials they could find in the forested larger islands. Of course she could have raised a bridge, or even caused the islands to join together, but nobody wanted her to, not even Suha. It was a challenge they wanted to be equal to themselves. As soon as it was first talked about everyone's eyes lit up as they saw that here at last was something difficult that they had a chance of doing without outside help. In their minds the bridge already swayed, majestic and graceful, creaking and moving with the weather, secure under their hands and feet with the comforting texture of the wood and fibres that those hands and feet had crafted lovingly from the giving forest; a true elven bridge.

They spent many hours praying. Their prayers were movements. Walking, gathering, beating long branches and vines into fibre, knotting, twisting, carrying new fallen trees, swinging the adze to shape wood into planks. Their lives became the bridge. This is what Zal remembered. Long months and days of the dream of the bridge, the quiet, the single purpose, the single mind, the emptiness and stillness as if the world had stopped and was waiting for them and would wait forever if needs be. They forgot their own names. When work was done and night fell they sang and played their instruments together, letting the music rise out of them in its own form. Their happiness built the bridge and when it was done they all stood on it at once, without fear, over the hurtling torrents of water far below.

Zal remembered the Bridge of Creation, where he was made, that moment with all of them there, looking both ways, safe in their own making. They held hands, a bridge on a bridge, from side to side of the narrow way, and they had a foot on both islands.

It was not even an elven bridge, as they had dreamed. It was too rough and ugly for that with its clumpy ropes and warped boards. It was their own.

Nobody spoke. There was no need to. They were where they belonged.

Over the years that followed many of the friends died on the Islands, including Sindri, their fragile defences weathered away by time. An elf was an aetheric being. Without a strong *andalune* the body ran dry quickly on the meagre energies of food and drink and breath alone. It wore out. They were old when they died, though some were younger than Suha. With each one that departed the abilities of them all to survive, their will and their energy, grew weaker.

Their passing broke his heart and one night, sitting over yet another body in yet another Silent Hut, he felt an inner voice speak to him and tell him to get up and go. As he packed his few belongings he had no idea where until he stopped outside Sindri's old hut for a moment of parting and then he knew, just as if she had spoken, that it was time to find his father. He closed the door of his own hut and fixed it securely with a twig, then called his mother's name to the wind, because without her there was no way off the Islands.

But her ship did not return. By dawn the ocean and the sky were as empty as a dry skull.

The five strongest who remained found him sitting on the shore as the sun rose, looking out to sea.

"I will stay," Suha said, knowing the truth of the white clouds and blue sky. She would never come. "You need me."

"You will go," they said. "We will find a way." And then, without a pause, they all looked at the bridge.

"No," he said.

"Yes," they said and left him there on the shore. They cut down the bridge and made its planks and ropes into a raft with a tatty sail of canvas sacks. A boat would be destroyed but his vessel was draftless. A few pushes and shoves with a tough pole put it safely over the corals. He sang Tanquo's song to the wind.

Zal remembered the bright flag fluttering day and night, night and day, snapping in the breezes with the rhythm of the wind, its patchwork colours valiant against the vacant horizon, a black peace against the shocking brilliance of the stars. They had clothed the sky for him.

Suha sang for days and at night drifted, his father's name a mantra he repeated until he slept—Sharadar Zanhaklion.

He came ashore without the raft. He woke half buried in sand. It was dark. He was sick with salt and rubbed raw by the sea. It was a moonless night, clouded, and the place was humid and thick with the sound of insects and frogs. He lay awhile, letting his spirit find the spirit of the place, connect with it, and use it to help him purge the ocean from his body. As he did so a silence came over part of the night.

The silence moved like a snake in the grass. It flowed towards him in a strip like a new river. Suha felt the small animals leaving as the raw aether moved in vaporous charm through the dark towards him. The sounds of nature died away, leaving a vast, demanding silence like an exclamation mark. Along the path of magic something trod towards him, its feet placed with exquisite sensitivity and care, making no disturbance. He felt it only as a beat inside his own *andalune*, a scenting curious, hungry presence, a mind listening, hearing him as he heard it. In that second he knew for certain it did not follow the trail of raw aether, it laid the trail before itself as a hunter sends his best dog ahead to scent out the prey.

Zal remembered the taste of salt and grit, the cold fear of the stalking thing taking over his brief gratitude for being alive. Thinking how dark it was—he couldn't see his hands.

Suha tried to move away but the line of aether followed him, unerringly, and behind it came the stealthy and near silent tramp. He tried harder, stumbling through an unknown, scrubby landscape. It came on closer, not too fast. It had time. There was a steady confidence to it that made him weary as it made him try ever more risky moves to get away.

He fell into gullies. He twisted his ankles among loose rocks. He tried to go faster. There were moments it seemed to have gone, but the silence didn't stop, not once. And then the line of aether, and then the footfalls coming. His fear grew, his anger, his rage . . . but in time they wore him out and finally, as he crawled on hands and skinned knees, there came a moment when he found he had stopped. He sat down and accepted that there was no escape.

Zal remembered lying curled up in mud trying to think of a solution, some trick of magic or power he could use—but he'd been brought up far from the skilled sorcerers of the world. His sum total of aetheric knowledge lay in how to light fires, put out fires, conjure water to rise from the ground, and heal by laying on of hands, as long as nobody was seriously hurt. None of his family had been able to demonstrate more, and besides, he scorned the power. He wanted to be like his brothers and sisters. He remembered the touch of the raw aether—a vapour full of promise that made him feel more alive than ever. He felt the tread grow strong in the ground and then there was a smell like thunderstorm air and a faint animal musk. He felt a large creature very close. The feel of its hot breath against his skin. Stink of old meat.

He remembered a voice smiling as it said, "I heard you," full of amusement and a slight uncertainty. "Get back, back, back Teledon." There was the sound of a light smack and the big creature stepped away and was replaced by someone with an *andalune* that felt like vibrant cold water running and the shock of cold air on a winter morning.

That was the first meeting with his father and the Saaqaa who was his charge and tracker.

Suhanathir went with his father back to the Night Land, far from the reach of the Alfheim he knew, into an even older region, where the monuments to dead gods were five times the age of any mark that the Light had to offer and where there was no writing, only pictograms, and everyone remembered the history of the world, yes, even as far back as the Blind Aeon. That had come after the Winnowing, an event they knew only the name of, and before that they did not remember anything at all.

Flashes from that time were many in Zal's sudden picture show.

The huge saurian Saaqaa, twice the height of any elf, gathered in their tented village at dawn, their violet, blue, and grey hides as prettily patterned as tigers and jaguars. Families of them asleep in piles in their half caverns, snoring the day away, tails curled around one another. Teledon giving him a ceremonial armband, made out of fallen feathers from a bird of paradise that were picked for their feel and not their colour . . . holding the delicate thing on one thick, clawed finger, his ugly, eyeless hammerhead facing off to the side and moving, always moving, to keep Suha in focus. Saaqaa were legendary monsters. Things. He never forgot the second he learned that they were people.

Deep night. Never light in any home. Fires during daylight only, for cooking or making. A life of hunting and much lying around in the various layers of the forest; floor, median zone, and canopy. Sleeping the midday away. Map reading the stars. Finding a second family in his father's house. Forgetting he didn't look like everyone else.

His father trained his aetheric abilities, mostly in deep forest retreat. Zal remembered sitting in natural pools of raw aether until his butt ached and his knees hurt and his patience was long gone, waiting for the revelation of the true nature of aether that Shar insisted was the only necessary knowledge for any elf. He remembered realising it one day and then going back and asking Shar if that was it; "Everything is the same," he said. "Every being is the same in eternal nature, in aether, but they're like crystal, and you can only be one facet at a time, outwardly, but really, you're the whole thing. And everything is like that. And the conscious things are more polished and definite, and the unconscious things are . . . like rough stones. And everyone is a facet of a much much bigger jewel . . ."

"Very wordy," Shar said, nodding.

"Well, couldn't you just have told me?"

"Nobody can tell anybody anything," Shar said, his hugely elongated and slanted eyes with their white inner membranes closed against the light looking ghostly and supernatural. "But everybody can find the truth. So, there's no need."

Suha rolled his small, wide open eyes.

He met Dar there. They spent years alone together, living in shelters built each night anew, running in the Night Land.

There followed many years of which nothing stood out exactly until Demonia. None of the long times of planning and plotting he and Dar and others had made, all for the overthrow of the Light. This was not to occur by outward forces, but by inward revolution. The White Flower would be a group of elves who were distinguished by their actions. They would not take up the ways of the enemy. Years of training. Years to creep forward with the plan, infiltrating.

He recalled instead the musical instants where, in free time, he renewed his passion for singing.

Suha joined the Jayon Daga after many trials. Meanwhile the hidden business of the White Flower crept on. Finally he sickened of waiting and began to doubt his vision. He already felt old and weary by the time he entered Demonia, weary enough to do or die. Travelling there was an attempt he felt he had to make, to prove that hard-won obvious insight about everything sharing a common centre correct. If all beings were only a facet of themselves then the other parts could be manifest, and if they were then there would be no more point in the divisions that so plagued his world.

Zal recalled his father's face on being told of Suha's great plan and its reasoning, the day before his departure: Shar looked resigned and disappointed.

"It will not change anything," Shar said, then hesitated.

"I am not trying to correct the past," Suha protested, believing it until he heard it when he knew he was lying. "I am not just taking up where mother left off." Twice.

Shar seemed to reach an inner conclusion. "If it is your desire, then I wish you well," he said, which was all he ever said. And then he did something he never did; he smiled and rolled his eyes, just like Suha, because he didn't understand and thought the plan was crazy, but he didn't mind.

That made Zal smile, falling as he was through the Void to uncertain death holding onto Mr. Head's sandy hand.

He barely survived Demonia. He remembered waking up in a canal in Bathshebat, coughing lagoon water and clinging to a lump of floating rubbish as fifteen imps jumped up and down gleefully on top of him, fighting each other with unalloyed savagery for the privilege of being the next in line to his ear and shoulder. The floating rubbish turned out to be the dead body of a demon with whom he had a vague recollection of fighting on the bridge above. He pushed it down in the shallow water, pressing it into the mud as he stood on it and managed to get his fingers over the lip of the bank. The imps swarmed up and down his arms, chattering.

"He's mine! I was here first! No good you being here. He's a moronic idealist who wants to save the world. That's MY speciality!"

"No no no, he's a crazed pseudoscientist with visions of grandeur and that's what I do best. I know all the best works of misinterpreted data, statistical analysis, and wishful thinking in the *entire* library, and that's more than you do, you son-of-a-monk!"

"Both of you are wittering fools! His biggest problem is his idolisation of his mother and the longing to become a worthwhile son who wins her approval. Oi, as if you had an inkling of the trouble in this boy's poor weary heart! See how his longing to conclude that dear relationship has strangled every impulse he ever had to be himself! He's a lost hero whose cause is his own redemption and I am the imp of lost causes so get off . . . Oof! That's *my* spot!"

"Gah! You pithering toadfleas! He's got a persecution complex a mile wide, any fool can feel it. It radiates out of him like the insincerity of an insurance salesman's smile. Why else would he come here, knowing we would only torture him to death? He does it to himself because he feels he deserves punishment for his failure to save the world. Why, it almost reminds me of that stupid human . . . the one with the wood. They never learn."

"Hey! He was *mine*! The point is, I saw him FIRST."

"I didn't say not, did I? Anyway, I was right there second in line on that one and in this case it's my show, so back off dictator-maker!"

Amid the yelling in tiny voices Zal heard a soft, strange laugh and, in spite of the imp on his head, clinging to the mat of his hair, looked up. A girl with a wolf's head was crouched near his hands on the bank. Her jaws were agape, panting slightly in the dawn heat of a new day, her pink tongue like a petal over the lower incisors. She held out her hand to him and her clawed fingers beckoned him to take hold. He got the impression she was smiling.

The imps shrieked and scolded at her and made pretend moves to attack. She ignored them completely.

"I am Adai," she said in a gruff, growling voice. "Come, pilgrim. Take my hand. Be not afraid that you near Hell's gate." She paused and her grin widened to laughter. "You are in the land of the free now, where the scum also rises."

He lay at her feet, vomiting pondweed while the imps screamed at her until she savaged one to death with a snap of her jaws.

The demons were worried he would die of his wounds so they let him accelerate Hell by taking him to a Hoodoo woman who gave him a dream vision; she sent his spirit into a parallel reality where he was more able, more lucky, better at being everything he had his heart set on.

Zal agreed because he thought accelerate meant it would soon be over.

He was in the alternate world for over a hundred and eighty years.

After the first month he reckoned they had stranded him for their own amusement. After the first year he gave up on getting out. He was a passenger inside his own head, a mute observer of his better self. He could only watch and listen as Suhanathir Taliesetra returned to the Lightside world and set out to gain power in Alfheim by approved methods, always intending, once he had it, to turn that power towards the greater good.

Zal in the Void remembered the Hoodoo woman. She was an ancient creation of driftwood tied together with ropes of seagrass, cackling, "I send him where all him dream come true!"

And so they had. Suhanathir Taliesetra rose to the top of the Alfheim tree and became High Lord, over all clans and all people of the Lightside. Along the way he didn't have to compromise too many principles, after all, when he had to lie to pretend to support the structure

then it was getting him where he had to be, dragging key people with
him. The details were not important in those years. The White Flower
was a rose that would bloom late.

When it did, his reforms required the exile or removal of his opponents. He had thought surely they would all come to his way of
thinking. It was so logical and, moreover, it was true. He applied magical persuasions in the manner he had learned from his peers: aetheric
seduction of the mind was always used to bring in stray sheep to the
fold. It would be better for them to live free and in harmony, so the
mild deception did not matter. It simply speeded the inevitable.

But to his increasing disbelief there were always dissenters, the
ones who wanted to return to the strong hierarchy of the High Light.
To maintain the effects of his changes to the social laws governing the
realm he was thus forced to keep that policed structure which many of
his companions viewed as the source of all the trouble. So he compro-
mised for authority's sake. He maintained the hierarchy to keep himself in charge. The Flower began to criticise him—where was his pro-
fessed free land? He showed them, sadly realising its truth, how total
freedom and equality would only give rise to another order because the
elves only understood order. They wanted it. There was no limitation
for anyone who wished to do as they will, but to protect what freedom
there was it was clear that he must stay in control of what forces
remained, as benefactor of course, as good spirit of justice. Better that
they who wanted no order, except the natural friendliness of one spirit
to another, be in charge.

A civil war fomented.

He prevented it by a quiet campaign of assassinations and bribes.
Every day found him signing warrants, issuing exile commands, beg-
ging for a recant from someone who spoke out against his lunatic poli-
cies of open borders and the sharing of all Light lands and wealth with
the shadowkin and even beyond, to Faery and to the hated and feared
realm of the Demons.

As the shadowkin began to spread into the Lightside there began to be open fighting between the races. To suppress it Suha sent soldiers to police the region. He had to grow his army to keep the peace. He redistributed ancient stolen wealth and was accused of colluding with shadow leaders to strip the light of all its value—of grand treason, and corruption. He was taken to trial and further charged with crimes against nature when some of the Jayon Daga, his secret service, turned on him and told stories of the executions they had committed in his name.

Suhanathir sat in his prison cell, baffled by the stupidity that was all around him, pressing him down, which would surely now find a way to kill him and move on to a fresh field of bigotry and slaughter, incensed by the removal of so much money and land, by the threat of the removal of more. Stupid people. He wondered how he had got there, even at the same moment he could see the path so clearly and every stone upon it was a good intention, a hard moral decision, a righteous way. How could it be that you might offer a perfect way to the people, and they would throw it aside in favour of the momentary gratifications of their own petty interests? He had had no life of his own for the last forty years. It had all been consumed by the endless struggle to survive politically. The costs had seemed worth it for the goal. But the goal was lost, and suddenly it was clear that those costs could not be repaid in any kind. They were outstanding debts upon his soul. So many.

Zal remembered his imprisonment in Suhanathir's world crystallised in that one moment in the cell. *So much struggle*, Suha thought, lying down to sleep because he had nothing else to do. Suha dreamed of a coloured flag, flying against blue skies, and tears fell in his sleep.

Zal, always awake for a hundred and eighty years, missing nothing, stared at Suha with hatred and pity and wished him dead.

At that moment the dream fell apart. He found himself looking at the Hoodoo woman, lying drunk and comatose on white rum and blood. She snored like a bull elephant, which was strange for someone whose nose was only a dark hole in a rotting piece of wood. Adai took his hand and helped him to his feet. His body was as wounded and sore as he had left it eighteen decades ago.

Three minutes had passed in Demonia.

"Come," said Adai in her growl, giving him no time to feel any of the joys of self-control again. "We must get you to Madame *quickly.*" She hauled him to his feet, her claws scratching his skin painfully as she pulled him with her down long streets and narrow ways where healthy, vibrant demons hooted and screeched at him and tried to rip his *andalune* free of his body.

At Madame Des Loupes's house they were granted audience immediately. She came out of her home to the street to meet them and looked down at him from one black eye. "Would you choose reality over the dream?"

"Always," he croaked, leaning on Adai's side, the cluster of demons around them becoming a crowd as they sensed the brimming of Madame's power and saw that its focus was the unheard-of being—an elf. He wondered why they all rushed back suddenly to the limits of the little square as he staggered in the light on his unfamiliar legs and felt Adai at his back. Her hands had become iron on his arms, holding him up and still. His eyes watered so he could hardly see.

"Then be free," said Madame kindly, and stabbed him in the forehead with her huge, black beak, splitting his skull.

Zal remembered that all right. It had hurt like nothing in the universe. She spoke into his eye chakra, the energy centre of all he perceived. "Let there be light."

Much later, in another agony in another region of Demonia, he remembered becoming demon, his wings unfolding and setting his clothes on fire. Everything hurt a lot in those days. He cried like a little kid most nights, but that was his secret. And one day he was walking down the street, a full and respected member of demon society, imp-free, and heard Sorcha singing. He joined in and started to follow her.

All day he followed her, harmonising on her tunes until she finally couldn't keep up her cold indifference trick and turned around.

"Are you like my shadow or something?" she snapped, melodious even in that.

"I'm your brother," he sang, as though in an opera, more sure he was right about this than he had been about anything.

She laughed instantly, enormously, enough to double over and nearly fall on the floor. The demons with her looked at him with suspicion and nervousness and envy. Sorcha wiped tears of flame from her eyes and straightened up, sashayed across to him, and stared him in the face, opening her big, full, red lips.

She looked. And then she sang back, "You are, you are, you are!" on a rising major chord. And continued singing in light operatic verse,

"How very dear peculiar, I wish you were my junior,
but sadly this effluvia of flame dictates a ru-li-er . . .
of matters rather magical and terrible and tragical,
I must admit you're logical and right and true and ad-mra-ble . . ."

She paused for breath and stood back, looking him up and down.

"Your visage most inimical, your nature but a principle,
you're sadly near-invincible, your ears are truly wince-able,
but you're contemptible and sensible and all that you should be.
As brother dear I'll take you then, though sad my heart to know that
    when
I want to slake a thirst for elf I'll be hunting them all by myself."

They stood facing each other, the entire street staring at them. A light jalopy fell out of the sky as its drivers forgot to keep windtalking in astonishment.

Sorcha grabbed hold of him and kissed him passionately on the mouth with a huge, audible-from-Mars kind of "Mwa!" at the end. She turned to the audience and sang,

"Be glad it's only me that has to suffer with the sibling curse,
for I can tell you all at once that at kissing he is not the worst!"

Then she added,

"Sons of the trees were once my favourite toys,
but now I charge each one of you to look out for Pinocchio-boy.
And if you listen not to me the fire of unrequited love shall burn
each and every one of you till you're done to a turn!"

She made the flourishing sign of a live curse with one red-taloned
hand and the mark flared in the air before her. Then she turned to Suha
and spoke normally, "So, bro, what's you called at home?"

"Zal," Zal said.

"Dinner's at six. Get lost, I need to hang with my girls and call
everyone in existence to tell them I was forced to sing a fucking impro-
vised aria by a hippie tree-hugger." She pointed. "House is that way.
They'll be expecting you by the time you find it."

He remembered standing in the dark room at Solomon's Folly, full of
a wretched desire to annoy the new bodyguard, to warn them that he
wouldn't be followed, to push them out of the danger zone as the
people who wanted him dead closed in. He remembered singing
"Blame It On the Sun," channelling Stevie Wonder's voice and then
laying eyes for the first time on Lila Amanda Black as she came into
his room, surrounded by huge magnetic fields that weren't all to do
with her machinery. He remembered stopping dead, his throat shut,
able to see her before she noticed him. She was close enough to reach
out and touch and he wanted to kiss her so much that if she had only
come one step closer, he would have.

Of course, she would have killed him. But it would have been okay.

It was a fitting final moment, Zal thought as he lost even the sense of Mr. Head's hand. He fervently wished Lila would be okay.

And then he heard a woman's voice singing, clear and true and light.

I saw three ships come sailing in . . .

"Heave to, my lads!" called a boy's voice from above him in the vast grey. "Look there, lubbers in the water! Fetch the grapples and nets and make haste! Turnabout turnabout, man overboard!"

A ship's bell clanged, mournful and true.

He heard the wash of the sea and felt the rise and fall of waves.

"What have we here?" said the woman's voice and he was suddenly being hauled up the side of a vast ironclad vessel that was as real and solid as true material but cold and weightless too. A ghost ship.

He landed on its deck shivering, his *andalune* half frozen by its gelid aether.

"What have we here?" echoed the boy, a coffee-coloured ten-year-old dressed in an outsize adult's navy uniform, adjusting his tricorne admiral's hat. His bare feet poked out beneath tattered blue trousers and a sword was fixed askew to his waist by a white leather belt wrapped around three times. It threatened to trip him up but he kept a firm grip on the hilt.

"Oh this is Half," said the woman's voice, moving closer through the thick fog that shrouded them all. "But who is his companion?"

Zal looked up into the unknowable face of Abida Ereba and said, "This is my research assistant, Mr. Head." He gave what he hoped was a winning smile.

CHAPTER NINETEEN

Lila felt a sharp pain in her ear and then the scratch of claws puncturing the skin of her shoulder.

"Ta Daaa!" Thingamajig declared, standing in showman stance with a huge grin on his face.

Max sat down on the sand, not entirely at her own will, mouth open. Buster and Rusty leapt up, barking furiously.

Thingamajig kept his grin going, though it froze slightly. "Not too late, am I? Am I?"

Keeping me for later in the show? Tath asked drily.

Lila didn't reply. She stood her weapons down and allowed the skin on her arms to remake itself. It did so slowly, like warm plastic melting together. The discarded sections withered in the sun. She hadn't even known it could do that. She dressed again.

The dogs circled anxiously around Max and whined. Max just stared and her T-shirt blew against her bony body like an old flag on a fallen pole. Buster whined and panted. Rusty cocked his head at Lila, ears going up and down in indecision.

"Begone," Lila commanded Thingamajig.

"But I . . ."

"Now." She was going to cry in a moment and she knew it wasn't for her. She didn't deserve it.

The imp prattled, "I can really help you out here. I am a trained counsellor and interlocutor for all kinds of disputation and debate. Family reunions are a speciality."

Tath did something Lila didn't understand but she felt his energy leap up through her shoulder and into the demon's tiny body like lightning. The imp squealed and snapped back to his stone form. Tath's whirling assumed a pleased pattern and his smugness filled Lila's empty stomach.

It also gave her the energy necessary not to cry. She brushed at her skirt for a moment.

Max's mouth worked. Lila could tell it was all the snappy one-liners that Max was thinking of but not saying. Smart, sassy Max who always had something to say about anything. Lila silently willed her to get it together. She hadn't wanted to reduce Max to a silent parody. She'd just wanted to get the horrible deed over with, to show the truth because somehow she couldn't bring herself to tell it.

"I . . . uh . . ." Max began. "I didn't know you could get that on Medicaid." The words ran out of her mouth on automatic, like she hardly knew they were coming. She looked up at Lila's silver eyes without changing expression and babbled. "Isn't it great what they can do these days? For a minute there I thought you'd turned into some kind of lethal weapon. That's the cool version, right? Maybe they forgot to do the one with the whisks and the dough hook accessory and the can opener. Nothing really useful for the home on there . . ." She trailed off and her mouth finished on open. She sucked in a breath and let it out slowly, dug her hands into the sand.

The dogs sat down together, starting to bore now the excitement was passed.

"Wh-what does it . . . I mean . . ." Lila stammered. "What does it

look like? Is it really bad?" She needed Max to tell her how it was. She
needed to know and only a sister who'd always known about everything
would know. Max would tell her what to do about it. Like always.

Max paused and covered up the smouldering stub of her cigarette
with a little heap of sand. "You know, I think you're on your own with
this one," she said after a while, then she looked back at Lila's face,
trying to meet her gaze, holding onto it as best she could. "It looks like
way outta my league is what. Some accident, huh?"

"Max," Lila said, tight as a drum. "I think Mum and Dad are dead
'cos of me. This."

Max continued piling sand for a few moments. She watched her
work. "Pyramids weren't built in a day, Liles. Think this is gonna take
longer to get through than just some talk on the beach, isn't it?"

Lila just nodded, waiting to see what Max's plan was but so grateful
that Max clearly had one. Her sister's face had gone hard but determined.
Lila had no idea sometimes where she yanked up her strength from. She
always looked like she was about to wither away but just when the chips
were down, Max would pull out a big hunk of grit from her soul and
start wearing away at the problems with it; tough cookie.

Max sighed. "Was that a demon on your shoulder?"

"Kind of."

"Anything else in the inventory?"

"An elf. Two. One dead. One not here. A faery. The one in the car.
A demon. Bigger. Not here."

"And that woman with the death-ray hair?"

"My boss."

"I didn't like her."

"Me neither."

"She's got victim eyes," Max said. "People like that . . ." But she
didn't have to go on. People with victim eyes were dangerous. Mom
had always said so. Lila wondered how she'd overlooked it for so long.

With a groan of exhaustion Max pulled herself from the sand and dusted her pants off. The dogs got up slowly and circled her, waiting for the homeward turn.

"Julie's getting married," Max announced to nobody in particular and stretched, looking out over the water of the Bay towards the far point where the glamorous districts of the city glittered with the obscene extravagance of casino lights and hotel billboards.

"I know," Lila said. "I heard about it."

"Yeah, but you didn't hear who to," Max said, letting her twiggy arms fall and slouching over to Lila to drape one of them around her sister's shoulders. "Sorry, kid. Had to come from someone. Roberto's the lucky guy."

Lila felt herself go frozen with surprise for a moment. She remembered, as if it were another world, that she and Roberto had still been dating at the time of her assignment to Alfheim. She hadn't thought about him in ages. She supposed she ought to feel something but she didn't know what it was. Suddenly her head was filled with Zal. "Good for them," she said vaguely.

Max looked into Lila's eyes, from one to the other. "Wish I knew what that meant. Time was I could see it."

"Meant good for them," Lila said.

"You're thinking 'bout someone else."

"See, who needs eyes when you've got a sister?" Lila sighed, glad that Max was there. She leaned her head forward until their foreheads touched for a long moment and Max didn't move away.

"And where's he?" Max said, moving first and starting them walking back in the direction of the house.

"I don't know," Lila said.

"Uh-huh. I guess it's time to cook spaghetti and chocolate cake then."

Lila smiled, a small, tired smile. "Yeah."

"Right." Max squeezed her hand on Lila's shoulder then let her arm drop so she could do that free striding walk that needed a good arm swing to help it along. They both dragged their feet.

"Did it hurt a lot?" Max asked quietly as they reached the end of the sand and began to cross the dunes towards the road.

"Yeah," Lila said and it was good to say it at last. She felt better.

The dogs hustled along ten paces in front, eager to be heading back, waiting for them to catch up every few strides. By the time they were in sight of the cars both of them were walking so slowly it was hard to keep going at all.

"Cigarette?" Max suggested, holding out her pack.

"Thanks." Lila took one and hesitated, then lit the blue pilot light that activated her flamethrower on her left arm. The flame jetted out of the tip of her middle finger and she stuck it up in the F-you gesture she'd always thought it must be meant for.

Max snickered and spoke around the filter. "Bit of overkill."

Lila lit her own and took a drag of the thick, mixed tobacco and hash. She grinned and flicked the light off, nodding. "Wait until you see me chop cucumber."

Max grunted and they stopped in unison at the corner of the road. "What does that woman want with Mom and Dad then?"

"I don't know," Lila said honestly. "But I'm going to find out."

Max nodded. "You seriously think it's your fault?"

"I killed a demon," Lila answered, glancing at Max to see if this made any sense and was surprised to see Max nod. "The timing looks like payback."

"You killed a demon," Max said. "Huh." She nodded, staring through her cigarette smoke into nowhere. "Just like that."

"It was accidental. Sort of."

"Goes with the job that goes with that lighter I suppose?"

"Right."

"Never thought of you as contract killer." Max snorted laughter and smoke through her nostrils. "I guess it's a natural progression from alcholic and gambler. Kind of a step up for us."

Lila looked intently at her sister, watching for a hidden agenda that was about to leap up and beat her but it wasn't there. The wry, self-deprecating half-smile that stretched her thin face was bemused and sad and nothing else. Max gave her a grin.

"Beats accountant anyway."

"I signed up to be a secretary," Lila said defensively. "I was going to pay for grad study." It seemed so far in the past.

"Spiderman did the same," Max said. "And it didn't work out so well for him either."

Lila took a drag and blew out smoke, internally watching her blood filters start to freak at the pollutants entering her finely tuned systems. A trickle of something entered her head and she felt her mouth stretch into a grin.

"Do you have web slingers?"

"I'll get some," Lila promised. "Mention it anyway. Don't think I actually have room. Not without starting to look like the Hulk."

"What do you owe them?" Max asked, watching the black car as the dogs whined and sat down on the grass at the roadside, cross to get so close to the house and not any further.

Lila shrugged. "About fifty billion. Just guessing."

"I'll tell you what you owe them." Max flicked her cigarette to the ground and stood on it. "Nothing."

"I . . ." Lila didn't want to admit it had never occurred to her that she didn't. "I didn't get a choice."

"Exactly." Max folded her arms and shivered, as if she finally noticed the breeze was chilly. Her skin was covered in gooseflesh.

Lila watched her own cigarette burning. She'd meant that she had no choice but to serve, to do the job or whatever was asked . . . She hadn't meant what Max had said at all.

She is right.

It was so long since Tath had spoken she'd forgotten about him. He almost made her jump.

"But . . ." Lila began. "I'd be dead you know and . . ."

Max smiled, the smile of comfort, the one you give to someone who's made a big mistake and is suffering the consequences, the one that doesn't help but shows you understand.

Lila pinched the cigarette out and dropped it. She saw Malachi coming back around the side of the house, hitching his perfectly hanging trousers. He opened the door of the Eldorado and the car rocked as he got back in. A strange pain was going through her, both physical and not physical. "We should go back," she said.

Max jerked her head in agreement and the dogs got up automatically. They went back to the house. As she went up the steps to the porch Lila felt and heard the wood bend under her feet and another kind of pain inserted itself just beneath her diaphragm. It was like that all the way in. A new room, a new object, a new pain.

She saw for the first time that they lived in a scruffy, rundown house. She remembered it as palatial and grand but it was only ordinary. There was a red security tape across the closed door that led into the lounge. She pushed the door with her fingers and it opened inwards. Max had already gone into the kitchen. There was a sound behind her. Lila turned and saw Cara Delaware opening the screen door.

"That's sealed for investigation."

Lila nodded, with every intention of investigating later. She left it for now. "What do you want?"

"Just here to help."

"You can help by being elsewhere," Lila said. "This is family time."

"We need to talk about Demonia," Delaware said. "The car will do. I know this is a difficult time but I know you'd agree that the matter is urgent."

Lila bristled.

She might have information worth knowing, Tath said, a cool spy where she was still just an angry daughter.

"Okay," Lila said. "Give me a minute." She went to explain to Max what she was doing.

"Sure," Max said with a twist of her near shoulder, the move of indifference. It looked like Max shrugged things off, but she never did. Her shoulders were bent as she went to clear the sink of what looked like a week's worth of unwashed pots.

Lila leaned across and put the radio on, tuning it to a pop station. She couldn't stand the grim silence of the house another second. Max sighed. It hurt again as Lila left. She put the light on. The yellow glow should have been cheering. It only lit up the room and revealed how cluttered and dusty it was. The table was covered with books on card games and recipe books, all jumbled in piles.

She was walking out when she saw the calendar. It was showing the same scene of Nova Scotia sunset it had shown the last time she was there. December, three years ago. The corner was curled and the colour faded.

Lila walked out and down to the waiting car. She nodded to Malachi as she passed him. He lifted a casual finger from the hand that was resting along the back of the front seats, a signal that he had something to say but he'd wait. A surge of affection for him made her feel suddenly vulnerable as she opened the door to the sedan and got in next to Delaware. She wasn't surprised to hear the locking system activate once she was inside.

Delaware sniffed, obviously smelling the smoke clinging to Lila's hair and clothes. "The department is truly sorry for your loss."

Lila nodded, saying nothing.

"Please, if you would switch your communications systems back into the Incon Tree—you'd have received a lot of news you need to know." She waited. Lila did nothing to increase her links to the outside world meanwhile. Delaware sighed. "It has been a lot to ask of you in the first year. I promise, once this is over, we can find a way to give you more time to get back some kind of life outside the service."

"You didn't before," Lila said.

"We weren't sure you could survive," Delaware replied. "And there are so many who would like access to your technology. We had to be certain you weren't at risk . . ."

"Oh please," Lila snorted.

"The demons and the elves have not tried to capture you . . . we thought . . ."

"No, they didn't," Lila interrupted. "They treat me like a person. Even the fucking elves, who see me as an abomination, didn't try to chop me up for study. A little light drowning was enough for them it seems. And the demons don't seem to care."

"The systems that make you are almost unique . . ." Delaware began. "We know that there are others who do want to see them, for study and for appropriation . . ."

"Well, you must have been pretty confident to send me to places where I was in so much danger then," Lila said. She was aware as she said it that of course they weren't. They hadn't known what would happen. They had only hoped she'd be up to the task. She took a sudden sharp breath. "Zal—you knew he'd be more than just a simple kidnap. You had to. And the demons . . . all these puffball assignments . . . they were field tests. You briefed me as if it was a real job, but it never was."

"We had no choice. Knowledge of what you were was bound to leak out as soon as you demonstrated your . . . abilities. The elves would never have cared so they were first. The demons are second least likely to be a problem and we needed someone who could get into their society in a way no ordinary human could. All those reasons were valid. And you know, spies operate strictly on need to know. You knew what you needed. That is how the job works."

"I didn't ask for the job," Lila said, shivering though the car was warm enough. Her shoulder ached. Her hip twinged. She frowned slightly. "What if I don't want it?"

There was a pause and then Delaware simply ignored the question. "Lila, did you discover how it was that Zal became a demon?"

Lila stared at the upholstery of the seat in front of her. "What will you do, if I don't tell you?"

Delaware had kept her dark glasses on. She turned to face the front of the car and said in her usual voice, "Don't fuck with me, Lila. This isn't the police force or some civil unit where you get to go to court for what you don't like. No, you didn't ask to be made. But we made you. And you are our machine. As I said, we'll do what we can to get you a life outside your role at Incon, but the job will always be first. It won't be much of a life. It isn't for any of us, for exactly the reasons we're sitting right here, right now." She lifted her chin towards Lila's house.

Lila was struck to the bone by this declaration. She was so shocked she could barely speak. She knew she shouldn't have been, should have been adult enough to know it and expect that under all the nice front and the kind professionalism of everyone involved lay only this cold, calculating usage. But oh, it was a cold new blade and it hurt all the same. Around her heart Tath was a slow sad spiral.

"I want my sister protected," Lila said, when she could speak.

"Demonia," Delaware said.

"I don't know the details," Lila replied, keeping to the facts. "He made a pilgrimage through Hell."

"Many demons do. Is it available to any race?"

"They seemed to think it was installed as standard on everyone who wasn't hatched from an egg," Lila said.

"It isn't a place?"

"It's everywhere," Lila said. "All over everything. In everything."

"Clarify." Delaware snapped.

Allow me, Tath whispered and Lila gave him control of her voice.

"Hell is a state of separation from god. Whoever is separated from god is in Hell, so wherever they go, there Hell is."

"It's a religious thing then."

"Spiritual, but even those without any sense of spirit may be in or out of it. No religion is required."

Delaware drummed her fingernails on the armrest, highly dissatisfied. "How does one exit Hell?"

"Through acceptance of what is."

"Oh what nonsense!" Delaware sighed. "And then what? What happened to him after that?"

"I have no idea." Lila took her voice back. "He must have made it out and then . . . there are demons known as gatekeepers who are guardians of the exit. They have to do something to mark it or . . . I don't know. Something. Maybe what they did changed him. But they talk about other races entering and leaving Hell and none of them are demons."

"That isn't it then."

"It seems like it's a prerequisite to whatever came after. Go through Hell. Maybe it's the test."

"We have no evidence of any other race being made demonic . . ." Delaware's agitation was almost visible as a fine shimmer in the air, she was so intent. "It's not enough."

"Why don't you just ask him?"

"He lied," she said.

Lila frowned. "What did he say?"

Delaware curled her upper lip in a snarl of contempt. "He said it happened in a party while he was dancing to Disco Inferno."

Lila bit her lips together. *I will not laugh. Laughing would be completely the wrong thing to do.*

"We need verification."

Tath took over, good tag-team buddy that he was at that moment. "You need another agent. Someone aetheric. Zal was fully adept. Humans will not make it. They are aetheric passives. To attempt to create a demonic form attached to their physical manifestation would compromise their biology." *Although*, Tath added thoughtfully to Lila alone, *there may be some scope elsewhere* . . .

Delaware turned her head sharply. "At last, something genuinely new and useful I don't have to extract from a printout."

"Sarasilien would have told you that," Lila retorted, inwardly giving Tath a stroke before she realised what she was doing. Tath gave no reaction, itself significant for him.

"We are investigating what happened to your parents." Cara changed subject without turning a hair. "We'll report as soon as we can."

"Where are they?" Lila asked, dreading the answer.

"An autopsy is required. The caskets will be returned in time for the funeral. Inform me when you know what you want."

Lila nodded and put her hand on the door handle, waiting. The locks didn't release.

"You're still on assignment," Delaware said. "We need you to find out the truth about Zal's transformation as soon as possible. Take the time out you need, then find out how it was done. Returning to Demonia might be unadvisable for the moment."

"Demons are involved with what happened here?"

"Just don't go back unless you have to. You know Zal. He might even tell you."

Lila braced her feet and free hand against the internal parts of the car, gently, and with her other hand sensors scanned the door for the locking system. It was a brute-force Z-bolt—big enough to stop a truck but there was a hinge point just inside the door interior. "Don't try to use my personal life as your easy ticket." With one swift punch she put her hand through the thin steel sheet of the inner lining, took hold of the turn mechanism in her hand, and undid the bolts, pushing the door open as they thunked back. As she put her legs out, careful of her skirt, she added, "You need better locks."

Delaware looked up at her from the car interior. "Just do your job. The rest is all your own. But where the job crosses with life, trust me, that never goes well." She leaned across and pulled the broken door closed to the latch by herself, shutting Lila out. The car engine came on and it slid smoothly back into the road, gliding away into the sub-urban commuter traffic in moments.

Was your life like this? she said to Tath, before she realised what she was saying. Her heart gripped in on itself and hurt. She apologised and he accepted the feeling in silence. Her face felt tired. She turned slowly and moved to the passenger side of the Eldorado where Malachi waited in easy silence. She got in and sat there, hands in her lap, watching a gash in her skin heal with bubblegum elasticity over the metal beneath. It was a pity her heart didn't do the same, she thought. That would have been the perfect agent; get cut up, suffer a few minutes, heal over, and pass onward to the next piece of business. That was what machines did, although they didn't even do the cut-up part first. She'd make a note to mention that next time they had her in to debug her programming. A trickle of suspicion about that ran through her; gut, skin, mind, and AI-self all at the same time. "You're our machine," that's what Delaware had said. And it had been Delaware who had delayed Lila's frantic first starts to contact people until she'd agreed to give up, wait until she was settled, just like the good boss said was best. Now she wondered if she'd been eating some kind of stupid pill in the food they'd given her, or maybe there was a switch somewhere that they'd managed to flick and turn off her self-will. The worst thing was the knowledge that they hadn't needed such a thing. She wanted to fit in so badly at work, even before the change, she'd have said yes to almost anything if it made the suits happy and got her accepted into the world of real jobs and security. After that she'd have done anything to pass for ordinary; no time was too long to wait, no test too tough. It must have been like taking candy off a baby.

Inside her rib cage Tath spread out and pulsed, his equivalent of a sigh—she knew it was because she'd hit the same nerve in him that the knowledge bit in her.

Some people are easy marks, he said and named them both.

Sometimes, she replied, as gentle with him as she would never be with herself. *And sometimes they wake up.*

"What do you want, Black?" Malachi said in his normal, easygoing tone, interrupting her gently. "We staying or going?"

She took a deep breath against the vast wall of sadness staring her in the face. "We're staying. Park on the driveway and get ready to eat enough pasta to kill a horse."

CHAPTER TWENTY

"**I**'m the Admiral of the Fleet," the coffee-coloured boy announced, sticking his bony chest out as he sat at the head of the table in the captain's cabin of the enormous ship. He was perched on three cushions atop the chair in order to reach the table and was rather unstable as the vessel moved with stately rocking-horse motions through its imperceptible ocean but, oddly to Zal, this only lent him gravitas.

The seats and table were suspended from the cabin roof by iron chains. This meant that all of them seated there were quite still while the rest of the ship tilted around them. A fluttering, bee-winged fey sprite, also able to move independently of the vessel, served steaming mugs of drink from a tray, wiping up spillages with a tiny white cloth that hung over his wrist. His akashic presence was powerful enough for him to lift the tray fully loaded, Zal noticed, and that was no mean trick for a creature the size of a small dog. The only thing that prevented the situation from being enjoyable was the shivering cold that permeated his *andalune* as each of the others came close to him. That, and the intense low-range vibrations of the ship itself: they were all ghosts, with one exception.

Abida Ereba sat slightly apart from them upon a large circular bed that was suspended on golden chains. The bed was covered in pink

velvet and pink ribbons festooned the chains. Cushions of every shade
of lilac and violet spilled over its surface and many had fallen to the
cabin floor where fey verminicules sprawled upon them, engrossed in
satin luxury, grooming their ratty fur and engaging in brief but frequent and enthusiastic mating. Zal didn't look directly at the Ereba.
He was afraid he might be struck blind. The closer his eyes got to
bringing her incredible form into view the more aroused he became
and he was convinced that a direct stare—even one which didn't
attempt to take so much as a professional interest in her beautiful curvaceous breasts—would result in an orgasm of apocalyptic proportions.
That would make him self-conscious, and he was scared about the
effect it might have on the ghosts.

He was also sure it was only her presence that prevented the Fleet
from consuming him and Mr. Head entirely and he didn't want to
upset her. The nature of ghosts was hunger. Even the one which had
sucked from his hand had been impersonal and relentless. It wanted
knowledge of form, and structure, akashic and material. It wanted to
know itself. It longed to become real. Zal could survive minor ghostly
maulings, especially as he was at the time tripping high on elemental
energies, but he couldn't survive being eaten all up. He didn't think he
would survive coming at the glance of the Ereba either. He'd looked
right at her in surprise the moment she spoke on deck as he tried to
smile and had immediately passed out as all the blood left his head.
Also, he was reasonably sure she'd been smiling at him and the feeling
had gone sweet and straight to his heart even if it was routed through
his crotch first. He thought she'd looked rather like Lila and wanted to
check but dare not.

The admiral took a long draught from his cup and stared with
abandon at Zal, then at the immobile seated statue that Mr. Head had
become. Ghosts were rarely sufficiently well formed to speak or exist for
long periods so Zal stared back with equal interest at these beings he
had never seen before. From her position at the side the Ereba regarded

them all with mild amusement. Zal enjoyed the aura of pure creative bliss she gave off. It didn't surprise him the verminicules were overpowered with sensuality. He felt that way so intensely he could barely get his mind to focus on anything other than generating soft-core imagery of Lila and the Ereba, individually, or together, undressing each other, the lissom elven goddess and feisty, human, angry girl Lila . . . which was surprising because, for him and Mr. Head, the ship and its crew really represented nothing so much as immediate and uncelebrated death. Still, it livened up a tense moment.

Sailors flitted around the room, drifting through the walls and leaving again much more like usual ghosts than the admiral. Their impermanent membranes flickered and shifted between this uncertain material moment and the shifted temporal dimensions of Thanatopia where they flirted with death. Bells rang and the vessel creaked. Sails flapped as they turned about before catching the wind again. Deep in the hull, enormous engines began to turn with a steady thudding.

"But who is you?" the admiral demanded, looking at Zal and spoiling a moment of reverie where Lila, getting furious with Zal for choreographing a tantalising striptease without joining in, was about to throw a priceless antique at his head. He started, and forced his eyes not to stray towards the Ereba.

"He is Half," Abida Ereba said again, as if that explained everything. "But I would like to hear his friend speak. What is his name?"

"Mister Friday Head," Zal said quickly, wondering if this were an interrogation where answers mattered. He was reasonably sure it was for his benefit since she must know already—anything of importance was a thing she knew. In between takes of pornography in his mind he wondered what she was doing with the ghosts here. He thought about his conversation with Malachi, and a little chill made his ardour go limp for a moment. He didn't even want to think about it in words. He didn't trust anything that could have an effect on the aether not to give him away.

The Ereba wasn't like other things; not of Void or any realm. She was Other. This fact screamed at him constantly, but it was largely blocked out by his body's aching arousal which saw fit to make endorphins, opiates, and arcanoids thunder around his system like crazy horses, pretty much stampeding everything in their path flat.

"He look like a toy this thing," the admiral declared, and Zal's weakened attention span was dragged back to the present. "He like a ghost. Somehow I see ghost inside. Like he a doll full of spirits."

"Yes," Abida Ereba agreed. "That is just what he is. Zal, you have made a golem who carries the dead of the long past, just as this ship carries the souls long forgotten of the sea."

"Then we and the elemental worlds is like each other!" the admiral declared, as if concluding a demanding puzzle. He looked at the Ereba with hunger for affirmation and she smiled at him. He seemed utterly unaffected by her, as if her generative aspects were unnoticeable to him. In fact as if any of them were.

She was birth, life and death. She was the in-between moments; time itself, and space.

Zal felt her watching him as she spoke to the admiral and knew she was once again doing something for his benefit. He began to sweat. The personal attentions of divinities was one more form of special treatment he felt he could live without.

"You ghosts are reborn of the living," she said. "The elementals are not born. They rise from Akasha, from the formless to the form, and fall back, and rise again without mind. Those that are elemental spirit forms come into minds, but of their own kind. You are more like the living, because you are the children of the spirits of the living."

"I saw primary elements," Zal broke in because at that second he was unable not to, his thoughts unstoppable. He felt like the words were ejaculate from his mouth, as if the Ereba had caused a mindgasm. "In Zoomenon. Numbers. Things like ideas. Protean concepts. Propositional components. Functions. Grammatons." He stopped, panting heavily, aware that his mind almost hurt with effort.

Energies in his nonmaterial bodies exploded out. Physically he was untouched but the rest of him was coming like a train. It was the oddest sensation he had ever had in his life, and he'd had a lot. "Mmnuuh . . . Ghosts are constructs, and elementals are strip-downs! Opposition. Organisation and entropy. Mutually . . . uuuhhh . . . incompatible . . ." Pleasure and release of a great idea, a great thought, a great insight, thrilled through him from his heart to the furthest reach of his outerbody, a dangerous few centimetres from the Ereba. She caressed its periphery lightly with her fingers, as though touching air, and Zal convulsed with ecstasy, blacking out for several seconds.

He came to some sense with his face on the table. He felt pain in his fingers and realised that he had dug splinters out of the wooden surface with his nails. His groin was wet and sticky. He felt as though he was floating on a little cloud.

The admiral, as immune to Zal's antics as he was to the Ereba, contemplated Mr. Head another moment and frowned. "He's full up. Who are they? They're not ghosts either."

"Half?" The Ereba's voice was lightly teasing. She stopped touching him and he found he could see again.

"Ah," Zal said. He attempted to draw himself up to sitting, and discovered every movement he made strangely exciting. He reached out for his cup in an attempt to find a distraction. It seemed to be rum and Coke, and that was old enough as a cocktail to be a ghostly item. He breathed over the aromatic liquid and then hesitated, tired, euphoric, thirsty. "Can I drink this without turning into a . . . thing? Or getting stuck here for eternity?"

"Probably not," the Ereba said and he sadly pushed it away from him. He could really have used a drink.

Instead he grabbed hold of the nearest solid object—Mr. Head's arm—and tried to address the admiral seriously although he wasn't able to speak other than in little spurts of words which were accompanied by jolts of delight through all his being. He had a stupid smile on his face.

"I found them. Most of them. In Zoomenon. Lying about. In a kind of hole in the ground. Tripped on them. Lucky really. They're not all here."

"And what happened to the rest?"

He knew when he was being tested. "I ate them. Had to. Survival. Ohhh!"

The admiral's astonished gaze now fixated on Zal's face once more. "You ate spirits? Those not yet dead . . . like we have to!"

"*You* don't strictly *have* to," Zal said quickly, not sure if the admiral was fully formed yet or still needed a lot of filler to keep him sustained.

"And you could have strictly died," the boy retorted, quick as a flash. So, not fully formed . . .

Zal shrugged. He wasn't used to ghosts that could reason and talk back. He had no idea what fully formed meant in their terms, since no ghost had made it that far . . . "Half shadowkin. Vampiric nature. Sort of." He was aware of the Ereba purring. The sound, barely audible, was vibrating his *andalune* body. He wanted to look at her to check if this counted as sex for her, just so he could know, but he also didn't want to die at such an interesting moment.

"The dark elves have much in common with us," the admiral said and stroked his chin as if he were much older, and bearded. It made Zal grin.

"The humans say we're all figments of their imagination," Zal said, trying anything for more common ground that might involve less discombobulation in the future. And for something that might make the Ereba talk, so she might stop playing with him. It cost him every bit of energy he had. "They say we're not exactly real."

"They make good fodder, the humans," the admiral stated, sitting back. "I like them best of all. The strength of their convictions is heady meat!" He thumped his own belly like a much larger man. "But let's hear the spirits talk. I never came across real living dead!" His eyes lit up with glee.

Zal risked a flick of the eyes so that he could get a sidelong glance of the Ereba, who seemed also to be smiling and attentive. She was still purring. The purr and the aura together made him almost insensible to anything else in the room. Zal felt himself adrift on a sea of hormones that was once again starting to turn the tide against his self-control. "Ah, Mr. Head. How's it going?" He braced himself against the swaying table and tried not to lean back from the clay creature too far.

Mr. Head opened his long, bow-shaped mouth and a thousand voices all spoke at once in a babble. He didn't have to move his lips. The voices were elven, but of a kind Zal hadn't heard before. Their voices had power. He could feel it beginning to affect the aether everywhere as soon as it started. He could feel it affecting him through his swoon even, in the fibre of his being. It was like being pulled in all directions, as if his insides were trying out different shapes. It hurt. He slapped his hand over Mr. Head's mouth in an automatic gesture, not even thinking before he had done it, and gave a cry of agony as his hand grew a mouth on the back and started speaking.

"One at a time," the Ereba said mildly in a voice that was sweet and quiet and carried through the din. Zal climaxed and felt the sensation shoot straight through his body into his damaged hand, obliterating the pain with pleasure as some part of the Ereba's *andalune* body took it away from Mr. Head and set it back on the table. She closed Mr. Head's mouth with her own hand and there was silence. "Little Star, why don't you speak first?"

Zal snatched his hand back and cradled it in his lap, scared to touch it. It felt as if it was his penis, shuddering and jerking with strange delight as it remade itself into an ordinary hand again. He wasn't surprised the Ereba could do that to him. She was the Namer and Naming was the summit of power. Most likely his reactions weren't intentional on her part, but just because everything about her was too intense for his system. He knew her in this form because it was her elven aspect but she had more. She could have any.

She gave him a sympathetic glance that stroked his whole body with a touch he could feel and said, "Rub it, dear."

Her joke made him look at her. *Oh dear goddess*, he thought, and blanked out.

Zal came to slowly, face on the table again. He was woozy with self-generated happy chemicals and saw no reason to move. Either the ghosts would eat them or they wouldn't. A girl was talking in that strange old language next to him. He heard her through a haze. She was saying that some people called Idunnai had forged something called a Brink. They had put prisoners on the Brink and spirits had come out. Sorcerers had controlled the spirits and sent them into the prisoners' bodies, to merge with their true forms and make a new kind of people. But it didn't work very often. Most of the prisoners became mad. They were hunted and herded through portals into Zoomenon where they fell to pieces.

The Ereba asked how many, and the girl said very many people. All who did not have magical ability. All. She said that the successful ones became sorcerers of a different kind. Not Idunnai. She gave an elvish word that meant face of shadow. Lothalan. These Lothalan were few. They were interbred with Idunnai mages. Some of their children were strong in magic, Idun throwbacks with powerful aetheric control. But some were weaker and stranger. She said most of these were sent away, told they were going to a new world through portals. It was a story. But it was not true. They were herded up and killed, their bodies sent to Zoomenon for disposal where it was safe to let them decompose. A few escaped and ran free. Monsters, she said. Not Idunnai nor Lothalan. Monsters without faces.

By this time Zal's ardour had cooled with the talk of aetheric engineering. He was only glad of the resistance that endorphins put up, and the fact that the Ereba's caress kept them circulating. The story made him want to stay where he was and pretend to be asleep. He could sense the attention of the ghosts in the room, listening with the same vigour they pursued all information; sucking it up like dry sponges.

"How long ago?" the Ereba asked softly.

The girl called Little Star said she did not know. She had lost count of time.

Then the Ereba said, "What would you like now, lost one?"

The admiral straightened, "She can join the Fleet," he said staunchly. "All lost ones may join. It's so. I made it so."

"She is no ghost," the Ereba said.

"She has a story," the admiral corrected. "And no material form. Few memories. She is only a dream walking."

"Is this the afterworld, is it the world of the dead?" the girl asked, hopeful. "We waited to get there. We thought it seemed long, but then, maybe it does to everyone."

"Nah," Zal said, eyes closed, face glued to the wood by drool. "This is the future. You're not dead. You just lost your body and now you have to share one with . . . whoever . . . whoever I didn't eat to stay alive. Welcome. Great to see you. Was I asleep there or did she just explain how the elves got into two different forms and that it wasn't evolution, or, not the usual sort?"

"Elves?" The girl repeated the word. It was clearly new to her.

"Shadowkin and lightside. Night and day. Light and dark. A world of contrasts, and other bollocks," Zal said. "I don't suppose you remember any names from those days, do you? You and your friends?" He was rather impressed with his skill at remembering to exploit any moment for its information. Almost a fey skill. Malachi would be proud of him.

"The mage who left us there," she said. "Lothanir Meyachi Saras Evayen of the House of Abhadha-Ilia," and here she used a word Zal had never heard, only read about in old grammar books. A bi-gendered pronoun. "Shya was against the actions but shya had no choice. All the others were against shyam." She paused. "You speak strangely. Are you one of the Lothalan?"

"No. Are you?"

"I was only a servant," she said. "Idunnai-ap." A girl of no power.

Zal was almost comatose. He was dimly aware that the Ereba was doing the equivalent of leaning on him because she didn't want him to do anything now. He felt incredibly good and incredibly sleepy. His hand was still on Mr. Head's arm and he was stroking it, and he hoped the girl could feel it. He would have liked to meet her and he wanted her to know he felt a bond to her, a complicated one, a personal one. But Mr. Head's arm was only pottery.

"From now on," the Ereba said, "each one of you may choose a destiny. Death, or residence within this golem until the time of its destruction. But if you stay you will speak only when spoken to and you will not control your vessel. What say you?"

Zal fell asleep to the sound of voices that slowly became soft and slurred like the wash of the sea. He held onto Mr. Head's arm. It was warm. He was inside a woman. That was nice. He liked her very much and it was good of her to give the lost threads their new chance at being woven in again, even if there wasn't much space for them left in the fabric after so long being lost.

CHAPTER TWENTY-ONE

Lila brought Malachi into the house, avoiding the closed, taped door, and said to Max's back, "This might be a bad moment but, Max, this is Mal, my partner. Work partner," she added the last quickly at the end, not wanting any romantic puzzles leading Max to make some joke or other. "Mal, this is my sister, Maxine."

Max turned around and leaned back on the counter, chopping board behind her and her paring knife dangling loosely from her fingers. Her kitchen presence was loose-limbed and deadly, in a quiet way. Lila wouldn't have wanted to be Max's sous-chef for anything. She always reminded Lila of Clint Eastwood when she was in her kitchen; languid self-possession, tough as nails. Lila used to envy her so much, she even felt it now. Inside her chest Tath snickered with recognition and she gave him an internal shove.

Max gave Malachi the once-over, leaving no doubt that he could be whatever he wanted as long as he understood that, in the kitchen, she was the king. King was the only word, not because Max did drag, but because she had that kind of authority. For a moment his natural jungle cat and her Clint-ness had a brief stare-down, fey to human and man to man. Then some barrier was passed. Mal made a minor tip of one shoulder and Max grinned with the left half of her mouth, arrogant and pleased.

She put the knife down and came forward to offer him a garlicky hand. His nostrils twitched but he took it without flinching. Lila knew how much he hated having clinging odours on him, so it was a mark of major approval on his part. She sighed, not even knowing until then that she'd been holding her breath.

"I've been done over by one of your lot in the past," Max said, as if she were making small talk. "So, just as a fair warning, and I'm not saying you will, but if you let anything happen to my sis, you're gonna be hamburger on my grill."

Mal raised his eyebrows and grinned. "Pleasure."

Max nodded, her eyes shrewd. "Always takin' it that you aren't responsible for everything else around here."

"That was the elves," Malachi said without a pause, dismissing the entire notion that faeries could be responsible for anything unfortunate. He sniffed, and Lila saw his glance flick to the pounds of ground meat waiting to be browned. "And the humans," he added, his eyes roving over the rest of the room before going back to Max, but lower; he tended to look up at her with his chin down, Lila noticed.

Deference, Tath said.

Maybe you should come out too, Lila said.

Do you really think that would be wise? Even your cat does not know me.

Mmn, Lila was suddenly unhappy at the idea of having secrets from Max, who would take it very badly if she knew. She wanted, needed, to have Max back on her side, where she belonged. But the elf's doubt was powerful, and she didn't say anything.

"Uh-huh." Max had dismissed Malachi meanwhile and turned back to her work, picking up the big knife and starting to create hundreds of perfectly square tiny bits of onion. "I heard a lot about faeries they . . ." She hesitated and then ploughed on with determination, ". . . have a big presence in the hotelinos."

Lila knew it was because the fey there were high rollers coming to cream the best of the luck, hotelino owners notorious for running untraceable scams, or call girls and boys offering special experiences for the endless supplies of tourists and businessman who made the industry run so hot. Whatever they did, they were better than the humans at the same game. It was a big sore point in the places Max worked. The only thing the fey weren't good on was cookery, but only because they had such varied tastes in food and most of them weren't acceptable to human palates or stomachs.

"That where you work?" Mal shrugged and made himself at home. He ripped a binliner out of a half-finished roll lying on the top of the refrigerator and started collecting up empty bottles and packets from their resting places all around. He glanced at the books on the table but only in passing, though Lila knew he'd be drinking in all the information about her family as if it were water.

"I was head of the kitchen at the Tropicana," Max told him.

"Was?"

"Relationship trouble. Never date at work."

Malachi grunted, momentarily poring over a folded issue of *Bayside Bugle* before stuffing it into his plastic sack.

Lila, not knowing what else to do, went to the cupboard under the sink and started to look for cleaning things. She was aware of Mal's expert forensic eyes and that they were probably reading a history of neglect here she wanted to wash away. Naturally, what sprays and detergents there were had either run out or crusted over entirely. The only clean cloth was a half a T-shirt balled up in a corner. Sponges and mops were balls of mouldy gruesomeness, stained and covered with ancient, congealed things. Dad never managed to finish a cleaning job. He just lost interest and threw things into the nearest hidey-hole.

She found herself crouched in the shadow of the open door by Max's legs, eyes prickling with tears, biting her lip. Max and Malachi had got into a casual get-to-know-you conversation that existed solely to keep everyone on an even emotional keel until they could get dinner over with. She ought to be participating to help things along. Lila bit her lips together even harder and reached behind the empty shoe polish containers to try and find any useful thing. She was momentarily surprised by a round dish of rat poison when the songs changed on the radio and suddenly she was surrounded by the funky, drum and bass hook of the No Shows' latest single.

She straightened up in surprise and hammered her head on the countertop. The tears she'd so successfully held back sprang forth and she was wiping them on the T-shirt when Malachi said artlessly, "Hey, this is Zal!"

"*. . . I bring you back from the dead, So I can kill you again . . .*"

Lila pressed the T-shirt against her face, trying not to breathe in. When she took it away she was able to straighten up and say, "Yeah."

Malachi was unconsciously bopping to the beat as he continued his leisurely circuit of their unhygienic home life. "Didn't he write this about you, Li?"

"What?" Lila didn't think that was possible. She hadn't even known him long enough.

"They recorded it just before you left for the tour. A last-minute thing. Released it straight to download. He wrote it the first night after he met you. What? Didn't he tell you?"

"Mal, I need a word in private," Lila said, without trying to sound annoyed. She gave him a look that said—should we really be talking about this in front of civilians? But Max was already half turned, her knife poised in midair . . .

"What else has been going on that I don't know about?" She looked incredulous. The No Shows were a popular band, comprising as many races and influences as they did. They were also the symbolic heart of the Otopian eclectic free-living culture, a reasonably sized social movement, which was nowhere bigger than it was on the Pacific Coastal Rim. Of course Max would have heard of them, whether she liked them or not. They were scene. Lila found herself opening and closing her mouth soundlessly like a fish.

"I still got tons of ammo and without even a scratch on my face . . ."

"It was part of a job, that's all," Lila said, abandoning the cleaning idea and thrusting the T-shirt down into Malachi's binbag with a glare at his smouldering orange eyes.

"Uh-huh," Max said, managing to make the sounds convey the impression that Lila had better spill the details now or later.

"Jobs are security protected," Lila said, pointlessly, since Mal had already breached the rules so far they were squeaking for mercy. He hadn't ruffled a hair either, as though he didn't care. Maybe he didn't. She paused to ponder that as he continued his cleanup and went out to take the bag to the trash bin.

"That's why Cruella is staking out the house?" Max finished chopping and started cooking at the same time as she drew her conclusion; another pale rider-ism. She found a clean glass and poured a shot of wine into it, handing it to Lila who slugged most of it in one gulp. The dogs began to snore contentedly in their double basket on the outside porch. It was a peaceful afternoon, with the exception of the sealed room preying on Lila's attention, like an unexploded bomb whose detonator was hidden, timer unknown.

"You know," Max stated, all her concentration apparently on her skillet, "it doesn't take a Sherlock to figure out that whatever's got her spooked is about Mom and Dad. And I bet you know what it is."

Malachi reappeared at that moment and went to the sink to wash his hands. Lila ripped him a piece of kitchen towel silently and handed it over. "No I don't," she said, noticing Malachi's ear tips twitching and knowing he'd heard enough to know what the conversation was about. She braced herself. "I was hoping we could find out before she comes back."

"We need magical powers better than mine," Malachi said, frowning as he wiped his hands clean, concentrating on every finger and nail. "Nec—" he began as Lila affirmed, "Necromancy."

The two of them locked gazes for a moment and smiled.

"Yo what?" Max said, half-turning.

But Lila was fully focused on Malachi for the moment, her grief forgotten. Remembered important facts sprang to her head and straight out of her mouth as they entered one of those brief periods of perfectly tuned partner-function. "Max saw a demon that looked a lot like Teazle. Doesn't have to be him, though. And his talents don't stretch beyond sending people into death, far as I know. I don't think he brings them back."

Malachi nodded. "Maybe coincidence. Lots of demons have similar colourings and shapes to the untutored eye. And no telling which of any of them is Teazle's form, since he can theoretically take any. Also, he seems to like you . . ." His lips curled into a snarl of disgust on the left side of his face, exposing his fang teeth. He screwed up the paper towel into a ball.

". . . somethin' screechin' screamin' poppin' breathin' waitin' at the end of the hall . . ." Zal sang cheerfully from the radio.

"I am here. Feel free to fill me in, only I thought you said something about talking to and/or possibly raising the dead," Max said, looking between them anxiously. Something spat in the fat behind her but she ignored it.

"I don't want to call anyone," Lila said, holding Malachi's amber stare and willing him to know why, which he always seemed to do: she didn't trust anyone but him.

He dipped his chin half an inch in affirmation. "I don't know any deathtalkers. You got a plan?"

"Yeah," Lila put her hand over her heart. "I got one. I investigate the scene and figure out whodunnit. Then we go fix that. During, or immediately after, that we find Zal before my ticket to prison in Demonia comes into force." She held up the wrist with the shackle on it. "We also watch our backs for a deadhead demon and a shadowkin elf terrorista with a grudge. And possibly there might be some trouble from expired duel notices I got . . . I'm still not sure how they work. And then . . ."

The doorbell rang.

Malachi was looking at her with his lower jaw hanging slightly open. There was a smell of blackening onion.

Lila breezed on. "I'll get it, while you fill Max in on the details. We need somewhere safe for her to hide out," she said, trusting Malachi to figure that out because she wasn't sure she could think of anywhere in the circumstances. She went out to reassure the dogs as they started barking, then locked them securely into the back porch.

Grudgingly, knowing it was dangerous because it linked her more comprehensively into the Incon networks, Lila set herself to one level below Battle Standard as she walked down the hall. She needed to get back to base and get information on this incident and other things, before they figured out she wasn't planning on collecting her retirement fund. That would need to be somewhere high and soon in the plan.

She scanned through the door and saw two figures, one tall and humanoid and one short with four legs. She opened it, her left hand hanging loosely in the relaxed state that allowed maximum reaction speed, ready to defend herself.

Teazle was standing there looking recognisable but peculiarly more human than last time, as if he'd been practising. He was smiling. In his hand was a lead, and on the end of the lead was a tan and white dog of nondescript breed with a fox's tail and husky ears, wagging.

"Okie!" she said in astonishment, bending down straight away to hug her dog.

Pleased yips and whines filled her ears for a minute, and a cold nose pushed at her neck through her hair. She looked up at the smiling demon who let the lead slip from his fingers as Okie shook himself and licked Lila's face.

"I'll be your dog," he suggested, his pale eyes shining. "Even though you seem to leave us in care most of the time."

From the back of the house Rusty and Buster barked harder.

"Where . . . how did you get him?" Lila asked, fussing Okie and ignoring Teazle's remark, mostly because she had no idea what to do with it.

"I'm very persuasive," Teazle said, tossing his hair over his shoulder with a grade-A camp flip of his head. "Also, I paid the overdue fees and the bills for his shots. Haven't you ever heard of Direct Debit?"

Okie sniffed her all over, whining a little as he smelled things she assumed he didn't associate with her, like metal and oil. In her chest a strange warmth. It was wrong to be happy in the circumstances, utterly wrong, but she was.

"Oojie boojie boozum poppet, yes, yes . . ." she said to Okie, burying her face in his ruff as he whimpered.

"Something's burning," Teazle observed, his stare never leaving Lila, though his nostrils widened slightly. She was sure by the tone of his voice he wasn't referring to the dinner but used the line he'd thrown her anyway.

"Pasta sauce." She straightened up, feeling obliged to ask him in now, her face heating up—which made her furious. "There's just one problem," she kept her fingers on Okie's head, stroking in his fur. "I don't trust you, and I don't invite people in that I don't trust."

There was a sharp tug on her ear and Thingamajig appeared. "If I might . . ."

"No," Lila said. Okie yipped and then barked loudly at the sight of the tiny demon atop Lila's shoulder, envy and anger warring in the sounds. "It's okay," she told him. "It's not another pet." The barking subsided to growls.

"You never called me Oojie boojie!" Thingamajig cried sulkily.

Teazle gave the imp a look that caused it to go still and silent. "What your debased minion means to say is that proposals, defence of your life, offers of service, and the return of lost loved ones are not matters a demon would attempt in order to deceive. If I wanted to do you harm I would take the straight way. To do otherwise is dishonourable."

"My sister saw someone who looks like you killing my parents," Lila said.

Teazle's right eyebrow lifted slightly. "You don't know what I look like."

She hated it when he was right. But she wasn't wrong either. "Which helps how?"

Teazle lifted his empty hands, palm up. His human version was utterly convincing, he even smelled right. She and the dog had both noticed. He sighed theatrically. "What must I do?"

Lila looked down at Okie. Rusty and Buster were pausing in their mini-outrages to listen periodically. A sudden inspiration struck her. She looked at Teazle and then at the front steps, pointing at them. "Sit. Stay."

The demon inclined his head to her in a bow, turned his back to the door, and sat down, resting his arms on his knees and looking out across the street.

"And don't let anyone in," Lila added, shepherding Okie through into the hall. "And no barking. The neighbours are having a good enough time already."

Teazle waved lazily with his right hand without looking back. She closed the door and locked it. That was dealt with. Sort of. She wondered if she could leave him there indefinitely . . .

Back in the kitchen, Max was snapping extra-long spaghetti in half to fit the only remaining pot as Malachi talked. They both looked up as she came in, and then down at Okie, and then up at Thingamajig, riding high.

"What did I tell you about door-to-door salesmen?" Max asked.

"Oh, this is *my* dog," Lila explained. "Someone brought him round . . ."

"Someone?"

"From the kennels," she said and continued rapidly. "Will dinner be ready soon? I'm starving . . ." And, since that statement got her past the table and to the back door, she reached out, opened up, and went out to introduce the dogs to one another without waiting for more questions she didn't want to answer.

"Sooo, this is your house!" the imp declared as the screen door hissed shut. It stared around, ignoring the dogs as they tried to jump up and investigate it. "What a tragic halfway-up-the-ladder place it is too. The suburban despair of the major Otopian communities rivals any torment a mere imp could dream of. So subtle, yet so completely overpowering. Why, I bet you were an anger-fuelled harpy on the path to middle-class redemption long before they pulverized you and made you into an actionbot. Oh, look, there's a guy in the next house taking photos of us. I guess you got to expect that what with the police tape and stuff all around the place . . ."

"What?!" Lila abandoned her daydream of barbecuing the imp on a stick and swung around to look. Sure enough there was a sudden twitch of curtains from the big beige fake Georgian opposite. Who lived there? She didn't remember. For an instant she moved forward, ready to march across and sort them out, take their stupid camera and smash it flat. Then she realised that the Otopia Tree would delete the images anyway, since it was illegal to distribute information about crime scenes except via the police.

"Some people are just bottom grubbers," the imp said scathingly. "No matter what they think of themselves. Total feeders. They'se the kind of crimes gets you made into lower than imps, into asprits who have only the power of swearing and the power of naysaying. Not here though. Here it gets you a fancy house. I sees that all through your world history. S'like none of you have a sense of what's right and wrong in a being. Youse never stop the worst ones when the stopping's good and you never hesitate to string up the good ones before they even finish a sentence." It spat a tiny burst of yellow flame and crisped a few strands of dry grass that poked up between the nearest rails. "Did you know lesser demons come here on holiday to feel good about themselves?"

"Shut up," Lila said. She calmed the dogs and prepared to leave them in the enclosed porch with bowls of dry food and water. Rusty and Buster were so soft they accepted Okie without a care. It was Thingamajig they didn't like. They all snarled at him and he cringed against her head and pulled faces at them.

She was with the dogs. The one thing that was spoiling her plan right now was the imp. She had to get rid of him, at least for long enough to let Tath out to examine the scene. Briefly she considered asking Teazle for advice, but she didn't want him any closer or to be more beholden to him than she already felt. She decided to take the demon's code at face value and said to the creature, "What do I have to do so you get lost for a couple of hours?"

"Not forever?" the imp piped hopefully.

Lila groaned inwardly. "I thought that was too much to ask for . . ."

"I *knew* you was starting to appreciate me! A'course you could kill me easy. I know that. But it's an honour to be asked, ma'am. An honour. Why, I could manage a little time perusing the city's fine sights I believe . . . let's say for the sum of not less than a hundred bucks?"

Lila straightened from filling the water dishes and frowned. "I thought imps were attached until Hell was all done? No reprieves."

"Of course *technically* that's true," Thingamajig declared, rubbing his paws together and looking hungrily at the dogs' dinners. "But for people who don't want us dead we can make a few rules bend. No harm in it. But afore I go I must remind you of the salient points of your personal Hell, as is my duty." It stood straight and put its hand to its heart. "You need to face up to the fact that you were sold out big style by a whole bunch of people who don't care about it one bit. And now you're a slave of the state, and everyone who had a hand in it has their own game to play that includes you but isn't about you. They care, sure. What's not to care about a huge risky investment that's running around with half a brain of its own? That's all they know. And they'll do anything they have to so you stay in line, even give ya a fake life and a nice dog and a house and some dates with a hot elf. Sure, it's true." He paused for breath. "Now gimme the hundred."

Lila sent a banking instruction via the Tree. "And, what can I do about it? If getting out of Hell is keeping it real . . . what do I do to achieve that?"

"You figure it out," the imp said, shrugging. "Not my problem. Listen to your heart, as my old mother never used to say cos no one in Demonia needs to know that. See, I already overstepped the line. My business ends with the telling it how it is."

Lila told it how to collect its cash from a bank outlet downtown.

"One thing," it said, letting go of its aching grip on her ear. "I do know 'bout Hell. You can stay if you like. Nothing in particular will happen. There ain't no special thing about it. Sometimes it seems much better than the real thing when you don't know the real thing and it looks like a lot of pain to get to it. You choose. That's all. Everyone got their time and everyone chooses. You get me?"

"Why did *you* choose it?" Lila asked.

The imp went quiet for a moment. "I wonder," it said, head hanging low, and then without warning transformed into a small orange fireball and zipped off through the unopened screen door into the garden air, leaving a tennis ball–sized hole.

"That's fifty bucks right there!" Lila shouted after it. The dogs looked at her. "Don't ask," she said to them. "It was a stray and I was tired."

Back in the kitchen the pasta was in the water. Max was listening to Malachi do a good impression of a secret agent with everyone's best interests at heart. They were both seated at the table. All the *Great White* poker magazines belonging to mother had been stacked on the counter. The top issue promised How to Hold 'Em Out for More.

"I'm going in to do the search," Lila said, at a break in Malachi's talk. "Stay here and I'll be back in ten minutes."

"I'll come with you," Malachi started to stand up.

"No," Lila held out her hand. "I've got the AI. I'll get whatever's there, then you can do an aetheric pass if you want to." It was a bit of a weak excuse but he saw her determination and sat back down.

"Sure, go ahead."

She nodded and slipped out into the hall. Her status was still high alert and she left it like that, pausing a moment to let her AI configure a set of responses to all her Incon instreaming commands so that people wouldn't think she was ignoring them. Then she checked the outgoing feeds and detached a minicam from a supply inside her arm cavity. She went upstairs and stuck it inside her room then switched all her outgoing information centres to that unit. It wasn't much of a ruse but hopefully she'd been so obedient in the past they'd fall for it if they chose to sneak an unwholesome inside peek on her where-abouts. She didn't linger to see what changes Max had made to her place, just went out again as though it was any other building she had to recon, but her cool left her when she reached the downstairs hall.

She stopped before the locked room and looked at the door. Dark fingermarks decorated the edge of it under the lines of red and white crime scene tape, left there by years of pulling and pushing without bothering to use the handle: hers too, she'd bet. With a jerk she pulled herself out of the reverie and looked more closely at the tape. It was the work of a few moments to pick the pathetic little doorknob lock, push the door open, and limbo under the thigh-height lowest line.

There were the cards, the vodka glass, the hollows in the sofa, the white piano, the dusty photographs missing occasional bodyparts at the edges. She waited for intuition or fear to hit her like oncoming cars in a lengthy train wreck but what struck her instead was the sense of how unreal the room seemed. She remembered it, but standing in it was like being inside a museum of her own life, so far removed that it might as well be archaeology. The feeling that washed through her was nostalgia followed by a lingering anxiety that made her want to leave as quickly as possible.

She bent down to look at the cards: two of clubs, six and nine of spades, Jack of Hearts . . . a shitty hand. The rest of the deck was sliding to the side towards the rimline of a splatter of dried vodka tonic. Next up: eight of spades. Why would that be face up? Maybe her mother had just picked it up . . .

Let me, Tath said.

She almost jumped. His presence had become so familiar she didn't know when he'd started to seem like part of her. "How?" she asked but he was already spreading out through and beyond her body, his aetherial form much stronger than she anticipated. Full of demon?

Has to be some benefit, he replied.

She couldn't really see his *andalune* body in this light, not in Otopia, but she had a clear sense of where it began and ended.

I need the whole thing, he said and suddenly she was immersed in him. They hadn't been like that since the night in Arië's palace. She knew that now, if anybody walked in, they'd only see elf. His power and glamour coated her absolutely as he took on his most articulate magical form. She shrank back to give him bodily control, surprised at the change that came with becoming the one who was inside. Last time he had been commanded to his performances. This time it was entirely voluntary and with that came a strange vulnerability she hadn't anticipated, hers and his. He enveloped her and infused her body but he didn't attempt to touch her mind, or heart. It was a peculiar tenderness. She was suddenly speechless in the presence of it.

But Tath, if he noticed, passed over the moment to briefly exult in his freedom. *Warp residue*, he said, and she had no idea what he was talking about—at least, she detected nothing. *It is everywhere in this region, like trash magic.*

Meaning?

A necromancer took them into Thanatopia; stolen away in time. He breathed, even though he had to use her lungs. He reached out and touched the cards, one at a time, with the tips of his fingers. *Regrettably I have no blood, else I could track the lines.*

Won't mine do?

No. He touched the glass and shivered, his entire form rippling with waves of aetheric disturbances. Lila was desperate to ask him what they were but she daren't interrupt him. As he worked she could feel his self-command. His revulsion was strong but he ignored it. There was so much she didn't know about the death realm, so much his work defied in the world of her human knowledge.

Can you tell who did it? Where they went?

Only by following the path. He went back to the glass and picked it up, holding it in his/her hand carefully. *It decays. Already it is very old.*

You mean go after them. Into Thanatopia?

Yes. Tath sighed and turned the glass over, looking at the thick bottom of the plain tumbler which was shaped like an irregular lens. *Time is place,* he said. *You think this room is in the same place that you left it, but every second that passes alters its position in the whole fabric. When your parents were taken, it was not from here. It was from Ago. Even the track of the world cannot go back to it though if you had a craft you might . . . but you have not. We cannot reach Ago from here without crossing over. We can only track in Thanatopia.*

Lila wasn't sure she got it but it would do. *And you need blood?*

I have the demon to ride. I do not need blood. The demon's spirit will take me over. But I need a living form in order to return. The part of us that passes into Thanatopia is not the material body, but the aetheric. But the aether cannot exist here without the material form and cannot return without one.

How did it take my parents? We're human. No aether.

Humans have subtle bodies that may cross over—I believe you call it astral travel. Those forms are quasi-aetheric. I know little about them. I have never tracked or spoken to human dead. He set the glass down exactly where it had been and went to sit down where her mother had been. He closed their eyes. Lila felt cold, jumpy. He was calm though across the surface of her skin Lila felt him scattering and jittering as though he was being electrocuted. He was strong, sad, determined. *If we are to find them at all it must be soon, within hours. I have no instruments or charms—nothing. Only my pact with the undead.*

The who? She wasn't sure she'd heard him right.

He ignored her. *Lila, if we are to do this thing you will have to come with me. We must go together. Otherwise I will be trapped in Thanatopia, as if I am truly dead, and I will never cross back. I have never attempted to carry a spirit, although I know it can be done. Just as I ride the demon, I can be ridden.*

Like a conga? She supplied the image of party dancers in a huge line.

Something like this. For a moment he almost smiled, the soft glow of affection blinking on and out in him like the glimmer of a distant lightning bug. *But you will be the one to carry me back because you are the only one who can find yourself in time on this side. Your astral form will call to and be called by your gross forms. As long as they persist you will be able to find them.*

He opened their eyes and looked around. *Other Necromancers have been here but they did not track. I feel their touches. Fey. They will have known it was a demon, and that it came here and left here through the dead gates into time. It dragged your parents with it.*

But they died . . . she said hesitantly.

Tath was quiet.

Tath, if they didn't die . . . why did they look so dead in the picture? Why have they been taken away to . . . She stopped suddenly. A shiver went through her that had nothing to do with him or where they were. Are they dead?

When a spirit rides through the gate the body left behind will maintain life unless it is so badly damaged it cannot. If it dies, then the spirit will remain in Thanatopia, as with any dead. If it survives, the spirit can return. But those who are not necromancers do not cross into or out of Thanatopia at will. Only one who has a pact with the undead has the ability to transect the barrier. If you are taken across, you must also be taken back.

So, they're what, stuck there?

It was a punishment of certain dynasties, Tath said tonelessly. He didn't elaborate and Lila didn't press it.

If they come back . . . does it matter how long has passed? Can anyone just come back at any time? She was trying not to hope, not to dream it could be fixed.

Return after the passage of years was the final part of the punishment, Tath said. *Entropy takes its toll. The longer the separation the worse the fit upon return, because time passes differently in Thanatopia. After a long time, there can be no reunion.*

Worse than death?

They are known as the Sundered. Lost souls who live and appear to be themselves, but they are constantly torn between realities. It is not a pleasant existence. They do not know if they are alive or dead.

Lila sat for a while. What happens to ordinary dead people, over there?

In the time of your life here you have a life in Thanatopia that is the same, exactly, in every way. But there you exist only in this astral form, as energy. On your death the body is released and you cannot persist in physical realities. Thereafter the astral self undergoes a brief incorporeal existence in Thanatopia. The living and the dead are present there, but in different forms. It is hard to say, without showing you.

So, I can talk to people who are dead?

Yes. You can even talk to them when they were still alive, but none who are not Necromances know this part. It is our secret.

She thought of it and he denied it at the same moment.

You cannot go back and warn them. The means of talking with them would only frighten them. It is rare any living person can heed the warnings of their deathform, especially humans. The astral does not speak with a voice. His conviction was clear.

Right, she said. If we're going, we're going. Let's get it over with. That spaghetti is going to be done in about two minutes' time.

As you wish, he said.

How . . . she began to say but the room had already vanished.

CHAPTER TWENTY~TWO

Zal woke with a start. He expected to see ghosts, hear bells, feel the ocean, but instead he heard the sound of distant TV and felt the sponginess of a hotel bed. He rolled over and found himself face to face with the implacable, gigantic, terracotta face of Mr. Head; in the near dark it looked like a giant black mountain.

He jumped so badly he almost ended up on the floor. Clutching the sheet to his chin he stared at the immobile features with their ever-open eyes. "A Buddha statue would never have done that," he said, accusingly, although he wasn't even sure exactly what he meant by it himself.

The clay man simply lay, an unwieldy statue that might have been stolen from some over-the-top hotelino tableau during a drunken binge. Zal stared around him, eyes adjusting to the blackout, and came to recognise the decor. He might be anywhere in Otopia, but he was in a Bellevue Deluxe apartment. It looked like the one he'd left behind in Illyria. They all did.

Another few moments revealed that he was fully dressed in his filthy, ruined clothing, boots and all. There was a certain sloppy kind of feeling in his pants but that was less dispiriting than he had thought it would be. He felt mildly pleased with himself for no adequate reason and then he remembered: Lila, Demonia, Malachi, Lila.

"What day is it?" he rolled over and picked up the telephone. "Hello, yes. Where is this hotel, please? Thanks. What's the date and time? Thanks. Send me a steak sandwich and orange juice. A bucket of orange juice. And some painkillers. No, the whole box. And get me a cab. To Ikea. Yes. Ikea. Yes, now. I know it's midnight. Sandwich, juice, pills, cab. Right."

Zal grabbed an apple from the bedside display and slipped out to the bathroom, practising his silent mode. However, he was so focused on what he was doing in terms of what he had to do once he got out of Otopia that he missed a move and caught his hip on the corner of the dressing table. It didn't make a big noise but it hurt and he realised he had got into the habit of holding his *andalune* clenched tightly inside because of the fear of the ghosts. It was making him human-clumsy. He had to take a moment and try to relax. It wasn't like him to panic and he didn't understand why he was doing just that. Realising his state made him sober, and that in turn let him know that he had been high.

A moment of calm let his nose tell him that silent was also irrelevant—he stank. Despite his need to get clean and dressed ready to leave he made himself wait to at least allow his spirit body to spread out. And then he realised that even though he had stopped and waited, and was fine and himself, it still had not released.

He tried again, not even knowing how to try since it had always been a completely natural thing to let that body spread out and move at its own will. Nothing happened. He bit into the apple, sure that the contact with one of nature's own objects would pull it forward from its hiding place. Fruit dishes featured large in his hotel orders for exactly that reason—since there was precious little else in a standard hotel room that was friendly to the spirit body.

There was a brief flicker in his throat, but something odd about it. The apple was tart. He swallowed and bit again, suddenly starving, his stomach painful as the first bite went down. There was a convulsion of sorts in his midriff where the two central chakras of his body held sway

and then the apple made contact with his buried body, caused the outward reaction he had hoped for, and it leapt free. Vivid yellow flame
erupted from his skin. There was a flare of heat, a stink of burning,
smoke in his eyes, and a tickling sensation all over as it burst free.

The smoke alarm went off with a sudden scream. Emergency
lighting came on automatically. He caught sight of himself in the
grand cheval mirror that had been hung over his vast bowl of fruit. He
was naked, white ash collected like snow on his shoulders and dusting
across his skin where his clothes used to be. He looked shocked and
thin and satisfyingly like David Bowie.

The door opened and two faery faces peered around it, hands over
ears.

"Don't look at me," he said, his voice sounding much more san-
guine than he felt. "I didn't do anything."

Once the hotel had been satisfied no damage other than minor charring
had been done he was permitted to go, but not before Poppy and Viridia
had attempted to get the full story out of him as he dressed. They
handed him items of clothing from arm's length and when he attempted
to go closer in an obvious play to put them to sleep they danced away
and threw pixie dust at him, all of which he could not avoid. Finally,
seeing that he would soon be falling under their spell if they managed to
get him many more times with the enchanted powder, he beckoned
them to the door of the bedroom and pointed inside.

"There is the greatest mystery of my journey, girls," he purred
smoothly, as though already fallen under their demands. "Mr. Friday
Head. An elemental creature of a kind not seen before, formed by my
own alchemical powers."

"Pnyeh," Viridia sneered, tiptoeing closer in spite of herself.

Poppy had more practice at resisting her curiosity, although not much. She wavered and looked at Zal with suspicion and admiration. "You? As if you aren't already some wunderkind in every respect, you are a student of the transformative arts as well? It is too much. Even if it is all an accident of the sort that seem only to occur to you, I think I will soon hate you."

"At last," Zal replied with a heartfelt sigh of relief. "I thought you'd never get the message."

Poppy bared her delicate little teeth at him.

Viridia, close enough to touch the golem, hissed suddenly and backed away, stamping a foot nervously on the floor. "Ack, it is a vessel!"

"Vessel?" Poppy was at her side in an instant, peering and sniffing at the immobile statue of Mr. Head.

Zal watched the two of them twine sinuously round and about the terracotta elf, keeping a safe distance as they traced and inhaled all they could of him. Their arms and fingers and the tips of their noses grew longer and more slender as they proceeded, beginning to sheer into spirit forms that shimmered like water. He felt the drawing, sucking force of their power rise from them as they vacuumed up aetheric information and permitted himself a fond smile. They were good and hooked.

As he slipped out, perfectly quiet and without incident this time, he heard them whispering to each other like two little girls.

"It's a chalice."

"A spirit chalice."

"A spirit chalice of great power."

"It is . . . it is a grail."

"Yes! Yes, a grail! That is what it must be."

"I never saw one before but I heard about them."

"Me too, me too. Lost in the long ago lands the last one, taken there by silly Famka into the big dark for safekeeping, but of course she forgets where she put it."

"It still counts."

"Yes. We have them all. Every last one of them. Well, nearly all."

"Not this one. We haven't this one."

"Yet. Yet we haven't . . ."

Zal stored that information as he ran down the fire escape and then
onto the back of the courier bike that had arrived for him. There was
some trouble to make the rider understand where he wanted to go and
that he wouldn't wear a helmet, but after slipping the man a hundred
Coast dollars he was on his way at a satisfactory eye-watering speed.

The Demonia portal was on the rise as he approached. He gave
brief thanks for twenty-four-hour furnishing retail and slipped out of
Otopian space and back to the park where he had set off much, much
earlier. The park was blackened and stinking of fire. Where the flutes
had been placed bare stubs of their bases poked from the ground. He
saw the charred remnants of bone where some revellers had not been
lucky and winced at the evidence that the elements did not necessarily
treat their adepts well. His own escape seemed suddenly much more
unlikely than it even had before and a brief swell of queasiness came
over him so that he hurried even faster past the spot, ignoring his
hunger and thirst, his contradictory feelings of strength and fragility.
His flare burned with a spiritual heat that his *andalune* now merged
with in a new way; though it was only visible on his back he could feel
its peculiar fire all over him and where usually he would have felt his
way as much by the living things in the area as by seeing where he was
going—sparks and tranches of life vibrant and singing to his soul—
now he felt everywhere the promise of combustion. He wondered if it
would wear off.

Singleminded running brought him quickly through the busy
streets where he ignored calls and rejoinders and demands for parties.
He was deaf to everything, thinking only of Lila and where she could
be. His ears picked up fragments of horrible things that made him run
faster. Of course she should never have come here with only a giddy
socialite like Sorcha for a guide, who had no idea how very different
human values and minds could be from her own and didn't care to

reason why. He recalled his own introductions to demon life and shuddered. He knew he had survived simply through a willingness to roll with anything, and a lot of unexplained luck. He had no values he could detect, at least not ones which related to other people, and so it hadn't been too hard. Even Hell was hardly more than a mild affront to the vestiges of his childhood assumptions and the relics of his elven upbringing, not the slaughterhouse of his entire identity as it was for some. He was shallow. It helped enormously. But Lila was not, and she was also cussed stubborn: he couldn't imagine her understanding the relationship between the trivial and sacrosanct the demons valued, and that would be the kind of combination that Demonia ate alive.

However, when he came to the Ahriman mansion and saw the white banners flying he stopped thinking at all. The servants averted their eyes and stepped aside even as they were doing everything they could to take his shirt and coat, usher him inside, guide him directly to people who were going to tell him what had happened. So he knew it was someone connected to him. There weren't too many of them. All reaction in him froze, waiting for information. It came too soon of course. Sorcha, alerted by her attendants, came running towards him in her mourning clothes. Like a crazy kind of antipope, he thought, marvelling at his own mind's desperate inventions to distract itself. She said only one word, "Adai."

And he breathed again, glad and agonised in the same moment. And then Sorcha explained the details and his pain and relief were overshadowed by anger. There was a still moment in which he knew that things between Lila and himself, hardly begun, would never be the same again. Guilt and grief sobered him, now that it was clear things were all too late. He collected the things he needed from his rooms in the house and instructed the chief of staff to summon a drake rider. For what he had to do he needed wings and the power of akashic flight through the interstitial. Then, finally, he went to the cabinet in the family War Room and took out the ivory compass that could always and anywhere find anyone who bore the Curse of the House of Ahriman, as Adai's killer must.

Sorcha followed him, like a lap dog. She was apologetic, he could tell by her silence. She didn't even try to ask what he was doing, just traipsed at his shoulder as he set the compasses and only then, as he stepped out onto the roof deck, she took hold of him at his belt. "I have to come too."

"It can kill you."

"I have to."

He nodded once and accepted her admission of guilt. "Don't do anything unless I fall. Stay out of it."

"Yes," she said.

The drake rider grumbled at the sight of two passengers. His beast, a semi-intelligent, self-aware creature, had a wingspan that dwarfed the Ahriman aircar balloon and barely fitted on the landing pad. Like Zal, it had an aura of aetheric spiritual energy that was just visible in the Demonia night—a shimmering ripple of luminescence like deep-sea plankton streaming off its chromatic hide. Trails of magic, rendered raw by its disruptive surfaces, gave it a fey look. Only where the harness was strapped to its upper back between the wings was there a clear space of unalloyed air. Zal avoided thorns and spikes and sat down, locking his legs into the strapping. Sorcha got up behind him and he felt her tie herself in place. Before them the skinny form of the rider twisted.

"Vengeance ride is it, master?"

Zal nodded grimly.

"May we have the compass?"

Zal handed the slender object over and the rider flipped it expertly into position at the front of her considerably more luxurious saddle seat. The drake turned its huge, ugly dragon head around and Zal saw the fine skin over the holes where its eyes would have been on a real dragon, veins gleaming blue-black and everything in between shining with a fierce internal white light. The light shifted as if it was water as the creature matched itself to the power of the compass. The rider spoke to it and it spoke back to her with a strangely soft voice. Then the rider said to Zal, "She says you smell of Zoomenon. She won't go there."

"No fear of that," Zal said, uncomfortably aware of the beast's unique combination of physical and aetheric power, and its mind, watching him closely. He allowed himself a look back into the sightless head, and saw nothing there he recognised although it saw things in him.

The rider muttered. "She says you have a dragon's mark in your mind." She sounded jealous.

"Another time I'd be happy to discuss it," Zal said with tight control, though it was news to him.

The drake tossed its head on the long neck with what was unmistakably the beast equivalent of girlish laugh; a natural predator recognising a kindred instinct. It kicked off the roof with a force that made the struts groan and creak. Tiles fell to shatter on the road far below as they rose with a dizzying speed and spiralled up and up and up into the thinning air over the city. Their way was full of small hover cars and the big forms of the main route zeppelins, but the drake navigated an effortless course between them, seeming to strafe the number 18 balloon and causing several of the more nervous passengers to scream and cower back from the rails of the viewing deck. The balloon pilot saluted the drake's flight with envy even as his craft walloomed horribly for a second or two before righting itself.

The compass meanwhile whispered to the rider with its own peculiar music and the rider took out her charmed spyglass and began to polish its nacreous lenses with a soft cloth.

Clinging to his waist, Sorcha hissed in Zal's ear, "We've worked on all the arrangements for the tracks. Even your recalcitrant DJ has let me bring her over. She's been doing drum tracks with Mizjah. Which reminds me. Where the hell have you been?"

Zal twisted around, his hands working carefully on the netspear they held. He let his anger show, "You deserted Lila for a *breakbeat?*"

"She's more than able," Sorcha retorted, guilt making her response less forceful than it should have been. "Anyway not just any beats . . . ones that open the gate to Joy. Besides. Why did you come and then leave without a word? If you'd just turned up to fucking dinner none of this would have happened!"

The drake rider demanded quiet so she could listen to the compass. Zal set his jaw, his back bending with the sudden pain of Adai's loss to try and protect his heart. Behind him Sorcha caressed his *andalune* with her hands in an attempt to soothe. Their small fight had had the effect they both needed—to bind them closer. He concentrated on letting the feeling flow through him as the drake abruptly changed course and the rider put the glass to her eye so she could see straight through every veil to the one physical dimension their prey had fled to.

"Alfheim," she declared with easy conviction, her voice a drawl so slow it was almost a purr.

"This is where you get off," Zal said to Sorcha, forcing himself to straighten up.

"No way!" she hissed, and she had a right to the pursuit if they kept to the letter of the law.

"Sorry," he said, jamming the netspear under his thigh and turning round to take hold of her, all vibrant and powerful and fragile as a hummingbird at the same time, her energy making his own tingle and scream. Her strength was no match for his and he used the unfair advantage to dislodge her. "But if I don't come back you're not going to end up at the mercy of the current rulers of my old hometown. Their laws are anachronistic beyond your wildest dreams."

She fought and scratched. The drake, sensing onboard mutiny, drifted low over the outskirts of Bathshebat, skimming the lagoon. Zal jerked Sorcha free and pushed her hard. She fell, her white clothes flapping and rippling like cloud around her. With the kind of presence of mind he'd always been surprised at finding in her she flung a small object back up at him, guided with a snatch of song. He caught it— her Songster—and with it the line she sent to his ear with the precision of tone for which she was famous, "Never go into battle unaccompanied . . ."

"Ready now?" the rider asked as the drake beat them out across the open ocean, wings adagio but their airspeed increasing beyond the physical limit of any living creature.

"Hit it," Zal said and the rider nodded with satisfaction, calling out to her mount. The drake opened her long, crocodile mouth and her inaudible cry sundered the divisions between worlds. They flashed into aetherstream, protected by the drake's aura of shattering disruption, and then she tuned herself to the frequencies of Alfheim and, with the sure power of like drawing to like, that place reached up and snatched them from nowhere. They soared in the dawn sky over the lumpy corrugation of a seemingly endless forest, the air colder and clearer.

The drake rested into a glide of satisfaction. The rider cleaned her lenses and listened to the compass. They turned and turned again and began to move silently away from the rising sun. Zal put the Songster over his right ear and adjusted the settings. Sorcha's funk-obsessed drum and guitars punched into him, honing his intent to a sharp point that he focused entirely on the gleaming, blunted tip of the netspear. Ten nets around its shaft clung as lightly as spider silk, the aetheric potential of their charms making his fingers prickle as he adjusted his grip and practised casting it clear of the rider and the drake.

The rider set her spyglass into its case at her side. "Did you talk to a dragon, then?" she asked, folding her arms.

"It talked to me," Zal said truthfully, trying to discourage conversation. He must have got better at demonic because she took the hint, or else she was already uncomfortable with the degree to which her curiosity had gotten the better of her professionalism.

She gave him a look of respect and nodded and for a moment he saw the drake look clearly at him through her eyes, a gaze much more penetrating and canny than any demon or human stare could have been. He looked back and the rider laughed.

"When will you stop your brief and petty squabbles then, I wonder?" she said, but it wasn't her voice and both she and he knew it and neither of them made an effort to answer the question.

The drake sailed him effortlessly to a place deep in the Shadowed Forest, a place he fully expected to find an escaping shadow assassin. There, where two glades met across a narrow river, they saw a typical Saaqaa campground looking deserted as always in the burgeoning morning light, only their cats and other diurnal pets lying about in the sunshine alone.

The rider pointed out one hut as they passed to the west.

"If your mages are good enough you can make the cast," she said.

He knew that she meant the spells on the spear would have to be powerful enough to pierce the physical barrier of the hut plus any charms that might be in its making, then accurate enough to find his quarry and tangle it without gathering bystanders into the merciless embrace of the net. She didn't mention the basic skill required just to get the javelin flying in the right direction at a reasonable speed and he hoped it was a matter of confidence in his reputation and not just the fact that she didn't care.

In his head it seemed like every musician in Demonia was doing their damnedest to make him feel like dancing; happy hard-core overdrive. In spite of the situation he found himself moving to the beat and the psychedelic sci-fi effect sounds that someone had gotten addicted to during the mix. Better that than anger or the grief; nothing made intent as pure as expanding, open, happy energies, whatever the source and whatever the target. They banked around for the pass and he readied the spear, turning himself and freeing some stiffness in his balancing arm.

The drake took a suicidally low line, aether streaming from her wings and scattering the birds. The sunning cats leapt and ran as her wavefront brushed them. Zal leaned out, sure and pure, the spot secure in his mind even as the actual camp flashed beneath him in a blur of earth and green tones. The spear flew from his hand, its line unspooling with a high whining sound from the reel attached to the drake's harness.

He felt the detonation of the charms—as if anyone in a radius of several miles could miss the aetheric retort—and then the line went hard and the drake snarled and the reel screamed and smoked and reached its limit almost in one second. It felt like an invisible hand swatted them, but then they burst upward, not down, and the harness slid and complained but they dragged what they'd caught with them. The drake struggled for a few moments as various bits of forest fouled the catch but its strength was easily equal to a hut roof, a few canopy branches, and some tangling vine. Zal only hoped the same could be said for whoever was in the net. The rider handed him the winding handle from its place at her saddlebow and he locked it onto the spool and began cranking as she recovered her spyglass and reoriented them for Demonia.

If there was a response from the shocked camp it came too late to bother them. Zal worked the line until the net was within the streaming wake of the drake's flight and aether stream, then they screamed their silent way home, leaving the fresh air of Alfheim's beautiful day before anyone could find them. The elves had no smash and grab equivalent of drake riders, no airborne terror, and now that they were gone, no proof of anything. It had been a matter of contention among elven sorcerers for centuries—why would the dragonkin favour demons and the fey? Some said it was a crime against nature, but it was never clear whose the crime was or what and, besides, dragons themselves favoured parts of Alfheim whether their relatives did or not. It didn't matter to Zal, only that he had the person he had to question.

At his request they steered away from Bathshebat and dropped him down at the Place of Stones, on the mainland, a region of bare rock that provided no cover of any sort for many miles. The marks of old duels were littered around like splashes of paint and he knew there were places where the ground emanated all the pain and dread of the defeated. With a shudder he felt himself reminded of Zoomenon as he dismounted.

"Return for me at dark," he said as the drake hovered impossibly above the ground on shivering wings that shattered the air into tiny ripples all around. He felt her energy beating the ground away.

The rider nodded as he slid down and landed on the rock some twenty metres from the motionless net. He watched the drake glide away several miles along the shore and then settle down to bask in the sun. Then and only then did he turn to the net. He switched off the Songster and put it in his pocket.

"Did you think you would escape?" he asked quietly in the old language, taking a dagger out of his boot as the words forced him to a genteel precision of baiting he so rarely enjoyed, coming as it did from the ancestry of manipulation and spite he despised. "Or did your master persuade you it could be done and you were fooled? If that place was your home then you're poor and stupid enough to be persuaded of almost anything. Tell me about your employment and maybe you can get out of this with your life, go back to foraging like an animal." He could see the body inside the netting stir and struggle to perform the magical movements of the Shadow Dance wherewith it could make the spell to become shadow but it was effectively trapped.

Zal sat down where he was and waited, turning the knife over in his fingers. The blade was cool and the point shining with a lacquer of Sorcha's venom—a poison that was harmless to him without her will to make it deadly. Not so for any of his enemies. For them it was attuned to his instruction. He could feel a fine thread joining him to its inimical substance, his heart to its aetherically bound molecules. There was so much about demons that was truly amazing. He found his interest focusing there for a time, to pass the moments as the elf in the net struggled with herself. The metal blade cut his *andalune* where it touched but he didn't mind the weakening—had learned to heal himself rapidly from all the assaults of metal. Besides, the injuries seemed deserved, he reflected—he had failed Adai, and an aetheric flaying was less than worthy of the offence. But then he caught himself and stopped. He hadn't become demon for nothing. The honour code of guilt and redemption was a futile path. Let the elves cling to it and their game of manners. He did not come so far to fall into it now.

He turned impatiently. "Must I wait forever?"

The sun was further advanced than in Alfheim and beat down with increasing vigour as it burned off the night's hazy fug from the shore. The captive elf writhed in discomforts of various kinds.

"You will kill me anyway," came the sullen reply at last.

"Do not count on it," Zal said, reminding himself suddenly of his father. "I do not have a merciful reputation in these parts. Now tell me who sent you and to do what. I have no doubt Adai was not your target, since her death seems almost a misadventure. Sorcha informs me you attempted to murder Lila but after making so much effort to enter a vast gathering of demons you bungled your single rotten shot and made a pathetic getaway attempt across the water—which anyone might have told you was the worst possible course."

"Anyone close to you!" the elf spat.

"I don't think so," Zal said smoothly. "Everyone in Alfheim could say that, although I suppose that if you had succeeded your reputation as an assassin might have come high enough to find the attention of a ruling family back at home. After all, for a little dirt grubber like yourself there's hardly any easy way to get a name for yourself. Nobody in Alfheim would take a challenge from you, being shadow and of low caste and from nowhere and of no family. You wouldn't even have been hired as a guard on a trade caravan." He pushed the line as hard as he could, sure that at least he was right about that part of her story. "A pity your archery is so weak."

"The white demon took my arrow!" she hissed. "My aim was sure. That creature had no way to avoid it. My poison was perfected. Nothing could have saved her."

"Then it was a careless act to shoot when someone like him was standing next to her. Wasting all your life's work on a moment's bad observation." He tutted.

"How was I to know he would sacrifice himself? He was of the family . . ."

Zal pounced. "Ah, he was of the family who set you up, you mean?"

"She had already killed the son. She was due to die. It was my job. There was no dishonour in it."

"But the family in question has bred the most deadly killer in all the worlds for ten generations. Do you think they would hire some filthy little elf for a task of honour? What were you to do when you failed them?" He could feel her hatred of him like a second sun, and knew he was right again. He felt sorry for her innocence and answered for her. "Of course, you'd kill yourself, like a good assassin, leaving some great death poem about your tragic little life so we could all have a good laugh over it. Did it not strike you that you might have been the evening's entertainment?"

She actually sobbed. "No! I had orders to kill her and if I could not then to kill you, your sister, or your wife. Any would do."

He felt inspiration come, as if she was willing him to know everything and was passing it to him, which, in a way she was . . . "But if you succeeded, what would happen? Lila would be dead. You'd vanish back to Alfheim with something and never darken their doors again. The Principessa would have given me a mortal insult and I would be obliged to challenge the house of Sikarza. Teazle would have to take up the challenge and I would die. Lila would be dead so the Otopians would have lost their most useful agent, the only one with any potential to become powerful in Demonia. The elves would have lost the only one with any sense, me. And then the Principessa would be able to rightly say her family had saved Demonia from an influx of foreign power and would move up to the top of the ruling families. That was a risk worth taking, even on someone like you. But you failed. Because of Teazle. That's very interesting. Like mother, like son, but a different game I'd bet. Teazle gains nothing much if his mother becomes a power in the region. Like her he'd be glad really to get rid of someone as annoying as his brother. His interests aren't remotely served by assisting his mother's schemes or Lila's death. He'd be much better off trying to marry her. Then he'd have foreign power and influence first in Demonia, plus the kudos of the most powerful partner who was already significant before she even got here. He's young enough to have a strategic brain left so of course he'd try that, and he'd be enough to scare off any other suitors for the time being. Except me. But I could be an added bonus if I also persuaded Lila to join with me. The combination of him, Lila, and myself would be a power structure unlike any other here, and possibly unassailable. It would be sufficient to found a new family line, one without any ties to previous or existing lineages. No more obligations to fulfil. And of course there would be Adai, the only one of us capable of producing heirs. What an interesting plan. The Principessa wanted you to forestall that, I'd bet, and you have. Anything you did she can claim is vengeance for that little runt of hers. She loses nothing no matter what happens and she stands to gain a lot. Unless Teazle does make it clean away, in which case she stands to lose her head. Of course, all that would rely on Lila being in any way marriageable, a thing the Principessa has probably failed to account for because she can't imagine anyone turning down Teazle whereas I can't imagine Lila saying yes to anyone. But whatever the reasoning, you're nothing but an embarrassment, a living endorsement, and unless you're prepared to make a full testimonial in court to clear Lila from any link to Adai's death, you're my business to dispose of."

There was a moment of sobbing misery from the net.

"Cheer up, it might never happen. I'm notoriously insane. By the way, what *was* that poison on the arrow you used? I didn't see too much of your shack but some of the totem poles had a medicinal look to them suggestive of some serious pharmacological interest. You'd find a very lucrative trade relation over here if you took the time to investigate it, should that be the case."

Between sobs came the words, "You are an abomination."

"Oh, you're not a believer, are you?" Zal summoned the energy not to groan and began to play with directing light beams over the surface of the rocks from the dagger blade, sending tiny focused golden glows over the netting. "Zal is a traitor to elves because he went off to discover what demons were all about and decided he preferred making music to waging war on his own people. Vulgar and tasteless . . ."

"You abandoned the shadowkin cause and the White Flower." There was some fumbling and then the elf poked her grey fingers out of the net. Held between them Zal saw a small white daisy, quite dried and flattened. "You were one of us."

Zal suppressed a shudder as a cold flicker went through him. "I *started* us," he hissed back.

"Lila murdered Dar. Everyone knows. He tried to save you from the worst of the Jayon Daga and now he's dead and you're gone. You left us to rot. Who do you think remains behind to champion anything?"

"Nothing's stopping you," he said, aware it was weak even if it was true.

"Dar begged you to come back but you stayed here for . . . for what? Music?" Her contempt was like a knife in his side.

"The music is important. And the cause is just another problem featuring in the same tired old drama," he said. "If we won we'd only take up power in the same form it has now and do the same wrong things over again. Besides, there was nobody with sufficient influence on the diurnal side to help us. We needed a better reason than simple injustice to turn them."

"Yes, and now that the cracks are spreading there is even more reason to stamp out the shadow filth for they all know we follow the wild streams and where do they come from but the cracks to the Void and surely we are farming the cracks to gain enough power to topple the light! Arië was their great hope for stability and you took it away. Now they have no reason not to openly exterminate us and that is exactly what they are starting to do. But you wouldn't know about that, since you are too busy singing songs and being adored by stupid humans who don't even care their world is falling apart. I was glad of a chance to kill you. Seeing you like this is worse than having you dead."

Zal didn't reply. He already knew everything she said was true, of course, and he was used to the truth and its pain so it didn't have the power to upset him now. He was thinking about Mr. Head, and his mother.

"Do you know how the shadowkin were made?" he asked, watching the sun's heat make Sorcha's poison gleam pale red. He moved across the rock to the net and poked the dagger through, making a small wound in the elf's thigh with the point.

She flinched, "What is that?"

"This? This is an aetherically attuned intelligent protein which will perform whatever work on you I ask it to, within reason. A poison, if you like. I could even tell you what I was going to have it do, supposing you'd tell me what poison you tried to use on Lila. Was it demon, like this one, or one of your own devising?"

"I made it," she hissed, trying to reach her leg and failing. She could barely breathe, the nets were so tight.

"And is Teazle carrying it now?" Zal asked languidly, as though they were enjoying the light and heat and the day. "Because killing him would be quite a coup. As much as a coup as finding out that the Saaqaa are elfkin, blood and aether, and that there could be no shadow if there wasn't light."

"How do you know that?" She gulped for air, beginning to pant now that the sunlight shone full on both of them.

"I found something."

"Your word is not enough."

"I have proof. And I will you to believe the truth when you hear it, just so we don't waste what time we have left on any unfortunate mis-understandings." He looked at her a long time to be sure she under-stood what he meant, that the poison was to have this effect, and as he saw her breathing calm he knew that she did. He could have lied about it and she wouldn't know, he knew that too, but he felt too jaded by the day's business to lie.

She waited, thinking, and then said, resentfully because he made her wait and ask, "So, how were they made?"

"By crossing light elves with ghosts. At least, I think they were ghosts. It's hard to say. The language she was using when she told me was so very old. I might have got the words wrong. Something that came out of the interstitial after they opened a portal onto the akashic plane and made people stand in the way. It's not always ghosts, is it? Anyway, the survivors were bred with various cocktails of other elves until they got the shadowkin. The by-blows who didn't fit the expected mould are the Saaqaa. Everything else got ported to Zoomenon and dumped, dead or alive. That was the Winnowing part. I guess the first bit must have been the planting part, and then the har-vesting part or whatever . . ." He stopped, feeling nauseous.

"Why?" she said after a long pause.

"I don't know," he answered. "But I'd like to. I have enough evi-dence, if I ever get time to go through it. That however would rely on me not being killed in the next few months. And we need to present it somehow in Alfheim. For that, people with brains will have to be alerted to the opportunity by people who know I'm telling the truth."

"You were right. I don't have any influence," she said, taking his point.

"I didn't say you could do it. I'm telling you this so you know I mean it when I say that either you get up on the stand and admit to killing Adai to save Lila from having to face a public trial or I will kill you. Your choice. The only one that interests me. I could care less about the shadowkin story. It's waited for millennia, it can wait some more."

"They will torture me until I confess the whole story," she said bitterly.

"Then you can just tell it all straightaway. They're not barbarians about it."

"And then what will happen?"

"The Principessa has her get-out clauses lined up. She won't care. She may take out some policy against you for failing to meet professional standards but given the thoroughness of the legal proceedings in the case against you I doubt it. Your shame will be enough for the demons. They'll consider you a fallen creature, beneath notice, so after that you can just leave. They won't pay you any more attention unless you fall foul of an imp. You can go home, do some gardening, brew a few more potions, turn into the mad lady who says the night hunters are elves too."

The sun was burning hot now. Zal could feel her waves of agony at the intense radiation and he sympathised with that.

"Take me where I must go to speak," she said.

He stood and signalled the drake rider.

"The drug was not a poison as such," she informed him as he cut the net free just enough for her to stand by herself. "It was a thanatritic, to collect the mind after death and distil it. A necromancer's tool, to extract information from corpses. It wasn't mine. The Principessa's agent gave it to me. The demon will carry it but it won't harm him. It may not even be enough to be active when he dies." She let Zal pull her to her feet and gave him a look of tired resignation. "I do make poisons. Just ones that kill."

The drake landed a short distance away and feigned interest in the horizon as they approached and made their way to its harnesses. Zal set the elf in front of him and held her in position since she was unable to use her arms or hands. Exhaustion and fear made her *andalune* body weak and he let her lean on him, her black hair soft against his cheek, her long ear twitching gently against his neck. She gave him a sad look as he set her down in the company of the demon police and made the necessary statements. Before he left he glanced at her and saw her vulnerability suddenly. It made him angry with her. He didn't intend to but he found himself saying, "I loved my wife," in a strangled tone, before turning and leaving on foot to begin the long walk to the Otopia portal.

The drake had long since departed and the afternoon was hot and humid. He was tired and sweating by the time he crossed over.

CHAPTER TWENTY-THREE

There was a shiver, as if the world had shuddered, and then Lila found herself inside the sitting room, just as before. But it was as she had never perceived it before. The room moved like an ocean. Everything that had been solid and material—the furniture, the walls—now possessed a quality she could only think of as subtle; their material certainty gone and their true nature as objects temporarily composed of energy in harmonious vibration exposed completely to her. And she was the same. And so was Tath. There was nothing in existence that did not have this evanescent charm. She saw at once how truly fragile everything was, how miraculous, how strange. And through everything that was surged deeper waves and movements, currents and flows, so slow and majestic in their tides that in an age of human time they would barely move at all, yet she could perceive their vital power, their unstoppable force.

Against this backdrop a burst of something as frail as a gnat's wing and as strong as stone dispersed and vanished into the subtle sea. She realised it was what remained of the demon they had used to come here: its spirit traces flying into the aetheric wind, borne away, lost forever.

"Holy shit," she said.

Tath agreed with her, grimly, his emerald and spring-green body enclosing hers. He was tense and wary, as if they were in danger. It seemed strange to her. Nothing here could be dangerous, because everything was revealed as part and parcel of one essential movement, one space, time, and wonder.

"Your parents are not here. Of course, we both would have known it if they had chosen to linger. To find them we can only go back to the last point at which they remained here, and then move into their after-life time with them. We must use the room to move back in time," the elf said quietly, his voice in her mind as soft as thistledown. "But I cannot do this myself. I must call one of the undead." He hesitated.

"What's the matter?"

He waited another moment and she felt his tension rise. "I can feel my death calling to me." His voice was wistful. Tired, guilty, he wanted to answer. But he only allowed himself a second of that and then turned away with an emotional jolt, forcing himself to resist. She was about to speak but he cut her off, opening his mouth and uttering the strangest call she had ever heard; silent to her ears but strong in her heart.

"You don't have to . . ." she began, determined to have her say.

"I do," he said. "Now be quiet."

They listened, still able to hear the small noises of the house, the retorts of the kitchen pans, the murmur of Malachi and Max talking, the scratch of a dog's foot on the bare boards of the back porch, the engine of a passing car. Then, beneath these gentle sounds, a yet more gentle tread came, vibrating on frequencies that didn't disturb the physical world of the living but only touched the subtle depths of this peculiar existence. Firm, steady, they came closer and Lila would have shuddered if her body had still responded to her feelings, which, she was surprised to find, it did not. In fact, she couldn't feel it at all.

Panic surged up as she realised she had lost her link to her AI, even though she didn't want it, and there was no contact with anything . . . nothing . . . she wasn't sure what she was feeling now because she couldn't . . .

Stop it, Tath snapped harshly. *You're fine. You're just not in your body anymore.* And to prove it he stood up and she went with him as though she was his puppet. Behind her, her body sat on the couch, eyes shut, pale and apparently motionless. He moved around with the lightness of floating in outer space and she saw herself remain, a punk puppet with the strings cut, her skirt across her legs that looked so human except for the fact that they were brilliant chrome to the hard black tops of her boots.

She supposed the feeling of disembodiment was no worse than the weeks it had taken to grow sensation into her machine prosthetics. At least, it wasn't too much worse and she took some odd comfort from the fact that then an elf had been with her too, in a similar role of care-taking: Sarasilien's nonintrusive but constant presence had saved her from despair. She got a grip and waited for Tath's instruction.

The footsteps reached the door. Through the material veil that interrupted it no more than a breeze, it crossed the threshold of the room and stood before them, human in form, its ears rather long, its body clad in nondescript grey clothing. It had no features: its form was blurred and full of movement like the most rough of pastel sketches that had been blocked with the basic colours and was awaiting a lot more work. The edges of it were uncertain. To Lila it seemed as if they simply faded into the space around them. And they shivered all the time, hazing the space around its body with an oil-sheen of flickering rainbow light.

It was surrounded by an area of influence—that was all Lila could think of to call it—in which everything of that place was under its control. Now she and Tath were included in that sphere and she felt its potential not only surrounding her but interpenetrating every part of her being. There was no need to speak, because all thoughts were understood, all desires known. Nothing could be hidden. She under-stood implicitly that she and Tath were being judged, though against what standards there was no knowing, and in this place of shared knowledge she realised the fine thread by which their lives clung to existence—this being had the power to sever them from the material world, to strand them here, or banish them far from either kind of reality, or sunder them to nothing. And there was no knowing why, or what it would do but now that they had drawn its attention they must endure its reasons because that was the cover charge for the living in Thanatopia.

Lila ought to have been more afraid now, she thought, but she wasn't. When her fate was certainly outside her control, she felt only calm. Tath was resigned. She realised he didn't expect to survive too many encounters with this place and its natural inhabitants, and that he had no idea why he had managed to become that most unnatural elven thing—a necromancer—when so many others had simply vanished from the face of existence for their presumption.

The undead being, that was not anything like the undead of story, and not like the living either, moved closer to them and Lila's vision of the room blurred as if she was moving into water. As though from the inside of a strange little fishbowl she began to see flickers of gold and silver light streak past the outside edge of the undead sphere, then colours moved. Darkness came, went, came, went. She realised she was seeing Time unknit itself around them. "Oh Tath!" she whispered, because they had got their wish.

His response was cautious, even sad. She didn't understand.

The streaking lights stopped and the room cleared. She saw her parents on the couch, as she had seen them in the picture—dead—and there, standing on the table, its foot by the overturned glass where vodka dripped to the floor, was the indigo-coloured necromancer whose room she had blundered into in the Souk. He held a bottle in one hand, was corking it shut. Then he shivered and turned to look behind him, straight at Lila.

She tried to grab him just on instinct, but with a grimace of fear he had winked away, into nothing.

Tath said he had taken the spirits and gone. Their undead guide agreed—they were already following; at least Lila thought so, for they were moving again but this time they left the room and shifted in ways she could not understand. Only through Tath's mind did she perceive them moving through space and time together within the secure shield. As they went Lila was filled with a kind of relief that there was no more to this than demon vengeance; it was not part of a greater and more mysterious plot. It was not the fault of the agency. But it was a small relief, soon gone.

You realise what this demon has? Tath asked her as they travelled.

Lila waited, guessing that "my parents' spirits" was not the answer.

Power over you, he supplied. *Like the people who made your machine body and mind. And those people have the other part of the power; the bodies. Soon there will come a moment when you must decide how much those lives, and in what form . . . how much they mean to you. What will you sacrifice for them? What gamble will you make?*

"My plan was to take them back and restore them without any deals," she said, but for the first time she felt uncertain. These few minutes had already revealed exactly how little influence she really had on the matter, at least in this place.

Tath's words came from his heart. She understood that he had already taken this choice, a long time ago. She didn't want to ask about it because his sad heart was enough to know that it had not worked out as he had wanted.

As long as you have strength and influence, people will always try to control you, Tath said wearily, accepting the fact he couldn't conceal anything from her. *How much is your choice.*

"They don't . . ." Lila began, but she already knew it was a lie. They did. In death alone would she be free of her body. She didn't need a textbook on master espionage to realise that the components that Incon had rebuilt her with would surely have some kind of external access control. The question was how much. She'd never let it bother her before. Denial was such a comfortable place. But of course, of course it was there: you only had to remember the horrible episodes of the faulty Battle Standard program to realise she was easy to take over and work remotely, a person whose conscious mind could be bypassed whenever some system decided the time was right. And now this. For the first time it occurred to her to wonder how, if ever, she could escape.

It was nice, to be innocent once, wasn't it? Tath whispered.

For a time she felt too miserable to respond, but from the depths of her being she found a grim voice that said suddenly, "Those days are gone and good riddance to them. You can't fight what you can't see. I'd rather buy the truth at whatever it costs . . ." but she faltered at the end because in her mind's eye images of her parents and her life, of her friends, of Sarasilien and Jolene and Zal and even Malachi, Dar, and Tath were playing and she wanted them all to be good, and on her side, and true. She wanted it so badly it seemed that it must be. And she saw herself pushing that image across a smooth countertop towards the demon with the indigo skin. His bloody fingers grasped it eagerly and slid it away. He was laughing and his blood splattered all over her and she was handing gold coins over to him, pouring them out of her pockets, from her hands, like water until he was buried in them, still laughing while from her head the happy pictures drained away like grains of sugar through an hourglass.

The interest rates are crippling, the elf murmured in agreement, privy to her vision.

It was the first time she had heard him make a joke like that. In spite of everything, she found herself smiling.

Their pursuit ended. With the softness of evaporation the undead who had carried them melted away and they were left standing on a grassy headland overlooking a sparkling sea. A few metres away the demon crouched, several bottles in its hands, its tail lightly lashing the green grass and flowers around it. Its grimace of agitation was out of place with the idyllic place. Behind it Lila could see many more of the undead—egg-shaped blurs of light—gathered on the shoreline below where ships of strange design were taking on passengers in steady lines: human, elf, fey, demon, animal . . . she saw many things. The ocean shone to the horizon, unbroken.

No spirit with a living body anywhere can cross this sea, Tath told her. *But they may travel on the ships if the undead permit it.* His tone told her he had never been there.

Aboard the ships yet more light forms guided the passengers to various places. The more closely she looked at them the more the shapes broke up until she wasn't sure she was looking at ships, or people, or animals, or ocean anymore. But if she looked away and glanced from the corner of her eye their storybook technicolour and clean lines returned.

The demon hissed. "To what pleasure do I owe your pursuit, elf? It's rare any of your kind would be bothered to learn the true arts of spiritual power. Come are you after some lesson, pup? Without the help of the Bright Ones you are surely no match for me. Their favour inclines me to mercy. Speak."

Tath sat down in the grass and ran his fingers through it gently. The demon was quite right. "I am after the bottle you hold which contains the stolen spirits of Lila Black's parents."

"Are you indeed? And why would that be? They are merely some personal trinket with which I amuse myself."

Tath's reply was delivered with the withering dryness Lila had only encountered coming from his lips, as though it was he and not the demon who held all the power. "Your knowledge of the family in question is sadly misinformed if you believe her loyal brothers extend no further than that. She is the beloved of Zal Ahriman and comes under his protection. Further, she is connected to his family in Alfheim, of which I am one cousin. So you and I have family business to dispose of via game or combat. I challenge you in this spot. Go no further before we are resolved."

As he spoke Lila was staring at the bottles, wondering which was the one . . . They all looked disconcertingly the same. Was one of them the demon's own life? And the spare? They seemed like nothing more than crystal vials in various hues of purple, glassy and ordinary.

The demon's long, crocodilian lips curled and Lila thought she saw disappointment. "Indeed I did not think she was so connected . . ." It paused for thought and winced, shivering all across its skin. "Though I owe her a painful death or two, you understand. Perhaps I might consider some leniency. You are a cousin, you say? I was of the understanding that Zal's elven family," it paused to spit with contempt, "had abandoned him for his heresies."

"That is so, but not all of us are so untrue," Tath replied smoothly. "And you do well to hesitate when you consider we are prepared to defend our own as you defend yourselves."

"I find it hard to imagine much threat from elves," the necromancer said, but something was clearly bothering it deeply about the situation.

Lila took over Tath's mouth. "Then figure out what an international incident is going to cost you when the Otopian forces come to figure out how to get your sticky fingers out of their business."

The demon jumped at the sound of her voice and peered more closely at them.

"Why, I did not see you there, Ms. Black. Truly you are more intimate with the elves than ever I believed possible . . ." There was a kind of wondering respect in its voice.

Lila sensed her chance. "If you will stop your duelling with me we could enjoy a more favourable relationship. Much better than the constant annoyance of trying to outwit one another this way."

"I am not sure." The demon considered its bottles and turned them over, switching them easily in the patterns of an illusionist shifting pieces around in the three-cup trick. "This duel has more challenge to it than any I have engaged in before. What cooperation could repay me with such interest or artistry?"

"Then let's fight."

"We are fighting," the demon replied with a shrug. "But the kind of fighting that few can manage for long periods of time." It held up one bottle to the light and squinted into it. "Attrition. Cruelty. The breaking of hearts and souls. Scattered wherever any leverage lies. Nothing left unturned. No place too low to stoop to. No trick too scurvy to discard."

"What were you planning to do with my parents?"

"I thought I might make a few more bottles, mix them all up, hide them away where you would have to look for them." It opened the one it held and shook it upside down . . . nothing happened. "Look, that one's empty. Now, your friend there will tell you that as time passes the chances of resurrection get very unfavourable, but as long as they are in my bottle the spirits of your dear departed won't go anywhere, won't age, can't decay. See." It picked up another of the vials. "You could keep them safe forever. No journey on the ships for them. Always with you. And if they don't rebel, you can let them out to talk with you here, in this place, at the edge of the world." It looked up at her through the vessel, one eye huge through the violet glass.

Lila listened to this, and the previous speech, and perceived with a conviction that she felt was new to her—not the demon's words but its intent, as though here only intents mattered and had any power. Not even actions were significant. Only the determination and vision of the individual, their concentration, their focus. The demon had no interest in giving her a quick or easy way out, for any price. She felt its contented commitment to lifelong struggle and pain, the way it was enjoying her powerlessness, her rage and grief. The more she tried to contend with it, the more powerful, in this plane, it would become and the weaker she would become. She might throw all her energy into its traps and feints, slaughter it a hundred, a thousand times . . . she wouldn't find its hidden life. And suppose she did, by some luck, regain the spirits of her parents—then what would she do? Defy Tath's knowledge and return them to a living hell? Let them wake up in some laboratory with the knowledge of what had happened and try to fit that into their ordinary lives as she showed herself to be this creation of technology returned to haunt them with her longing to go back to times that were already over? Even if, in the best of scenes, they loved her and used the experience to remake their lives in better ways . . . what was to stop this creature doing it all over again, whenever it wanted to? Or worse? She knew the ways of demons.

What happens if they are in the bottle, but can't go back? What if the bottle gets opened then?

Then they will take the ships, Tath said.

The ships are just some kind of metaphor, right? I mean, they're not really ships are they?

No. They are the undead shepherding the dead in forms that are easier to under-stand than the true spirit. As they cross the ocean they will change and the dead will take on the same forms, and then the dead will be free to return to Akasha as compo-nents, no longer conscious, no longer the individuals they were. Like biological death, they will be the basic matter of energy once again.

So, that's it. No afterlife?

What is done is let go, the elf said hopefully.

Then let's go, she said to Tath, silently. Now she knew why he had been sorry to get her wish answered.

"Leaving so soon?" the necromancer said with mock politeness as they stood up. Beneath them ships were pulling slowly out of port and setting sail. At the edges of vision other ships were taking shape in the shallows, like dreams forming on the brink of night.

"You win," she said, the words coming calm and steady from her. "I'm going home. I think that any court will recognise your grievances as repaid. It's over. Congratulations."

The demon stood up. "You can't get out of it as easily as that . . ." But it sounded uncertain.

Lila shrugged. "I'm through with you, though I can't speak for my friends and relations. I'm going to be getting married to Teazle Sikarza by the way. I'll try and talk him out of taking you up." Where the last part had come from she wasn't entirely sure, it more or less appeared in her mind and out of her mouth simultaneously and as she said it she realised she was smiling and that part of her, a large part, was pleased with the idea. Of course, a second later the other parts of her that considered it a shocking and dreadful and impetuously insane idea started clamouring for attention but they didn't manage to dislodge her smile nor the small glow of satisfaction she felt deep inside.

You are an education, Tath whispered to her, mild as the Sahara.

The demon clearly thought so too. It jumped up anxiously and paced after her through the lovely grass, carrying its vials carefully. "Supposing I were to return your parents to you now . . . might we consider the matter concluded honourably? You have murdered me twice, attempted, but I am still alive and here they are, also, capable of being returned to life. Quite unharmed."

"Well, but that's not certain, is it?"

"Only days have elapsed in the physical dimensions. As long as the bodies live there should be only minor . . . discombobulations. Consider—necromancers and yourself are all spending time travelling away from the world of the living material objects . . . and we shall return, many times."

Nobody truly living spends more than hours here, Tath told her privately. *The upper limit recommended by the undead is four hours of time passing in the world of the physical body. The astral form of the self loses its ability to connect with the physical body effectively very rapidly once it moves beyond the immediate threshold of the timeline, as we have, in moving here. There is a half-life period of six hours in relative time.* He paused, and then added with a quiet but clinical perfection. *I know how you feel, but I advise against any attempt to resurrect your parents after this interval.*

The demon waited anxiously as Lila pretended to consider, though she was responding to the elf.

People in comas come back after years, she said.

People in comas are not in this region, he replied. *They rest or travel within the world of the body silently, until they are able to reconnect or they remain on the same timeline boundary with their physical world, like ghosts. When we first crossed over, we might have stayed there without suffering decay of this sort, but I have witnessed untimely resurrection of people who had travelled far from the Material Rim. Do not think that his offer is a fair exchange.*

Can I talk to them, here? she asked.

It is possible, Tath said.

Lila held out her hand. The demon gave her one vial, a blue, teardrop shape the size of a small beer bottle with a stopper on a fine golden chain. As she took it from him she felt its peculiar substance more like her energy body than not. It might have been true glass in the physical world but here it was a tough knot of energies, cold to the touch, impermeable, and dense as lead.

"We're quits," she said, without sparing another glance at the creature. "Get lost."

The demon backed off a couple of steps and gazed with resentful precision at Tath. It bowed with grudging respect and then vanished abruptly in midstraighten.

Tath's nervous tension eased slightly although he retained a vigilance Lila didn't care for.

"Isn't it safe here?" she asked him, looking at the bottle, at the stopper, at the chain. She wondered what she'd do if the demon had stiffed her and there was nothing inside it.

"It is not safe anywhere here," the elf replied.

Briefly, Lila caught the impression of a thoughtscape—Tath's experience of this world. She saw the light forms of the Bright Ones and the spirits of the newly dead, but also regions so vast and strange there were no words to adequately name them. In those places were other beings, akin to the Bright Ones, but dark, or coloured with flickering sprite fires, their fields of energy shifting unpredictably to forms the eye could tolerate and forms that became flat fields of unknown dimension because they had topographies too alien to be understood. This was a world of intent, of consciousness reduced to its purest form, before words and images took hold of it and marshalled it into orderly possibilities or familiar dreams. Many of these other forms did not have the pleasant aspects of the Bright Ones. They shifted, subtle and ill-willed, self-absorbed, beyond appeal or understanding. Those were the things he feared, their billion forms and their unknown states. It was a wild place, with one border on the akashic region of true pure interstitial aether, one on the material realms of possibility, and one that was made of pure consciousness or mind where the only limits were the limits of imagination. Within that region worlds took shape and were born, as here across this visionary ocean they lost organisation and died into the chaos of raw energy.

Against such a place one elf and one human were simply brief instants of passing organisation and potential interest, for chaos was all the same, but actualised entities were unique and peculiar, perhaps with minds that could make or direct. They were prey; tiny fish in the sea.

Great spirits may survive well here, Tath said, but his voice didn't hold out the conviction that either he or she were among this sacred number.

And what makes a great spirit? Lila asked defiantly.

Perfect Realisation and Conviction, came the reply. *Be quick with your dealings. We are far from the Rim, and time is running fast there, at the edge of the wheel.*

Lila didn't move. She didn't have much conviction herself that opening this bottle wasn't akin to some kind of murder, since surely she held the power to save them? Would Max understand the difference? Did she herself? And then, that fleeting black little whisper in her mind that said, oh, maybe the elf is lying to you. Don't you remember Alfheim? How they can wait, and turn and trick you and lie? To whose advantage does this turn?

And then again, in her hands, Mom and Dad, their entire lives and hers and Max's all in the balance of that bottle. Would they want to go back? Did she want them to know that their fate here was her fault; an awful, stupid mistake?

A sudden rage gripped her. No, it was not her doing that any of them were here at the end of everything with their ordinary lives undone. She had not asked to be the agency's ignorant pawn in that first ill-fated journey to Alfheim. She had never asked for her own metal resurrection. She would not give the people who were responsible for this a moment more of her suffering—and then her heart hardened with a clever determination she did not like—and she would not give them any more leverage against her.

With shaking hands she uncorked the bottle, surprised at how ordinary it felt, a little action that meant so much. It felt like nothing.

They were there in the field with her. Mom, looking faintly astonished, as though she'd suddenly been dealt five aces. Dad, a little dishevelled as ever, slightly blundering, staring around him with relief and a touch of despair.

"Lila?" said her mother. "Is that you?" She was peering, as though she couldn't quite see, the beginnings of a hopeful smile on her face.

"Lila's here?" said her father, turning and only then appearing to see her. "Oh my god! It really is! Lila! Lila!" and he swept her into his arms, crying and lifting her up at the same time.

"Oh no," said her mother, joining the hug fiercely. "If you're here then you must be dead after all. We hoped so much that you were out there, somewhere."

"I'm not dead," Lila said, feeling torn apart by joy and heartbreak, happiness and despair. "I'm alive and I came here to find you."

"My baby," said her mother softly, proudly, holding tight. Nobody said anything or moved for a long time but Lila felt the growing unease of the elf, withdrawn inside her, and finally she made herself speak.

"Mom, Dad, do you know what happened to you?"

They let her go slowly and looked at one another with faces that were full of trouble. "Not exactly," said her father first. "But we know . . . this is death, isn't it? Something came and killed us. Hardly felt a thing, just a cold cut, and then we were gone. Caught us arguing . . ." He looked ashamed.

"Don't," said her mother, taking her father's arm gently. "Not now." She gazed at Lila with eyes that were suddenly much more acute and with it than Lila was used to, as though with losing her bodily existence she had shed all the frustrations that had held her back in life and forgotten them in the same instant.

"I wanted," Lila stammered, "t-to rescue you. But I-I don't think I can after all. In fact. I have to go in a moment and . . . I wanted to . . ." But she was crying too hard to continue and her throat was full of feelings that were too big to say.

There was a moment of silent communication between her parents, fast as light, and she thought for an instant that Tath reached across and spoke to them in some way but it was too quick to be certain.

"No," her father said and put his arm around her shoulders and his face against the top of her head. His voice was steady. "We talked about this when we realised what was happening. I don't know how we knew that but we did. Soon as we crossed here. It was like we just had known it all our lives. When you cross over, really cross, you see things differently. How it was, what you were, what you did. We don't want to have to go back and carry on with that now that we've been here."

"But you could change things, fix things," Lila sniffled. "If you can see, then it could be so much better."

"Maybe," her mother said, and glanced at the ships. "But your spirit guide here doesn't think so. And I feel so calm here. It's peaceful."

"But if you go, you'll just disappear!" Lila cried. "And there's so much I wanted . . . wanted to . . ."

"Lila, this was the right thing," her father said. "God knows, after all the mistakes we've made it's kind of a miracle that one of us could make this choice, and it's a terrible thing, I know. But you didn't cause our deaths, Lila. You aren't to blame. And we're not unhappy, look at us. We had our moment and we had you and Max and those were the best times anyone could have, even if they were shitty sometimes."

"You could hang around and be ghosts," Lila said. "You can live along the timeline. You'd see us."

"And do what? Haunt your every waking minute?" Her mother stroked her back. "I know you don't want to say good-bye. But think about it this way—how many people never get this moment and wish they'd had it all their lives long? We could have just been flattened in a car crash and you'd never see us again."

"But I have to . . . I want to say so many . . ."

"We know," her father said, smiling with the ease of quite a different man, the one that she knew he had always wanted to be, and had drunk to forget. It was strange to have that person suddenly there, as if all the broken pieces of his life had suddenly fit together in a second. It was a great mercy, Lila felt, a grace that none of them had ever expected could exist in any world they might see. Her tears were happy, as well as sad. "We love each other. We understand it all. There's nothing to forgive and no reason to be sad now."

"But I won't see you!" Lila said pathetically. She didn't want to admit in that second just how much and for how long and how badly she yearned to be held close and safe in the comforting touch of their embrace, nor that she didn't know how to go on if it would never exist again.

"Lila," her mother said, taking her hand. "Oh." She touched it carefully, then held it as she always had. "What a clever thing . . ." She glanced with concern at Lila's tear-stained face. "Better than the original I bet. Anyway, it's not important. Your guide is saying that you will die too if you stay here any longer. It's time. I know you're not ready, but we are. You must never worry about that. Go on home now. We have other things we have to do and better places to go."

"No, I can't," Lila whimpered, as weak as she had ever been, longing to be different, longing to be stronger and better and more sure. She thought that they would remonstrate with her as they always had, and say things like she should look after Max and had work to do and must be strong and look after her sister and do well . . . but they didn't. They held her quietly and their calm slowly passed into her, she didn't know how, and finally she was able to let go of her own free will. She still felt all the terrible feelings of loss and fear, but they were not in control of her any more, and she realised for the first time that it did not matter that she had those feelings, instead of other ones that she thought she ought to have. She was as she was; not the perfect older sister, or the best daughter, or a credit to them, or a good girl, or a feisty hero, or a perfect and unruffled cyborg servant, or any of those things. There was no description that fit and it was not important.

Her parents took one another's hands, rather awkwardly as their union hadn't been the most amicable of things, and they held on with the carefulness of little children. Then her mother paused and turned back for one instant, a faint smile on her face although Lila could see tears there too. "Always remember," she said, with a wink and a wicked grin. "Aces high."

Please, Tath whispered.

Lila closed her eyes and thought of home.

CHAPTER TWENTY~FOUR

She was cold as ice, heavy as stone, dry and aching as though she had run to the point of collapse. There were shooting pains in her shoulders and thighs. Tath curled up slowly like a decrepit and arthritic cat in her leaden chest. Lila opened her eyes and found herself staring into the face of one of the agency technicians. He shrieked and dropped some small piece of handheld technology on her stomach. Above her lights glared from a low, white ceiling. Cables of various colours snaked down from tracks above her. The stink of overcleaned vinyl was overlaid with the curiously out of place odours of fresh forests, spicy musk, and garlic.

"She's awake." It was Zal's voice, coming from above and behind her. She tried to move but her body didn't fancy the idea much and made her wince with pain and stop. Belatedly she realised she was lying on a gurney, but her head and upper body were cradled on the pillow of Zal's legs, his hair long enough to tickle her forehead as he leant over to look. He laid his hand gently against her cheek and she pressed into his touch, amazed to find herself comforted by it more than she could say.

She heard someone sobbing. "Max?"

"She's with me," Malachi reported from a short distance away.

Lila slowly tilted her head to look but was distracted by a shimmer above her. Between the light fittings, so camouflaged he had been invisible, Teazle hung from the roof as lightly as spiderweb. His long, dragonish neck uncoiled and twisted so that his head came down close to hers. His eyes were the white of arctic winter, with just the faintest hint of blue. His triangular ears pricked up and he made a distinctly doggy whining sound, then opened his long, fang-lined mouth and let his indigo tongue hang out. He licked her nose. "There are a lot of other people coming and going with devices and so forth. Do you want me to kill them for you?"

"No," she said reflexively although she privately liked the idea. "What are you all . . . doing here?"

"While you were gone Max found you and thought you were dead so she called the agency and they came along but Teazle, Okie, Rusty, and Buster kept doing a good job of maiming anyone who came near the house until I came to talk them out of it," Zal explained patiently. "After that we were all under arrest and agreed to accompany you here to the medical facility. Well, they didn't want us to, but we insisted, didn't we, Mal?"

"A lot of people insisted," said another familiar voice from a different side of the room. Lila grudgingly and with difficulty pushed herself up a little so she could look around. Sarasilien was there, sitting back with an expression of mild amusement on his face. Dr. Williams was beside him, a world-weary kind of smile attached to her as though she had stuck it there for a party. Several technicians were loitering next to her, including the one who had recovered his instrument from her blanket. The dogs were lying around underneath their seats, bored to sleep.

"We're difficult to resist, when we insist," said Zal, pulling her back against his body and holding her close in his arms, his face next to hers. His *andalune* body wove around her like smoke. She could feel a grim determination in him that was completely at odds with his facile surface.

"If all the reserves weren't out dealing with this crisis I can assure you resistance would have been highly effective." Cara Delaware stepped forwards, her face as icy as her tone of voice. She held herself upright as though she was starched, though her face was almost grey underneath her makeup and her eyes were rimmed with the red of exhaustion.

Teazle snickered, a highly unpleasant sound, and began to stalk Delaware with his gaze. She gave no sign of noticing which Lila took as a sign of extreme fatigue or stupidity.

"What crisis?" Lila murmured, closing her eyes so she didn't have to see something so unpleasant as Cara staring at her. She felt sore and tired in every possible way. Zal crooned softly into her ear. She wondered if he knew about Adai.

"You can concern yourself with that once you are certified fit to return to work," Cara was saying. "Everyone else may be released after interview if they are satisfactory."

"The Otopians are experiencing many strange night haunts and encounters with what they think are extraterrestrial beings," Teazle hissed. "Creatures which defy all natural law." He drawled the word "natural" with extreme contempt. "They suppose they are under attack or the threat of it and have sent all their forces to capture and command one of these creatures."

Cara's lip curled, "You are not here to speculate upon classified . . ."

Zal coughed and interrupted. "I don't want to spoil your party or anything but don't you think it's time you dropped the bullshit and adapted to what you've got in front of you?"

She turned to him with icy composure. "And what might that be?"

"A crossworld group of uniquely powerful allies, all brought together by the person you thought you'd just use as a robot spy."

"You have no power within your individual races or worlds. Skills and strength maybe, but no authority . . ." She glanced upward at Teazle's dangling form, his wiry and muscular body apparently hanging from no more than a cursory connection with some flimsy ceiling tiles, and flinched slightly. "Not any more," she added.

"She's right," Teazle said in his harsh garble, words half swallowed and liplessly delivered with all the promise of a B-movie monster. "We haven't got any authority here, or anywhere. You're a crazed heretic pretending to be a pop star who used to be a half-assed secret service employee. The faery hasn't got the loyalty of a mayfly or the attention span of one either, even in human guise. The sister's an out-of-work chef who just managed to burn spaghetti, and I have better things to do than be bossed around by some human jobsworth. We should leave the humans to their hysteria with the moths and take off for a better place." His speech was an open invitation, and Lila sensed a rise of energy in Zal correspondingly. She could feel his smile in the swirl of *andalune* he bathed her in and the beginnings of a conspiracy of sorts— they were plotting something, or beginning to execute a plan of their own and even though there was almost no magical power in the place they had enough between them to manage something before the day was out.

There was the sound of guns being cocked. Lila craned around and saw armed guards on the door. Some guns pointed at Teazle, some at Zal, some uncertainly at the floor.

"You're not going anywhere," Delaware said. "Liabilities all. You've said enough in the last ten minutes to ensure your incarceration as security liabilities."

"Where are my parents?" Lila broke in. "Have you released them?"

"In their current condition the doctors say there is some hope for recovery . . ."

"They're dead," Lila said.

The room was silent. Delaware bit her lip, apparently only then realising her misstep in revealing that they had at least lived until recently.

Lila felt Max staring at her. "What do you mean? They were dead before. Weren't they?" Her sister looked at her accusingly and then at Delaware and then at Malachi.

"You were keeping them on ice just in case they were capable of being returned, right?" Lila asked, speaking to Delaware but looking at Max. "Maybe you could have sent me to Thanatopia to recover them, found out how to use that place, like a necromancer. That's the reason you'd give me to go there. Or you could trust them to be the ballast keeping me flying right."

"We need every piece of information we can get," Delaware replied, cool and stony faced. "You and every other human knows that. All the others have the advantage of prior knowledge. We know nothing. We have to do everything we can to ensure our security and safety. I hardly need blackmail to make that an essential goal."

"There's a lot of holes in Demonia," Zal said conversationally. "Like in Alfheim. But nowhere near as much cracking as there is in Otopia. It's getting worse. I hear the faeries are none too happy about it either. I hate to interrupt again but it seems like there are some larger issues of the moment here that nobody is addressing. If I were you I'd be wondering if the incursion of outsider creatures here wasn't related to that. Maybe you'd like to make a note of it." He smiled at Cara though there was no smile reaching his eyes.

Delaware gave a nod and one of the technicians did something on his notebook.

Lila's AI sprang to life. She had got used to its quiescent state and having it suddenly appear in her consciousness, as big as she was, was a terrible shock. Her awareness expanded and at the same moment she felt herself seamlessly overridden by this second system. She felt so loyal and grateful to the agency, how could she have allowed her personal life—however tragic—to interfere?

Tath, who had been weak and silent until then, suddenly stirred inside her chest.

"Yar," Malachi said with uncharacteristic droll annoyance. "I'll be having that if you don't mind." He held out his hand and the notepad spun out of the technician's grasp and flew across the room straight to him. He caught it in midair, releasing the still-sobbing Max who put both hands over her mouth and stared with disbelieving eyes.

"It won't do you any good," Delaware said. "We have others, and we have the codes. We can reset them faster than you could try to crack them."

"Time to go, lads," Malachi said and the technicians sidled up towards him.

"Graham, Yvonne," Delaware snapped, but her commands went to deaf ears.

"Don't get me wrong," Malachi said idly, as he was flanked by white coats. "I've nothing against you and your operation. I've been glad to help you and I'd do it all again, I will do it all again, but I have some interesting affairs that have to be settled first, namely, you have to give Lila autonomy, or as from this moment the fey will cease all diplomatic friendliness with you. And that could be disturbing at the present time, since I believe you will be needing us to help you deal with your—little problem."

"But . . ." spluttered Delaware, turning to Sarasilien and Dr. Williams.

"Faery dust is persuasive," Sarasilien said, giving Malachi a glance of respect. "And to human senses, virtually undetectable. Dr. Huggins and Dr. Peacock here are under his command until it may be washed off."

"You are the magical expert here. It's your responsibility to be on guard for this kind of treachery!" Delaware snapped at him.

"I have been in the laboratory for months, attempting to resolve the issues with the Bomb Forensics Team, aside from that brief interlude with the elves and their quest to hunt down Zal. Besides, Malachi has clearance to do as he likes. It was part of his remit. He is within his rights to use minor magical persuasions against lower-ranking officials if he suspects them of unethical practices."

Dr. Williams turned to regard Sarasilien with new interest. She followed the conversation like a small owl, her head turning eagerly to each new contribution.

"So you're prepared to betray us all?" Delaware sneered.

"You are in no immediate danger, so betray is a foolish word." Sarasilien barely moved from his upright position. "But Malachi is not the only one here who foresees bad consequences for your use of Lila as a remote-controlled device. Even if it were unobjectionable, the opportunity exists for her to be subverted and used against you as Malachi has proved."

"The other reason none of this will ever work," Dr. Williams spoke up, "is that as it stands the agency and Lila are now mutually opposed to one another's interests. Either you all work together in a spirit of trust and cooperation or the entire matter will end very badly indeed. Cara, this is your problem. You can't do this with rules and force from on high, mostly because none of these people respond to it. It's time for a different approach."

The younger woman stared at her with rigid dislike. "What had you in mind?"

"I was thinking you might take a holiday. I've already written you a note. Overwork can be a terrible thing."

"I have no intention of leaving at a crisis period . . ."

Dr. Williams looked dismayed. "Oh, but I already sent it. Your authorisation is here. Plus, the Director has been so pleased with your work that he's arranged a promotion for you on your return. You can go anytime you like. Your replacement is on the way."

Teazle snickered. "That's more like it. Finally a bit of interest. Mutiny, and no telling at what level the commands really come from. I like it."

Delaware had gone a deathly, speechless white.

At that moment a fiery ball, smoking faintly, pushed its way through the wall and darted to Lila's shoulder. With a small popping noise Thingamajig manifested and took a look into the surprised faces around him.

"Ooh, not a moment too soon! I'm sensing a lot of anger in the room, a lot of restless spirits filled with the vibes of inadequacy and confusion, mingled with just a piquant hint of incompetence. You, you lady," he pointed to Delaware, "have done a masterful job here." He bowed deeply and dug his claws into Lila's shoulder with a shiver of satisfaction. "So, how is everybody doin'?"

There was a moment's thoughtful silence as everybody stared at the imp.

Then Delaware turned and stalked from the room, pushing past the armed guards without a backward glance. They heard her heels in the corridor fading away to quiet.

"Was it something I said?" Thingamajig asked, his eyebrows raised almost higher than his head.

Sarasilien turned his head towards Dr. Williams. "Do you suppose she will make a valuable enemy?" Everyone listened, temporarily stunned to personal silences by the sudden turns of events. Lila noted the AI signing Delaware off the authority listings, but nobody appeared to replace her.

"Her losses are her own affair," Williams said with a sigh. "She simply wasn't suited to the position by temperament, which caused her to make several unfortunate misjudgements, and that's true enough to be the entire reason I will ever give."

The elf nodded slowly, his lips pursed forwards in the common human manner of someone who is considering a strangely intriguing and impressive manoeuvre.

"I can't see a replacement," Lila said, all her attention focused on Dr. Williams, but as she spoke the omissions from the roll began reappearing in her knowledge—Malachi was reinstated where he had been deleted when she awoke. Sarasilien's cautionary status was dropped and his privileges restored. Her own file, that had always been brief and to the point, suddenly expanded, like a concertina; chock-full of new information. Her seniority was upped five levels, putting her on equal footing with Sarasilien himself for clearance and command. It was like watching flowers bud and bloom in seconds of time-lapse film. And then new blooms came: Zal's name appeared, and Teazle's too . . .

At this point Dr. Williams, who had been quietly fiddling and muttering crossly at her personal interface Berry, pulled up what Lila was seeing and projected it shakily onto the far wall across Malachi's and Max's heads so that everyone else could read it too.

"I've been doing some adjusting," she said, reaching into a pocket for her glasses, shaking the arms out carefully and putting them on her face. "And if you are agreeable, Zal and Teazle, I would like you to consider this proposal . . ."

She got out the light pen from her top pocket and started sketching lines. She drew a band around Lila, Zal, Teazle, and Malachi. "This would be the outside operations group. Which leaves myself and the office and technical staff as your base resource team." At this point her own name appeared: Dr. Williams, Director of CrossWorld Resources and Operations. She circled it into the much larger list of people who worked at the agency. "Whilst of course Lila's responsibility is to Otopia, naturally, I wouldn't expect that of outsiders whose interests may lie elsewhere. This group is to be created solely for the purpose of investigating common crossworld problems and resolving them to mutual satisfaction. If you don't want to participate then you must say so now because it's high time we paid more attention to interesting reports like this one . . ." She fussed with the Berry and murmured, "Stupid machine . . . such little buttons . . . come on, damn you . . ."

A video clip appeared as Max and Malachi sidled out of the way and came to lean against Lila's bed. Teazle swivelled his head around to look the right way up at it.

On the image a human presenter and a demon who looked like a cat-person looked with slight stage fright at the camera but began without preamble. "We are part of the mathematical analysis teams who've been working on the physics of what we know about the new cosmology since the Bomb . . ." The human, a young man, cleared his throat and glanced at his colleague but continued. "We've been studying the crack patterns in the various regions and comparing them with what is known from akashic science about I-space. We've also been consulting with groups about unexpected phenomena . . . wherever we can get that information. You're now a part of that organisation. It's not exactly government from anywhere, but we are funded and . . ."

"Digression," murmured the cat.

". . . um . . . the point is that we have reason to believe, if our equations are right, that there is a fundamental instability governing the space-time and aether matrix which permits our worlds to coexist. It is getting worse and various activities increase the instability . . . however, the major point about our research is that we think the primary cause of the problem is: our theories predict the existence of another world. But nobody seems to be able to detect it." He glanced at the cat who nodded sagely. "The fact that it isn't there, apparently, means that the fabric of our dimensions is starting to rip itself apart and there's nothing we can do about it. It's reasonably slow. We think years, not months. A decade to fatal instability. Before that . . . we don't know what will result as things get worse. But they will get worse, probably in unequal jumps." He paused and took a drink from a glass of water that had been out of shot.

"But," the cat interrupted in a smooth, soft voice, "we think that if this world could be found and somehow reintroduced to the matrix, the pattern will stabilise. The equations clearly predict that the presence of the seventh realm would balance everything out. It's because it's not there that everything is starting to warp. Everything points to its existence."

"How could it exist and not be there at the same time?" Zal asked the recording, just as the cat continued.

"Of course it seems impossible for something to exist, yet not be there at the same time. We have postulated that maybe it does exist but has become separated from our continuums in some way and is therefore only detached and not nonexistent in the greater cosmos. If it has been destroyed or failed to arise then, of course, nothing could be done. Demonia, Alfheim, and Faery also note for the records that the instability issues were present, yet at much lower levels, prior to the QBomb event in Otopia. We never considered looking for other worlds before now. If there is evidence . . . I am not allowed to discuss it here. Another department will take care of that. That concludes the summary findings."

The recording ended.

"Well, I think that says it all." Williams switched off the display and put her Berry back into her pocket. "Now, staff if you would return to your duties I will take Lila and her sister home and assist with the arrangements for the immediate return of Mr. and Mrs. Black. If that's all right with you, Lila?"

Lila took a deep breath, "I think I'd like to be alone for a while," she said, and got down from the gurney. She gave Zal a nod that said he was included in "alone" and gave Max a small smile of apology. As she passed Malachi on her way out he signed that he'd look after Max and she picked the technician's device from his hand. The soldiers guarding the door stepped aside for her silently.

As she was walking Lila re-cued her access to her AI and set it to full interface. The extra machine mind lay seamlessly with hers. She only had to think for all its possibilities to be controlled: she closed the door behind her and locked it, using her new security permissions to invoke Protocol 111b (higher-ranking agency staff are temporarily counter-manded in event of emergency or suspicion of threat) to ensure it could not be overridden. She did the same thing to the control system in her hand, locking out all others from access—and not only to this single unit, but to all units of any kind containing the same program.

On her shoulder Thingamajig tugged at her hair but she ignored him and began to walk down the hall, orienting herself via her internal schematic of the building. "Where are we going?" he piped. "Are you on some mission?"

She didn't answer. Inside her chest the exhausted Tath watched her with quiet interest. Her feet took her at a steady pace through doors she had never had cause to open before, their locking mechanisms opening at the touch of her fingers. As she walked she also opened up regions inside the secure zones of the AI systems where the hot-working copies of several million different operational programs were kept, located the ones which gave remote access to her internal software and hardware, and watched them closely. Meanwhile she was really looking for a master command somewhere in the whole works—several security levels higher than she was allowed to command she knew it must exist: a means to shut her up and shut her down. As that was going on she took a cursory glance at the flow of comms traffic to see what was bothering most of the other agents.

Weird reports of supernatural events flooded the lines.

She turned into an airlock and waited for it to cycle, reading all the time: all over Otopia, mostly in regions of isolated country, people were reporting strange creatures, humanoid but greyish with red eyes, who could move at incredible speeds and seemed to haunt certain places. They also told stories of strange people arriving late at isolated places and asking favours, who then made cryptic warnings about impending disasters, usually minor, although one of these had occurred shortly before the collapse of the entrance to a lead mine in which two men were killed. It made peculiar reading but less peculiar if you were armed with the knowledge that these things were almost certainly unknown people from a known place. The media was rife with speculation that they were undead, vampires, and ghouls that were coming through from Thanatopia—a place never out of the popular press. Lila was ready to discount this, as they sounded quite wrong

for that. In any case, although they were disturbing, they so far posed
no threat she could see.

She put the matter aside as the airlock opened and let her into the
machine room deep in the basement, where some of Otopia's most sensitive computer systems were encased in carefully designed sarcophagi.
The people who worked here were mostly maintenance engineers and
they were few and far between, doing regular checks at times that
didn't coincide with her visit, so she was alone.

"Whaddya gonna doo?" Thingamajig asked with abominable
enthusiasm, looking all around them for something that he, perhaps,
could get stuck into vandalising.

Lila moved to one of the interface access points, opened the cover,
and pulled out the relevant cables. She plugged them into her arm
where the technicians usually applied their much smaller portable
units to her and continued her search for the trojan while she reset the
airlock system to 111b rules, shutting everyone else out.

By this time there were various other people attempting to figure
out what was going on and taking moves to prevent her damaging the
main setup. They locked her out of personnel files, spy data, and all
secure processes important to their main operations but she was only
interested in certain parts of her own programming. Thanks to 111b
she was temporarily allowed to isolate herself by her own command—
she guessed it made sense that she ought to be able to if she were being
interfered with and was a danger to others. But it went both ways. If
she were being ridden by a programmer it would be the ideal opportunity to break into the entire network. Nothing was perfect. She
stared for a second at the 111b rulings and saw, underneath it, some
special addenda which stood out with the oddity of their statement:

Agent Black Systems Exception—this unit is considered secure to
all outside systems . . .

There followed a great long swathe of information she didn't
understand which referred to high-security documents she was not

allowed to access. Her AI mind summarised it for her into a single conclusion that stopped everything she was doing except the AI's regimented search for the trojan command.

The security people did not regard her as a hackable item, due to the fact that the systems which had been used to create her were of a type not available to any known technology-competent race. There was mention of a thing called the Rosetta Artifact and the fact that her machineries were of a different order to the rest.

She was absorbing this when her AI abruptly halted the trojan hunt. All interface attempts went through this object, or program— the Rosetta Artifact. The machine she still held in her hand, and the others which were really only simple interfaces, used a single programmed password to initiate a command switch from her to themselves. Cracking an unknown password of unknown dimensions would take longer than her reactor would last. It was impossible. For a moment she sagged literally with the weight of failure.

Meanwhile, as she had been involved in this brief minute of study, the imp had walked down her arm and was amusing itself with the wiring, tying knots of various sorts in the unused cables. "Mm," it said as it felt her spirits sink. "At least you tried though, eh? Better than sitting there listening to all that guff and waiting for them lot to try and make a decision. Suppose there's nothing to be done. You didn't think they'd let you get away did you?"

She had already gone through several scenarios and a host of searches, looking for the physical location of the Artifact. It was not listed anywhere.

With a jerk she tore the cable inputs out of her arm and sat down on the floor. The determination that had driven her here, certain direct contact would make a difference, certain she could do something, was gone. The only possible action she could think of was to find the Artifact. Even then she might be unable to do any more than hold it and know it was the immovable object in her way to freedom.

The signal for an incoming call flashed on in her vision. She knew who it would be suddenly without needing to look, and answered silently.

"Lila?" Dr. Williams voice was gentle and concerned. "I suppose you've found out now, about yourself and the codes. I'll be waiting, when you're ready to talk."

Lila cut the line and rescinded all her commands, letting the doors open.

The imp was murmuring to itself, ". . . rabbit goes over and down through the hole, then around the tree root . . ." as it tied a particularly complicated hitch.

"There's no way back," she said to the air. Tath sighed.

"Back to where?" the imp asked, tugging to test the strength of its work.

Lila got to her feet, feeling another twinge in her hip. "Let's go," she said and waited for the tiny creature to walk its way back to her shoulder.

The imp moved slowly and pouted its lower lip, "Don't you resent me no more? Time was you'd just have left without me."

Lila looked at the ugly thing for a second. It sat uncertainly on the ruined shoulder of her suit like a tiny god. "You're just another one like me," she said and passed through the airlock silently on her walk back to the exam room.

CHAPTER TWENTY~FIVE

" ...**C**rossworld group of uniquely powerful allies?" Teazle was
saying to Zal with incredulity. "What is this, a comedy?"

Zal shrugged and made a so-sue-me face. "The woman was so
annoying. I couldn't help myself."

They turned around as Lila came back and everyone looked at her
with a variety of concern, expectation, and curiosity.

"Are you all right?" Zal murmured.

"No," she said. "I wonder if you all would mind moving to another
room so that Dr. Williams and I can talk alone." She glanced quickly
at Zal and Max to see if this request had upset them, but if it had neither of them were showing it. Malachi spoke in warm tones, ushering
everyone competently away, diverting them with suggestions of drinks
and untangling the dogs' leads from the chair legs. At last Lila and the
doctor were left together in the cool, clinical light.

"That was quite a coup," Lila said.

"A necessary one," Williams replied. "Cara has become too nervous
to be effective. And who is this?" she indicated Thingamajig and
looked at him with interest.

"This is what you get in Demonia when you go to Hell," Lila
informed her, knowing that Thingamajig was in one of her reports and
she didn't need to go into excessive details. Williams was simply
making pleasantries of a kind to pave the way to other things.

"I'm a Lord of the Infernal temporarily inconvenienced by a curse: overcome by your plight and beauty I have become your companion in adventure and adversity and analysis," Thingamajig corrected her haughtily. "I'm as good as that elf or that faery any day of the week."

Inside Lila's chest Tath was laughing but his amusement didn't touch Lila's personal core of sadness. She shared a frank meeting of eyes with the doctor.

"I don't like the world I'm in," she said. "I don't like what happens in it. I don't like the agency for lying. I don't like myself for believing in the best all the time when I should have been paying attention to what was really true."

"You like Zal," the doctor countered with her trademark mild tone. "And Malachi. You have your sister. You seem to have collected a couple of demon admirers. That's more than most people can say."

"Yeah but this girl here used to believe in things," the imp said with great feeling. "Like truth and justice, and adventure being a nice thing, and heroism and salvation and a whole bunch o' other candy-sweet nonsense that you people like to fill your heads with morning, noon, and night. So what you're offering her is a couple of sensational lovers, some friends, and a relative in exchange for the universe. I hear a lot about elves in the bedroom department and we all know demons are worth the cover charge but still you haveta consider what that weighs up to when it's matched with your great and powerful motivating abstractions like goodness and purity and rightness and the work ethic and the notion of the world being a good place to live in which is continually moving towards a state of bland but acceptable pleasantness. The faeries sure did a number on this place and no mistake."

Williams regarded the imp for a moment. "I see that my services in the psychological department are under threat here. Are all imps this way?"

"Few of them with my intellect or hidden arcane powers of insight, ma'am," Thingamajig said modestly.

"I don't like being reduced to a two-minute magazine piece either," Lila added. "Although you're right." She twisted her head around to look at the imp. "Get lost again. I have something to talk about you're not allowed to hear."

"Just because you ask so nicely," the imp said and bounced off her shoulder, immensely pleased with itself. Somehow it flattened like a shadow and was able to slide between the door and the frame in order to get out.

Williams watched it go and then looked up at Lila. "Change your mind about Alfheim?"

"Everything about everything in these cases is wrong," Lila said. "Including me. What I did was wrong, but I had to do it. I never thought I'd be the kind of person to be in this position. I feel cheated, like someone should have told me how it is and I should've had some box to tick Yes or No. You should have told me about the real reasons I was made. You should have told me about the Artifact. Delaware should have admitted she wanted to use my parents as a good excuse to find out about the necromancers. I should have paid more attention to the real differences between my world and the demons' so I didn't end up starting more wars than I can handle. I should have objected right from the start. But none of those things happened. And I hate that. I resent it. I want everything to be otherwise. I want to be right. I want to be good. I want to be blameless. I want to be able to fix things. I want to be free. I want to be normal. I'm not any of that. And there's something wrong with me. My arms and legs hurt at the joins. Zal's wife—I didn't even know he had one—is dead because of me. I don't know if he knows yet. And Mom and Dad are dead and now I have to tell Max it was my fault. And the only thing I feel able to do is stand here and whine to you about it like I'm four years old. And I hate that."

"So, what are we going to do?"

"We're going to figure out what's going on is what," Lila said. "And if you've got that Artifact hidden somewhere then you'd better hope it never gets into the wrong hands. I'll be looking into it, and if I find it I'll take it for myself. You can be sure of that." She left her statement there, to allow the other woman time to offer an explanation or to object, but the doctor just nodded.

"There's a lot of work to do, and not much time. And you have some grieving to do, and other people who need attention. You'd better get to it. When you're ready, check in with the medical staff but it's up to you when. We're here to help you."

"Sure," Lila said, letting the word be as ambiguous as it possibly could. She left the door open on her way out and went to find the others. They were in a small staff lounge. As she approached she heard them talking and the sound of a dog crunching a biscuit. Without knowing exactly why she found herself stopping outside before they saw her.

"For the last time, who doesn't like disco?" Zal was saying. "Disco was one of the great unifying and emancipating forces of modern musical history which broke boundaries of race, class, and gender iden-tification. Plus, it sounds fantastic. I'll tell you whose soul doesn't dance when it hears disco, wankersouls, that's who. Disco is a celebra-tion of everything that binds us together. And it's fun. And it feels good. And I'm sick of the rest." He sighed on an inward breath and then outwardly too. Then he said much more quietly, "Plus I always wanted to be like James Brown, or, in a pinch, Olivia Newton-John."

"You're older than you look," Malachi murmured. "At least you have the hair for the second one."

"I like disco," Teazle said, in his human voice. "But I don't like this coffee. What's it made out of? Cat piss? It'll never catch on."

"He's right," Max sounded weary. "When Lila comes we can get something better . . . I mean . . . can we go now? I want to go home."

Lila walked around the corner and stood in the doorway. She tried to smile and she thought she almost succeeded. "Come on," she said. "It's time. Let's go home."

ABOUT THE AUTHOR

JUSTINA ROBSON was born in Yorkshire, England, in 1968. She studied philosophy and linguistics at University. After only seven years of working as a temporary secretary and 2.5 million words of fiction thrown in the bin, she sold her first novel in 1999.

Since then she has won the 2000 amazon.co.uk Writers' Bursary Award. She has also been a student (1992) and a teacher (2002, 2006) at the Arvon Foundation, in the UK. Her books have been variously shortlisted for the British Science Fiction Best Novel Award, the Arthur C. Clarke Award, the Philip K. Dick Award, and the John W. Campbell Award.

In 2004 Justina was a judge for the Arthur C. Clarke Award, on behalf of the Science Fiction Foundation.

THE NO SHOWS US. CYNIC GURU

Through the agency of arcane powers beyond imagination Zal's band, the No Shows, have been in collaboration with real-world band Cynic Guru, so that together they are able to bring you a free track for your entertainment. Listen live to "Doom,"* at www .thenoshows.com.

This page is dedicated to **Cynic Guru** as a thank you for allowing themselves to be temporarily possessed by beings from beyond. They are:

Roland Hartwell (vocals, violin, guitar)
Ricky Korn (bass)
Oli Holm (drums)
Einar Johannsson (lead guitar, vocals)

They also write and record many great songs entirely their own that have nothing to do with channelling the mystical aether of imaginary space-time. More information about them, their tour dates, and their music can be found on their Web sites: www.cynicguru.com and www .myspace.com/CynicGuru.